ECHOES OF SILVER

LIZ DELTON

TYTAN
THE HOLLOW ISLES
ROKHOLD
MAR NEVAN
THE TWIST
KING'S MOUNTAIN
AREM
THOAN
GHORVOST
GREEN'S TAVERN
THE GOLD WOOD
RAYVA
BELTA
CARRIAGE HOUSE
THORNKILL
NOVA ISTRA
HOLVDAN
THE SALT SWAMPS
BARD'S REACH
VIREN
RESBROK MANOR
SOUTHMARCH
ASHBROK MANOR
VERINDAS

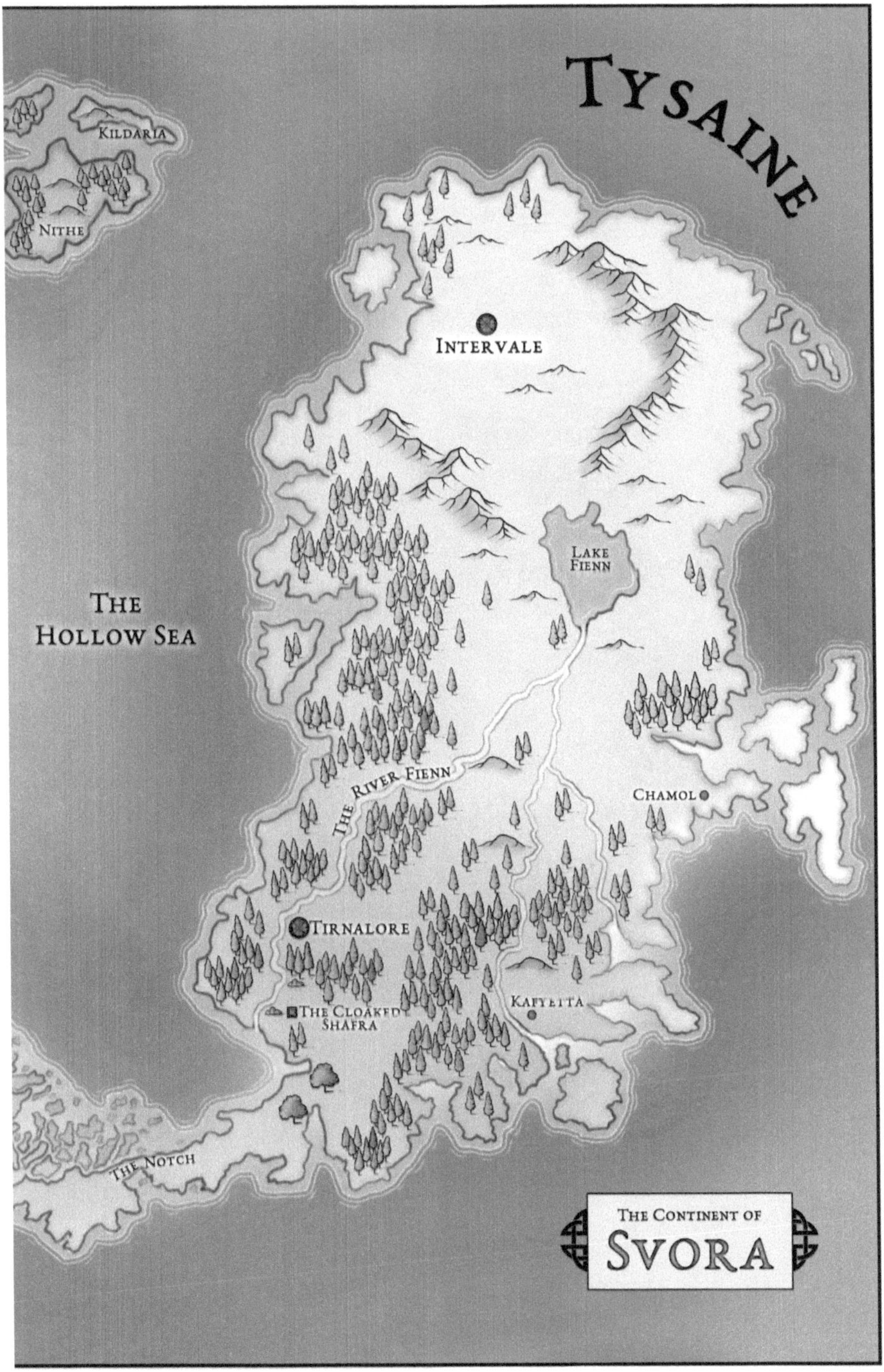

TYSAINE
KILDARIA
NITHE
INTERVALE
THE HOLLOW SEA
LAKE FIENN
THE RIVER FIENN
CHAMOL
TIRNALORE
THE CLOAKED SHAFRA
KAFYEITA
THE NOTCH
THE CONTINENT OF SVORA

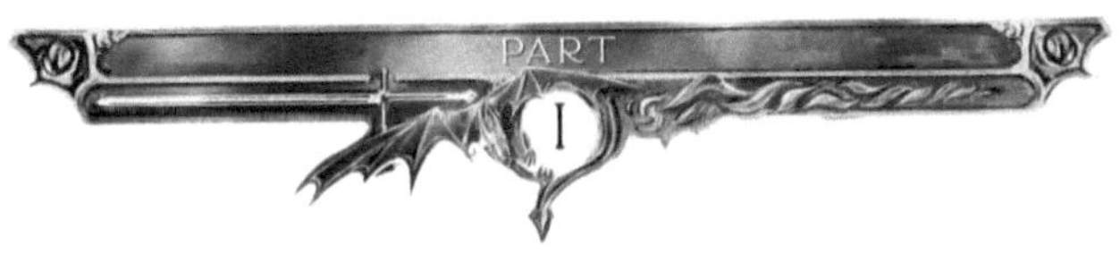

THE WALLS OF MAR NEVAN

LIESS

"You're next, Astor," Djuren growled, knocking into her shoulder as he stalked out of the throne room. A splatter of blood marked the skin beneath his crooked nose, and he carried his left arm awkwardly, the dark gray sleeve dripping with bloody water.

So Rhivven had broken Djuren's arm and nose during his interview. She wasn't so sanguine about her own appointment with the king either.

The door boomed shut behind the briigard, and Liess straightened, thumbing the axe at her belt. King Rhivven had requested her presence two days ago, and she'd ridden like a dragonet on the wind from the salt swamps back to Rayva.

Two silverswords she didn't know stood at attention on either side of the door, their weapons glinting in the early morning light that shone down from a tall, mullioned window high above them. Wordlessly, she did as she was bidden and yanked open one of the doors, her stomach muscles clenched tight.

Liess forced her hand down from her axe as she strode into the throne room—running her thumb along the leather guard always comforted her. The edge of the leather was worn from the gesture; only a thin layer still covered the blade's edge. But Rhivven knew about that particular nervous habit of hers, and she didn't want to give him any reason to think she was uncomfortable.

His long silver blade called to her well before the man himself came into view. It had been this way since she'd crossed over—weapons called to her, so clearly that she could sense their locations far better than she sensed the proximity of their owners. And Rhivven's sword was no exception. The weapon was old, a chip or two down its length only adding to its wickedness without making it any less dangerous. It radiated a gnarled, hungry power, much like the man who wielded it. Beside him sat an even more powerful sword, the likes of which she'd never sensed before. She felt something akin to the majestic wonder she'd felt when visiting the holy shrine at Mar Nevan. An almost religious sense of awe stole over her at the sensation of the new sword leaning against the throne.

Flaxen hair slicked back under his new crown—one that until recently had rested on old King Haemond's head—Rhivven turned his face toward her. Liess had been there when Rhivven had the old briigard, Haemond, killed. Silverswords would always rule Tytan, and Haemond would have given the country away to his mage-blooded son. The Bard's-cursed son who had slipped out of Liess's grip.

"My king," Liess said as she sank down to one knee on the stone pavers at Rhivven's feet.

Bloody water from a recent healing pooled beside the throne. She ignored it. Liess noted the red sister lurking on the dais behind the carved wooden chair, head bowed and red hood shadowing her face. At least King Rhivven had allowed Djuren to heal after his apparent beating.

Liess swallowed the hard lump in her throat.

Her head still bowed to the cobblestones, she could hear

Rhivven drumming his fingers on the wooden armrest, tapping them in a beat seemingly known only to himself. "Liess," he said, as plainly as if stating that blood was wet.

"Your Highness," Liess said, resisting the urge to extend a thumb to stroke her axe.

"I received your report of the incident at the Tysainian border." She stared even harder at the cobbles, noting that he hadn't invited her to rise. "Your failure to capture Prince—no, he's not a prince anymore." He growled. "*Procuring* the coward Devryn was the reason I entrusted you with the responsibility of the Tysainian checkpoint, so assured was I of your loyalty."

Liess fixed her gaze on a tiny chip of stone that was coming loose in the grout. From the way Rhivven went on, she could tell he wasn't yet inviting her to speak. She studied the tiny grains of sand framing the loose stone chip.

"This was your sole responsibility," his voice ground out like shifting gravel. "And yet you report that Vaelor Resbrok, that cursed son of Viren and Devryn's sworn protector *slipped through your grasp.*"

She'd had to report it. Rhivven would kill her outright if he'd heard of it from anyone other than her. Even though none of the other 'swords at the checkpoint had survived the encounter, and she had been betrayed by Ziggrune, Liess knew in her bones that Rhivven would have found out somehow. He always did.

"Rise," he barked.

By the time she rose from bended knee, his gnarled sword was at her throat, and his stubbled chin inches from her face. A jolt of electric energy tingled from her chest and ran all the way down her body. He had a good hands-breadth of height on her. The silver ring in his eyes seemed to cut right through her, just as sharp as his enhanced swiftness. Her silversword crossover had heightened her sense of awareness and strength—and an axe wasn't known for its speed. Rhivven, on the other hand, had been gifted with both strength and speed.

"Djuren says you plot against me." He spoke so quietly the tiny hairs in her ears stood on end.

"I do not, my king," she said levelly. The only way to survive an encounter with Rhivven Reynolt, the Butcher of Viren and new king of Tytan was to remain level. Every breath, every word, calculated. Calm. She had spent enough years by his side in the enclave to know that fact.

He pressed the sword into her neck, and she felt the jab of one of the jagged chips in the metal. "You worked alongside Vaelor here in the castle before King Haemond's death, did you not?"

She could feel his hot breath on her cheek, tingling over her ears, and she leveled her own breath. "I did, Your Majesty."

"And you plotted with him to rescue Devryn, did you not?"

"No, never, King Rhivven." She let out the controlled breath.

Pain collided with her cheek, making stars burst in her eyes and tossing her bodily to the ground. She caught herself just before her right shoulder smashed onto the cobblestones, but a kick to the gut came next, and she doubled up on herself. His sword remained loose in his grip, the knowledge giving her a modicum of calm in the tormented storm that was Rhivven Reynolt.

"You plotted with him and allowed Devryn to escape. How else could the prince have gotten to Tysaine?" he demanded, standing over her and lifting his jagged blade—she could sense it all. Liess held her breath. "I've received a report that the former prince is in Tirnalore, safe and alive—the pathetic little kirich. You yourself told me that Vaelor Resbrok broke through the checkpoint." He took a step closer to her, and the tip of his sword penetrated an inch or two into her shoulder.

She tightened her gut, preventing any cry of pain from escaping. His silver-ringed eyes bored into her own. "I do not conspire with Virenish animals," she hissed. "The prince was not in the carriage. While I was fighting the traitor Ziggrune, I saw only two women inside." She had, of course, stated these facts in her report, but she was not going to remind him of that.

Pain wrenched from the wound in her shoulder, where his sword now twisted, and a cry escaped her lips unbidden. She locked eyes with him. "I speak the truth, my king."

He didn't release his sword or divert his stony gaze. "But it is *easy* to lie, little Liess," he said in a low gravelly voice. "Liess...lies. Liess lies..."

She couldn't rip her gaze away from his if she'd wanted to, those silver rings cutting through her even deeper than his sword. She felt blood trickle under the back of her arm as he pushed the blade in just a little more, as if testing to see if she were indeed made of flesh and skin, and how far it might cut. Men and their swords.

Liess grimaced. "I speak the truth," she repeated, then gasped as he chose that moment to withdraw the sword with a parting twist in the opposite direction. "I swear it!"

"Get up," he ordered, turning his back on her to return to the throne. "You're getting blood all over my floor."

She kept her eyes on him, as one might watch a feral bear that had wandered out of the woods and into a village, making her movements slow and obvious. He stalked back to his throne, which allowed her to rise and cup her hand to her wound to prevent further blood spillage.

This seemed to be the right thing to do, as Rhivven sank into his throne like a man lowering himself into the finest hot spring bath, his arms stretched lazily along the wide armrests. Blood and violence always had that effect on him.

Liess's gaze flicked involuntarily to the red sister behind the throne, who studiously pretended not to watch the proceedings.

"No holy water for you," Rhivven growled. "If you are not a traitor, then you are a failure, Liess."

She lowered her gaze. "I know," she said throatily.

"Come closer."

Her hand firmly pressed against her bloody shoulder, she counted her steps and made her way up the dais toward the throne. His sword was sheathed, and his knees spread wide on the old oaken throne. She didn't like towering over his seated form— it went against every rule of obeisance and formality that she knew—but there was no direct order she wouldn't follow, and the look in his eyes continued to beckon her closer.

Her insides fluttered like a creature was loose in her bowels as she continued to advance on her seated king. Finally, when she stood no more than a handspan from his left knee, he raised a casual hand for her to stop. Her gaze landed on the foreign sword propped beside the throne. Rhivven never used any weapon other than his own Welded sword.

He sat at ease, head resting on the tall, polished wooden back and fingers drumming out his particular rhythm on the armrest. Quicker than seemed humanly possible, he snaked his hand out and grabbed her limp left forearm, yanking her face to his level. Agony lanced through her wound at the movement, and she fought not to scream in her king's face—and to keep her other hand steady so as not to drip blood on him. The battle for calm raged inside as she focused only on her breathing. It was her heartbeat that betrayed her, thumping wildly in her exposed throat.

"Ah, there it is," he whispered, eyes darkening. "Finally, a crack in the infamous armor of Liess Astor." His lips almost formed a smile, and she tore her gaze back to his eyes.

In response, his hand crushed her forearm where he held it in his cruel grip. He took a deep breath like a man sniffing a full dinner plate set before him. Liess clutched her wound even harder, wondering if she was bleeding all over the king. But what could she do about it?

"You will make it up to me by tracking down our lost prince," Rhivven said, hardly raising his voice from his gravelly whisper that made the hairs on her neck stand up. His other hand reached up to grab the back of her neck and force her head closer, thumb pressed just under her ear, as his voice lowered to a whisper. "If you succeed, I am in need of a queen to give me heirs. But if you fail, I'll spill your blood across this floor."

FIG

"Wait." Vaelor's hand landed heavily on Fig's shoulder as they hurried through the Gold Wood.

"What is it?" Mairead hissed.

Fig glanced around the Gold Wood. The golden auran trees sparkled in the twilight, their glittering essence drifting down from the gilt leaves and filling Fig with an indescribable sense of power. She reached out with her senses while being careful to keep her magic in check. The Gold Wood amplified her powers, and she didn't want to accidentally burn the place down.

Vaelor froze, listening. She caught his eye, and her chest constricted a little. Ever since his sword had broken in the Hollow Isles, red had seeped into the silver rings in his eyes like the most unwelcome rust.

"Nothing," Vaelor said after a moment. "I thought I heard—"

A loud *clang* cut through the forest, loud enough for Fig's normal senses to hear it. She whipped her head in the direction they'd been heading—Emrah's tower.

Clang.

The sound was coming from the hidden clearing, Fig was sure of it. She warily eyed the whorlthorn bushes that protected the clearing and attempted to pick her way through without getting stabbed.

An arm wrapped in leather bracers brushed them aside for her. Vaelor.

Together, they cautiously stepped out into the sunny clearing, the familiar tower rising above them. Fig smiled at the sight. An old stone tower with three stories and a pointed roof, all for one little dragonet and his small hoard of gemstones, was nestled here in a small valley and surrounded by tall auran trees, away from the silversword patrols. It was like paradise, except for...

Clang.

Without a word, Vaelor stalked forward, hand on his sword hilt. Fig watched as he headed toward the tower with a sword they'd stolen from a farm in the Virenish highlands. The shattered remains of his Welded sword were kept safe in the bag slung across his torso. But though Vaelor had survived his sword breaking back in the Hollow Isles when Dev's brother—whom they'd long thought dead—had attacked, it had changed him. She could tell something was wrong every time she looked into his red-ringed eyes. She never thought she'd miss the ring of silver there that marked him as a silversword.

"What is that?" Fig hissed.

"Someone's inside," Mairead whispered.

"I thought the dwarves had returned the tower to Emrah?" Sparks danced on Fig's fingertips, and she did her best to rein them in. She ran her thumb nervously over the tips of her other fingers in a familiar rhythm.

Vaelor didn't respond; he only stalked toward the front door of the tower, which was propped open. Fig shared a look with Mairead, and they followed.

Mairead nervously adjusted her red hood. She still wore the cloak of the Sisters of Morgha, despite being ousted from the sisterhood for her curiosity about silversword matters. Fig wasn't convinced Mairead ought to continue wearing it, but the tattoos on her hands branded her a sister, so she looked even more suspicious without the cloak.

Vaelor pulled up short. Keeping his back to them, he motioned for the women to move around to the side of the clearing.

Fig hastily complied, furious at the intruder. She dashed through the low grass with Mairead at her heels. This was *Emrah's* tower—the only solace she'd been looking forward to after weeks of tromping through Viren. They'd been on the run since their ordeal on the Hollow Isles, when they'd found out Dev's older mage brother had survived the silversword ritual despite everyone thinking that a mage crossover meant sure death. Instead, Shadryn had transformed into something far deadlier, with black ice that could break even Vaelor's weapon.

They'd endured weeks of wet feet as they slogged through the salt swamps taking roundabout ways through the lowlands so as not to be seen, then hiding out in old barns and copses of trees in the highlands, and finally, stealing through the Tytanian countryside, until they'd slipped into the forbidden Gold Wood in the night like the wanted criminals that they were.

The broadsheet Mairead had swiped in Verindas had said as much. They were wanted for aiding the traitor prince, Devryn Verrence. But Dev was the true heir to the throne of Tytan, despite his psychopath brother Shadryn still being alive, and the slimy briigard Rhivven currently sitting on the Rayvan throne.

Fig was getting *really* tired of people taking things that weren't theirs—including Emrah's tower. She stomped up the grassy incline at Vaelor's side, flames crackling at her palms.

Vaelor's red-ringed eyes flashed toward her, but he said nothing as he put his back to the tower wall just outside the door, his sword at the ready. She was used to his silence by now. Ever since his sword had broken, he'd been more guarded with his words than ever before. He gave her a nod.

Clang.

"Hello?" Fig called, pitching her voice loudly through the

open door. All her focus went to the flames at her palms; using her magic here in the Gold Wood, the one place that amplified all mage's powers, was particularly dangerous, but she was getting much better at controlling it.

The clanging inside stopped, and they heard a curse and muffled shuffling. She could see the large raised hearth was lit from the dim red glow that emanated through the door.

"Who's in there?" Fig demanded. "I'll have you know that the owner of this tower will be in a mighty rage—"

"Oh, aye? Is he here?" a voice grumbled. A shadow passed into the doorframe. Silhouetted in the red light of the hearth was a short, stocky figure. He wore a heavy toolbelt, weighed down with all manner of tools—among them a massive hammer. His right hand twitched toward the hammer.

Fig straightened, her ember-hot fingers twitching as well. "What does that matter? We're his representatives. Who are you, and what are you doing here?" Emrah was in Tirnalore with Dev and Ziggy, but she didn't need to tell the dwarf that.

The dwarf stepped out of the shadows, the glow of the hearth outlining him in the dim red light. He put a dark hand comfortably on his hammer, its handle decorated in dwarvish runes. Fig doubted she could *lift* such a large hammer, let alone walk around with it casually attached to her hip. She swallowed.

"Knoll," he grunted in the deepest timbre, dreadlocks shifting off his shoulder as he inclined his head.

Fig glanced at Vaelor. His grip on the placeholder sword was tight and ready, but he remained quiet.

"Excuse me?" Fig said.

The wrinkles around the dwarf's eyes deepened into dark black creases, and Fig thought she saw a smirk behind his dark braided beard, which shifted along with his dreadlocked hair. "Name's Knoll," he repeated, his voice still low.

Fig reined her flames back in and turned to Mairead with a slightly exasperated look. Mairead, panic flitting over her freckled face, began, "Um, well, Knoll, as my friend here mentioned, we know the owner of this tower...and we would just like to know what you're doing here?" Her voice rose in pitch until the end of her sentence was nearly indiscernible.

The dwarf turned his attention to Mairead and took in her red robes. Mairead crossed her hands in front of her as befitted her station as a Sister of Morgha, the red runes trailing from the tips of her middle fingers to her wrists on clear display. Mairead also had a mark on her palm—a runic brand that labeled her as an outcast of the sisterhood. But Knoll didn't need to know that, which was why Mairead kept her palm pressed to her robe.

He bobbed his head. "Begging your pardon, Sister, but I was given permission to use this tower."

"By whom?" Fig demanded.

Knoll gave her a cursory glance, and a great sigh rumbled out. "Noblest Firth of Clan Feijowa, if you must know."

Fig closed her eyes slowly, running an idle hand across her stomach. Firth had put an axe through her belly, the injury almost killing her...twice.

"But we settled with Firth," she said heavily. "The Feijowa have no quarrel with Emrah or the rest of us."

"I don't know about any quarrel," Knoll grumbled with a shake of his head. "I only asked to use a hearth."

"And you know nothing about Emrah, or...anything?"

He shrugged thick shoulders clad in leather. "Just need the hearth."

"Well," Fig said, exasperated. "Do you mind if we come in, then? We've been on our way here for weeks now, and..."

"Doesn't matter to me," Knoll said. He turned his back on them and trudged back toward the hearth.

Fig shook her head slowly. What did she care if the dwarf had set up shop in the base of the tower? She just needed a place to *sit down* for the Bard's sake.

"Fine. Great," she muttered, motioning the others in behind her. As soon as she'd hitched up her satchel and strode over the threshold, a calming earthy scent stole over her. The dwarf wiped sweat from his brow as he settled back in front of the hearth, ash streaking his dark brown skin. He looked older, though his black dreadlocks showed no signs of graying. Fig had a hard time telling ages in dwarves, as they lived longer than most, but the wrinkles around his eyes and a weariness in his gaze gave her some clue. Knoll settled a white-hot piece of metal on an anvil with tongs and raised his massive hammer. *Clang.*

The sharp scent of metal invaded her senses, mixed with the heady earthen aroma she often sensed around dwarves. They possessed an obvious skill with earth and metal, although their magic was strongest in the ancestral home of the King's Mountain —no, the dwarves called it the Great Mountain—much as the mages' magic was strongest here in the Gold Wood. It was no surprise to Fig that both domains had been claimed by the silver-swords as the dominion of the crown.

She dismissed her concerns over the dwarf and long-dead politics and headed straight for the staircase that wrapped around the inner wall of the tower, trudging toward the second level. Thoughts of collapsing onto the nearest alcove quickly flew from her head when she crested the next floor. A deranged chuckle ripped from her. Half the beds—rope hammocks built into the wooden alcoves that lined the tower walls—were burned away or charred.

"Fig?" Mairead asked, putting a hand on her arm.

She shook her head. "I— There's more on the third floor," she said, not mentioning that it had been *her* who'd burned these bunks on their last visit to the tower during their fight with the Feijowa. They'd worked everything out with Firth a few days later, when they'd all escaped the Burning of Nova Istra, as it was now being called. Incinerating the whole port hadn't been her intention when she'd teamed up with one of the Feijowa dwarves to create a distraction and flee from the silverswords, but it had worked. After escaping the flaming harbor, Fig and Dev had sat down with Firth, the head of the Feijowa clan, and reluctantly entered a bargain.

Fig had expected the dwarf to ask for the Mountain in exchange for the clan's support of Dev's claim on the throne, but instead, Firth had told them of a weapon. The Sword of Morin was made from a unique metal called bloodril—a weapon that could make the silverswords even more powerful. Bloodril was an element worthy of the gods, according to the dwarves, unlike the trivial iron or steel that made silverswords stronger when they were bonded with their weapons. But now, that sword was in the possession of the silverswords.

Knoll's presence here didn't bode well for their peace with the Feijowa. Perhaps they had left him to keep an eye out for Emrah and his people. Or perhaps the dwarf really did just need a hearth.

Fig sighed as she continued to the third floor, her footsteps growing heavier with each stair. Finally, she lifted her gaze to the wooden ceiling, embedded with the gemstones Emrah had collected over the years. There were lumpy white stones with veins of green, glassy blue sapphires with sharp edges, and tiny, sparkling, cream-colored affcrvatz. They all winked down at her from where Emrah had embedded them in the ceiling, scorch marks framing each one.

She missed the dragonet. But she would rather he stay in Tirnalore—if Dev still had need of him. Dev and Ziggy were up to who-knew-what with the Fienn-Da, the underground mage organization in Tysaine that dealt in smuggling and thievery, among other things. But Dev had wanted allies, and the mage organization had seemed their only choice. Not to mention, they'd keep Dev safe if he was part of their crew. She just hoped he was keeping out of trouble.

"What is this place?" Mairead asked, setting her pack down on a low bed farthest from the top of the stairs. She tested out the hammock with her hands and, finding it satisfactory, sank down to sit, immediately pulling off her boots and lining them up beside the bed.

Fig frowned in thought. "I'd thought it was some kind of old tower for the Sisters of Morgha with the old water pump down below."

Frowning, Mairead shook her head. "Nothing like I've ever seen."

"Hmm," Fig said, claiming the bed next to Mairead and

throwing herself onto the hammock. A pleased groan escaped her as she stretched out and closed her eyes for a few seconds. "I could sleep for a week."

Vaelor claimed the bed closest to the stairs, and Fig's heart wrenched when he placed the pack with his broken sword on the bed with utmost care.

She caught the glint of silvery-red rings in Vaelor's eyes as he watched her, and she gave him a smile.

"Is that how long you're planning on staying here?" Mairead asked, going through her own pack.

Fig stared up at the hammock above her. "No," she said quietly. "Vaelor and I need to get to Mar Nevan as quickly as we can. But you...you should stay here while we do that."

At least Mairead could rest while Fig and Vaelor searched for answers about how to fix his sword.

Mairead cleared her throat awkwardly and turned toward Fig. "Actually..."

Fig sat up, tossing her legs over the side of the hammock, and waited for the girl to speak.

"I'm going to go home," Mairead said. "For good."

FIG

"Just go," Fig urged the next morning.

"But *he's* down there," Mairead hissed quietly as they lingered at the top of the stairs.

"I doubt he means us any harm. He's just some dwarf."

Fig caught Vaelor's gaze, and he lifted a shoulder. He didn't seem to see Knoll as a threat either. She had actually felt safer last night, knowing the dwarf was on the base floor of the tower as they slept. Of course, she and Vaelor still took shifts watching over the third floor, but still...

"We need water and food," Fig reminded Mairead, poking her in the back. Her announcement about leaving to go home last night still felt like a sharp pain in Fig's side.

"Of course," Mairead finally muttered. But still, she stood there.

Fig shook her head and squeezed past the girl, a light chuckle on her lips. "I'll go first, shall I?"

Knoll had woken them all up with the clang of his hammer at

sunrise, but having fallen asleep well before the sun sank, Fig felt better rested than she had in weeks despite sleeping in shifts. But now her other senses were making demands of her—and they really needed to find some food and water.

Clang.

Fig reached the bottom of the staircase, the other two coming down behind her. A sense of loneliness sank into her as she thought of traveling on without Mairead. Vaelor, with his shattered sword, seemed to trudge on as if only a fraction of himself remained. Though he was vigilant and watchful as ever, more than melancholy had settled over him. It was like his body was merely going through the motions. She tried not to wonder about how the silversword ritual might affect someone's *soul*.

Of course, Mairead wouldn't have gone with them to Mar Nevan—the holy city was the last place someone burned out of the sisterhood should go—but Fig had assumed they'd reconvene and continue their journey together with Mairead after they'd found their answers.

Mairead hadn't said much after the atrocities that had befallen them on Nithe. When Fig and the others had taken the ship from the Hollow Isles, Fig had fully expected Mairead to disembark in Tysaine and head back to the Narndian Cathedral where she'd been welcomed and given a position to help heal people—with no strings attached. But Mairead had remained on board, keeping her reasons to herself.

Fig had gotten the sense that Mairead wanted nothing further to do with the sisterhood after her ordeal in the Hollow Isles. And after hearing about the other time Mairead had been forced to do a crossover, it made sense. This wasn't just about healing. The goddess Morgha had two aspects: life and death.

And Mairead had seen too much death. Though Fig would miss her terribly, it was probably best to send her home.

"Good morning," Fig ventured when she spotted Knoll. He had his back to them and was working at the anvil he'd set up in front of the raised hearth. The stone hearth jutted out from the wall in a semicircle, a quarter-sphere hood enclosing it from above.

The dwarf grunted in response, though he at least caught her eye. She took that as a greeting, and continued on out the door.

In the sunlight of the Gold Wood, Fig inhaled the honey-like scent of the auran trees, filling her lungs and chasing away the mantle of loneliness that had begun to settle on her. What she wouldn't give to spend all her days here in the Gold Wood. But she had given up that dream when she'd quit the Carriage House —the only crown-sanctioned way for mages to live in the sacred forest. *Except, of course, when offered refuge in illegal towers owned by dragonets...*

"I'll hunt, and you two get the water?" Fig offered when the others joined her.

Mairead blinked in the bright sunlight, raising her red hood to throw her pale face into shadow. Vaelor nodded and led Mairead to the southeast, perhaps remembering the location of a stream from their previous hurried flight from the tower.

Alone in the tower's clearing, Fig practiced sending out a few bursts of flame. She had never hunted before they'd returned to Tytan, but necessity had driven them to it as they trekked through Viren. Vaelor was built for sword combat and had offered to acquire tagor meat, but Fig and Mairead had ruled that out as an unnecessary risk. It had been painful for all of them when they'd passed by Resbrok House—no one more than Vaelor—but the danger their mere presence would be putting Vaelor's family in was too great a risk.

Flames roared from her fingertips—ten or fifteen spans long —but far too wide. This was the benefit—and sometimes the hindrance—of amplification in the Gold Wood. She tried again, tightening her connection and therefore tightening the tendrils of fire. When she was satisfied, she nodded to herself and strode off into the aurans, the taste of golden honey coating her tongue.

An hour later, she had two small vorse eagles for her efforts, each a little charred around the edges.

She found Mairead outside the tower when she returned and deposited the birds into the red sister's waiting hands.

"Thank you," Fig said, not looking at the partially burned birds. Mairead had a better stomach for such things and had taken on the role of dressing the kills without complaint before they could be cooked properly.

"Vaelor's out gathering more wood," Mairead reported, "but we'll need to ask Knoll for the hearth, unless we want to start a fire out here...?"

"I'd rather not," Fig said. "The chimney is more efficient at hiding the smoke."

Mairead nodded then scurried away to pluck and prepare the vorse eagles. With a final glance out into the trees, Fig knocked once on the open doorframe as a polite warning before she made her way inside.

"Knoll?"

He looked up at her, hammer raised mid-strike.

"We'll need use of the fire for cooking," Fig stated plainly. "But you're welcome to join us for dinner, of course. Also...while I have you. If there's any way you could start work sometime *after* sunrise, the Bard knows, we would appreciate it. Just for tomorrow. We'll be leaving tomorrow evening."

Knoll stood one step back from the hearth, somehow unbothered by the heat or the massive hammer in his casual grip. Barely any sweat graced his dark brow.

Fig swallowed, waiting.

"Oh, aye," he finally said in that deep baritone that seemed to penetrate a particular register of her ear canal.

She nodded once in acceptance. She appreciated a person of few words. Each word carried more weight. "Thanks."

When the hearth had burned to embers, casting the ground floor into shades of red and black, and the smell of roast meat from their long-finished dinner had begun to fade, Fig found herself alone with the dwarf. The trailing ends of Mairead's red cloak swished up the stairs and out of sight as she headed up to bed, yawning. Vaelor had gone outside a few minutes earlier to walk around the perimeter of the clearing and check for danger amid the aurans. Outside, gold sifted down like glitter from the trees, offering weak light through the sacred forest.

Fig seized her mug of weak ale that Knoll had begrudgingly shared with them. It was long since empty, but she didn't know what else to do with her hands. She should have gone up to bed when Mairead had made her excuses for the night, but Fig wanted to make sure Vaelor returned safely. "So Knoll, what are you..."

"It was you," Knoll interrupted slowly.

"What?"

"You. I was supposed to meet you in Green's Tavern. Going on a month ago now."

Her jaw dropped, and she considered draining the warm dregs of her mug to cover the awkward moment but thought better of it. "I...Green's Tavern," she said ruefully. "By the Bard, what a night that was." Vaelor retrieving her from the tavern and bringing her to Dev, whose father had just been killed. The fight with half a dozen silverswords that had followed. And the beginning of their search for allies.

Knoll grunted, shifting on his stool. He still had his hammer at his hip, and Fig saw the runes etched deep in the metal running down the handle. The patterns danced in the light of the flickering embers. "Oh, aye?"

"I'm sorry I couldn't meet you," she said, setting her mug down on a nearby stool.

"Aye, well, I know who you are now, after hearing you talk to the others," he rumbled.

After all the times Fig had wondered where her life would be now—if only she'd stayed in Green's Tavern that night and followed through with the job—she had to ask. "What *was* the job? You were looking for a fire mage, right? Bruna said..." She trailed off, her heart constricting as she thought of her friend whose life had been cut short in a whirlwind of paper and silversword blades.

Gazing into the hearth's embers, Knoll didn't say anything for a moment either. "I *was* looking for one when I first came back to Tytan. Don't need one anymore."

They lapsed into an uneasy silence again, and Fig wondered whether she should just go to bed. She could wait upstairs for Vaelor to come in. Her gaze landed on the tools that Knoll had neatly organized around the room, and an idea sprang to mind.

"Knoll," Fig said, "I don't suppose... Do you know anything about fixing silversword weapons?"

He eyed her warily. "I can fix a sword—a normal one at that. But a Welded weapon?" His gruff demeanor seemed to slip for a moment as his eyes softened. "You might need the red sisters for that. I only study metals, I'm not much one for magics. Normally, those swords don't require repair."

Fig hung her head. "Of course. We're headed to Mar Nevan next."

Knoll stroked his beard in thought. "I don't know what goes into their rites," he said slowly. "But I've seen the ancient Svoran runes they use. Written in blood and holy water...well, that's a powerful combination. I'm afraid you'll need to find someone versed in silversword lore—if you can't go to the enclave directly."

Fig pressed her lips together in a sad smile. They certainly couldn't go to the enclave—and she was sure Knoll knew that. "Thank you."

"But if you just need a sword fixed, I'll be here. Blacksmithing is in my blood." He coughed out a laugh at some private joke.

She nodded, and somehow, she no longer minded the idea of the dwarf staying. "We won't be here much longer—though I wish we could."

In response, Knoll took a swig from his mug. Then he returned his attention to the embers glowing in the hearth, and Fig did the same.

FIG

At the edge of the Gold Wood late the next evening, Fig drew in one final breath of the honey-scented air. She glanced back in the direction of the tower one last time. Gold trees glinted amid the dark of night.

Their stay at the tower had been far too short, although they'd finally gotten to sleep in—with Knoll waiting until an hour after sunrise to begin his work. They'd tarried on the third floor for much of the morning, adjusting their gear. In the afternoon, Fig and Mairead had gone to bathe in the stream, then foraged for blackberries to eat and embergold leaves to make tea. It had been a blessedly unhurried day. The three of them finally had time to catch up on rest, taking turns sleeping despite Knoll's constant hammering and clanging downstairs.

Mairead put a hand on Fig's arm, the red sister's tattoos glinting in the gold glitter sifting down from the aurans.

"Maybe we can come back someday," Mairead said.

Fig nodded, jaw tight. "Maybe." Emrah's tower was more of a

home than she'd ever had—save the Carriage House deep in the Gold Wood. *Mages are meant to live in the ancient wood. It's in our blood.*

"I could take you through the Twist," Mairead offered for the fifth time. As they left the Gold Wood behind, the Mountain loomed ahead of them. "I've been on meditative passages through there more times than most of my contemporaries."

"Absolutely not," Fig told her. "You're not going near Mar Nevan, it's too dangerous."

Even Vaelor grunted a negative reply, his rust-red eyes flashing in Mairead's direction. He had freshly shaved the sides of his head when he'd taken his turn bathing in the stream, and he'd redone the half dozen braids laced through his straight blond hair, so a few beads clinked together quietly as they walked.

"Are you sure you don't want us to travel with you to Thoan first, though?" Fig asked.

Mairead shook her head and lifted her skirts to step over a rutted cart track. "No, it would only take you longer. You need to fix Vaelor's sword. That's more important."

It wasn't long until the glow of the Gold Wood was no longer visible over Fig's shoulder, the few times she turned around to look back. Fig's desire to remain safe in the tower was strong, but she couldn't look in Vaelor's eyes without seeing something wrong. She was going to help him fix it, no matter what. He had broken his sword saving her from Shadryn's black ice, and she would do anything for him.

They took their time walking so they wouldn't *look* like fugitives who'd chosen the cover of night for their trek. The half-moonlight guided their way to the sleepy village of Arem, nestled at the bottom of the rocklands.

A dwarf woman greeted them at the tavern looking cheery despite the hour—it was well past midnight. Fig secured a room for Mairead, who settled in while Fig ordered food. Then she sat with Vaelor at the end of the long table that took up most of the ground floor. She leaned over and asked, "Do you want to stay the night before we attempt the Twist?"

"If you do," was all he said. He lowered his head, a few of his braids falling forward.

Fig ran a hand through her curls, nervous as she suddenly remembered running her hand through his blond braids during their brief kiss aboard the *Trevena*. That moment had felt like fire scouring her soul...now only embers on the verge of ash remained. Those feelings had been snuffed out along with his broken sword.

He had saved her, only to lose his soul...or so she couldn't help but think. The life was gone from his eyes anyway, replaced by that bloody ring. She couldn't rightfully answer the call of those feelings. Not now. Not until his body and soul were intact.

Soon their end of the table was filled with food and bolstered by Mairead's presence, but the three remained quiet. Whether it was the late hour—so late it was actually early the next day—the grief that preceded Mairead's departure, or simply that they'd run out of words after these last few weeks in constant company, Fig didn't know. She merely tucked into her meal of potatoes and tough shafra meat, covered in a decadent gravy to mask the toughness.

Once or twice during their meal, Fig brushed the corner of her mind searching for her connection to Emrah but found that he was nowhere close enough to speak into her mind.

A loud scrape drew Fig's attention from her nearly empty plate, where she'd been toying with one of the few peas that added color to the brown meal. Mairead was standing and had evidently said something to her. Fig blinked, trying to remember.

The pale girl tugged on her red hood. "I *said*: you two better get going before it gets any lighter out."

Fig nodded, coming to her senses and finally noticing the impending dawn that peered through the tavern windows.

"Of course. You're right." Her words choked up at the end, and she clamped her mouth shut. This was it. After all they'd been through—Nova Istra, the salt swamps, Tirnalore, Nithe—she had to say goodbye to Mairead. Again. She'd already said goodbye once at the cathedral in Tirnalore. But this time was different. And she could understand why the girl wanted to go home. Fig's throat felt tight as she swallowed.

Mairead flung her arms around Fig. Red curls spilled out from under her hood, and their clean scent flooded Fig's nostrils. A weight crushed her chest that wasn't from Mairead's own body pressed against hers.

"I don't want to leave you here," Fig blurted out.

Mairead only squeezed her tighter.

"But I wouldn't let you come, even if you wanted to," Fig said, wiping her eyes with her hands behind Mairead's back where the girl couldn't see.

Mairead pulled away and looked Fig full in the face. Fig did her best to blink away the traitorous tears. "You'll do fine. Just find Sister Avelina, like I told you before. I would trust her with my life. Mother Savidah... She might have the answers, but..." She turned her palm over to briefly display the circle of runes that had been burned into the skin. "Don't go to her unless you absolutely *have to*. Sister Avelina should be able to get you into the ancient archives, at the very least. I've seen plenty of texts on silverswords there—far more than I read during my own training. She'll know where to find them."

Fig nodded. Mairead had explained this as they'd trekked through Tytan, but she recommitted the names to her memory once more.

"And"—now it was Mairead's turn to choke up—"g-good luck on the Twist. Be careful. I hope we cross paths again sometime, Fig."

Stomach in knots, Fig watched Mairead turn and head up the stairs. It wasn't goodbye for good, Fig told herself. Once they found their answers in Mar Nevan, they could go to Thoan and make sure Mairead was settled in. Still, she couldn't help but wonder if she would ever see her friend again. She met Vaelor's bloody gaze and swallowed.

"The Twist, did you say dearie?" a voice called from near the tavern's front door. A cheery dwarf stood there, laden with a pack and bundles of rope. The door slammed shut just behind him, and Fig caught a glimpse of the glowing light of dawn.

"We better get going," she said to Vaelor, ignoring the dwarf.

"You're not walking to the holy city without a guide, *surely!*" the dwarf said, taking a step toward her and Vaelor. He put a scandalized hand on his long ginger beard, his rosy cheeks pushing up into his wide eyes. "It's more treacherous than the tagor-infested waters of the salt swamps, my dears! A good guide will get you where you're going." He waggled a gnarled finger at her, a glint in his eye.

"No, thank you," Fig said, with the shadow of a smirk as she thought of the salt swamps. "We don't require a guide." If Mairead could traverse the Twist, then so could they.

Many pilgrims visiting the holy city crossed the Twist—it was the only way to walk to Mar Nevan on foot. The boat ride from Thoan was expensive and—for Fig and Vaelor's purposes—not as private as they wanted, as it was often chaperoned by silverswords or representatives of Mar Nevan.

"But—" the guide began.

Vaelor took a step forward, and his towering form was all the invitation the guide needed to move out of their way. The dwarf leaned an elbow on the bar top, and called after them, "May Morgha show you her caring side then, dearies!"

The tavern door slammed behind them, and they turned their faces toward the Mountain and the clear path through the rocky terrain beside it that led to the Twist. They began their trek in silence, and Fig wondered if their entire journey would be like this. Silent walks and the occasional muttered word from Vaelor, now that cheerful Mairead wasn't here as a buffer.

Fig glanced at him out of the corner of her eye. She *knew* something in him had broken with the shattering of his blade. She had to help him fix it, after everything he'd done for Dev...had done for her. And it began with the Twist.

When the sun peeked over the edge of the Mountain, Fig turned to look at the sight, and thought she saw something over the Mountain, though she was unsure whether it was a bird or her much-longed-for dragonet companion. Or maybe just a wisp of smoke.

They were exposed on the path that led up to the Twist—this was the first time they'd traveled in full daylight in what felt like forever—but the silverswords didn't patrol this far north. If they had business in Mar Nevan, the 'swords would take the ferry from Thoan; the main reason Fig had wished to avoid it.

The leafy green trees outside of Arem were quickly replaced by scrubby bushes and the occasional hunched tree, its bark gnarled like arthritic limbs. Despite the lack of foliage, Fig kept thinking she heard something in the brush, like a bird flitting about. Vaelor didn't react, though, so she brushed the thought aside and kept trudging onward up the rocky slope.

A few weathered wooden signposts marked their way, carved runes with their cavities dyed black from age. Fig didn't allow herself to think the trail too easy—she was well aware it had only just begun—but so far, it was merely an upward slope on a rocky path.

When they reached the first narrow pass, where the Twist truly began, Fig paused for a moment to collect herself. Until now, their path had been cradled between walls of craggy stone on both sides. It had risen for hours, causing sweat to grow at the small of her back, until finally depositing them at the edge of a great crevasse—where the path narrowed to a stone ledge hugging the sheer rock wall that jutted from one side.

According to Mairead, the goddess Morgha had walked this path in her travels across Tytan, sensing her true purpose lay in the rocklands beyond. The ordeal had taken the goddess countless attempts to reach her destined purpose deep within the mountains. When storms pushed her back, she'd had to turn away, only to retrace her steps with more vigor, pressing onward. When a rockslide deterred her, she'd found a safer passage. Her footsteps had worn down the stone in her many attempts to reach the heart of the rocklands. And when she finally reached the site of what was now Mar Nevan, she had blessed the waters there, making abundance and generosity flow freely. And of course, the sisters, in all their wisdom, had maintained the path as nature and Morgha intended without the help of any bridges or guardrails, to test those pilgrims who walked in the goddess's footsteps.

Suddenly Fig wondered if they should have hired the guide, with his helpful coils of rope to keep them from falling to their deaths below. She frowned as she looked down into the crevasse, as deep as the great Library of Tirnalore was tall.

Fig tried to catch Vaelor's eye. He, too, was studying the path ahead and seemed to sense her gaze, but he didn't meet it. He glanced toward her—not at her. She let out a quiet sigh.

"Are you ready?" she asked. A sound in the brush behind her made her whip her head around, but she saw nothing except a fallen twig. Perhaps a bluebird had been following them all this time, looking for food in the barren scrub.

Vaelor was finally looking at her now, that bloody ring in his eyes meeting her gaze. Her stomach twisted. She expected him to make his usual low grunt of agreement, but instead, he sighed and said, "You shouldn't have to do this."

She gaped at him, her heart suddenly racing in her chest. "But I want to."

He moved as if to step closer to her, but then stopped, boot scuffing the dirt. Fig's right hand clenched, her nails digging into her palm as she studied his face. Normally, his visage gave away nothing, as if the sword breaking had robbed him of all emotions. But Fig sensed the pain just behind his tightened expression.

She strode toward him, wrapping her arms around his strong chest and arms, which hung at his sides. Weeks ago, on the *Trevena*, she'd been this close to him. Closer. She'd felt his lips against hers... But that was a lifetime ago. Indeed, it felt as if Vaelor had lost his life that day and hadn't been the same man since. She couldn't, in good conscience, treat him as if a great injury or tragedy hadn't befallen him. But she could offer him comfort.

Moisture squeezed out of her eyes as she closed the lids as tight as her embrace, small and ineffective as she felt. Slowly, so slow she hadn't thought it would come, big arms circled around her back, hands wrapping around her shoulders just as a lock of soft blond hair fell in front of her face.

She didn't know how long they stood like that, frozen in place at the head of the Twist.

An unexpected raindrop finally drew them apart, and Vaelor's voice rumbled out, "Let's go."

FIG

The ledge would have been treacherous even without the sudden spattering of rain, which pelted Fig as she focused on her footing. The path was only wide enough for them to walk sideways in single file, and she took the lead, Vaelor following. When they'd started an hour ago, she'd only felt a few raindrops— what had appeared to be a lone cloud in an otherwise entirely sunny sky—but now the rain had returned in force.

"Bard strike it," Fig spluttered, her fingers scrambling on the rock wall at her back for the illusion of support. She knew she wouldn't be able to grip *anything* should she slip, but she spread her hands out behind her anyway as she edged along sideways. "Good thing you're not in armor, Vaelor."

She thought she might have heard him chuckle, but when a rock underfoot skittered over the edge of the cliff and fell into the crevasse, she swallowed the lump in her throat, watching it skip and bounce off a few outcroppings on its way down. The other side of the crevasse was thirty span or so away—a completely sheer cliff face—and she couldn't make out the bottom with all of the jutting rocks and scraggly trees below.

The rain chose that moment to beat harder, running cold down her face and chest and soaking her tunic. Knowing there was no way out but through, she kept edging along with frequent glances back at Vaelor who had even less space to work with on the ledge with his bigger frame. A faint rumble emanated from the clouds above, echoing over the Twist. It was immediately followed by another rumble—but this one Fig felt in the rock she clutched desperately. She felt it through her chest as she dug her fingers into the rock, fraying a few of her short nails. Vaelor's fingers suddenly covered her right hand, and she gripped him back tightly, gazing at the clouds that had darkened with frightening speed.

Bright lightning forked across the now swirling dark clouds, followed too quickly by a loud boom as the wind picked up. Vaelor squeezed her fingers, the only point on her body that wasn't flooded with fear and tension—the one warm spot in the cold. And despite the fear freezing her feet with the next rumble of thunder and the sky quickly becoming a canvas of black clouds and flashing light, she took another step to the left. One step after the other, barely lifting her feet from the stone as she scuttled on. She hadn't realized storms could come on so quickly up here in the rocklands—she'd never been this far north. She would never take a single raindrop in a sunny sky for granted again.

Then a voice in her head nearly caused her to fall from the cliff. *You're not in the middle of that storm, are you, you daft Svoran?*

Vaelor gripped her hand even tighter when he felt her body shift in surprise. She narrowed her attention back to her feet and took another step, while responding to Emrah, *Unfortunately we are,* she told him. *I wouldn't blame you if you wait it out.* Despite her words, her heart leapt at hearing the dragonet's voice. If he was close enough to speak to her mind—even if she had to wait out the storm—he'd be here soon. Between that and Vaelor's sturdy hand in hers, she felt a burst of strength that kept her feet moving.

Drakioryn's claws, Emrah said, *I'm not scared of a little storm.*

A flash of lightning illuminated dragonet wings in the next instant, their green and gold glinting mutely. She lost sight of him in the next moment as a gust of wind scoured the cliff. It was all she could do to focus on her footwork.

Keep going, Emrah urged. *Just a little farther.*

Fig could tell Emrah had projected his words to Vaelor too. There was something different about the quality of Emrah's voice when he spoke only to Fig—it carried less of an echo than when he spoke to everyone. But *she* was the only one who could respond inside the dragonet's head. That was the nature of their unique bond, something that was still a mystery.

Fig's searching fingers curved around a big bend in the rock, and she turned to see a small inlet, a cave of sorts with an overhang. The inside was dry, thank the Bard. She lurched inside, her chest filling with warmth at the thought of a respite from the storm and the sheer cliff face. As she reveled in the safety of the dry crevice, water dripped from her nose and hair. Her clothes were beyond soaked, like she'd been swimming in the Hollow Sea.

Her fingers shook as she reluctantly let go of Vaelor's grip, and he settled into the small niche with her. It was only big enough for the two of them. They couldn't even bend to sit down. She hugged her back to the side wall, trying to make herself as small as possible so Vaelor could come all the way out of the rain.

Scaly wings fluttered inside, spraying them with a slew of fresh raindrops.

"Agh," Fig said in surprise, wiping her face as Emrah settled on Fig's shoulder. There wasn't anywhere else for him to land.

Oh, please, Emrah shot at her. *You're wetter than a tagor in the solanse.*

She snorted, smiling at the familiar weight of the dragonet on her shoulder. "I know, I know. It's *so* good to see you, my friend."

His scaly snout bobbed against the side of her neck, and she reached a hand up to pat the top of his head and run her fingers down his wet scales. Warmth seemed to glow just under her skin.

Fig shifted, trying to find a more comfortable position, which only moved her closer to Vaelor. He was trying to wring his hair out without getting any more water on her—a feat in itself. Heat flooded her cheeks as she brushed against him. Emrah remained on her shoulder, looking at her with a mixture of expectancy and sly cunning.

"Well?" she said, "What news from Tysaine? How are Dev and Ziggy doing within the Fienn-Da?"

Emrah's claws padded her shoulder softly as if he were a cat. *They're fine,* he told the two of them. *Not much headway with Evandahl, though. He's not ready to throw away decades of careful consideration for one crown—his words, not mine.*

Fig nodded sadly. Of course the leader of the Fienn-Da wasn't ready to jump straight into Dev's campaign to reclaim the Rayvan throne just yet. The man ran an entire operation across Tysaine and had the resources and people to track down whoever and whatever he needed. With a crew of talented mages at his disposal, Fig and the others had thought him the perfect ally. But he had his own plans—his own desires for the future. And had been ready to skewer Fig when he thought she'd betrayed him. They had to tread carefully.

"And helping him get the last remaining auran seed didn't win us his trust?" Fig wondered in annoyance, remembering the dim gold glow of the endangered seed inside the stolen chalice.

Not enough collateral, it seems, Emrah commented. *He's a transactional man, that one.*

"I noticed," Fig grumbled.

Emrah bobbed his head. *So he's making Dev and Ziggy work for the crew, doing jobs in Tirnalore—*

"What?" Fig demanded. She accidentally brushed up against Vaelor's leg. "They're doing jobs now? I don't really care if Ziggy wants to help the Fienn-Da rob people, but *Dev?*"

A few sparks shot from Emrah's snout and quickly sizzled out in the damp air. *He knew you would be mad. But if you want him to gain Evandahl's trust, this is the only way.*

Fig bit the inside of her lip. She knew it was true, judging from what she had seen of Evandahl's nature—but Dev could be such an idiot sometimes, even if he did have formal training from the Carriage House to control his air magic. What if he got caught by the Tysainian blackguard and brought before King Artaxis? The last heir of House Verrence would be a valuable political tool, and from what Fig had heard of the king, Artaxis would likely hand Dev over to Rhivven for the right price.

"I know," Fig sighed. "I'm just worried about him. Trying to be a good advisor, eh?"

Emrah bumped his head into the side of her neck again, and she closed her eyes.

We all have our parts to play, Emrah spoke into her mind.

We do indeed, she responded.

After Emrah expounded on Dev's most recent escapade with the Fienn-Da—a heist led by the sound mage, Fang, to retrieve a vile potion from an aristocrat who shouldn't have had it in the first place—the dragonet stretched his wings as far as he could and announced, *I'm going to find another cave if I can.*

"Wait," Fig said, before he lifted his claws off her shoulder. "Will you stay a while? Or are you heading right back to Tirnalore?"

And leave you here in the middle of the Twist? Bard's quills, no. You need me more than they do, my friend.

Relief flooded into Fig's core. She had told Emrah his priority should be to keep watch over Dev—him being the true heir to the Rayvan throne and all. But the truth was, she would rather keep the dragonet close. She watched him sail out of the crevice, only to catch a stiff breeze that lifted him up and out of sight.

I'll come find you when the storm's blown out, he told her a minute later. *I found another cave not far.*

Is it any bigger than this one? Fig joked weakly. *I think I'm going to have to sit in Vaelor's lap if I want to sit down.*

A scratching in her brain made her think Emrah was chuckling across their connection. *Sorry. When I said* cave, *I should have called it a svorcat hole. It's barely big enough for me, Svoran.*

Fig turned to give Vaelor a tight smile as another flash of lightning forked across the sky. He turned his briefly illuminated face toward hers, his rust-tinged eyes glinting in the lightning. The thunder that rumbled over the Twist and their tiny crevice came a few seconds later than usual.

"That's a good sign," Fig said, her voice coming out low. "Maybe it's starting to move away from us."

The wind still scoured the cliff face, tugging at Fig's wet clothes. A shiver seized her whole body, and suddenly Vaelor's arms shifted around her.

"You're freezing," he murmured in her ear. His hands moved, and soon she found herself wrapped up in the big Viren's arms, his warmth quickly taking the chill from her flesh.

"How in the Bard's scrolls are you so warm?" she demanded into his chest. She was thankful Emrah had left, as she felt her neck heating from more than just Vaelor's body temperature. She leaned her head against him.

A deep rumble sounded, not from outside, but from within his ribcage. A chuckle. Hope sprung in her heart at the light-hearted sound, one she hadn't heard in a while. "I run warm," he admitted.

"Lucky for me," Fig said through teeth that chattered, regardless of Vaelor's warmth embracing her. She was soaked through to the bone, and the rain showed no sign of letting up. Between the moisture and the wind that brushed its cold fingers across their cave entrance every so often, they might be in here a while.

One of her hands somehow traced its way through Vaelor's hair, finding a braid, then toying with the bead in it. A current of electricity seemed to be running through her whole body, most of which was pressed against his. But after Nithe...

"Vaelor," she whispered.

"Mmm?"

Another shiver ran through her. "Is everything..." The electrical current seemed stuck in her chest, making her heart pound furiously. "When your sword broke. Are you...? Are you all right?"

He drew in a deep breath, and she relished the feeling of his chest expanding as he breathed. "I...I don't know, honestly. At times I feel normal. Others, it's as if I've died again and am...not really here." His voice grew quiet, but with her head on his chest, she grasped at every word.

As if I've died again, she thought, placing her hand more firmly on his chest. "Are you worried?" she asked, her voice barely audible.

"About dying?" A chuckle rumbled through him. "If I was going to drop dead, I think I'd have done so already."

Fig swallowed nervously. She recalled Ziggy saying something similar. But what if it didn't happen right away? His life could be slowly leaching out of him.

"I lost my fear of dying when Rhivven killed me with my own sword, anyway."

"Rhivven?" Fig demanded, her head rising so she could meet his eyes, and the silvery red rings there. "He...did your crossover?"

Vaelor nodded. "That's how he became the Butcher of Viren."

She stared at him. After a minute or two, he took a deep breath and went on. "We stood in a line on the battlefield. Mist hung on the highlands. The final battle had gone through the night. By sunrise, all who remained were either dead for good—or dead and revived by the ritual. They brought a pair of red sisters... and one of their wagons I used to see trundling through Verindas to deliver holy water. At least I got to see the sunrise with fresh new eyes," he ended softly.

Fig's mouth trembled, and she snaked her hand up to stroke

his cheek. There was moisture at the corner of his eye, and she wiped it away with her thumb. He blinked and looked down at her. The red rings glinting in his eyes constricted.

And suddenly, it was like they were back on the *Trevena*, and his lips crashed down on hers like a wave in a storm. Her hand clutched the back of his head as she responded to the kiss, and his arms tightened around her body as if he were clinging to a life raft.

Finally, when they broke apart, she gasped, "I was afraid..." His sweet breath filled her senses, and she shook her head. "I was afraid that after your sword broke you had changed—that I didn't—"

"No matter what is taken from me," he said, reaching up to move a wet lock of her hair out of her face, "or *how much* is taken from me, know this: I want you, goldfire. And I won't let anyone change that."

FIG

The storm raged into the night, and though Fig was perfectly content being held by Vaelor, she began to sway on her feet while lightning rent the darkness. Despite her jest to Emrah about sitting in Vaelor's lap, she realized the maneuver wasn't even possible in such a cramped space. So she dozed where she stood, encircled by warm arms, lulled by the symphony of thunder.

Hope you two are decent. The words intruded into her dreams. Fig's eyes jerked open, and Vaelor clutched her tighter lest she tumble from the side of the crevice.

Emrah! she admonished in her mind. *Of course we are!*

Her neck flamed as she came to her senses. The closeness between her and Vaelor had been so intimate—more than any romantic encounter she'd ever had—and the two of them had been fully clothed and merely held each other all night.

Groggily, she realized the morning air outside was still—and, even better, dry. She stretched, extending a hand beyond the crevice, and the green and gold dragonet dropped down onto her arm. She chuckled. "Good morning."

She couldn't resist trailing her other hand down Vaelor's torso in parting as she slipped out of the cave and back onto the path so she could stretch her aching limbs. The sky was a pleasant blue once more, peppered with innocent-looking clouds.

"Well, now we know not to trust a few raindrops," she muttered. She was having a hard time not smiling—the storm had brought her Emrah, though not directly—and she had spent the night pressed up against Vaelor, wrapped in his arms. She'd had so few precious moments in these last months.

Shaking her head, she glanced at the man in question and offered him a quick smile. "I don't suppose you got any sleep either?"

He shook his head, running a hand through his hair. His eyes were the same as ever, but the expression around them seemed less strained.

"Do you know how much farther we have to go, Emrah?" Fig asked.

The dragonet lurched into flight and rose high above them. *I have no idea. Do you want me to scout it out and see?*

"No," Fig said quickly. "We'll get through when we get through. If you could just scout immediately ahead of us for anything on the path we should know about."

Emrah bobbed up and down in the air, and she took that as a yes. He darted off, leaving her and Vaelor with the arduous task of sliding along the ledge. But the air was fresh, the sun wasn't beating down on them yet, and her limbs were grateful for the movement after a cramped night. Her fingers skidded along the rock face at her back.

"You really didn't have to do this, you know," Vaelor rumbled after a while, when they paused for a brief respite to break their fast. Fig made sure her feet were solidly planted before trying to reach into her small pack that hung at her side, but then she felt large fingers cover her own hand as Vaelor got the food out for her. She smiled as he handed her an oat cake and a slightly bruised apple.

"What?" Fig asked, taking a bite from her oat cake. "Cross the Twist?"

"Come to Mar Nevan. Help me fix my sword."

She pinned him with a look. He didn't turn away. "I guess I didn't make it clear last night," she said quietly, hoping Emrah wasn't eavesdropping. "But I want you too. And I want you to be whole."

"As whole as I'll ever be," he muttered.

Her hand snaked up to grab his, and she squeezed it. "You are whole. And deserving. Now let's go get the sisters to tell us how to fix your sword. It's no different than if you'd broken a leg, in my opinion."

Strong fingers squeezed hers in return, and he let her have her hand back as they finished their food.

With one last glance at Vaelor beside her, she stood and continued on, ready to face Mar Nevan.

<hr>

The holy city lay much farther down the Twist. A collapse on the trail set them back several hours, time they spent shifting rocks out of the way. Fig feared they might have to spend another night on the cliffs. Emrah was a gift from the gods, able to topple rocks out of the way without fear of falling down the cliff, but Fig had to move some of the heavier ones. Eventually they were on their way again, the tips of her fingers a little bloody.

"I wonder what it would have been like if we'd hired the guide," Fig mused later that afternoon as they faced a sizeable gap in the cliff path. At the tavern, she'd assumed the dwarf just wanted their coin. Her respect for Mairead, who had crossed this path more than once, was increasing by the moment.

Only a few hours away, Emrah reported encouragingly, swooping overhead.

"I'd really like to get off this cliff while we still have daylight," Fig said.

Vaelor offered his hand so she could steady herself. Fig took it and eyed the gap. She tested the sturdiness of the edge with her foot, and crept all the way to the end, the toes of her boots hanging over nothing. Then she lifted her front leg and tipped her balance to cross the gap, Vaelor's steady hand giving her a boost.

Relief flooded her as her second foot followed the first and she landed on the other side, but that relief was short-lived when the rocks beneath her feet began to crumble. Her arms pinwheeled. Claws raked across her skin, yanking her forward in a flash of green scales. She stumbled, thrown off balance once more—but this time forward. She staggered farther away from the crumbling edge, clutching the rock face.

Panting, she turned back to look at the edge, then up at Vaelor who was staring at her.

"Well," she breathed. "Watch your step. Thanks, Emrah."

From her safe point, she pressed a foot to the remaining rocks at the edge to test their stability. One piece crumbled away into the crevasse, but the rest seemed secure. With his longer legs, Vaelor was beside her in no time, quickly moving away from the unreliable edge and urging Fig onward.

Two hours later, just as she was squinting in the waning light, the path suddenly widened to reveal a large rocky shelf. After a few hasty footsteps, she flung herself onto all fours, feeling the ground underneath. Emrah chirped, flying in circles overhead.

I can see the glowing lights from Mar Nevan, but it'll probably take you an hour on foot, he reported.

"I can hardly even think about standing right now," Fig said, "let alone trying to get our answers from the sisterhood. We'll camp here tonight. Well, a little farther away from the edge, perhaps."

Vaelor gave a low chuckle and set down his bag. Fig rolled over onto her back, feeling the solid rock beneath her, and closing her eyes. She was almost asleep when Vaelor offered her some food. They shared a few apples and some hard cheese before finding a better spot to sleep for the night, lying side by side to look up at the stars. Emrah drifted off somewhere farther into the rocklands, promising to keep watch.

They were cradled on either side by the mountainous rock walls, in a path that should lead straight to the holy city. They were close. Fig felt Vaelor's hand in hers just before her heavy eyelids enclosed her in darkness.

Fig drained the last of the water from her waterskin just as they rounded a bend in the path. Though a bed of rock hadn't been particularly comfortable, she'd had no trouble sleeping last night, the sheer weight of exhaustion keeping her shrouded in sleep until the warm sunlight had peered over the mountainous peaks.

Before them stood a sheer rock wall, shaped not by nature, but—according to legend—by the hands of dwarves. Perfectly flat, with detailed parapets and interwoven carvings in the wall separating it into various rectangles, it spanned the distance between the rockland peaks as far as they could see.

"The walls of Mar Nevan," Vaelor said in quiet reverence.

Emrah made himself scarce, soaring out of view.

Fig stared at the walls in awe. Even from here, she could see the craftsmanship. They could hear the *shushing* sound of water, but none was in sight—only the stone wall facing their path and the two guards in red standing at attention on either side of the open arched doorway, their red cloaks fluttering over black armor. The legendary Brothers of Morgha. Fig had never seen a red brother before, and she'd only heard scant rumors about them. They never left Mar Nevan, and while the sisters were blessed with healing magic, the brothers possessed something different—though what that was, no one knew. Fig had never cared...until now. She and Vaelor headed for the doorway. Runes framed the arch, the details carved deep into the stone.

She eyed the two guards nervously.

I'll meet you inside, Emrah told Fig. She thought she spotted him out of the corner of her eye; anyone else would think him a bird high on the drafts of wind above them.

Be careful, Fig warned.

They kept a steady pace toward the archway, weary pilgrims whose exhaustion was genuine. Through the arch, she could see activity inside the holy city: servants bustling about, vendors hawking their wares to the pilgrims, and red sisters calmly proceeding through the chaos in small groups, their red cloaks fluttering serenely behind them.

That's a wholesome welcome, Emrah said, jerking Fig's attention away from the inside.

What? she demanded.

Look up.

As they drew within half a dozen paces from the two guards at the gate, she saw six red-cloaked figures hanging evenly along the wall above the gate. She hadn't noticed them before—they were positioned between the wall's designs. Hanging there, blood staining the stones behind them, the rust-red darker than their pristine cloaks. Six Sisters of Morgha.

Fig tore her eyes away and back to the guards at the gate, who were now studying her and Vaelor. Her mouth seemed to glue itself shut.

Red runic tattoos similar to Mairead's ran over each man's left eye. The two guards nodded for them to proceed but remained silent. Her stomach in knots, she led Vaelor into the holy city in search of answers. It was too late to turn back now.

Why would they kill their own priestesses? Fig wondered to Emrah as she and Vaelor slowly entered the crowd. The gate they had come through wasn't nearly as busy as the rest of the city;

most people arrived by boat, except for the few pilgrims committed to the old way—coming on foot. Indeed, Fig noticed several reverential glances aimed their way, when people realized they had come from the Twist.

Drakioryn's claws, I wouldn't know, Emrah replied. *But you might want to find out.*

Fig nodded to herself as she studied the square tucked within the mountain peaks. The *shushing* sound she'd heard was coming from a waterfall at the north end of the square, crystal clear water cascading from the rocks jutting high above and falling into a large pool with decorative stone walls containing it. Stalls had been carved from rocky ledges, forming permanent structures for vendors selling food and red sisters presiding over the sale of various charms—prayers wrapped in blessed red fabric embroidered with runes—or silver statues of all sizes that had been dipped in holy water.

She didn't see any silversword presence, which was good for them—however, that meant that Mar Nevan was killing their own and hanging them on the walls as some kind of example. Fig didn't know which was worse. She eyed a red brother posted at the fountain as they passed. Pilgrims tossed coins into the fountain, making wishes for the Bard knew what. Fig nudged Vaelor briefly and they detoured over to the fountain. She dug her hand deep into her pocket for a copper and flipped it into the fountain, her thoughts on Vaelor's sword and leaving the city safely.

These weren't the holy waters of Morgha no, those were deep in a cavern inside the temple—but surely this pool had its own magic.

Mouth watering at the smells coming from the food stands, Fig dug in her pocket for a few more coppers. "Food?" she asked Vaelor.

He nodded, and she caught a glimpse of his former self when he said, "Yes, please."

Fig tried not to waste too much time scanning the food vendors, but they were scattered around the square, with long lines already forming at some of them. They finally settled on one who sold meat pies, half-moons you could hold in your hand filled with savory shafra and a tangy *soratillo* sauce that Fig had only ever tasted in Tysaine.

When they'd finished eating, they turned south, where red lanterns painted the way up an enormous stone staircase leading to the main temple.

"We find Sister Avelina," Fig muttered to Vaelor, taking his arm as they mounted the stone steps, "and then leave the way we came."

He nodded, silent, though she saw him pat the bag containing his broken sword.

They could camp out on the wide ledge before attempting the Twist again, safely beyond Mar Nevan's walls.

"And then I think we should head back to Arem and find Mairead—if she hasn't already left for Thoan. We should...um... warn her..." She trailed off. Vaelor had also seen the women hanging from the walls. Mairead had been kicked out of the red sisters for refusing to perform a silversword crossover—one she had still been forced to carry out, including the part of the ritual where the person was killed by their own weapon.

They passed two red sisters coming down the steps, and Fig stepped into their path at the last second. "Oh, excuse me!" Fig said. "I don't suppose you know where I could find Sister Avelina?"

The girls went pale and shook their heads, bustling down the staircase even faster.

Fig met Vaelor's red-ringed eyes. She couldn't help but wonder if Sister Avelina was one of the sisters hanging from the wall, but she kept going—the only place they would find any answers was inside the temple.

Finally, they crested the top of the stairs and were greeted by the late morning light filtering through some old red alvar trees. The temple spread out before them, dark wooden entrances set into the mountainside, with three cavernous openings leading inside. A trio of red brothers manned the entrances, exhibiting the same red eye tattoos and solemn silence as the others.

Pilgrims filtered in and out of the temple. Fig and Vaelor joined the throng, entering through a wooden foyer bedecked in paintings of Morgha—one was even painted directly onto the high ceiling, the goddess's face bright on one side and shadowed on the other.

Next was a simple chamber with a small stone fount at the center, where the ceiling opened up to the sky. This fount, a red sister was explaining to some other pilgrims, was one of the first the Sisters of Morgha had used to heal with the holy waters. Now it was accessed with wooden ladles and used to cleanse pilgrim's hands before they entered the temple proper.

"Excuse me," Fig said, stepping closer as the sister finished her explanation to another pair of pilgrims. She lowered her voice. "I'm looking for Sister Avelina. Do you happen to know where I might find her?" Fig held her breath.

The girl, a young dwarf, fluttered her tattooed hands and clasped them in front of her. "I'm sorry, no."

Fig shrugged, hoping to convey that she wasn't *too* concerned about finding Sister Avelina. "Oh. No matter. Just an old friend wanted me to pass on a greeting."

That made two sisters now who couldn't—or wouldn't—help her find Sister Avelina. Mairead had insisted she was the one to help them, the only one they could trust.

Masking her concern, Fig bent down to pick up the old wooden ladle from the side of the fount. She dipped it into the water—which, according to the sister, contained only a drop of the holy water—and poured it over each of her hands to cleanse herself before entering the holy place. Then she passed it to Vaelor, who solemnly repeated the ceremony, whispering what might have been a prayer under his breath. Having been brought back to life by the sister who performed his crossover, Vaelor knew firsthand the power of Morgha and her holy waters. Fig had also been healed by them before, though she would never know what it was like to undergo the silversword ritual.

Or so she hoped.

Dev's brother Shadryn had been eager to induct Fig into his sick plans, attempting to make her a "silvermage" as he had called it. But she would never forget Afrith's botched crossover, and the black flames that danced just under the mage's skin before they were snuffed out, like the life from his body. Mages weren't meant to undergo the crossover. Shadryn, now endowed with powerful black ice magic, was a solitary rogue accident. Abandoned on the Isle of Nithe, Fig was sure his plans to take back the Rayvan throne hadn't been snuffed out, only delayed. But before she could help Dev take back the throne, she had to help Vaelor.

After passing through the fount chamber, they delved deeper into the temple, where the silence around them grew into a palpable weight in the air. The walls were less polished, and soon became rough-hewn stone, with ancient runes and sigils carved at intervals in the path. Red lanterns lit their way, and they walked by a dozen more red sisters passing through silently.

Finally, they reached a simple antechamber, where the silence was broken by the sound of trickling water. Vaelor adjusted his hood, and the two of them exchanged a look before passing through the last remaining doorway, a simple arch, carved all around with an interwoven pattern.

A pair of red brothers were stationed in the shadows just inside the door. Fig moved alongside the other pilgrims who'd filtered in with them. Despite the number of people, the chamber was silent.

A pool of water greeted them, larger than the entire square outside. The surface was still, save the corner nearest them where a trickle of water ran down the rough rock face from somewhere unseen.

Fig could see the bottom of the pool. An ethereal silver glow, so subtle she wasn't entirely sure it was there, made the clear water visible throughout the whole cavern. Two red sisters stood solemnly by the pool's side, facing away as though guarding it from those who wished to see it. Fig's hand tightened on Vaelor's arm, which she had almost forgotten she had been holding.

They stood in awe for longer than Fig could tell, listening to the gentle trickle of water, and gazing into the ethereal glow of the water. These were pure healing waters—not the watered-down version she'd seen the effects of before. These waters had been responsible for a myriad of healings across the centuries, as well as countless deaths brought about by silversword crossovers.

Life *and* death, like the goddess who had blessed them.

FIG

Fig didn't know how long they stood there, too entranced to move, until the sound of footsteps behind them jerked her to attention, and she saw another set of pilgrims come through the doorway. She nudged Vaelor, and they headed toward the exit, passing by the two red brothers. Others still lingered in the chamber in reverent silence.

Before they could decide where to go next—Fig had vague ideas of finding the archives since they were supposed to be public—a red sister approached them. The dwarf girl from before. She clasped her tattooed hands in front of her, eyes cast down.

"I know where Sister Avelina is," she said quietly. "She's just very private. I can show you to her now."

Fig dropped Vaelor's arm and narrowed her eyes at the dwarf, unsure if she could trust the girl. "We have a mutual friend is all. We had...hoped she could help us find something in the archives," she said simply.

The dwarf bowed her head slightly. "Of course. Sister Avelina knows everything about the archives."

Fig's hand snaked out, and she grabbed the girl's arm. "What's going on with the sisters on the wall?" she whispered. If this was a trap, she at least wanted a bit more information.

An incomprehensible look passed over the dwarf's face before she spoke. "They dissented."

Fig's fingertips warmed, and she let go of the girl, rubbing her thumb across her fingertips to keep the sparks from escaping.

"And Sister Avelina wasn't one of these dissenters, correct?" Fig demanded.

The dwarf shook her head. "No. She's in the archives."

"Very well," Fig said.

I think there's a good chance we're walking into a trap, she warned Emrah. *Just so you know.*

A snorting sort of sound came across her mind, and Emrah said, *You would, Svoran. Just be careful.*

I'll try. Maybe look for other ways out of the temple for us?

Already circling the paths and streets around the grounds.

It warmed her a bit, knowing Emrah had their backs, even if they were heading for trouble. They followed the dwarf down one of the hallways leading off the main one, passing more rooms and more corridors. Groups of red sisters walked by, going about their business with their heads down. The deeper they ventured into the temple, the warmer Fig's fingertips grew. She brushed her thumb along her fingertips nervously, and a few sparks scattered to the floor, but no one else was around to see them. She was starting to wonder if she was moving closer to Emrah—with the way that he magnified her magic—or if it was merely her rising anxiety.

Finally, the hallway opened to a large antechamber, where a massive arched wooden door stood, one side open wide. The dwarf held out her hand, beckoning them forward, her eyes still cast down.

Only a few pilgrims and sisters were in the archives, though red lanterns burned brightly from the walls, and large chandeliers hung from the wide-open ceiling, shedding more light on the stacks than the windows could provide. Rows of books filled the center of the wood-paneled room, and square cubbies holding scrolls lined the walls, with spiral staircases at the corners leading to the open second floor. A nearby sister with dark skin and shiny black hair spilling from under her hood looked up from a large tome as they entered. Her gaze went to the dwarf that had led them there. The aura of silence grew heavy with tension before anyone spoke.

The dwarf said quietly, "These are the ones I told you about." Then she quickly excused herself and practically fled back down the hallway, leaving Fig and Vaelor staring at Sister Avelina.

"What's—" Fig began.

Sister Avelina's dark, heart-shaped face pinched in worry. "Who sent you?" she hissed. "What do you want?"

Fig glanced around the archives, but no red brothers lingered in stoic silence, and the few others inside were intent on their own work. "Mairead said you could help us find some information—on how to fix a broken silversword weapon." There was no sense drawing it out.

Sister Avelina shuddered, her gaze immediately flicking to catch Vaelor's red-ringed eyes. He stood rigid beside Fig, his broken sword in the bag he held over his shoulder.

"I can't," Avelina said quietly, shaking her head.

"Can't? Or won't?" Fig demanded. "Mairead said you—"

"*Mairead?*" Avelina hissed. "If *Mairead* were here, she'd be hanging on the walls with the others, the—" She gasped, turning back to the large open tome she'd been studying before they'd found her.

"They dissented," Fig said in an equally quiet voice, her suspicions confirmed. "Like when Mairead refused to perform a crossover?"

Avelina stared down at the tome, her eyes wide as if she'd finally learned the truth about why Mairead had left the sisters. She ignored Fig's question. "I can't help you. You should leave." Her gaze flicked between the two of them. "Mar Nevan isn't safe."

Fig? Emrah suddenly said in her mind.

What is it? We found Avelina, but she isn't helping.

I was wrong, he said. *There* are *silverswords here.*

"Was it the silverswords?" Fig asked Avelina, an unpleasant current running through her nerves. "The 'swords strung them up there, or…"

Avelina's eyes grew wide, and she stared vacantly, without looking down at her book, breathing hard.

Then Fig heard footsteps coming down the hallway toward them. Her nerves jumped like they were aflame. The other side of the double doors swung open, revealing not a contingent of silverswords, but five red brothers, their red cloaks fluttering over black and silver armor. They all had red runic tattoos over their left eyes —distinct from the red sisters' tattoos on the backs of their hands, which helped them heal people. The rune lines started above their eyebrows, running onto their eyelids and down to their cheekbones. Only the Bard knew what their purpose was…or what the brothers were capable of.

The man at the front beckoned to Fig and Vaelor. "Come. Mother Savidah requests your presence."

To Fig's relief, the red brothers left Avelina alone. Even though she had been curt, it was clear she feared retribution. Fig glanced up at Vaelor, whose face was steely, but he squeezed her arm before they followed the red brothers down the corridor. Fig thought briefly of their night on the cliffs, wondering if that was all the time they would get together. And whether it was the mother or the red brothers who were responsible for the barbaric punishment.

Fig wasn't sure which scenario was worse.

The red brothers led them back in the direction of the main pool, then one hallway farther, bringing them to a large stone chamber. The walls were rough rock, marking it as one of the more ancient chambers, and a small trickle of water fed a rough-hewn pool beside the entrance. The water didn't have the same ethereal glow as the holy pool. The woman at the other end of the room, however, gave off a silvery presence of magic Fig wasn't familiar with. It wasn't the taste of honey like the Gold Wood or the sting of copper that wafted from silversword weapons. It was something sharp and clean.

The woman stood beside an ornate wooden chair, posed *just so* as to not look like a throne upon its dais. The holy mother of Mar Nevan ruled here, that much was clear.

A black veil covered one half of her face, and as they grew closer, Fig could see that most of the brown skin on that side of her face was covered in red runic tattoos, similar to the red brothers, but fuller. The interwoven runes went from her hairline to her jawbone, running in a line through her left eye and branching out all the way from her earlobe to the centerline of her nose. The other half of her face was clear, with no veil or covering of any kind. Her hands were decorated like the sisters with healing tattoos. She wore a red gown with black lace and high shoulders, and a collar that rose high above her shoulders at the back. A thick black braid settled across the shoulder without the veil, running down to her waist.

The red brothers fanned out into a line, each falling to a knee with a fist to their heart, then rising to their feet just as swiftly, and marching silently from the room.

The chamber positively dripped in red light—not only from the red lanterns hung at intervals along the walls, but the stained-glass windows on the farthest wall behind the high priestess, where the sun was throwing deep red hues through the glass as it began its afternoon descent.

Fig's heart raced as she stood with Vaelor on the red carpet. She had no desire to bow or offer any kind of obeisance; she wasn't a priestess here, and though she believed in Morgha, she had no love for the mortal politics of the goddess's religion.

"Only fools would enter my city," the woman said in a deep, scratchy voice, "and expect me not to notice them. A fool with a broken sword, and his fiery companion, both wanted across Tytan for treason."

Fig swallowed the lump in her throat as she sized up the head priestess. They were alone with her, but the strange silvery magic emanating from the woman gave Fig pause, much like the tattoos covering half the woman's face. She knew the Sisterhood of Morgha could do more than just heal with the holy waters, but she didn't know exactly what they could do, and that terrified her. The magic of the water was mysterious and deep.

Vaelor stood stock-still beside her. She wanted to reach out to him, and by the Bard, she wished she could speak mind-to-mind with him now like she did with Emrah. Because, somehow, she didn't think they'd be able to fight their way out of this one.

Fig's mind whirred. If there were silverswords here, that didn't necessarily mean the sisterhood had aligned itself with Rhivven's cause. The silverswords needed the sisterhood's cooperation to perform crossovers, and the sisters no doubt wanted the silverswords' business. Fig frowned. "Perhaps we are merely pilgrims seeking Morgha's wisdom."

Mother Savidah chuckled, her surprisingly deep voice scratchy as she said, "Aren't we all? Come, sit," she urged.

Fig's shoulders had crept up to her ears, and she forced herself to relax as Mother Savidah indicated a set of chairs near the dais. Mother Savidah perched herself on the throne chair while Fig and Vaelor sank down onto the low cushioned chairs awkwardly. A red sister emerged from some hidden doorway at the back of the room, carrying a tray with a red glass teapot and matching glasses.

"You seek information," Mother Savidah said without preamble. Her gaze cut from Vaelor straight to Fig. The sister poured the amber-colored tea into their three glasses and left, but no one touched their drinks.

Fig didn't know how much to divulge, still unsure about Mother Savidah's possible alignment with Rhivven and the silverswords. Mairead had said only to trust Avelina, but that hadn't exactly gone well. They were in the tagor's den now...

"We do," Fig admitted. "But we can understand if you're not in a position to give it."

Mother Savidah's eyes narrowed at her. "Positions are relative to time and advantage. What is it you want to know?"

Fig thought her reply over carefully. "What will the cost to your advantage be in exchange for that information?"

A chuckle burst from Mother Savidah, and her eyes alighted. "Oh, I like this one. Such...spark. You want to know how to fix the sword," she said plainly, picking up her glass and taking a sip of the tea with her bottom two fingers outstretched.

Fig paused, wondering how Mother Savidah had known about that. She could have deduced it from the red ring in Vaelor's eyes. It wasn't exactly easy to hide, even under a hood. And she was certain that the events on Nithe were known only to those who had been there, so for Mother Savidah to know about the sword... Fig's gaze wandered to Vaelor's bag, which held the broken pieces, and back to the tattoos around Mother Savidah's eye. She drew in a breath.

"Yes." It was Vaelor who spoke. He cleared his throat and continued in his deep timbre. "If you know it is broken, then you know I need to fix it."

Mother Savidah's gaze landed on the bag as if she could see through to its contents—Fig wondered wildly if she could. "A Welded weapon is a tenuous thing. Life and death magics interweave with the weapon and its wielder. Fixing one..." She waved a hand slowly, searching for words.

"Can it be done?" Fig asked quietly, intent on Mother Savidah. If she was offering them even this much information, perhaps she wasn't aligned with the 'swords after all.

"It would take—"

The chamber doors burst open, revealing the same red brother who had led them here earlier—only this time, he was flanked not by his brothers, but by men and women clad in silver from head to toe, Welded weapons at their sides. The scent of copper permeated the chamber.

"By the mother," Mother Savidah groaned quietly. Then she grabbed Fig's wrist. "It can be done, but it needs to be bound once more—like your connection to your familiar, but that in itself is incomplete—"

"How do you—?"

"There's no time. Fix the sword first, then bind it. The magic still lies deep inside, but it grows weaker each day. You'll need—" Mother Savidah let go of Fig's wrist and rose to her feet as the silverswords moved closer, composing her face into the calm mask she'd greeted Fig and Vaelor with.

Fig and Vaelor followed suit, turning to face the newcomers. Vaelor ducked his face farther into the shadows of his hood. By the Bard, they were trapped...

Emrah? she called in her mind.

"Mother Savidah," one of the silverswords said, offering her a sloppy bow. "You didn't have to apprehend them yourself." He eyed the tea on the small table in disdain. "Or entertain them."

Mother Savidah's high lacy black shoulders rose and fell. "A distraction until you got here, Captain Djuren."

Fig's downcast gaze swiveled to meet the head 'sword, who she recognized from Nova Istra. The man who'd stolen the dwarves' ancestral sword—the Sword of Morin, made of an almost-mythic metal that would make any silversword damn near immortal should they Weld with it.

Heat rose in Fig's veins, and she could feel the well of fire deep in her core, ready to burst free. How had Rhivven's lapdog known they were here?

But Fig wasn't entirely convinced that Mother Savidah had betrayed them either, after she'd divulged the information about Vaelor's sword. She caught the high priestess's eye, and the woman stared at her. The woman seemed to be trying to convey something more than words.

"What is this about?" Fig demanded, attempting a distraction. At the same time, she reached out to Emrah, hastily filling him in on the situation.

Djuren swaggered forward, hand on his sword. The ring of silver around his eyes contracted as he got closer, and his nostrils flared. "I think you know very well, fire mage," he spat. "You and this—this *man*—are wanted by King Rhivven. And does he have plans for the both of you. Alive or dead." He looked over Vaelor like he was muck with the audacity to stick to the man's boot.

The silverswords had a deep prejudice against the Viren, whose oath lay not with the silversword enclave but with the House of Verrence.

Fig caught Vaelor's eye, then sent one more instruction to Emrah.

"Well," she said. "I'd quite like to remain alive, wouldn't you, Vaelor?"

With a whispered word, Fig flung her hand out, casting a wide circle of flames between them and the half dozen silverswords. Mother Savidah flung herself backward, escaping the circle entirely by vaulting behind her throne with the swiftness of a much younger woman.

Vaelor drew his replacement sword and planted his feet wide to meet one silversword who had tossed care to the gods and flung himself through the thick flame wall with a shriek of pain. Their weapons clashed in a sharp din that was quickly drowned out by a burst of breaking glass behind them. Emrah sailed overhead, bits of red glass scattering off him as he flapped his wings, sparks sifting down amid the sound of stained glass shards clattering to the floor.

Flames erupted from Fig's palms, aimed straight at Djuren. Power surged through her veins, doubling the size of the fireballs.

What now, Svoran? Emrah asked.

That was as far as I'd gotten, she admitted, sending another burst to keep Djuren at bay should he decide to brave the flame wall. Vaelor dispatched his opponent with a kick to the chest, sending him back through the flames. His companions yanked him shrieking from the fire and dragged him back to safety. Djuren had started to circle them like a caged beast—only Fig and Vaelor were the ones trapped.

"Goldfire!" Vaelor called, grabbing hold of her arm and drawing her attention to the back of the room. Mother Savidah had pulled away, and though it was clear her instinct was to run, doing so might signal guilt to the silverswords. The high priestess's gaze kept darting to a small dark doorway behind her, where the red sister had appeared earlier. Vaelor pulled Fig to the edge of the circle. "Let's go," he said into her ear.

She sent another burst of fire at Djuren and his companions, dropping the circle of flames and sprinting for the doorway, Vaelor's hand at her elbow. Emrah kept up his harrying, swooping down upon the 'swords and showering them with bursts of flame and sparks.

I'll go out the way I came in, Emrah told them. *I'll meet you outside.*

Thanks, Emrah, Fig called gratefully as she reached the small arched doorway. It led into a dark hallway where a dim red light glowed at the far end. She didn't voice her thoughts to Emrah about *if* they made it outside. It was probably best not to put those thoughts into words.

FIG

They could still hear shouting from the high priestess's chamber when they reached the end of the corridor where a single red lantern hung at a crossroads of hallways. Fig chose a random direction away from Mother Savidah's chamber. When she turned to look back, all she could see were the red rings of Vaelor's eyes glinting in the darkness as he followed.

Finally, they reached another corridor intersection—this one much larger. The high ceilings revealed rock and carved runes, which she barely glimpsed before running into a red sister in the dim red light. Fig was forced to throw her arms around the girl to steady herself. "Oof! Sorry!"

"You!" the sister said. Fig recognized Sister Avelina's heart-shaped face immediately. "What are you—what's—"

"I'm sorry," Fig said again. "We need to get out of here—it's the silverswords. Is there any way—"

Avelina shook her head violently. "N-No—" Avelina yanked Fig into the shadows of a doorway. Vaelor stood guard, melding into the shadows beside them. "You should head for the boats. They'd catch you too fast on the Twist. There should be one last one leaving tonight."

"But won't the boat—"

"Here," Avelina said, jiggling the handle of the door they stood next to. She disappeared inside for a second, then returned with two red cloaks.

As Fig threw one over her shoulders, a clamor arose down the servant's hallway, and two silverswords emerged from the darkness into the dim light of the vestibule. Djuren roared and charged at them.

Vaelor swiftly unshouldered the bag that held his sword and shoved it into Fig's hands. "Please, keep this safe," he said. Then he whirled to meet Djuren.

Avelina tugged on Fig's arm, but Fig pulled away, slinging the single long strap of Vaelor's sword bag across her chest and shifting it so that it hung behind her back where it would be safer.

Flames erupted at her hands, and Fig turned to face the silverswords. Vaelor moved with inhuman speed to meet them. He swept one 'sword's legs out from under her, then rolled across the hall to avoid Djuren's sword. Two more silverswords appeared from a corridor, and Fig sent flames roaring in their direction.

But the flames only got halfway across the vestibule before they flickered and died as if snuffed out by an invisible hand of darkness. *What in the name of the Bard...?*

Wondering if something was wrong with her magic, she reached deep into her core, feeling the strength of her inner flames. Everything seemed normal, so she summoned gold fire to her hands again, looking for an opening in the fight.

Vaelor slammed against another silversword's chest, locking weapons. He wrenched himself free to avoid Djuren once more, then swung his replacement sword at the man to keep him back.

A gasp escaped from Avelina, who had frozen by the closet door, eyes wide.

Glowing red runes appeared to hover in the shadows of

another dark corridor, then a red brother stepped into the vestibule close to where Vaelor was fighting.

Expressionless, the brother lunged forward, executing swift movements with his hands, the red tattoos around his eyes glowing brighter. He made a final pushing movement in the air toward Vaelor, who had just grabbed hold of the silversword about to stab him. Vaelor shoved the silversword woman in front of him at the last second. She collapsed to the floor, dead.

Vaelor backed away from the red brother, who turned his attention to Fig and Avelina. Glowing tattoos glinted in her direction as the silverswords engaged Vaelor once more.

Fig raised a shaking hand, her flames bursting in a fresh surge of magic. The red brother continued forward, his shorn head glinting in the red lantern light as his hood fell. He began a rhythmic dance of controlled hand movements, and Fig's flames guttered and went out, just like before. The red brother's lips curled up in half a smile. Fig's eyes grew wide. There wasn't something wrong with *her*—he'd snuffed out her flames with his magic.

She tapped into her core, delving deep for the searing heat of her magic—connecting to the flames along the inner pathways of her magic. Gold fire shot from her palms once more, strong at first, but just as quickly snuffed out by more of the brother's gestures.

Avelina yanked hard on Fig's arm, pulling her out of the way as the red brother threw his hand in a pushing motion toward her. Something slammed into the wall beside them, unseen but hard enough to crack the stone wall. His magic.

Fig stared down at her hands helplessly. The red brother seemed satisfied that Fig was out of the fight, and turned his attention back to Vaelor, who was fending off two silverswords at once. The fourth lay on the ground, unmoving. Djuren hung back with the superiority of his station, uneasily eyeing the red brother, his sword raised should his lackeys fall. The brother began working his magic, this time aimed at Vaelor's back.

"No," Fig growled, yanking off Vaelor's bag and shoving it

into Avelina's hands. She launched herself forward, hands formed into claws as she gathered flames.

The red brother paused in his signing, turned, and made a pushing motion toward Fig instead.

Everything went black as a crushing weight slammed into her chest.

She blinked and sparks shot from her fingertips. Everything was quiet, peaceful, even. Where was Vaelor?

She gasped and felt a small hand grab her shoulder. Sister Avelina.

"Where are we? Where's Vaelor?" Fig demanded. It took a second to realize she was sitting on the ground, her back against a stone wall. It felt like she'd fallen off the Twist, and if the immense pain gathered in her torso was any indication, she wouldn't be surprised if it was entirely black and blue. She put a hand to her chest and felt it rise and fall painfully with each breath.

They were at the end of a narrow corridor. Vaelor's sword bag sat in her lap. Avelina knelt beside her, her tattooed hands placed perfectly on her knees.

"No, no, no," Fig muttered, sparks jumping in her fingertips as she felt around her. "I have to go back for Vaelor."

Avelina stared down at her sadly and shook her head. "You can't. They will have taken him to the brothers' sanctuary. We'll have to leave now if there's any hope of surviving."

"No, no, no," Fig repeated, trying to scramble to her feet. It took some effort, but she made it, her gaze sweeping the dark hallway Avelina had evidently dragged her to. "Where are we? You have to bring me back to him!"

Avelina put a finger to her own lips. "Please!" she hissed, "Be quiet! We're not far from the path that leads to the docks, but I couldn't drag you down there without arousing suspicion. He told me to—"

"*He told you what*," Fig said in a quiet deadpan, the question more like a statement.

"He told me to get you out and to 'fix it first,'" Avelina said, sticking out her chin. "And now I have to leave Mar Nevan too. Brother Gevalin saw me, knows who I am. They'll kill me, and they'll kill you too."

"What is going on in Mar Nevan?" Fig asked through gritted teeth. *Emrah?* she called loudly in her mind. "*Who* strung up your sisters?" Sudden anger sparked through her, as flames surged across her knuckles. Avelina had taken her away from Vaelor, and now he was... Dead? Held captive by the ruthless red brothers or the silverswords? She had no way of knowing.

"We have to get to the dock before the last boat goes out," Avelina urged.

"*What is going on here?*" Fig demanded, stomping her foot.

Avelina bunched her hands into fists. "The 'swords came. They met with the brothers behind Mother Savidah's back. They've convinced them to join Rhivven, promising scores more crossovers as long as we cooperate—so, of course, filling our coffers. Those who questioned—"

"Ended up on the wall," Fig finished. "So it wasn't Mother Savidah, and the brothers are no longer under her control." Fig shuddered at the thought of those glowing tattoos and eerie fighting techniques, able to snuff out her flames and kill with a few hand signals. The tattoos under their eyes must be imbued with the holy waters, giving them access to magic.

"We have to get to the dock now," Avelina repeated. "The 'swords won't take the last boat—it's one of the smaller craft meant for holy water deliveries, not large groups of pilgrims. But once word reaches the rest of the brotherhood, they'll probably shut down the dock, if they haven't already..." Now she was rambling.

Fig, Emrah's voice came.

Have you seen Vaelor? she asked, desperate.

I saw them bring him to a large building off the main temple. He's alive. There're scores of red brothers there keeping watch. I heard Djuren say they're bringing him to Rhivven.

Fig's heart wrenched. *Then they'll keep him alive. There's... there's no chance I can get him from the red brothers. Just one of them snuffed out my magic with a flick of his fingers. But if they're bringing him to Rhivven... That's my only chance.*

Avelina stared at Fig pleadingly.

Feeling like she might throw up, Fig nodded.

The red sister sighed in relief and pushed the door open.

Fig followed, feeling as if she'd left part of her own soul behind. She wondered whether Vaelor could feel it even more acutely, since she was now carrying his Welded weapon—a piece of his own soul—away from him. And all she could do was try and fix it.

***

Two girls in red cloaks emerged from the temple's back door and walked swiftly in the dusky mountain light.

Avelina is leading me to the dock, Fig told Emrah. *Please, will you watch over him?*

Emrah's voice came immediately. *Go, Svoran. Get out of here. I'll keep an eye on Vaelor.*

Mother Savidah wasn't working with them, she babbled. *The 'swords converted the red brothers to their cause.*

I'll keep watch. You need to get yourself out now.

Tears began running hot down her cheeks. *Please,* she added.

She let Avelina lead her down a worn path that brought them to a set of ancient stone stairs. Behind them, the city square was alive with the sound of pilgrims purchasing trinkets or heading back to their taverns for dinner. There was even lute music wafting from somewhere. With each footstep, guilt pricked her skin.

Her thoughts began to formulate another possibility. What if she went back and waited for them to bring Vaelor out of the red brother's sanctuary? But while they were in the holy city, they were at the mercy of the red brothers with only two ways in and out even if Fig could manage to get past the brothers with their uncannily fast magic.

They got to the bottom of the steps and followed the worn path along the mountainous seaside, Vaelor's sword bag thumping against her hip. She clutched it tightly, running her fingers over the canvas to feel the pieces within. *Fix it first.*

"Please Mother Morgha, please, please, *please*," Avelina chanted. They hurried around a rocky outcropping, and Avelina let out an immense sigh of relief. "It's still here. Quick. Hurry!"

Fig could see lights down at the harbor. A lone boat sat at the dock, surrounded by a flurry of movement as the dockhands readied it for departure.

Doing her best to watch for rocks so she wouldn't break her ankle as they rushed, Fig followed the girl, keeping her borrowed red hood over her head. Her heart raced, knowing what she was leaving behind. Her vague plans of waiting for the silverswords to come out of the temple with Vaelor were quickly coming to naught. If she got on that boat, she was leaving him behind.

Fix it first, he'd said. Could she really leave him like this? If he were killed, the sword would be useless. But she and Emrah— against a contingent of silverswords and who knew how many red brothers, who she couldn't even fight?

Hot guilt swamping her chest, she allowed Avelina to lead her onto the dock as the girl did her best to calmly tell the captain they'd be accompanying the shipment tonight. Fig's eyebrows drew together, but then her gaze landed on the large barrels stacked on the deck of the boat. Holy water.

Fig schooled her face and gazed out at the dusky sea, as if for all the Bard's quills, this was something she did every day. Her insides churned with turmoil.

The captain welcomed them aboard without a single question, affording them a place of honor away from the few pilgrims catching the last boat of the day.

Fig thought she was going to throw up still as she gazed up at the silhouette of Mar Nevan high up on the cliffside. Vaelor...

How could she leave him behind? She couldn't. She didn't care if the red brothers were stronger. She started to stand, ready to leave the boat, when she saw a large group of red brothers descending the mountain path. It was too late. Fig fell back into her seat as the boat jolted away from the dock, quickly claimed by the current.

She clutched the bag holding his sword and let the tears flow as they bobbed through the strong current heading south, where —hopefully—her chances of rescuing him were higher.

A dozen sets of red tattoos stared toward them from the darkening cliffside.

Fig awoke several hours later with her head on Avelina's shoulder. She quickly righted herself. The sister appeared wide awake, and Fig offered her apologies.

"It's no trouble," Avelina said softly. Indeed, many of the other passengers were asleep on their neighbors' shoulders, many exhausted after an exciting day in the holy city.

Fig's day had been far too exciting for her liking, and in the worst way possible.

She clutched the sword bag, hugging it to her chest and hating herself. Hating Avelina for dragging her away from Vaelor—for listening to his pleas to send Fig to safety.

She hadn't heard anything from Emrah back at Mar Nevan, but the distance would soon bar any communication. *How* she would find out what was going on with Vaelor was up to the Bard now.

She thought back briefly over what Mother Savidah had said about Fig's familiar connection, and how it wasn't complete. Perhaps that was why she couldn't speak with him over long distances. Fig still didn't understand how he'd become her familiar in the first place—let alone whether the connection was complete. But perhaps there was a way to strengthen their connection...

Every time her thoughts drifted away from Vaelor, returning to him was all the more painful. Disgust riddled her core at her cowardice in abandoning him. A growing part of her was sure she could have fought harder and helped him stand against the 'swords or the red brother. She had barely even *tried*...

But the memory of Vaelor handing his broken sword to her—before the fight had even begun—made her heart wrench. Had he intended to fight all along so she could escape?

She closed her eyes, and moisture trickled down her cheeks once more. She quickly swiped it away with the backs of her hands.

"Will we reach Thoan tonight?" she asked Avelina. At least, she could reunite with Mairead, warn the girl about the silver-swords and red brothers' crusade...

"Thoan?" the sister said. "The holy water shipments always go to Rayva for distribution. We're headed to the capital."

FIG

Fig watched the glowing lights of the Rayvan harbor with an increasing sense of dread, clutching the bag with Vaelor's sword tightly to her.

Rayva. The last place on the continent she wanted to be right now.

"Bard's broken quills," she muttered, as the docks came into view across the night-dark waters. She sat up straighter, adjusting the hood of her red cloak.

Avelina sat pin-straight as always, staring ahead.

"Where are the barrels headed? Do we need to stay with them?" Fig hissed quietly in the girl's ear.

Most of the boat's other occupants were still asleep, nodding off on their neighbors' shoulders or chins tipped toward their chests, but the trio of crewmen were wide awake, watching the boat's progress with a keen eye. The captain stood in front of the stack of barrels, stroking his dark brown beard.

"The boatsmen normally deliver the barrels to the temple, but since I said we'd accompany them, we have to follow through. The boatsmen aren't part of the order, but they'll report straight back to Mar Nevan after the delivery. The water's distributed all across Tytan from here, but the first stop is at the temple in the castle district. It's the largest temple in Rayva."

"Of course it is," Fig muttered to herself.

She kept her head down until she felt the boat bump up against the dock, and the calls of the crewmen hitching the boat to the posts began to wake the other passengers. Soon, Avelina was pulling her to her feet, and the two of them proceeded down the gangplank at the behest of the captain, to await their watery charges.

Fig's stomach roiled in turmoil as she turned her back on the capital city to watch the barrels' progress. Somewhere behind her, Rhivven sat on the Rayvan throne, which by all rights belonged to Dev.

She clutched the sword bag to her side. Surely the silverswords would bring Vaelor here to meet Rhivven. They'd said dead or alive, but from everything she had seen and heard of him, Rhivven was a man of spectacle. He would want to make an example of the silversword—or at least, mete out punishment personally. Vaelor was not only Virenish but had crossed the enclave and helped the crown prince escape a coup. So perhaps a trial, ending in a predetermined verdict, of course. Or maybe the false king would skip any kind of pretense and go straight to public execution. She swallowed the lump in her throat. Though every instinct screamed at her to get out of Rayva as fast as she could, she knew she had to stay in the city and wait for Vaelor.

They would certainly bring him by boat; even in his melancholy state, Vaelor would toss the other 'swords off the Twist, should they try to transport him that way.

She barely noticed the others disembarking, sleepily talking to one another about their experience in the holy city as they headed home to bed. What Fig wouldn't give for a nice warm place to call home right about now. The closest thing she had to one was Emrah's tower, but now, Knoll was there...

Fig's heart lifted as she thought of the dwarf, and she knew exactly what she needed to do once she found Vaelor. The dwarf would fix the sword, no questions asked. After that, they just needed to figure out what Mother Savidah said when she told them to bind it to him.

Bolstered by some semblance of a plan, Fig fell into step beside Sister Avelina as the boatsmen loaded the barrels of holy water onto a cart pulled by a solitary old mare, with room for a single driver at the front.

She shared a look with Avelina and wordlessly urged the girl to take the driver's seat. The boat's captain helped Avelina up into the seat, then tipped his cap at the two girls and returned to his work on the boat. Fig had no choice but to follow Avelina and the cart out of the harbor, even though she'd rather lie in wait, watching for a boat to come from Mar Nevan.

Her feet reluctantly trod the cobblestone streets as she focused on keeping her back straight and appearing as serene as Avelina, since she also wore a red cloak. She kept her eyes on the wheels as she walked beside the wagon, taking deep breaths. The familiar sights and sounds of Rayva had set her nerves jangling. A miasma of scents ranging from the sharp tang of silverswords to the smell of mud caked in the cobbles, and of course, the towering statute of Tesvier the Relentless—a carved monument which featured the silversword's double-sided axe in formal rest at his feet. From here, she could see only his head, covered by a helmet with winged sides. She tore her gaze back to the wagon wheels and took shallower breaths.

Unfortunately, the wagon's path led them closer to Tesvier's statue, which towered three times as high as the two-story buildings surrounding it. She couldn't help but look up. The silversword king—a Verrence, of course—stood straight, both hands on the axe handle, the weapon's head filling the space between the statue's feet. The face was indiscernible through the helmet, but its wings flared in the pre-dawn sky, silhouetted by the half moon lurking behind bright white clouds.

In the square itself, Fig saw dwarves lingering amid doorways and at the heads of alleyways. The way they loitered made her wonder if they were homeless. She'd never seen *any* homeless gathered here in the castle district—other parts of the city were another story. She didn't think their presence by the statue of the Verrence king who'd claimed the ancient Mountain for the crown was insignificant. Avelina steered the cart onward, though Fig would have rather abandoned it somewhere; surely the sister felt an obligation to bring the holy water to its proper place.

A pair of silverswords strode down the street toward them. Heat danced in Fig's core, and she fought to keep the sparks in, making her fingers stiff so she didn't accidentally brush her fingers together and release them. Which, of course made her look extremely odd—walking with stiff arms and splayed fingers—so she balled up her fists and stuffed them in her robe pockets, trying to adjust her shoulders to look as serene as Avelina. Fig had to give the red sister credit—she possessed a deep well of calm for someone who'd wronged her own order and was marching into the briarwolves' den just to deliver holy water.

The approaching silverswords didn't head for the holy water shipment but a grouping of three dwarves who had gathered in the doorway of a closed apothecary. Fig trained her eyes on the holy water barrels, glimpsing the scene in her periphery. Shouting from the doorway commenced, and a thick scent of earth wafted toward her so strongly she might have been walking on a dirt path and kicking it up herself. No one knew much about dwarven magic besides the dwarves, but there was *something* about them and their affinity for the earth and metal.

The sound of fists striking flesh filled their ears as the wagon rolled out of the square—until a sharp cry and a gurgle rent the air.

Fig clenched her fists harder, hoping she wouldn't singe her disguise.

"How much farther is the temple?" she demanded quietly as the buildings lining the streets enclosed them. "Can't we just leave this here?"

The other girl glanced at her, the white of her eyes bright on her shadowed face. "No, we can't. Another block or two. I can't remember. I don't normally leave Mar Nevan," she added in a hoarse whisper.

Perhaps the sister's well of calm had a leak in it after all.

The street transformed into a more pristine path with red lanterns lining the stone walls. They passed under stone archways, and Fig spied a tunnel ahead, its deep shadows marred only by the dim red glow within. She shot a panicked glance at Avelina. She hadn't expected a tunnel to lead into the temple, but it made sense for important holy water deliveries. Except they would be trapped for certain in less than a minute if they encountered anyone who noted their presence.

"Avelina," she hissed over the creaking wagon wheels. "We can't go in there."

The sister's eyes widened, and she shook her head. "We have to—"

Fig grabbed the girl's arm. "We're close enough, aren't we?"

Avelina's throat bobbed as she swallowed visibly. "I suppose," she whispered, looking around for a second before lowering the reins.

Fig helped her down, and they left the mare standing at the edge of the tunnel, the holy water as close as it would get. Part of Fig wanted to smash the barrels for what the sisterhood had allowed to happen. The red brothers had taken control—but some of them had tried to stop it. Some of the sisters had also resisted. They just hadn't survived the ordeal.

Her stomach in knots, Fig grabbed Avelina's hand and led her back the way they'd come. They turned off the street before they reached the Tesvier statue square, and she hastily guided Avelina down a side street. She kept her pace to a light jog, though she wanted to sprint through the streets of Rayva and never look back.

Anyone who noticed her light jog would assume she just wanted to get off the dark streets and home safely. Sprinting, on the other hand, would look guilty at this time of night—something reserved for careless thieves and fools.

As she reacquainted herself with the streets, she found her feet leading her to the one place she thought could be safe. The surrounding streets became grittier, the buildings more dilapidated, and her thoughts whirred as she considered what to do.

"Black End?" Avelina demanded, when they were a couple blocks in. She dug in her heels and tried to wrench her arm out of Fig's grip. "Oh no—"

"Yes," Fig replied. "Now take off those robes." Fig quickly disrobed and balled the red fabric into a heap.

Avelina's jaw dropped, and she looked down at herself in the dim light spilling from a nearby tavern, the Hart's Demise. "I—no —I—"

"Please," Fig urged. "Red sisters draw notice, and that's not something we need right now. We should get you some gloves too. That's how we got in trouble with Mairead. When she stopped wearing her robes."

Eyes swimming with unshed tears, Avelina just stared at her.

"I'm sorry," Fig said, hugging her ball of robes to her stomach. "I really am. This is probably—well, this is all my fault for approaching you at the temple. But Black End is the only place in Rayva that I have anyone who might pass for a friend."

Avelina stared daggers at her as she also removed her robes. She wore a simple brown and cream tunic and loose pants underneath, a brown rope belt around her waist. "Maybe after all of this is over, you'll tell me everything that happened to Mairead," she growled. "I have a feeling we didn't get the whole story."

"I'd be delighted," Fig said without emotion. Pressure filling her chest, she glanced down both sides of the street. Only a few people milled about the tavern, which seemed usual. Fig just hoped the few people she knew and half-trusted were still around. In recent years, she'd tried to distance herself from Tytan's underbelly, and with the coup, there'd been plenty of upheaval everywhere. She didn't know who was on which side of things anymore.

She sighed, bringing her attention back to Avelina, and her

gaze softened. "Do you have family? Anywhere outside Mar Nevan that would be safe for you?"

Avelina didn't look at her, instead staring down at the neatly folded robes in her arms. "My parents still live in Pan Vidda, but I don't have any money, any—"

Fig nodded. "Right. Good—that you have a place to go, I mean. And that it's not on this continent. Here, take this." She shoved a fistful of coins at the girl—money sent by Dev.

"But won't they ask for papers?" Avelina said. Her voice sounded as if all her hopes had been crushed—the promise of home barred by something so trite as *papers*.

"That's one of the reasons we're *here*," Fig said, waving one hand vaguely. A wave of vertigo hit her when her thoughts immediately shifted to Bruna, and she had to steady herself on the wall of the building they stood next to. The thoughts were swiftly replaced by melancholy when she realized she had been thinking of her friend as if she were still alive and could still forge the best documents this side of the Notch.

Fig took a steadying breath. "Look, I'll get you some papers so you can get out of here. You'll be safe in Pan Vidda. Just do me a favor, and next time you pray to your goddess, say one for my friend Bruna, will you? She was...killed...at the beginning of all this mess. I don't know if it'd be worthy coming from me."

Avelina's brows furrowed. "Why, of course it would. Just because I bear these tattoos doesn't mean I'm any more worthy of a person than you."

Fig shrugged. Avelina didn't know anything about her past or what she was willing to do. She turned and glanced at the tavern, the place she'd go first, but a soft hand on her arm drew her attention.

"My station in the sisterhood only means that I've been bestowed with Morgha's power to heal. But death comes for everyone." She grimaced. "Which sounds really ominous when I say it like that—sorry. But it's true, Morgha comes to everyone. And that means we're all equals in the end."

Fig gave a nod and attempted a smile. "Thanks."

FIG

Fig was nursing her second glass of ale in the Hart's Demise when Harryn dropped into the seat beside her. Avelina nearly jumped out of her chair but snatched her empty glass as if to keep it away from the man. His hair hung in greasy curls that couldn't decide whether they were brown or gray, and the sharp scent of ashbar smoke clung to his clothes, stinging Fig's nostrils. His face was worn and weathered after fifty years in Tytan's underbelly.

"Well, well, well," Harryn drawled, pulling a flask from seemingly nowhere and taking a swig. Fig's stomach leapt. While she'd seen Harryn's particular magic before, it now reminded her of the mage she'd met—and killed—in Tysaine, who could make knives appear and disappear. Harryn's was different, though; he could make anything appear or disappear in a certain small radius around himself. Certainly handy for a thief. "If it isn't Fairaleigh Veil, by the Bard's lucky quill. Been seeing your face around a lot." He tipped his head ever so slightly toward the spot by the tavern door where several fliers plastered the wall.

Fig leaned back in her chair. "I'd say it's nice to see you, Harryn, but the bartender took so long delivering my note, I was starting to think the two of you had turned me in." She gave him a charming half-smile.

He chuckled, which turned into a fit of coughing. "'Course not, Fig. You know I wouldn't do that to our kind."

"I thought I knew a lot of things, Harryn," she said wearily, "but the rules are changing all the time."

"Indeed they are, indeed they are." He glanced at Avelina, then lowered his voice. "What is it you need? I know you wouldn't come to Rayva if there wasn't a good reason—blimey, you're not here for the tournament, are you?"

She leaned closer against her will, her nostrils wrinkling at the strong ashbar scent. "What tournament?"

His thick graying eyebrows dug deep ridges into his forehead as they rose. "King Rhivven's holding a tournament for some ancient dwarven sword—figured that might be why you risked it..." He jerked his head again toward the fliers.

Covering one with her face was a royal-looking flier she hadn't noticed before. Between the crests and flourishes, she could make out only a few words: *sword — glory — power —*

"Bard's broken quills," she grumbled. "No, we're not here for some tournament. I'd like to get out of Rayva before it starts, if I can. No, I need papers for my friend here to get a boat to Pan Vidda."

Harryn gave Fig a sad smile. She knew he must have been hit hard by Bruna's death. Bruna had introduced Fig to Harryn in the first place, back when Fig had been looking for legitimate mage work. He'd been able to give her a few jobs she didn't morally disagree with and never gave her a hard time about turning down the more unsavory jobs.

"That I can do," he said, the flask appearing in his hand once more.

"And I need to find Conham," she added quietly. She needed

to get into the castle—that's where the 'swords would bring Vaelor once they arrived in Rayva—and Conham was the only one who might be able to help her.

At the mention of the man's name, Harryn's swig turned into a double. He coughed and cleared his throat. "Might take a bit longer, that."

"Papers first," Fig said. "And if you know of somewhere to stay while I wait…" She hoped Vaelor would land in port tomorrow, but if the silverswords took a boat to Thoan to avoid notice and traveled the rest of the way on land… Well, she had no way of knowing when he'd enter the city. She'd just have to wait until she heard from Emrah.

Harryn nodded gruffly, stroking the gray bristles on his unshaven chin. "Aye. I can try. The city's filling up with all the news of this tournament. But there might be a safehouse I know of… Aye," he said, still nodding.

Fig watched him go, riddled with apprehension.

He'd promised he'd be back sometime before sunup with the papers, at which time he could take Fig to the safehouse. So Fig ordered another ale, and the two girls moved to one of the more secluded booths at the back wall of the tavern to wait out the night. Avelina, hands hidden below the table, asked the bartender for a cup of tea when she came to bring Fig's glass.

"Are you sure you can trust that man?" Avelina asked around a yawn.

Fig had to work hard to stifle a yawn of her own. She pushed the ale glass away and toyed with the ring of liquid it left on the table in front of her. "Course not. But he's the best we've got."

Avelina stared at her.

"I'm sorry," Fig said, shaking her head. "I'm dead tired. And I've known him for a few years. He's given me work before. I just hope whatever he's doing for coin now is better than whatever reward they're offering for me."

"What have you done, exactly?" Avelina said, brows furrowed. "I know you came to Mar Nevan about a broken silversword weapon, which was unusual in itself—"

"It's a long story," Fig said. "But we do have some time to kill." She took a deep breath and glanced around to check for unwanted listeners before beginning. "So one night, I'm in a tavern waiting for a job, and that very same Bard-cursed silversword lays his hand on me and says..."

By the time Harryn returned, Avelina was asleep—her head rested on the table, red robes folded beneath it like a pillow. Fig had had to reach over and rearrange the girl's hands, so her tattoos stayed out of sight.

The mage slid onto the bench next to Fig, and at once the smell of ashbar smoke assailed her, jolting her senses awake.

"Good news is," he began, "Jaffid was around and drew up your papers."

"And the bad news?" Fig said, narrowing her eyes.

"I didn't say there was bad news," he said, coughing and clearing his throat. "Just some...*mediocre* news, you might say."

Fig rolled her eyes.

"Conham's gone into hiding, but I have a contact who can find him."

Biting the inside of her lip, Fig nodded. "I'm not surprised he's in hiding. But I really need his assistance—and soon."

"I can put a few people on it...but they're working blokes."

Fig was already reaching into her money pouch. She counted out five gold coins just by touch before pulling them out and sliding them across the table.

"That'll cover the papers," he said easily, an official-looking envelope appearing in his hand out of nowhere—or more likely, magically whisked from his pocket.

Five more gold coins in front of him, Harryn smiled, and nodded at Avelina. "There's a ship heading to Pan Vidda at daybreak and another at sunset."

"I'll get her to the docks before daybreak," Fig said, relief flooding her chest. And maybe she could keep a lookout for a boat coming from Mar Nevan while she was there—she might not need to break into the castle after all.

Harryn nodded, taking another swig from his flask, which then disappeared. "And I've got a place for you in the South Ninth district to wait out Conham."

"South Ninth?" Fig asked. It was a residential dwarven district, and an unlikely place if the silverswords were looking for the Fire Mage Traitor, as the flyers were calling her.

After giving detailed directions to the place, Harryn bid her goodbye with a promise to check back in two days with an update on Conham. Fig thanked him and slid another gold coin into his palm as she shook his hand goodbye. Hopefully, she wouldn't need Conham, but she couldn't make any assumptions.

An ancient clock hung on the wall, showing several hours remained until daybreak—and Avelina's departure—so she let the girl sleep a little longer. Guilt seeped into her chest the longer she looked at her. Fig had completely upheaved the girl's life. But then again, the red brothers had strung priestesses up on the wall at Mar Nevan before she showed up, and Fig could have very well saved Avelina from that fate. She just had to get the girl on the boat.

Fig had no desire to drink the warm ale left in her glass, and she leaned back in the high-backed booth, when her hand landed on the bag containing Vaelor's sword.

A jolt of energy zinged through her, and she ran her fingers over the canvas, feeling the pieces inside. The heavy hilt was the most obvious. Its weight in her hand filled her soul with guilt. She glanced around the tavern but couldn't see any of the other patrons from here. A pair of voices were talking by the fire at the other end of the room, so the tavern wasn't completely empty, but she felt secluded enough in the booth.

She began pulling out the sword pieces and placing them on the worn wooden table, thinking of Vaelor as she did. Piece by piece, sliver by sliver. She hoped to all the Svoran gods that Vaelor had found them all, in his scramble to get them while they fought off Shadryn.

Finally, the shards lay assembled before her, and the enormity of the sword's brokenness came crashing down on her. How in the Bard's name were they going to fix the bond between Vaelor and his weapon?

Mother Savidah had implied that the magic remained, but they didn't have much time to bind it to Vaelor again. Fig could picture the magic sinking deeper into the shards, until eventually, they'd be unable to draw it back out again. And if the same went for whatever magic was inside Vaelor...

Her stomach in knots, Fig reached over to inspect the pattern carved into the hilt but carelessly caught her forearm on one of the shards. "Ouch," she hissed, drawing her hand back. A droplet of blood ran down her forearm, right next to the two scarred semi-circles from when Emrah bit her that day in the Gold Wood. Her eyes widened.

He'd bit her. Was that why they had a bond? He'd ingested some of her blood?

And when Mother Savidah said their bond was incomplete... Fig had to suppress a wild sound of amusement that burbled up her throat at the thought of asking Emrah if she could ingest some of his blood to see if that would complete the bond. But perhaps it had some merit, after all. Her mind raced as she blotted her cut with the red robes sitting in her lap.

When the silverswords crossover, they're bonded to their weapon, she thought. *Though they call it Welding—probably because it sounds more mysterious. They spill blood on their weapon, in the form of the runes the sisters put on it. And then the weapon draws blood, killing them.*

She packed up the sword pieces with care while her thoughts raced through blood and bonds, death and weapons. Things were starting to make sense. She had barely realized Emrah had bitten her at the time. And who in all the Bard's tales would think to exchange blood with a dragonet to bond with one? And the sword... Her plan became clearer and clearer.

She just had one problem: she still needed to get Vaelor back.

CHAPTER 11

FIG

With the sword packed away, Fig reached over to wake up Avelina.

The sister's bleary eyes met her gaze in confusion, then quickly shifted to sadness and worry. Fig's face crumpled. "I've got good news," she offered weakly. "Here's your papers. And there's a boat for Pan Vidda at daybreak. We should head to the harbor soon."

Avelina schooled her face and accepted the papers gratefully. "That is good news. My parents will be glad to see me, and I..."

"I'm sorry you had to give up your life in Mar Nevan."

Avelina paused. "It was time. The other sisters...and what the red brothers were doing..." Her voice cracked at the end.

Fig nodded. "I'm still sorry. Are there Sisters of Morgha in Pan Vidda?"

"Not really. It's quite far to transport holy water to, and Morgha isn't well known there. But I think I'll just be glad to be home. I spent most of my time in Mar Nevan in the archives, as it was. Perhaps I'll find a library to work in."

With a sad smile, Fig pointed at the girl's robes. "Here, give me those. I thought we might stash them with the bartender—"

"What?" Avelina said, pulling them closer to her chest. "N-no."

Fig sighed. "Two red sisters disappeared last night, abandoning the holy water delivery, remember?"

"But I...I wanted to keep them," Avelina said in a whisper.

"Do you know when the boatsmen set back out for Mar Nevan?" Fig asked her. The last thing she wanted to do was take away the one thing Avelina possessed from her time at the holy temple, but if they were searched, the robes would condemn them quicker than a tagor bites.

"Daybreak," Avelina admitted forlornly.

"So they'll be in the harbor too." Fig looked over at the bar. "Wait here."

After some convincing—and relinquishing her stolen robes as part of the bargain—Fig slid back into the booth with a few items courtesy of the bartender.

"Here." She handed Avelina a leather satchel, a worn brown cloak, a small wax paper-wrapped bundle of food, and lastly, a pair of thin leather gloves—those had cost two whole gold, as they belonged to the bartender herself and she hadn't seemed eager to part with them.

Avelina started to put the food into the leather satchel, but Fig stopped her with a look.

"The satchel is for the robes," Fig explained. "Just carry the rest. Keep your hood up, and for the love of the Bard, put the gloves on and keep them on, got it?"

Avelina nodded gratefully, pulling on the gloves and then the cloak.

Fig tucked her own bundle of food under her arm and cocked her head toward the tavern door. Then they headed out into the late-night air tinged with the light blue of coming dawn—each desperately clutching a bag that contained an object dear to their souls.

The dock was the good kind of busy. Enough people around that two potential travelers such as themselves wouldn't be scrutinized by the roving silverswords. Word of Rhivven's tournament had traveled fast from the looks of those coming off the recent ships. Fig hadn't put much thought into the tournament, except that she hoped to be long gone from the city before the silversword presence swelled even more, but perhaps the event would serve as much needed cover for what she would have to do to find Vaelor.

Fig and Avelina kept their hoods up as they sought out the boatmaster and quickly secured passage on the large ship leaving for Pan Vidda imminently.

Though Fig desperately wanted to leave the docks once she had booked Avelina's fare, she had to see this through—she was, after all, the whole reason the girl's life had been uprooted. So together, they located the *Jeffries*, Avelina's ship, where a rope over the gangplank prevented passengers from boarding too early. Fig kept a cautious watch on the smaller boat a few docks down that was preparing its return to Mar Nevan. The boatsmen welcoming passengers didn't seem too bothered, and Fig hoped to the Bard they hadn't heard anything strange about the holy water delivery last night.

"Are you sure you don't want to come too?" Avelina asked quietly.

Fig shook her head. "No." Pressure settled on her chest at the single word.

Avelina extended a gloved hand to touch Fig's arm.

Soon, the rope on the gangplank was swept aside, and Avelina was hugging Fig goodbye. Fig urged her aboard the *Jeffries* swiftly, bidding her all the Bard's luck. Once the ship pulled anchor and began to drift away, Fig released a heavy sigh. Some of the pressure in her chest eased, but not all. She felt a pang of guilt for sending

Avelina off alone, but the girl would be heading home to safety. It was the best Fig could do for her.

Now *she* was alone in the middle of Rayva, with an impossible task before her. One of many, it seemed.

Fig watched Avelina's ship for a long time—or, rather, she appeared to be watching the ship. She was actually scanning the horizon for incoming boats from Mar Nevan. When a small fishing boat came in from Thoan, she remembered that most of the boats leaving Mar Nevan were going to Thoan. She heaved in a deep breath as she watched a pair of silverswords approach the fishing boat, swaggering aggressively to the old dwarf captain and demanding his papers.

She turned her back and stole away from the port as quickly as she could. It was risky to linger anywhere. As she walked, she debated whether she ought to hitch a ride up to Thoan, where she would be more likely to intercept Vaelor, but as she calculated the time it would take, she knew it would be a stupid gamble. What if she missed him and then lost her chance of rescuing him here in Rayva as a result?

Her stomach began to grumble as she headed toward the safehouse. She didn't think it was from the mediocre ale from last night, so she nibbled on one of the hard rolls in the waxed paper bag. But as she trudged the streets, once so familiar to her, she knew the sour feeling in her gut had nothing to do with food.

Harryn had said he'd come in two days with news of Conham. But Fig didn't know if she could wait that long. She wasn't sure how long it would take the silverswords to return to Rayva with Vaelor—or even worse, what if she was wrong, and they'd kept him in Mar Nevan and exacted Rhivven's punishment there... No, she couldn't think about that. Her footsteps slowed and her vision blurred. She swallowed the bite of bread that had been in her mouth. It revived her a little.

No, no, Rhivven will want Vaelor brought before him. Rhivven was, after all, the one who'd performed the crossover, turning Vaelor into a silversword. Surely Rhivven would want to exact revenge with his own hand, to have Vaelor brought to the feet of his stolen throne.

She swallowed the lump in her throat and picked up her pace, trying to focus on her rough plan: keep away from silversword notice and find Conham.

Flourice Conham had been a revered member of the court until his retirement shortly after Queen Eileigh's death. A mage with the ability to affect the color of any object around him, he'd been an invaluable part of the queen's entourage for obvious wardrobe reasons. His retirement hadn't gone over well with King Haemond in his grief, and Conham had taken up residence in Black End, where most untethered mages ended up, or at least, where they spent a great deal of time.

The silversword coup must have driven him farther underground. He was likely the only person outside the castle who knew how to infiltrate it.

Fig looked up when she reached the street corner, only then realizing she'd eaten her entire roll. She brushed the crumbs from her fingers and rolled the bag back up. She'd found the street Harryn had told her about and made her way down it. The road was narrow with deep muddy cart tracks; there were no cobblestones here in the South Ninth district. Fig heard a baby crying, and a dwarf man burst out the door—amplifying the crying sound briefly as the door swung open. He hurried down the street, bleary-eyed and mumbling something about goat's milk.

The sun had begun to shed some light on the city, but Fig clutched her arms about herself to ward off the chill as she approached the building in question. She thought about walking by the safehouse and around the block to survey it but figured she might look more suspicious if she was seen walking back and forth around the area. Best not to draw any more attention to the place than necessary.

The neighbor's house—where she was to inquire—was shaded by an awning, so when she approached the door, she didn't immediately see that it was already wide open.

She halted in her tracks, arm raised to knock. Then she

dropped her hand and peered inside, her heart thudding in her chest as she stood in the doorway. Furniture had been knocked aside, pottery smashed on the floor, and tracks lined the floor—they looked like boot heels digging into the floor as their owner was dragged out the door.

Fig turned to leave but was met with a wall of silver.

"What are you doing here?" the silversword demanded, hand on his sword as he blocked her from the street.

Bard's quills, what are the chances?

Fig kept her face down, pretending to lower it out of respect. "N-Nothing my lord, I was sent by my cousin to ask Barley for some goat's milk," she blurted out. It was the first thing that came to mind. "But I think I got the wrong house."

"Barley?" the silversword drawled, most of his face hidden by his helm. "Is that right? You sure you're not a friend of the old dwarf conspirator Barrow who lived here until very recently?"

A hand gripped her chin and forced her to look up at him. Heat surged in her chest, though she reigned in her sparks. But as the waxed paper bag slipped out of her grip, she felt it disintegrate between her hot fingers.

But the silversword paid it no attention, his focus fixed on her face. Then a smile began to form at his mouth, the only part of his face she could see besides his steel-ringed eyes.

"Came a long way for goat's milk, eh, fire mage?" he whispered, his breath hot on her face.

Her nostrils flared as she glanced at the street. "Briigard," she cursed, swinging Vaelor's sword bag behind her to keep it safe. Flames leapt to her hands as she pushed the silversword away—or tried to, anyway. He didn't budge at her touch, but he *did* jolt away from the flames. Luckily, she hadn't gone inside the house, so her path was mostly clear. But the silversword was fast.

He whirled behind her to get away from the flames and grabbed her biceps. She slammed her hands back, striking armor—and earning nothing but stinging palms. Then she used her full weight to hang from his grip, kicking a heel into his armored legs.

"Argh!" he cried, releasing her.

She scrambled away. Somehow, she'd struck his knee without meaning to. He was down on one knee, clutching the other, but an instant later, he surged to his feet, drawing his blade.

He was Welded with a sword, a common enough choice, which gave him unnatural strength. He roared, swinging the weapon up to strike. All she had to shield herself were her own two hands.

At that moment, the ground rumbled, like the earth itself was shaking. Fig dropped her hands involuntarily, palms parallel to the ground, as if that would steady her—or the earth. She wasn't sure which.

In his bloodlust and rage, the silversword barely seemed to notice. Fig tried to scramble away, but the shaking ground made that difficult. She threw herself down and rolled, trying to put some distance between them.

But the ground wasn't just shaking—it was *moving*. Moving, in fact, right between her and the silversword. A lump of earth rolled directly toward the 'sword, as if the mud and dirt of the street had become a wave in the ocean. The swell struck him hard, knocking him down.

Fig lunged to her feet, not bothering to glance behind her. She raced down the street, and by the time she got to the corner, she couldn't feel any shaking—except in her own hands.

When she chanced a backward look before turning the corner, she glimpsed the silversword still struggling with the riotous earth, unable to stay on his feet. And just before she darted out of sight, her lungs burning and her feet nearly tripping in the cart tracks, she saw a curtain drop on one of the windows near the safehouse, concealing an unfamiliar dwarf behind it.

FIG

Afew blocks away, Fig finally stopped running, ducking down a narrow alley and throwing herself in the lee of a short set of stone stairs to hide. Her hands were still shaking. She sank to the ground, back against the wall, and clutched her knees as she regained her breath. *What in the Bard's name had that been about?*

She patted her pockets and bag, making sure she still had everything. By the Bard's luck, nothing had happened to Vaelor's sword. Her coin purse was deep in a hidden pocket in her tunic, so the only thing she'd lost was the rest of the food she'd gotten at the tavern.

She knew dwarves possessed earthen magic, but they kept the specifics to themselves. She had always thought it was more of an affinity for things like earth or metal. Considering the earth had only rioted right where they were fighting and not anywhere else on the street, Fig was certain that someone had interceded on purpose. If the owner of the safehouse had been taken, his neighbors might have wanted revenge on whoever took him. There was a lot she didn't know about the dwarves as a people—they kept their secrets within their clans ever since the fall of the Mountain. She had never seen so much of a dwarven presence in Rayva before, either.

But now she had no safehouse, no friends, and no one else to turn to. She wondered if Harryn had turned her in but shook her head at the thought; the silversword hadn't realized it was Fig until he'd peered into her face—and her visage had been plastered all over Rayva. Now, word would get out that Fig was in the city. She needed to get out of here. Now.

It felt like she was abandoning Vaelor all over again as she picked herself up and left the alley, heading for the closest city gate. But she couldn't stay. Hoping the Mountain Gate wasn't as heavily manned with silverswords as the more popular Bard's Gate would be, she struck out with her head down. She brushed herself off as she strode down the streets, vowing to return for Vaelor. Harryn had said he needed two days to get a hold of Conham, and it would likely take just as long for the silverswords with Vaelor to arrive from Thoan.

Until then, she wasn't safe here.

Her flight from the South Ninth district was uneventful until she rounded the final corner and came face-to-face with a wall of people. She clutched the sword bag as she waded into the crowd mostly consisting of dwarves. Fig caught snippets of muttered conversations, all about the tournament—and the fabled sword.

"Can't believe he got the Sword of Morin..."

"Morgha take those silver briigards..."

"Valencia said..."

"...take it back."

Fig almost stopped in her tracks listening to them. Of course. Harryn had said the tournament was for some ancient dwarven sword—she just hadn't realized he meant the Sword of Morin. But why would Rhivven just give it away in a tournament?

Well, he can't Weld with the sword himself, she thought, pushing against the current to try and reach the gate.

It was lucky she wasn't the tallest person in Tytan, otherwise she'd have stuck out like a tagor at a tea party in the crowd of dwarves and drawn unnecessary attention from the silverswords at the gate. By the luck of the Bard, she wasn't the only person attempting to get out of the city instead of in.

She held her breath as she passed under the large gate, its stone pillars carved with interwoven designs, much like the walls at Mar Nevan. After dodging a few more dwarves, she gained a clear path and released her breath slowly, her nerves still on edge. She stuffed her fingers into her pockets to avoid spilling any sparks.

"Oy!" A call came from the gate. "Girl!"

Fig turned her head on reflex and swallowed. The nearest silversword eyed her up and down. He couldn't see her face with her hood up, though—and wearing a hood wasn't unusual, especially not for someone leaving this gate. Heat burst to life in her chest, and she focused on breathing. Had he recognized her?

She cocked her head toward him and politely inquired, "Yes?"

"You're not leaving Rayva before the tournament, are you?" he asked incredulously.

The heat in her chest guttered like a candle flame when a door opened, replaced by relief. "Oh, yes, well, I've got some errands to run before then, you know," she said in her sweetest voice. "But I wouldn't miss it!"

He shifted, his boyish face breaking into a grin as he put a relaxed hand on his sword.

She smiled, angling her head so he could see only her mouth from the shadows of her hood. "Good day, sir," she said, and turned on her heel, walking purposefully away from Rayva, and following the call that sang in her blood—of honey-scented air and glittering gold.

ECHOES OF SILVER

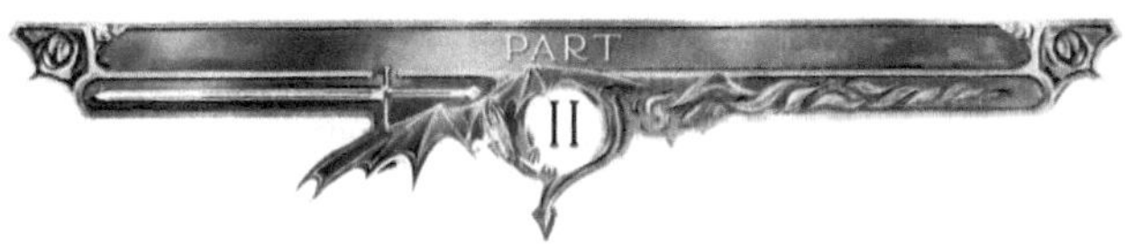

THE LOST HOUSE

DEV

Dev stared down at the slip of paper and shook his head, sighing. Fang had given it to him last night, after they had transported unlabeled cargo up the River Fienn to one of the small villages on the shore, but Dev had been rereading the note all morning at his little corner desk in his quarters.

The Snake's head might have been cut off, but the poison remains. Black ice is ever invisible. -TE

He knew what it meant—he'd easily figured it out the first time he'd read it. Thomat Evandahl, leader of the Fienn-Da, usually referred to Afrith Senaka as a snake, and it was clear that some of the briigard's agents were still roaming free. And black ice... He shuddered.

His brother, whom he'd thought dead for over a decade.

They'd left the former prince in the Hollow Isles with no

means of escape, his advisor Afrith dead on the floor. If only they'd been able to defeat Shad, then Dev's path would be clear—well, as clear as it could be after having the throne stolen out from under him by the head of the silversword enclave.

But now he had his brother to worry about with every waking moment. Whether Shad had more support lurking in the shadows on Tytan or Tysaine. Whether—no, *when* the briigard advanced into Tytan and tried to take back the Rayvan throne.

The note offered him little relief. Evandahl was traveling across Tysaine on Fienn-Da business and had contacts all over the continent, and this was *all* the information he could offer? Dev scoffed and crumpled up the note, exchanging it for his milky tea. It had grown cold sitting on the windowsill by his desk, but it was delicious at any temperature. The cook in their little house in Tirnalore really knew his way about the kitchen and the right ingredients to buy at the markets.

Their little safehouse was lucky enough to have a cook; Dev had seen some of the other safehouses and storage locations along the River Fienn, and this was one of the nicer ones. Perhaps Evandahl had afforded Dev some courtesy after all, as the heir to the Rayvan throne.

His door burst open, and a tall, muscular blonde woman bustled in, flinging herself down on a second bed against the far wall.

"Ugh, Ziggy," he said, pinching the bridge of his nose. "How many times do I have to tell you, shut the Bard's-blessed *door*, will you?" He got up and crossed the small room to close the door, then picked up his tea, and sat back down on his bed.

"Not afraid of a little svorcat, are you?" Ziggy said, reclining with her eyes closed.

"I'm not afraid of it," Dev bristled. "But the *hair*, Ziggy. It's atrocious." He brushed the imaginary hairs off his deep plum vest. Then on second glance, he noticed there *were* some long golden svorcat hairs on the vest. He sighed and set to picking them off.

"I told you," she said. "Get some Tysainian tunics. You won't see it on the lighter colors." She wore a cream tunic with matching loose pants, her sword strapped to a wide red belt decorated with gold.

Dev shook his head. He didn't have much left from his life as crown prince of Rayva, but he would laugh in the Bard's face before he let go of the one thing that remained—his sense of self. He had tried the Tysainian tunics and baggy light fabric pants meant for the arid climate but hated the way they felt, favoring the well-tailored pants and vests in the style he'd grown up with. And besides, the darker colors suited him. He didn't care if Ziggy or anyone else thought him vain. But he did care when he was covered in *fur*.

"I'm still surprised Fang's dog gets along with the fluffy little fiend," Dev muttered. Fang had acquired the svorcat last week and let it roam about the safehouse the three of them shared with a constantly rotating number of Fienn-Da mages—depending on their missions.

"Ursa's a sweetheart," Ziggy said, her eyes still closed.

"And why are you so tired? *I* was the one on the overnight run." Dev huffed. He knew he was being irritable, but the note from Evandahl was like a finger poking a wound, all the terrible things about Shad and Afrith he'd attempted to bury in his mind for the last month given new life. Shad was still out there, and so was some part of Afrith's network—they'd failed to put an end to it on Nithe. *He'd* failed, and Vaelor's sword had broken in the process—an unheard of atrocity for a silversword.

Ziggy scoffed, crossing one foot over her knee and rubbing it. "Oh, you must be the only one who didn't sleep last night, you poor king. I had to go down to the Cloaked Shafra on the foot-path—if you must know—and was down there since midnight putting out a little fire with the blackguard. But it's done now, and Evandahl should be pleased."

Dev's lips parted in surprise. "Oh. I had no idea."

"Of course not. You weren't here either."

She sounded too exhausted to care, but he apologized anyway. "I'm sorry, I—thank you for all the work you've been doing for the Fienn-Da. I know it's on my behalf, and…I appreciate you."

"Well, well, well," Ziggy said, finally sitting up and propping herself against the wall with one knee pulled to her chest. "The prince-king apologizes. What's gotten to you today?"

He met her smirk with one of his own and shook his head ruefully. "Word from Evandahl. No news on Shad except that some of Afrith's network might remain. It was just vague enough to be unhelpful."

Ziggy frowned. "You'd think Evandahl would be more concerned about Afrith's spies in Fienn-Da territory, after the way they almost got the auran seed."

"Right?" Evandahl still had the precious seed in his possession, though the Bard only knew whether he wanted to plant it or use it as leverage. But the auran trees on the continent had been dwindling for centuries. The tiny golden seed was more than just a *seed*—it was power for the mages. The return of healthy auran trees meant stronger mages everywhere. Dev's intentions to sidle up to Evandahl and glean his plans for the seed had been fruitless thus far; the leader of the Fienn-Da had been traveling ever since Dev and Ziggy joined up.

Ziggy went on. "And all the work the two of us have been doing for him, should have earned you more...more..." She waved her hand searching for words.

"More assistance from our new allies," Dev supplied. "More information."

She nodded. "Well, at least Evandahl doesn't think we owe him anything anymore."

Dev snorted, patting his pocket and the healthy pouch of coins there. "True. Being part of an underground society of mages doing illegal activities has had its benefits."

A brief whining outside the door announced the arrival of a newcomer moments before the knock, then Fang barged into the room, Ursa at his heels as usual. The dog came up to Fang's hip, his black ears alert as he sniffed the small room from his place by his master's side.

"You know," Dev said, "knocking implies you're going to wait to be allowed in, right?"

Fang rolled his eyes, crossing his arms over his chest as he lounged in the doorframe. "Not when you're living in a house owned by the Fienn-Da, kingling," he said good-naturedly. "And here I am with good news for you and all."

Dev gave him a look.

Fang grinned. "Word from Rayva. That old sword you were looking for? The pretender on the throne is holding a competition for anyone to win it. He's spread the news all across Tytan."

"What sword?" Ziggy asked, eyes narrowed at Dev.

He avoided her eyes. "An ancient one the dwarves were looking for. I thought it might help gain their favor and assistance in taking back the throne. The Feijowa clan told me as much."

"Vaelor told me about that. Isn't that why you blew up Nova Istra?" Ziggy said. "And you just want to *give* it to the dwarves?"

"That's *not* why Nova Istra blew up. The dwarves tried to pay Emrah to—anyway, that's not important. I just thought the sword might gain their favor."

"True," Ziggy said, drawing her other knee up to her chest to massage her other foot.

While Dev had worked with the Fienn-Da for the last month and seen firsthand how the organization could 'acquire' certain things, he'd asked Fang if he knew anything about the Sword of Morin and to keep an ear out for it. Surely it would help Dev's cause to have the dwarves on his side, particularly if the Fienn-Da was a dead end.

And a tiny voice in the back of his head had wondered about another possibility. The dwarves claimed the sword was made from some mythic element they had found ages ago. If Dev Welded with the Sword of Morin, he'd be the most powerful silversword on the continent, able to take back the Rayvan throne and have a better chance of keeping it out of Shad's hands. Mage and silversword, with a powerful weapon.

He knew—*he knew* it was a bad idea. Afrith had died during his crossover, never to be brought back. Mages weren't meant to cross over. But Shad had survived, and they shared the same blood. Dev also knew quite well that he'd be making a permanent enemy of the dwarves if he took the Sword of Morin for himself.

"Right," he said, shaking his head. "So Rhivven's just going to give the sword to anyone?"

Fang shook his head. "I doubt it. He'll probably want them to cross over with it."

"Likely. I'm sure he's torn up that he can't have it for himself."

Ziggy snorted.

"No one's ever tried to Weld with a second weapon, eh?" Fang mused.

Shrugging, Dev said, "I doubt it. Sounds just as dangerous as a mage trying to cross over." He felt a black shadow of guilt wrapping around his words. No. He would give the sword to the dwarves, if he managed to get his hands on it.

"So when's the competition?" Dev asked.

"Word's just started to get out," Fang said easily, "Corava's Day. About a week away now, right? 'S all I know. The criers and fliers just talk about the glory, not so much what the competition is exactly. Anyway, I gotta run to the market for some sardines to feed Miraculis." A smile lit up his face when he mentioned the svorcat. "I'll see you two at the dock later."

Dev nodded, remembering the upcoming run. He took an idle sip of his cold tea. Fang left with Ursa, thankfully, shutting the door on his way out.

"You're not..." Ziggy began.

He looked up at her, perhaps a little too quickly.

"You're not seriously thinking of going into Tytan—to *Rayva* —just for the *dwarves*, are you?"

"The dwarves are a ready-made ally for my cause. The silver-swords wronged them too—"

"Passing over that it was your ancestors," Ziggy cut in.

Dev waved a hand. "Two centuries ago. But if I can get on the throne—if a Verrence rights that wrong and returns the Mountain to the dwarves, then I'll gain a powerful faction of allies in Tytan."

"But I think you're missing the part about you going to Rayva," Ziggy said, looking at him like he'd been deep in his cups at the tavern. She shook her head. "I'm coming with you."

"I hoped you would," he said, energy filling his veins at the idea. He'd been idle for too long, sitting around in the safehouse and getting nothing from Evandahl. Sure, they were busy most nights doing work for the Fienn-Da, but it wasn't helping him get his throne back. "The dwarves are at least on the right side of the continent," Dev added. "And I need to be in Tytan, doing something. We know Shadryn could have more allies somewhere, and I need to reclaim the throne before he does."

"I think you've been with the Fienn-Da too long, my prince-king. Got a taste for the risk, now, do you?"

He let out a sharp chuckle, finished the last of his cold tea, and set down the cup with a flourish. "Why, yes. I quite think I do."

MAIREAD

Mairead stepped off the wagon, grateful to find solid ground, and adjusted her brown hood. The farmer's donkey brayed as she walked past, an arm raised in thanks to the driver, who was already unloading the potatoes and cabbages he'd brought to Thoan. Mairead had paid him early this morning when he picked her up in Arem. She'd lingered an entire day in Arem just in case Fig and Vaclor changed their minds about crossing the Twist. A thunderstorm had rolled through while she cowered in her room at the tavern, and she prayed all night to Morgha that the two had crossed safely. If everything had gone smoothly with their trek, Fig and Vaelor should be in the holy city right now.

She stretched her fingers in her new leather gloves, which fit in perfectly here in the shadow of the rocklands, where a slight chill dampened the air this close to Corava's Day. A Virenish festival in origin, the custom had been observed across Tytan for decades. Black streamers would soon decorate doorways like the wings of

Corava's crows, to prevent wandering souls from entering the homes they used to live in. Mairead didn't think that was true, of course—Morgha guarded dead souls once she took them in her arms, or else they went to the pits of Malhela. But the frivolity of the black streamers everywhere, the sweets, and the crow masks weren't something she looked down upon either.

Each step she took back into Thoan felt like a surreal dream. Nothing had changed. There was the Brewer's house on the edge of town with its mismatched windows. There were the stables where visiting pilgrims boarded their horses before going to Thoan's port and continuing on to Mar Nevan. Mairead had watched them for seven years as a child. They would arrive in Thoan appearing the same as everyone else, then return some days later with a distinct look of wonder in their eyes...and an almost mystical aspect about them that Mairead could never quite put her finger on. That is, until she'd visited the holy city herself, when she'd finally been allowed to go for her training. And now that city was closed to her forever.

Her family's house was across town. She stuck to the outskirts and less-traveled roads to avoid notice as she wove her way through the town. She was glad she'd removed her red cloak back in Arem—she'd stick out like blood on snow in the dreary rock-lands landscape this time of year.

Her parents had moved from the farm years ago, settling into a plot of farmland in eastern Tysaine, but Mairead had never visited. Only her great-uncle remained at the family house, but he always welcomed anyone in the Joiros clan. They'd once hosted someone whom Mairead was told was her second cousin twice removed, hailing from far off Chamol in Tysaine. The girl had brought *kafye* and delicacies from her home and stayed with them for a month. Mairead would be more than welcome, even if her great-uncle discovered she'd been kicked out of the Sisters of Morgha. He had, after all, not quite approved of sending an eight-year-old alone to the city to become a priestess.

Perhaps conjured by the thoughts of her fellow sisters, Mairead's eyes were drawn to a break between buildings through which she would catch sight of the only fount in Thoan—a place Mairead had once visited dozens of times a week, often getting underfoot of the sister there. Sister Francine. Mairead had always called her Sister Fancy, since before the age of seven she had a hard time pronouncing *r*'s.

A place where a dead woman in a red cloak now hung, her feet dangling five feet off the ground, her body swaying from the rope attached to the steeple on the temple roof.

Mairead's heart stopped. She peered between the two houses toward the fount. Was that... Sister Francine? Who could have done such a thing? Should she—

Footsteps ahead made her jerk back into motion, not wanting to be caught gawking at the horrible sight. Hadn't anyone else noticed? What if someone caught her looking and pinned the murder on her? But it was only a lone silversword on patrol, and he didn't even spare a glance at the sister. Mairead's gut clenched.

Ahead of her on the road, two children approached, laden with empty baskets headed for the edge of town, where farmers like the one Mairead had ridden in with were beginning to set up their wares for the day. Mairead nodded at the children and continued in the direction she'd been headed, even though every instinct told her she should leave Thoan at once. Run.

But where else could she go? She had secretly hoped Fig and Vaelor would come see her after their trip to Mar Nevan... But perhaps she should have voiced that to Fig, knowing the mage might respect Mairead's wishes to be done with the danger of their quest, leaving Mairead safe in her hometown.

Safe...

Her thoughts darkened. If a Sister of Morgha had been hanged here in Thoan, and everyone seemed to be going about their business, what had befallen Mar Nevan? Had Mother Savidah ordered this? She was beginning to realize nowhere was safe.

Heart thumping, Mairead kept a watchful eye about her as she took the long way home, avoiding any paths near the temple. The last thing she wanted was to get close enough to see the face of whoever hung there. Whether it was Sister Francine, or another red sister, she wished to Morgha to never find out.

She stuffed her hands into her pockets, even though her gloves covered her tattoos. Finally, when the houses grew farther apart down the dirt roads, she was able to spot the Joiros farm. It was a large farmhouse with the wraparound porch slouching a little, and a barn behind it. The goat pastures and fields spread out on either side.

Her eyelids fluttered, and a rare smile returned to her face. Folly, the old goldhound was growling from the corner of the barn. A voice from the house called out to quiet the beast, and Folly lapsed into silence, but the dog continued looking in her direction and wagging his tail.

Then, Folly's attention shifted down the road the other way, where a fast moving wagon approached the farm. Mairead looked left and quickly found a section of fence to hop over, into the field that abutted the farmhouse. Her skirt snagged on some thorns, and she fell over to the other side, landing in the long grass.

Maybe it'll just go by, Mairead thought hopefully, trying to peer through the grass. But the carriage wheels and the pounding of horse's hooves ground to a halt. Folly growled, but a stern command quickly silenced him. It hadn't been her great uncle's voice—likely whoever had been in the carriage, because she could now hear the newcomer's tones rising and falling among the sounds of her uncle's steady voice. She couldn't make out anything they were saying.

Sighing quietly, she got on her hands and knees and stayed out of sight with the fence and overgrown grass to hide her as she crept closer and closer. She thanked the holy mother Morgha that she was already wearing dark brown, or she'd have grass and mud stains all over the knees of her only dress.

"—assure you, I will," her uncle was saying.

"That's what you keep saying," the other voice said. It rang with something unsettling, sending a shiver down her spine. Mairead wouldn't be surprised if it belonged to a silversword.

"And *I* keep saying, *she's not here*."

There was a pause, and Mairead's heart hammered into her throat. She felt like she was going to be sick, on her hands and knees as she was already, her stomach rebelling at the idea that some silversword was harassing her poor great uncle looking for *her*. Why were they here now, after she'd been kicked out of the sisterhood months ago?

There was a strange choking sound, another pause, and then the stranger said, "You know what will happen if we find out you're lying."

Mairead seized the grass at her fingertips as she tried to peer through it to see what was going on.

Without preamble, the carriage began to speed in her direction, and Mairead dropped flat on her stomach as it passed. She listened for several heartbeats, the grass tickling her face unpleasantly, until she scrambled closer to the farmhouse. Before she could decide whether it was safe to go check on her uncle or not, she heard him curse, and the front door slammed shut. She let out a full breath there on the edge of the field with the house in full view. So he was all right then.

She pulled back into the long grass. Whoever was in that carriage was looking for someone, and she would bet all the Bard's stories that it was her. She couldn't put her uncle in danger by coming to the house, especially if they were already threatening him.

At that moment, Folly began a ruckus of barks, and Mairead hissed. He must have caught her scent. Her eyes wide, she watched him bound toward her. His tongue lolled out in a canine grin, and he continued to bark his greetings.

"Shh!" Mairead admonished, torn between fear at being discovered, and an attempt to cover a smile so as not to encourage him. "Shh!"

But it was no use. Folly came right up to her and nearly bowled her over from her crouched position in the grass.

"Folly," she admonished lovingly. "You're going to—"

The back door of the farmhouse opened and swung shut with

a loud bang. Mairead looked up to see Uncle Howarth standing there, a crossbow pointed straight at her.

He whistled to Folly, who gave up on licking Mairead to sit at attention for his master. Uncle Howarth whistled again, crossbow still trained on Mairead crouching in the tall grass. But Folly didn't obey the command, his wagging tail breaking through the obedient stance cheerfully.

Before her uncle lost patience with the dog, she glanced around quickly then threw back her hood, revealing her red hair and calling quietly, "Uncle, it's me." She put the hood back on immediately, even though this stretch of Thoan contained only her and Uncle Howarth—and Folly of course—as far as they could see. She didn't want to chance another carriage coming along.

The crossbow dipped, and Uncle Howarth stepped down from the back step. "Mairead?" came his gravelly voice.

She nodded fervently and scrambled to her feet, crossing the distance between the edge of the fence and the house in only a few heartbeats, Folly at her heels.

Skidding to a halt a few feet from the steps, Mairead met Uncle Howarth's eyes, and he closed the distance between them, lowering the crossbow to the side and throwing his other arm around her.

"Mairy—you shouldn't be here," he said, the words rumbling through his chest right into her. "They're looking for you."

Tears threatened her eyes. "I was afraid of that. I wasn't even going to come to the house once I saw the carriage—"

He pulled away, then looked around at the empty land around them. "Come inside," he insisted.

"I shouldn't..."

He took her arm gently and ushered her toward the door, his crossbow at his side as he continued to watch the road and surrounding fields. Folly remained outside, obediently watching the fields.

The tears broke through once she inhaled the familiar scents of home—not only because she couldn't stay, but because for so long she had considered Mar Nevan home. Her own family's farm had been the place she'd wanted to leave to begin her journey to priestesshood. And look where that had gotten her.

She dashed the moisture away before it could track down her cheeks and took in the kitchen. A large wooden table, where food was prepared and meals eaten, filled most of the space. A bucket sat on the counter full of soapy water. It looked like her uncle had been cleaning dishes when the carriage arrived.

"Who was that?" Mairead asked, letting the strap of her small satchel slip down to the crook of her elbow. "A silversword?"

Her uncle hissed and shut the door. He secured the lock and twitched all the curtains shut, casting the kitchen into darkness that was only penetrated by the hearth. He set about the room grabbing things at random—a couple of apples from the cupboard, the big kitchen knife, a cloth—lurching around as quickly as someone of his age could.

"You shouldn't be here, Mairy," he said, finally turning back to her. His pale face was lined with more wrinkles than she remembered, which wasn't surprising, but at the moment they were all pulling his face in a look of concern. He shoved a bundle of items into her hands, all wrapped in one of the kitchen cloths and tied on top. "I want you to go out to the barn and stay there until we can get you out of here—"

"I *shouldn't* be here, Uncle," she said, shifting the bundle to sit better in her hands. "Wait... is the kitchen knife in here?"

His solemn face cracked in a slight smile. "Best not cut yourself, eh? Good thing you have those gloves on."

Mairead looked at her gloved hands and frowned. "It's to hide the tattoos," she said, the truth spilling out like water from a broken jug. "The sisterhood put me out after I complained about...well, the silverswords and a crossover."

Uncle Howarth visibly shivered. "I thought you wouldn't have to do any of those so soon." He shook his head. "We can catch up tonight. For now, I want you in the barn in case *he* comes back."

She was about to protest when a knock came at the kitchen

door. She nearly dropped her bundle, her eyes going wide. To her shock, Uncle Howarth lurched forward and yanked the door open, revealing a stretched-out version of a familiar face. Golden-hued skin with half of his chin-length hair pulled into a bun at the top of his head, he slipped into the kitchen as comfortably as if he lived here.

Mairead took a step back, but by the goddess, she was fairly certain this was not the man who had threatened her uncle. As if to prove this point, Uncle Howarth slapped his hand into the newcomer's, and they both shook jovially.

"Well, this works out perfectly," Howarth said, looking between the two of them. "Mairy, you remember Derrinahl, don't you?"

She stared at him, trying to picture the face smaller, the body less muscled and tan. "Of course," she said, a smile coming to her face unbidden. "Didn't we used to dig trenches in the river mud? And play marstones—"

"At the farmer's market on the back of the cabbage cart," he finished with a smile, one eyebrow cocked. "I thought you became a red sister." His gaze went to her gloved hands to look for the tattoos, then he glanced over her cloak which was very clearly *not* red.

She sighed, trying to think of what to say, but her uncle rescued her.

"Derrin, Mairead needs to leave Thoan—do you have room in the shop for her?"

Her eyebrows furrowed as Derrin ran a hand along his jaw. "I do, but not for long. Father will need to clear out the back room soon to make way for our new press."

Mairead wasn't sure her eyebrows could furrow any farther. "Excuse me, Uncle," she interrupted. "But what exactly are you talking about? I can leave, you don't need to—"

Uncle Howarth turned to her. "Derrin's parents still run the printing press over by the port. He can hide you until you can get on the first ship out of here."

"Ship?" Mairead squeaked. She cleared her throat. "I've been trekking all across Tytan—and Tysaine, mind you—I know I'm putting you in danger by being here, but I'll find my own way."

Her uncle stared at her like she'd grown an extra head. "Mairy—Mairead, I thought the sooner we got you out of Tytan the better."

"I know about the wanted flyers, but—" She paused, making up her mind. "I'm going to head back to Arem to find my friends. They went to Mar Nevan to look for some information. But I'd like to meet them when they return, since it's not safe for me here. I can't endanger you, Uncle. I didn't realize the silverswords would be looking for me here—"

He grabbed her gently by the arms and looked into her eyes. "It's not the silverswords. It's the red brothers. They hanged Sister Francine."

MAIREAD

Derrin left almost immediately, promising to be back after dark with his wagon. Mairead had a precious few minutes to clean herself up while her uncle prepared a meal for her. She didn't want to stay, putting her uncle in even more danger, but she felt obligated to let him help her.

She peeked into the bundle he'd hastily put together and found it contained some food that would keep on the road, the kitchen knife, and—her eyes watered at the sight—a bar of soap made from the farm's goat milk.

After cleansing her hands with the same type of goat's milk soap in the washing room, Mairead felt she could breathe a little easier. That is, until she came back out into the kitchen and saw the silhouette of her uncle sitting there with his crossbow on one knee, pointing it at the back door.

She hugged her arms about herself and slipped into the chair next to him, immediately reaching for the plate of food he'd set out for her. Casting all manners aside, she hungrily made short work of eating. Words spilled out between bites, the chance to speak freely just as nourishing as the food as she explained everything that had happened to her since she'd taken up her post in Nova Istra—from the *solanse* to Tirnalore, and all that transpired on Nithe.

It wasn't until she was swallowing her last bite of bread that her uncle spoke. He was looking at her hands.

"And they did that to you?"

She looked down. The brand on her right palm was visible as she idly clutched the side of the plate. Uncle Howarth and her parents had seen the healing tattoos down the backs of both hands after she'd been honored with them, but not the circular brand filled with runes. She nodded as she swallowed the bread, surprised that the brand was what most interested him in her tale.

"Yes, the 'swords forced me to kill a man, and then do his crossover. I had the audacity to complain."

Uncle Howarth bowed his head. "Audacity is sometimes all we have to retaliate against the unjust. Of course, I've had the audacity all these years to keep on living, despite these old bones —the unjustness of age and all."

An unwilling chuckle escaped her, and she pushed her chair back to go wash up, but Uncle Howarth grabbed her plate. "You rest," he said. "If you've been tramping across the continent, I think I can walk to the wash bucket."

Folly barked outside, and Mairead got a crick in her neck from turning too quickly to look at the sliver of darkness visible through the curtain on the back door.

"It's just Derrin," Uncle Howarth said, not even glancing up.

"How do you know?"

"Folly growls when it's anybody else. Well, he barks for you too. Barks are for friends."

A smile warmed her face. "You trust Derrin?" she blurted out.

Howarth dipped the plate in the washing water and began scrubbing it with a rag. "With my life. When you went to Mar Nevan—by the Bard. I almost forgot—" He set the plate down in the wash bucket, forgotten, as he grabbed a towel to dry his hands. "Although, how could I? The red brother showed up right after."

"What is it, Uncle?" Mairead demanded.

"This came for you a week ago." He took a scroll from the top of the dresser where they kept their clean dishes and held it out to her. "I didn't know what to think of it. You hadn't been here in so long. Then the red brother came to Thoan, and Sister Francine..."

Mairead would recognize Mother Savidah's seal in the red wax as long as she lived. She inhaled sharply and recoiled, even though the scroll was across the kitchen. Shaking her head, she whispered, "I can't touch that. That's how she branded me. But why would the holy mother send me anything, *and now?* And the red brothers..." she trailed off, completely at a loss. She'd barely encountered the Brothers of Morgha during her time in Mar Nevan. They spent most of their time in their sanctuary, meditating and doing who knew what. The only times she'd crossed paths with them was when she walked the Twist—it was tradition for them to guard that post, but perhaps that wasn't the case anymore, if one was here in Thoan, outside the holy city.

They *never* left the holy city. Not as long as anyone could remember. During late nights in their shared dorm, Mairead and Sister Avelina had occasionally hypothesized that the brothers must have holy orders to protect the source of Morgha's waters. Mairead had once suggested that the sisters represented Morgha's healing side, and the brothers represented the goddess's death aspect. Avelina had looked scandalized, and they never spoke of it again. But why else would they have different holy tattoos? What kind of magic did they even possess?

The back step creaked, and Howarth went over to unlock the door, letting Derrin inside.

"We need to hurry," Derrin insisted. "My sources say a barge from Mar Nevan has been spotted off the coast, full in silverswords. If we move quickly, we can get out before them."

Her uncle deposited the scroll on the worn table, and Mairead stared at it.

What could Mother Savidah possibly have to say to her now?

There was no way she'd risk any sort of branding or other magic that the scroll might contain. She couldn't touch it.

She took over at the wash bucket while her uncle locked the door behind Derrin and the two of them had a hasty conversation.

As soon as the dishes were set to dry, she turned to face them. "I don't need to get on a ship. I'm going back to Arem to look for my friends."

"They went to Mar Nevan, you said?" her uncle asked, sharing a look with Derrin.

She nodded, her thoughts jumping to the sight of Sister Francine hanging from the temple. If that had happened here in Thoan... What in the great mother's name might be going on in the holy city?

Fear for Fig and Vaelor struck her—along with another, deeper feeling that soured her stomach: relief that she was safely out of harm's way. Suddenly, getting on a ship didn't seem like such a gods-cursed idea.

"No," she whispered to herself. Then, louder: "I'm going back to Arem. Even if they're not back, I might try to meet them on the Twist."

Derrin's jaw dropped. "Meet them on the—"

"I've crossed it a dozen times," she said dismissively. "They'll need my help."

Disdain for herself oozed through her. She had sent Fig and Vaelor on a dangerous path to a place far more troublesome—all for the promise of returning home. Of being safe. Something she wouldn't find here.

"Very well," her uncle said, a new light in his gaze as he looked her over. "But you should still go to Derrin's shop. It's on the way out of town. The red brothers know this is a place you might go —that's why they've been coming here these last few days. Go on to Arem and find your friends."

She nodded firmly. "Of course. I don't want to give them a chance to—" Her throat constricted, and her words failed...except for the ones inside her head: —*hurt you.*

Her uncle shoved another bundle at her—he must have gathered it when she was washing up earlier. It was soft and, by the feel of it, likely contained extra clothing—something she desperately needed. She set it on the table and flung her arms around her uncle; he stumbled a little, then stood firm.

"Thank you, Uncle," she said, inhaling the familiar scent of soap.

He patted her back, and she dashed away her tears before pulling away.

"But I do think you should take this," her uncle said, picking up the scroll from the holy mother and holding it out.

She swallowed, unsure. Finally, she held out the sack with the clothes, and let him slip it inside, so she didn't have to touch it. Maybe when she found her friends, she could have Fig open it for her instead...

Whether it contained some kind of apology or a curse...she wasn't about to find out now.

Mairead glanced around the kitchen one last time, soaking in the sight of home as much as she could, until finally her eyes landed on Derrin. She was struck with the sudden memory of pushing him into the muck at the riverside once, for no good reason. Her face warmed, and she hefted her two bundles. "Let's go, then, shall we?"

Folly let out a quiet bark at once they stepped outside, and Mairead soon found a wet snout shoved into her hand. She shifted her belongings and got down on one knee to throw her arms around the canine. Derrin took her bags and quietly disappeared around the far corner of the farmhouse. Mairead hugged Folly, straightened, then rubbed the old boy's head one last time before turning to face her uncle.

"Uncle, I'm sorry I put you in any trouble—"

"It is no problem at all, my dear. I can tell you are on the side of good, and protecting the good is worth any trouble."

A smile bloomed over her face, and she flung her arms around him one last time. "Thank you."

"You'd better get going," he said, patting her back.

She smiled sadly at Uncle Howarth and took her leave, stealing into the dark night air, Folly sniffing her heels one last time before she rounded the corner. Derrin pushed himself off the side of the house where he was waiting and went to give his donkey a pat on the flank before launching himself up into the one-person driver's seat.

It was clear Mairead was to sit in the back, so she hastily mounted the small plank that served as a single step up and made herself as small as possible next to the two sacks her uncle had given her. Derrin turned around, holding up one edge of a dark tarpaulin. Mairead cocked her head, and he pantomimed throwing it over her. She nodded, then took a deep breath as if she were going underwater and ducked her head as he covered her.

Under the cover of the tarp, she couldn't even get a last look at the house as the wagon lurched into motion and the donkey trundled onto the dirt road in front of the farm.

Mairead bit down on the inside of her cheek, chewing the skin. The sound of the hooves and wheels grew much louder, and Mairead wondered if they had only just gotten onto the road, but she could have sworn...

The sound passed them—another carriage heading for the farmhouse.

Mairead sat up straighter, the tarp going taut over her head. "Derrin," she hissed. "Derrin!"

Derrin was either choosing to ignore her or couldn't hear her whisper-shout over the sound of the wagon, so Mairead found the edge of the tarp and flung it back, leaning over to poke him in the back.

He twisted around to look at her, wide-eyed. She could barely see his expression in the last of the light radiating out from the house which was becoming increasingly distant. He mouthed "red brother," and it felt as if the bottom dropped out of her stomach.

She slammed her hand down on the edge of the wagon between her and the driver's seat. "We have to go back!" she hissed. She didn't care what magic the red brothers might possess

—that was her great uncle back there! And the one who had visited earlier had said they'd be able to tell if Mairead had come. With the strange magic granted to them by Morgha, she didn't doubt it was a possibility.

He shook his head violently. "Not a chance in Malhela. I watched them hang the red sister and—"

Mairead scooted to the end of the wagon and jumped down, her dress billowing around her. She trudged away from Derrin and offered him no further explanation. If he'd seen what the red brother had done to Sister Francine, then surely, he knew how much danger Uncle Howarth was in if the brothers knew Mairead had been there.

She should never have come to this Bard's-cursed town.

"Wait—Mairead!" Derrin hissed.

She turned, half-expecting to see him following her, but instead, he was tossing her sacks out of the wagon toward her. The briigard! She scowled at him—the coward was still going to leave without her—but she reached for the sacks automatically. Something fell out of one, and she picked it up in the dark.

Her fingers touched the paper before she realized what it was. Too late, she realized it was the scroll. Its hard round wax seal had broken open somewhere between being stuffed in the sack and falling out of it.

Her hand shook.

"Wh-What's wrong?" Derrin asked, lowering the reins he'd been about to snap to get his donkey's attention.

She glared at him. This was all his fault. "I—I shouldn't have touched this! It's from Mar Nevan, and who knows what the holy mother did to it... You know, they can do far more with that holy water than just heal..." The last part she babbled almost to herself, and her eyes darted toward the farmhouse. She couldn't see much —only that the same carriage as before was parked outside...and a strange red glow was coming from inside the house.

She tossed the sacks back on the ground along with the scroll. She could deal with that later. Right now, her uncle needed her.

Before she dashed toward the house, however, she lurched

back to grab something from one of the sacks. Sharp silver gleamed in the dim light coming from the house, and she pointed the kitchen knife down as she started running.

Trying not to picture another horrible brand burning into her skin, she raced back down the road, going for the back door. Something inside the house was still glowing red. She broke into a sprint.

Folly barked as soon as she rounded the corner of the back of the house, but there was no helping that. At least her uncle would know it was friend, not foe.

When she returned her attention to the back door, she saw what was glowing red, a blurry string of sigils she recognized from her training—except these sigils were coming from inside, and she was seeing them *through* the closed door. Sharp lines with half-moons dissecting them, another with diamonds layered over one another, simply floating in the air inside the house.

She gasped and ripped open the door as fast as she could. Whatever magic the red brother wielded, it was like nothing she had ever seen or heard of before. How could she see it through the door?

Her uncle lay on the floor, his crossbow knocked to the side as the red brother stood over him like a vorse eagle about to swoop down onto its prey.

The sigils now appeared more defined, hanging in the air in front of the red brother. Another glowing sigil appeared when he signed in the air with careful movements. Mairead knew that sigil —the inverted *Y* with a horizontal line through it hung in the air like the symbol of death it was.

But how was he doing it?

She lunged in, darting in between the overlapping diamonds sigil for finality, and the one for death, and the kitchen knife in her hand seemed to act of its own accord.

It pierced the red brother's gut, a painful place for a mortal wound—she knew this very well after healing a few stomach wounds—but it was the only opening she had seen between the red glowing sigils that appeared with his movements.

His face went blank, and his jaw slackened. He looked at Mairead, and then down at the blood on his hand that he'd drawn to his wound. The sacred tattoos trailing over his left eye dimmed along with the red glowing runes that hung in the air around them. He slumped to the ground, knees first, then fell onto his front with sickening finality. Red blood formed a pool around him, matching the color of his tunic under the black leather armor.

She barely registered her uncle's voice; she couldn't make out the words as he scrambled back from the fallen body, clutching a bloody spot on his head.

The sigils in the air had faded until they were no more than a memory. Who was this red brother, and how did he wield such power? She stared at the body on the floor.

The body on the floor.

There was a body on the floor of her temple in Nova Istra, blood mixing with the water spilled on the flagstones. The fount was only a few steps away, but it would never wash off the blood on her hands.

There was a body on the ground in the courtyard at Nithe. Shiny boots and a black and purple wound on the head; she thought she could see the skull bone through the hair. The blood wasn't on her hands—but the water didn't bring him back. She had killed him, anyway.

"Mairy!" her uncle was shouting. His hands were on her shoulders, shaking her. Somehow she was crouching on the floor.

She looked up at him. Her eyes were so dry they almost hurt. She blinked. She'd been staring at the body on the floor, which Derrin was now studying, his hands on his hips as he assessed the situation.

Mairead glared at him. What was he doing back here? He'd all but abandoned her uncle. Part of her wanted to fling those words at him, but her mouth wouldn't open.

She turned her attention to Uncle Howarth. He was rubbing the back of his head and favoring one arm in particular.

Uncle Howarth enveloped her in half a hug, but she could still see the body over his shoulder. Where had the red glow come from? Why had red brothers been sent from Mar Nevan? Tracking down an errant sister or two was hardly cause for sending out the sacred order.

Derrin cleared his throat annoyingly. "We need to get rid of this."

Mairead ignored him and tried to find her feet. Her uncle helped her up, and she swayed for a second before she found her balance. It was then that she realized that the knife was still in her hands. She dropped it immediately. It clattered to the floor, and the three of them stared at it.

Without a word, Mairead went to the washroom and closed the door behind her. She began to wash her hands carefully and meticulously, as she had after each healing at her fount in Nova Istra—covered in blood, holy water, and who knew what else.

After she'd finished scrubbing the skin until it was raw, digging under her fingernails, and glancing idly at the tattoos on the backs of her hands, and the hated brand on one palm, she realized...*there was no new brand*.

It was only when she walked out of the washroom and caught sight of her reflection in the hallway mirror that she noticed the red tattoos framing her left eye.

CHAPTER 16

MAIREAD

Mairead's hand went to the red tattoos. A single straight line ran from above her eyebrow, down over her eyelid, and underneath her eye. It was dissected by a series of sigils, only some of which she recognized. There was a *Y*, but with an extra line going upwards that she recognized as the symbol of life, the opposite of the sigil the red brother had signed in the air. Next, a series of half-moons, arrows, dots, and lines all symmetrically dissecting or parallel to the main line.

What had the holy mother done?

She ran her fingers over the marks. They felt old—like they had healed years ago—and yet, they gave off a faint red glow, as if she'd just been imbued with the holy water from the sacred pool.

Irritated muttering echoed from the kitchen, and her hand dropped. She stared at her reflection for half a minute longer, then stuck out her chin and returned to the kitchen.

Her uncle peered at her curiously when she returned, and she gave him what she hoped was a reassuring nod. She was all right for now. She had dealt in blood for years, what was a little more? He was likely curious about the new tattoo, but he didn't ask, and she was grateful.

"We need to do something about this," she said quietly.

Uncle Howarth picked up the knife and dropped it unceremoniously into the empty wash bucket, grunting in the affirmative.

"This?" Derrin demanded, waving his hands. "*This* is the dead body of a *red brother*. How did you possibly— How could you even— I've heard they can take down *silverswords...*"

Mairead shrugged, wondering how he knew that. "I don't know, I just saw an opening between the sigils and took it. And we—"

She had been looking over at her uncle, who still stood at the wash bucket by the window, when she noticed the faintest red glow in the distance—out in Thoan proper. She dragged in a breath. "How many red brothers are in Thoan?"

"There were three," her uncle said quietly.

The breath in her lungs turned painful as the red glow she'd been studying in the distance split into two distinct dots. From what she had seen of this red brother, she was certain she didn't want those red dots coming any closer.

"We need to get rid of him—*now*—and get out of here."

"Wh—" Derrin began.

"Now!"

The only relief, as the three of them hoisted the body up and out the back door, was that the two red dots hadn't moved toward them yet. It seemed that touching the scroll from the holy mother had given her the power to see the magic of Morgha that resided in the brothers. And she had no desire to see that magic—or those sigils—up close again anytime soon.

Uncle Howarth began work on the blood on the floor with some lye, while Derrin and Mairead carried the body past the barn and toward the river. She had to use all her focus to hold onto the ankles and had to admit she was glad that Derrin was here to help with this part.

She wouldn't speak to him, not after he'd abandoned Uncle Howarth. Wasn't he supposed to be a friend of the family? Why had he been trusted to smuggle her out of Thoan in the first place? She shook her head, turning her attention toward the moving water ahead. As they approached the edge of the water carrying the body, Mairead tried not to think about how she used to play here every day as a child.

They silently agreed to walk a few steps in, and after a few swings, hoisted the body as far into the deeper part of the river as they could. There was a sickening splash as it hit the water, then the body of a sacred Brother of Morgha began floating downriver.

Mairead stayed where she stood, knee deep in the river, while Derrin splashed ungracefully toward the shore. She cupped her hands and bent down to scoop up a handful of water, which she raised level with her heart, and began to recite the ancient prayer:

> "Bless the body,
> Bless the soul,
> Bless the time spent here an—"

Her voice cracked, and she couldn't go on.

How could she bless this man, who had taken part in killing one of her sisters? Who had been about to kill her uncle? The sigils she'd seen hanging red as death in the air made his intent at the end clear.

Death and finality.

She sighed, letting the water fall and turning her back on the river, then dragging her feet out of the water when she reached the shore. Derrin had waited for her, but she didn't look at him. She sought the two red dots to ensure they were the same distance away as before.

They headed back up to the house in silence. When they passed the barn and Folly joined them, Derrin finally spoke. "You shouldn't have gotten out of the carriage."

Ire boiled hot in her throat. "What, and let that brother kill Uncle Howarth? Some friend you are."

"That's not what I meant," he said. "I don't think they would have hurt him. You're a red sister, aren't you?"

"No—yes," she corrected. "I am. But I would swear once again on my oath to the Holy Mother Morgha that Sister Francine could do no wrong, so I can't think of any good reason the brothers would have to hang her. And my uncle? That brother was about to execute a killing blow. This has something to do with the coup, I am *sure* of it," she added to herself. Why else would the sacred order of brothers leave Mar Nevan?

"The coup?" Derrin asked. "What do you know of it?" His words didn't sound condescending, as she might have expected—only a hushed demand for information.

She checked the Bard-cursed red dots in the distance; they still hadn't moved. Her voice softened as she and Derrin drew close to the back steps. "More than almost anyone left in Tytan, probably."

"Truly?"

"Truly."

"Tell me, what happened to Prince Devryn? King—I mean. I know he escaped Tytan, but we've been looking—"

"We? We who? He escaped, and—gods, there's so much more to it than that." She wasn't sure why she was bothering to tell him anything. He had always been curious when they were kids, and she could see that same inquisitive, alliance-seeking boy under the man.

She put her hand on the doorknob, "I'll tell you on the way to Arem. But we have to get my uncle first. You're both coming with me."

CHAPTER 17

DEV

Dev inhaled the increasingly familiar scent of salt water and used a wisp of purple wind to urge their small boat along faster in the dark.

"Oy," Ziggy hissed, raising her oar as she twisted to look at him. "What's the point in me paddling if you're just going to mess up my steering?"

"Sorry."

To Dev's surprise, Vilvan glanced back at him with a half-smile, short leaves bristling as he moved. The swamp dryad had been teaching Dev the finer points of steering crafts with air magic whenever they did these late-night runs. Of course, Dev had trained at the Carriage House, but he hadn't put his magic to much practical use since his school days.

Normally they were out on the river, where the Fienn-Da did most of their smuggling, but tonight would be different. Tonight, they were out on the Hollow Sea. Ziggy dipped her oar back into the water, where they paddled along the edge of the isthmus that linked Tysaine and Tytan. The Tysainian gate towered to their left in the dark, a massive stone archway with two towers and a wide parapet between them, guarded by the fierce blackguard. The bleaks—as the Fienn-Da called King Artaxis's soldiers—were barely visible from where they paddled. About a dozen of them were stationed at the gate, the numbers increasing by the day, it seemed. King Artaxis wasn't oblivious to the coup in Tytan and had been stricter about who he allowed to cross into his country. Or perhaps the Tysainian king feared the silverswords taking the gate—or *his* throne next.

Dev breathed a sigh of relief as they rowed away from the gate, its bulk looming into the darkness, until eventually, it was swallowed up in the black. Their next obstacle was the silversword checkpoint.

After silently gliding past a sort of no-man's-land between the two posts, beacons of light shone out at them from the isthmus. Vilvan steered further out into the sea waters, which were unpredictable and known to be the home to the deadly tagors. It was safer to stay close to the land—if the silverswords didn't kill them upon sight. They had to tread a fine line of distance from shore, which was why Vilvan always led these kinds of trips into Tytan; the dryad was an expert on the water. Dev held his breath as both Ziggy and Vilvan lifted their oars. The swamp dryad gave the slightest push with his magic—Dev hoped the dim green glow would go unnoticed—and they relied on that to glide past the checkpoint.

Tonight, Dev would return to Tytan.

Over the last few days, he'd coordinated this with Evandahl—who, despite being away in Chamol on business, had agreed. Sometimes the Fienn-Da helped smuggle more than just *things* between the two countries and across Tysaine. Sometimes they dealt with people: mages looking to escape Tytan, mostly, or the types of people who preferred to remain unseen and anonymous. Dev didn't know who they were smuggling out tonight, but their contact in Tytan would be ready with the group at the pickup location. There had been a steady trickle of mages and others who opposed Rhivven's rule, and Evandahl was only happy to help the refugees—for a price.

Vilvan had done this a dozen times by now. He would be returning to Tysaine with the refugees, while Dev and Ziggy would not.

The bright lights of the silversword checkpoint drifted past slowly, making it feel as if the boat was stationary and the lights were moving instead. Ziggy shifted quietly in her seat, and Dev turned to look at her, but she just shrugged, a quizzical look on her face.

Minutes dragged on, until finally—finally—the lights faded into nothing. Dev didn't envy Vilvan for having to make the painstaking return trip with the Virenish craft packed with refugees.

"Nearly there," Vilvan said so quietly Dev almost didn't hear him. "I can feel the heart of the *solanse* growing closer."

Dev gazed at the dryad in wonder. Vilvan was still on his *voixage*, a pilgrimage of sorts that all swamp dryads of a certain age were required to undergo, leaving the salt swamps for a "short" period of fifty years to travel the world before they put down roots—literally—when they returned to their ancestral home. Most dryads made the most of their *voixages*, traveling and exploring the continents, but others—like Vilvan's love, Fenra— despised leaving the *solanse*. Dev knew that Vilvan's dream had been to work at the library of Tirnalore, but when he was told he wasn't qualified, he had begun working with the Fienn-Da instead.

Vilvan steered the craft carefully around the viragrove trees and cedar knees that had begun to crop up in the dark water like knobby fingers and limbs reaching for them. The dryad used more of his magic, and the gentle green glow aided in navigating the salt swamps. Dev both wanted and *didn't* want to see more of the water—afraid he might glimpse a set of tagor eyes lurking beneath the surface, watching.

Finally, a yellow glow bloomed to life just up ahead.

Vilvan made a pleased sound and adjusted the boat's trajectory.

Ziggy shifted suddenly, making the boat rock in an ungainly way.

"Ziggy," Dev hissed. "What in the Bard's—"

"I'm sorry," she said, her voice sounding odd. "I thought I heard something, but I don't know…"

The boat bumped into a soft bit of land, and Vilvan seized the nearest cedar knee with his willowy fingers, securing the craft. Dev had to practice patience as the swamp dryad fussed over the boat and finally let his two passengers off. Vilvan then turned toward the dryad on shore, and the gentle green glow emitting from his short leaves brightened.

Fenra stood there, a soft yellow glow about her long leaves trailing down her back. The two dryads wore matching tagor-tooth necklaces, and Dev couldn't help but smile at the sight of their reunion. They intertwined their long bark-covered fingers together, gazing into each other's faces in a surprisingly intimate way for such a small touch.

"Fenra?" Dev asked. "What in the Bard's name are you doing here?" He knew Fenra lived in the *solanse*—which her elders had only allowed because she was employed at Vaelor's family home, House Resbrok. Dev gingerly stepped onto the squishy earth of the smallish island they'd docked at. A handful of people stood there, bundled in cloaks and clutching their meagre belongings.

Vilvan turned to shine his grin on Dev. "It was Fenra's idea. The house she works for has been helping us find—"

Ziggy drew her sword in a ring of steel.

"Ziggy, what's—"

But the silversword wasn't listening. She advanced on one of the refugees.

"Ziggy!" Dev hissed.

The refugee took a surprised step back, her face hooded by her cloak, but as she shifted, Dev caught the distinct glint of a silver ring where her eyes should be.

The refugee—a silversword, by the gods—drew a wickedly sharp axe from beneath her cloak.

Dev unsheathed his dagger, shifted closer to Fenra and Vilvan, and pulled on his magic.

The other refugees scattered in fear, some splashing into the water. The small swampy island they all stood upon wasn't big enough for such an altercation, and a dwarf woman clutching a child barreled past Dev to push her way onto the boat. Steel rung out as Ziggy's sword made contact with the axe, then she tried to complete the arc and twist the axe wielder's arm away with little luck.

The other refugees crowded toward the boat, and Dev would have gotten thrown into the water had he not steadied himself with a burst of wind. Fenra did her best to bark some order into the refugees while Vilvan stood his ground beside Dev. *What in the Bard's name...*

Ziggy fought like a dark beast bounding from Malhela, her sword swinging expertly in the cramped island space. Viragrove trees pinned them in on a few sides, and murky water framed everything.

Two sets of silver-ringed eyes danced in the dark.

Ziggy's opponent swung her axe with equal speed and precision—one swift strike clanged against Ziggy's sword so hard Dev felt it reverberate across the little island. Not certain how to help, he watched, stunned, as Ziggy pressed on. Dev stood guard with Vilvan in front of the refugees as Ziggy finally gained ground, pinning her opponent against a viragrove tree's exposed cage-like roots.

The hood of the stranger slipped, revealing the unmistakable harsh blonde haircut of a woman Dev had all but forgotten: Liess Astor of Southmarch, one of the 'swords once sent to kill him. He growled, clenching his dagger tighter. If Ziggy wasn't so close to the woman, struggling to keep her pinned, he would have hurled his dagger as hard as he could, assuring the speed with an extra burst of wind. Vilvan put a hand on his chest, and Dev backed down—this fight was personal for Ziggy.

Ziggy locked her sword Mystic across Liess's throat, pinning her against the cage of viragrove roots.

"I thought I could hear your axe!" Ziggy snarled in her face. "Yours has the most bloodthirsty song of them all. I should be able to hear it across the continent!"

"And you're supposed to *be* across the continent," Liess seethed, her brow furrowed in annoyance and anger.

"You were coming for us?" Ziggy demanded. Her sword grip tightened, and she shoved Liess back down from the woman's sudden struggle.

Liess chose to clamp her mouth shut then, gazing back at Ziggy with a fierce glint of silver in her eyes.

Dev came over behind Ziggy's shoulder, dagger still drawn. "She was looking for us."

Ziggy nodded.

"Well, lucky for you, *'sword*, you found us," Dev told Liess.

The air changed behind Dev, and he turned to see Vilvan standing there, his light green glow illuminating more of the small island. "What will you do with her?"

Dev adjusted his grip on his dagger, and Liess chose that moment to attempt escape from Ziggy's hold. Liess kicked her feet out, trying to sweep Ziggy's legs, but Dev sent a surge of amethyst wind to push Liess harder into the viragrove roots.

"You don't think..." Dev began, glancing at the boat and thinking aloud. "No, you can't take her to Evandahl. I guess that means *we'll* have to do something about her."

"Why don't I just kill her?" Ziggy said.

Dev frowned, staring into Liess's silver-ringed eyes. The woman spat at him, and he deflected it with a wave of his hand. "She could be useful. She's close to Rhivven."

"Yes," Ziggy said slowly, as if he were daft, "but *she's close to Rhivven*."

Dev ignored her and turned to the two dryads waiting by the boat. "We'll deal with her. Vilvan, you should get the others out of here."

Vilvan nodded, his eyes glowing yellow as he flourished his

hand by way of a dryad goodbye, then he turned to embrace Fenra. Dev looked away, startled again by the intimacy of such simple gestures. It must be a dryad thing, he thought, or perhaps the love between the two was greater than he was used to seeing.

When he turned back to look at Liess, he groaned. This was *not* how he wanted to return to Tytan.

DEV

"You can take her to the lost house," Fenra said, once the glow from Vilvan's leaves faded into the dark swamp. She clutched her own fingers together, her glow also fading a little. Dev felt a little sorry for her. "That's where we hide the refugees."

"The lost house?" Dev asked, shaking his head to clear it. They were supposed to be making their way up to Rayva. They only had a few days until Rhivven's tournament, and Dev still wasn't sure how he was going to get into the city undetected. But no, now he had to deal with Liess gods-cursed Astor.

But perhaps this was the Bard's blessing in disguise.

"Sure," Fenra said, idly elongating her willowy fingers so they resembled sharp sticks as she eyed the hostile silversword. Fenra's gentle green glow was the only light they could see by, and considering she was their guide, Dev agreed.

"Wait a moment," he said, thinking again. "Wouldn't that compromise your safehouse if we bring her there?"

Fenra shrugged. "She was already in there. That's where I brought all the refugees from."

Dev's eyes bulged, glaring at the silversword for infiltrating their operation.

"Take her axe," Ziggy insisted, still pressing her sword to Liess's throat.

Dev watched Liess as he approached her weapon, its blade in the soft mud at their feet, and picked it up. Liess's fingers twitched as soon as he touched it.

"If you think it's all right, Fenra," Dev said, "but how will we—"

A creaking sound sent a shiver up Dev's spine. Roots surged up from the ground, a green and yellow glow emanating from them as they snaked like vines toward Liess. They wove around her wrists and ankles, until finally Fenra smiled and said, "There."

Ziggy dropped one hand from her sword and cocked her fist back, just as quickly sinking a punch into Liess's face. Liess, already disoriented, fell back upon the hard roots with a resounding *crack*.

"Ziggy!" Dev hissed, rushing forward. "I told you not to kill her!"

"Relax, my king," she said. "That wasn't her skull cracking. It was the roots."

He huffed, but she did appear to be alive; her breathing was shallow, and her nose was seeping blood.

Ziggy nudged Dev out of the way. "Hold onto that," she told him, nodding at the axe.

Dev clenched the handle, feeling a sense of revulsion like he was carrying someone's bloody limb around. Though not a silversword himself, he had grown up respecting silversword weapons. You never touched someone else's Welded weapon with your hands. A guard's gauntleted hand had slapped him at the age of four ensuring he learned that lesson. The guard had, of course, been taught an even harsher lesson when the king found out what he'd done to the prince.

Ziggy crouched down and shoved her shoulder under Liess's

armpit, easily hauling the woman onto her back with her unnatural strength. Liess couldn't fight back—thick roots wrapped around her limbs.

"Lead on," Ziggy told Fenra.

After only a few minutes of navigating the swamp on foot, Dev was soaked, disgusted, and on edge. His clothes were wet up to his stomach, and he was constantly scanning the darkness for a set of tagor eyes. He was also fairly certain he wouldn't see it coming if a tagor lunged at them from underwater. So he was relieved when Fenra halted, holding up a long finger.

She didn't speak. Dev adjusted his grip on Liess's axe, not wanting to use it; although, he might have to since he'd put away his dagger.

Something was moving toward them.

"Is it too late?" a newcomer hissed into the darkness.

"It is," Fenra replied. "*What* are you even doing out here still?"

Dev peered past the dryad to look. A young boy was steering a small Virenish craft in the waterway beside them, and another person sat behind him.

"Perrin?" Dev asked, incredulous.

"*Vir dan,* Dev!" The boy appeared noticeably older, even though it had only been a few months since he'd seen him. He'd cut his tightly curled black hair, so that only a thin black fuzz covered his dark skin, but the same mischievous grin shone out at Dev.

At that moment, Liess stirred, and Ziggy moved with her. The roots snapped as the silversword chose that moment to break her bonds.

Dev used a gust of amethyst wind to push Perrin's boat safely backward. Ziggy grappled with Liess, who wasn't fighting Ziggy as much as she was fighting to get *away* from the woman—and toward Dev.

Now that he thought about it, she wouldn't have tried to smuggle herself across the continent for just anyone. Rhivven must have sent her. Dev had been too caught up in his plan of getting to the tournament to even think about it.

An arrow came from nowhere, sinking right into Liess's leg, earning a growl of pain.

"I've got plenty more where that came from," Perrin said, standing perfectly balanced in his boat with his bow aimed at Liess and another arrow nocked.

Liess snarled and snapped off the protruding arrow, tossing it aside. She lunged for Dev again.

He beckoned to the wind and formed it around himself, a thick curtain of amethyst blowing her back. They had to contain her somehow, or Ziggy might be right—they would have to kill her just to get her to stop. She was close to Rhivven, from what he'd heard. She had, after all, been in the group sent to kill Dev. She had to know what Rhivven's plans were, or something that could help Dev reclaim the throne.

At worst, he could use her as leverage. He had to start thinking like a king.

He swept her feet out from under her with a gust of wind, and she fell flat on her back. She twisted to the side, dodging a blow from Ziggy's sword that Dev barely saw coming. They had to *contain* her.

Then, the familiar sights and sounds of the salt swamps soaked into him, stirring a memory of the night he'd been taken from the dock at Resbrok and giving him an idea.

Connecting with his inner magic, he summoned a desperate gust of wind, one that wove toward Liess. She could see it coming, of course, but as she moved away from it, Ziggy swung at her again, and Liess had to twist away—right into Dev's amethyst wind.

It wrapped around her torso, pinning her arms tightly, and squeezing—condensing. He expected her to break it, to wrench her arms free. Her hands writhed at her sides, but her arms seemed frozen in place. It took only a second for her to begin running again—straight at Dev, her head down as if to plow right into his face.

Ziggy stuck out a swift leg, and Liess toppled to the ground just as Dev summoned another dense slip of wind. He floated it quickly to hover over Liess's legs, where Ziggy now pinned them down with her own strength.

Liess lay face down in the mud.

Ziggy let out a low whistle. "Gods, Dev, I didn't know you could do that."

He shook his head. "I didn't either." There was a lot the Carriage House hadn't taught them, and he was loath to admit that Afrith's skills had inspired it.

A massive push against his magic made him sway on the spot, and Ziggy came over to grab his elbow. "What is it?"

"She's pushing against the bonds," he said. "I'm not sure how long I can keep this up."

He normally used air magic and immediately released it. Perhaps that was why this kind of magic wasn't taught—maintaining it took quite the toll. He also suspected that the enclave hadn't wanted mages trained in combat.

Perrin kept his bow trained on Liess as he hopped off the boat. "Who's that?" he asked, eyes wide.

"We'll explain later," Dev said. "Right now, we need to move, get to the lost house or—"

A grin broke out on Perrin's face. "Oh. Well, you're already here."

Fenra smiled at the boy as if sharing an inside joke.

Dev sighed wearily.

"Where is that, exactly?" Ziggy demanded.

"Hold on," Perrin said, reaching down to pull his boat all the way onto the shore, and holding out a hand for his passenger to disembark. Frowning, the small woman accepted his hand and stepped gingerly onto the muddy bank. "Oh, this here's Midruna. She was supposed to be on the boat tonight."

Midruna lowered her head and muttered something about being late, then twisted her hands.

Another push from Liess made Dev's knees buckle. He tightened his connection with his inner magic, focusing on the bonds.

How in the Bard's name had Afrith kept up those bonds on Dev when he'd taken him all the way to Nithe? Perhaps air magic *was* weak, like his brother had said.

"Hurry up," Ziggy barked out to the others, her eyes on Dev.

"Sorry," Fenra muttered, then lifted her hands, elongated fingers glowing brightly.

The waterway beside them began to drain as Fenra pushed the water away, and Dev saw the need for Perrin to put the boat on land. The guttural sucking of moving water echoed through the night-dark swamp lit only by Fenra's green glow. Dev stared in awe as the muddy bank revealed a set of stone steps leading down to the waterlogged door of a small house, embedded in the muck— which mere moments earlier had been hidden beneath the surface.

He let out a strangled chuckle. "There aren't any tagors in there, are there?

Ziggy lifted the prone form of Liess, no longer struggling, as they all descended the slimy stone steps, being careful to watch their footing.

Perrin eased down his bow in order to yank on the water-logged door. It took a few tries, but eventually, it swung open with a groan, and he beckoned them inside.

Dev peered in but saw nothing but darkness. "Got any light?"

"Oh, *va*," Perrin said, scrambling back up the stone steps to retrieve a lantern from the boat. Once he was safely below the steps again, he made quick work of lighting it. The flickering lantern light revealed the sunken house in menacing detail. Soggy viragrove leaves hung from the doorknob, and all the windows had been boarded up, the wood waterlogged and swollen. The entire facade was buried in the surrounding mudbank. A slight breeze fluttered around Fenra as she concentrated on holding the water back, but she seemed to have no difficulty. When Perrin headed inside with the lantern, Dev and the rest followed.

Dev's boots squelched along the wooden floor, which was coated with a surprisingly light layer of mud. Where they stood was barely bigger than the room he and Ziggy had shared back in

Tirnalore, though a couple doorways led off from it. Perrin found a hook on the wall and hung up his lamp in a practiced way, then he hurried back, struggling to close the door securely. The boy nodded at Fenra.

The swamp dryad raised her arms, then filled herself with an even brighter green glow. Dev felt more than heard the shift of the water outside, filling the waterway back up. He wondered how watertight this dilapidated wooden cottage possibly could be, but not a single drop of water entered, even after Fenra had dropped her arms and the water outside seemed to settle. He suspected the dryad had something to do with the small house's continued dryness, because there was no way those boarded up windows were remotely watertight.

He might have helped her air out the soaked planks a little more, if he hadn't been so focused on keeping Liess from escaping her bonds. She tested them every so often, though not as violently as before. Dev figured she was waiting for a moment of distraction, and he wouldn't give it to her.

"What is this place?" Ziggy said.

"It's the lost house," Perrin said easily. "We use it as—"

Dev shook his head, nodding at Liess. "You can tell us later. We need somewhere to keep her for now." He didn't want to let anything slip in front of Liess, and he still had no idea who the woman that Perrin had brought—Midruna—actually was. The woman in question shucked off the small bag on her shoulder and made herself at home.

"I can't wait to hear what your *mazir* thinks of all this," Dev said quietly to Perrin, a smile cracking through his concentration. He wondered just how in the Bard's name Perrin had gotten involved in smuggling people out of Tytan—but if Fenra was involved, the real question was *which* of them had started the illegal activity and encouraged the other.

Perrin grinned. "Oh, she doesn't mind. And Taskor keeps an eye on her—they're engaged now, you know. You can keep your silversword down here," he said, hurrying over to one of the doors in the small house. "It's drier in the basement. And the door locks."

Dev and Ziggy quickly moved the silversword down the narrow staircase, depositing her in the empty room. It was, indeed, drier in the basement. And it didn't smell like rotting wood and muck but...people. It smelled as if a group of people had been living down here recently. All of the marstone pieces on the gameboard suddenly lined up with the realization. The refugees Fenra had led to Vilvan earlier in the night had come directly from here. Liess had also been in this "lost house" as Perrin had called it.

After he acquired rope from somewhere, Perrin came tromping down the basement steps to help secure Liess, and the three of them followed in silence. Dev was eager to get out of earshot of the silversword who'd mucked up his plans. A silversword of any worth could easily break free from simple rope, so Ziggy wrapped it around her as many times as she could, using a series of complicated knots. Dev had no hope that the rope would actually hold her, but if she were also locked in here, it was good enough for now. They shut her in the basement, and Perrin locked the door.

"It's watertight down there—so insulated she won't be able to hear anything."

"Thanks, Perrin," Dev said, his shoulders finally relaxing as Perrin brought out some stools from an evidently airtight closet —the second door in the lost house. "So what is this place? Your safehouse, obviously. But Liess was here already since she was with the refugees. Can she breathe down there?" He was babbling a little, but the night wasn't exactly unfolding as planned.

"'Course," Perrin said. "There's a few air pipes that come up into the reeds above." He gestured vaguely above them.

"So, what," Ziggy said, wandering around and eyeing Midruna in the corner. "You keep the refugees down in the basement, and flood this room on your way out?"

Perrin nodded, grinning.

"And who're you?" Ziggy demanded of the woman in the corner.

The pale woman cowered after glimpsing Ziggy's silver-ringed eyes, but she stuck out her chin and stammered, "M-Midruna, my lady. I was late getting to the safehouse..."

Her story seemed to check out with Perrin and Fenra, who didn't seem surprised. "How long have you been doing this?" Dev asked.

"We started a little after you left Viren," Perrin explained. "*Mazir* kept hearing about people who couldn't make it through the Notch, and she thought, well—"

"It was *her* idea?" Dev asked, snorting.

"*Va,* of course," Perrin replied with a grin.

"And where did this place come from?"

"Oh, it was an old cottage of Lady Atricia's that sank into the *solanse* decades ago. We made some improvements."

"Does she know you're using it?"

Perrin gave him a sly look. "Not exactly. But the less the Viren nobles know the better. And she did agree to help me and Mazir. We just didn't tell her exactly how she'd be doing it."

Dev chuckled and shook his head. "It is a fantastic idea. And you just safehold everyone down there until the crossing?"

The boy nodded. Ziggy cleared her throat, giving Dev a significant look.

"Oh, right," Dev sighed, then drew himself up. "Well, the Bard threw this wrinkle in our plans, but I can't possibly leave that silversword here with you. She's probably already broken free of her bonds."

Perrin crossed his arms, glancing at his bow and arrows which he'd propped against a wall.

"I don't want to kill her," Dev said. "She could be useful— she's close to Rhivven, and the briigard's sitting on my throne."

Midruna gasped, and Dev turned. He'd forgotten the woman was there.

"Sorry, love, I didn't properly introduce myself, did I? King Devryn Verrence, at your service."

Midruna stumbled to her feet and bowed clumsily, muttering, "Apologies, Your Highness, I didn't kn-know—"

"Well, of course you didn't—you're trying to get *out* of Tytan. When's the next crossing, anyway, Perrin?"

"Not for another fortnight. You'll be safe down here until then," Perrin told the woman. "Well, once we get the silversword out of the basement. They charge by the boat, so we try to fill them up."

From the way Perrin said *they*, Dev assumed that Vilvan's involvement meant the Fienn-Da were charging the Resbroks for these trips across the Hollow Sea, which didn't surprise Dev in the least. He would have been more shocked if Evandahl had been offering mages and refugees an escape out of the kindness of his heart.

"Why are you were escaping from Tytan, if I may ask?" Dev said to Midruna gently.

She looked down at the floor and twisted her hands in her lap. "I'm a mage, Your Highness."

"The Carriage House..." Dev began. The Carriage House got its orders from the crown—and that crown currently sat on Rhivven's greasy head.

Midruna shook her head. "It's not safe. The silverswords are there permanently now, always watching. But then I started hearing about mages disappearing," she added in a whisper.

"At first, I thought it was just people leaving the country. You know," she said, her face coloring, "we were all looking forward to having a mage on the throne, Your Highness. After Rhivven took the throne, some of the other mages were afraid. I knew some of them were fleeing. But there were others..."

"Others?"

"Mages who I knew would *never* leave the Carriage House, disappearing overnight. Some I knew personally. I don't think they left on their own. So I decided to go myself, before I was taken too."

Midruna gave a jaw-cracking yawn then, which seemed to remind everyone just how late it was. Dev and Ziggy were fairly used to working through the night at this point, and he suspected Perrin and Fenra were too.

"I suppose we should all rest," Dev said, looking around at the small room.

"Normally, we use the basement for sleeping," Perrin said, pulling some blankets from the watertight closet and glancing around at the damp floor.

Dev brightened and got to work drying out the soggy room. Now that he wasn't struggling with Liess's bonds, he found the mundane task far easier than before. Warm air currents flowed over the floorboards, drying the surface so they could put blankets down.

Midruna was the first to fall asleep, her mouth open and her head facing the lantern light. Ziggy parked herself next to Dev. He had no intention of sleeping, and instead reclined on his blanket with his arms crossed, thinking.

Fenra didn't rest, but Perrin guided her onto a stool so she could get off her feet while she kept them all from drowning.

"How long can she do this?" Dev whispered to Perrin as the boy came to sit next to them.

"Oh, all night. We normally leave the refugees here and go back to Resbrok, but there've been a few times when the silver-sword patrols got a little too close to the lost house and we had to stay overnight too."

"They've been patrolling the *solanse*?"

Perrin nodded. "By boat. They've strong-armed a few of the noble families to lend their expertise in navigating the swamps." He wrinkled his nose in distaste.

Dev's gaze wandered up to the ceiling and he shook his head. "I know you've been smuggling people south, but can you help get us north?"

Ziggy interrupted. "I think you're forgetting one thing, my king"—the title sounding more like a teasing endearment than true fealty—"the 'sword in the basement."

"I haven't forgotten her," Dev ground out. "I was merely avoiding that subject until I came up with a brilliant idea for her."

"She's not going to talk," Ziggy said.

He frowned. "We'll see about that." He got to his feet.

"Now?" Ziggy demanded.

"You're the one who brought her up," Dev said. "Besides, were *you* going to sleep?" He gestured around at the underwater implications.

She snorted, tossing her hair over her shoulder. "No, I wasn't. But maybe a little torture will make me sleepy."

DEV

B*ard bless it*, Dev thought to himself as he descended the basement stairs. *What am I even doing?*

Ziggy had gone first and given him the all-clear. Apparently, Liess hadn't broken free of her bonds, nor was she standing at the bottom of the stairs waiting to ambush and kill him. Ziggy had her arms across her chest, giving him a smug look as he approached. Liess, on the other hand, sat slumped against the wall, her hands still tied behind her back and her legs bound together. Dev narrowed his eyes.

"I checked her hands, don't worry," Ziggy assured him.

"Good." He didn't think for one second that the rope was hampering Liess's escape, no matter how good Ziggy's knots were. She was waiting for her moment, that was all.

Dev stood staring into Liess's face, as if waiting for someone to tell him what to do. But the lost house was silent, surrounded by the waters of the *solanse*, and the only things he could feel were the beating of his own heart and the somewhat stale air caressing his skin.

The air. It would be easy to take it away from Liess to get her to talk, a small pocket without air wrapped around her head. He'd done it to Shad, when his brother had tried to force Fig to cross over. He'd had to protect Fig; there was no guarantee a mage would survive the event. There was certainly no guarantee that *he* would.

But with the promise of the Sword of Morin, making him stronger... He could take the throne back from Rhivven.

And then, he would resume the long line of bloody Verrence silverswords on the Rayvan throne. Was that what he really wanted?

Liess stared back at him, daring him, her silver-ringed eyes boring into his face. During the coup, she'd been sent to kill him. Only Vaelor had protected him. Somehow the thought of his silversword friend bolstered him, and Dev stood straighter.

"I don't expect you to tell me anything, quite frankly," Dev said. "And I'm not going to torture it out of you."

Ziggy *tsked*, disappointed.

"Then what do you want with me?" Liess demanded, her silver eyes rolling.

"I want you to tell me why your king is holding a tournament for a dwarven sword."

She scoffed, shaking her head, though it was clear from her expression that thoughts whirred in her mind. "Only the Bard knows."

"You know."

She blinked several times. "And why would I tell *you*? A weak mage who can't even lift a finger for his throne."

"You owe me."

A peel of laughter rolled out of her, then she made a show of closing her mouth.

"You tried to kill me. I haven't killed you. Therefore, you owe me."

"You were going to make a very poor king with these bargaining skills, *my lord*."

Dev ran a hand through his hair. "What makes you think I'm bargaining? *I'm* not staying here," he said, waving a hand to indicate the submerged house. "But *you* will. I'll take the dryad with me, and someone will forget to close the basement door. It'll be out of my hands."

She stared at him, the silver rings cutting into him. She had to know about the tournament. Dev was sure there was a catch. What of the dwarves? Surely they would come in droves to reclaim the sword. And no matter who won it, Rhivven would want to control that person. What was Rhivven playing at?

Before Liess could respond, a thump sounded above, followed by the quiet trickle of water.

But it wasn't trickling long. They could hear water rushing into the lost house, and soon it began pouring down the basement stairs in a strong torrent. Ziggy and Dev raced for the stairs, pushing through the current that rushed around their feet. Liess yelped and staggered to her feet.

Dev's mind raced as he and Ziggy fought their way up the stairs toward the door, not really caring about what might happen to Liess either way—he hadn't been entirely sure he was going to follow through on his threat. He'd assumed he'd uncover *something* from the gods-cursed silversword before he had to make that decision.

Ziggy had gone up the steps first amid the waterfall, but something pushed her back, and she slammed into Dev's chest, knocking the wind out of him.

The two tumbled back down the stairs, colliding into Liess, who had—of course—chosen that moment to break free of the ropes. Water rushed around the trio as they fought to disentangle themselves, the current making things even harder. Water rushed into his nose and mouth as Dev struggled to untangle himself. *What in the Bard's name—*

Ziggy growled, fighting off the water and Liess's unhelpful limbs as she got back to her feet in the rushing waterfall at the bottom of the stairs. The basement had filled so the water was now up to their chests.

"What in Corava's grave is going on?" Ziggy seethed, racing back up the stairs. Dev quickly followed.

"*What happened?*" Dev demanded. He'd never known Ziggy to be clumsy, and the current wasn't strong enough to push a silversword down the stairs.

"Something pushed me—the damn stair moved!"

A roar behind Dev caused him to whirl just in time to see Liess barreling for him, intent on sending him right back down into the watery abyss. He pushed a gust of air at her, twisting it as quickly as he could to wrap it around her wrists and contain her again.

Ziggy, either unwilling to risk another fall down the stairs or in defense of her king, darted past Dev and brought her sword to meet Liess, whose axe remained in the upper room.

Liess wrenched her hands apart, evading Dev's admittedly disconnected wind. He pushed himself up the stairs sideways, watching Liess fight unarmed—using inhumanly fast attacks to bat Ziggy's sword away. The water had risen until it was only a span from the low basement ceiling. Dev reached the top step, wondering what could have possibly thrown Ziggy down, when he felt the wood move under his feet. Prepared for it, he placed his hands on the wall on either side of him, lifting his body up. Somehow, he knew it wasn't the water that had moved the plank.

"Perrin!" Dev cried as he burst into the room. "Fenra?"

No answer. The house was empty, save for the water rushing in through the cracks in the walls and windows.

Over the rushing sound of water, Dev heard an eerie cry, like a pained howl in the night. He didn't know what sound tagors made, but he hoped to Morgha that wasn't it.

Ziggy spilled into the room behind him and slammed the basement door shut, panting. "I kicked her down into the water," she said, breathless. "It'll give us a few seconds before she's—"

Bang.

The basement door—thick wood that had been reinforced to

make the basement watertight—crashed open pushing Ziggy to the floor. The surface of the water in the basement rose to meet the floor, and Dev rushed to the front door while aiming a strong gust of wind at Liess, giving Ziggy time to get back on her feet.

Without thinking, Dev had sent Liess flying toward the place where her axe rested against the wall. "Gods!" he growled.

The silversword cheered in exaltation, lunging toward her axe. Even across the room, Dev saw something in her change when she was reunited with her weapon. Her posture exuded strength and confidence as she straightened, a violent zeal in her silver eyes as magic shifted in the air.

"Now you're a dead prince," Liess said.

"That's *king* to you," Ziggy shot back, raising her sword.

At that moment, a louder howl came from outside, and the water began gushing into the house at an even more alarming rate. Wood had broken off the windows, even though the planks were nailed from the outside. Dev had to steady himself with a gust of amethyst wind as a wave of salt water rushed into the room. Ziggy and Liess were trading inhumanly fast blows, and the water around them had taken on a red hue, but Dev couldn't tell which of them was bleeding.

The lantern that Perrin had hung high on the wall was the only thing lighting the small space, and Fenra's green glow was nowhere to be seen.

While Ziggy fought off the crazed silversword, Dev sloshed his way to the front door. Though he could provide himself with air underwater, he didn't want to be trapped in here any longer. And he still didn't know what in the Bard's name had happened up here—or where the others were.

He reached the door, but it wouldn't budge, no matter how hard he pushed. The pressure of the water must be too much. He gathered as much air as he could and pushed with both his hands and the purple gust. Flowing straight at the door, he shoved. But the water was stronger.

With a great effort—grunting and straining—Dev gave another push. He was prepared for more water to come in, but he wasn't prepared to see a slab of wood blocking the way. Perrin's boat lay flat against the door, pulled by the draining suction into the house.

Dev banged on the door with his fist, dropping the wind with a groan. "Fenra!" He hammered on the waterlogged wood. "Perrin!"

Dev glanced over his shoulder and saw Ziggy on her knees, her cheek bloody and her sword raised over her head as she tried to hold off Liess. He sloshed over, the powerlessness of his magic weighing on him as heavily as his soaked clothes. He pulled as much air magic as he could from his core, twisting it into a dense pocket of air, and threw it at Liess, who was forcing her axe down on Ziggy's weapon.

The air was strong enough to make Liess stagger back a step, knocked off balance in the already tenuous situation with the swirling water. It had almost reached their hips.

Liess snarled incoherently as she raised her axe again.

"Liess! Gods, would you bloody *stop?*" Dev demanded, yanking more air and forming another dense pocket to throw at her.

"Never, you coward," Liess said, her face pinched in hatred. "It's my job to bring you before Rhivven, and by Morgha's bloodstained hands, I'll do it."

"Ziggy, the boat's blocking the door—see if you can open it," Dev called hurriedly, already twisting his hands to connect with the air around Liess's head. He had no other choice.

The silversword noticed immediately. Her roar of anger was cut short as Dev pulled all the breathable air from around her face. A swoop of nausea hit him as the reality of what he'd done sank into him, but there was no other way. Not anymore.

She staggered toward him, half swimming now as the water had risen to their chests. Dev jumped backward, pushing against the current toward Ziggy and the door. How had the window planks broken and flooded the place? And where in the Bard's *bloody* quills were Fenra and Perrin?

He kept up the air pocket around Liess's head—or lack of

air pocket, really—as the silversword struggled toward him. Ziggy slammed into the front door again, sending a jolt through the whole building. Dev didn't think the current should be strong enough to hold the boat there, but he was an air mage, not a water mage. No, Fenra was supposed to take care of that last bit.

Another wave roared through the openings, pushing Dev off balance. His head went underwater, and he found Liess's hands on his neck.

His head broke the surface, but the crushing hands were still pressing on his windpipe. He didn't let go of the bubble around Liess. He grabbed at her hands with useless fingers. It was like trying to move a statue's hands from around his neck.

"Stop...and I'll...stop," he gasped.

She stared at him, her eyes bulging. She could have easily crushed him, snapped his neck or broken his windpipe. But she didn't. She wanted to bring him to Rhivven alive.

Ziggy slammed her body against the front door again, but with the water so high, she had almost no momentum. Dev could only hope that once the building filled with water, the door would float away, released from the suction.

Water sloshed over Dev's mouth, and the edges of his vision started to blacken. He stared back at Liess, a choking sound emerging instead of the words he had hoped to win her over. The waves kissed the ceiling, and the lantern finally went out.

Complete darkness swallowed them. Had Dev not already had a silversword's hands around his throat, he would have feared unseen tagors were somehow lurking in the blackness, the taste of salt water on his tongue pervading his senses. His lungs screamed for air, and it was about to get worse as the space between the tops of their heads and the ceiling filled with water. There was only one way to get Liess to trust him.

The water gave a final surge, covering their heads entirely.

Dev reversed the bubble over Liess, giving her breathable air. He formed another bubble over Ziggy, and one over himself. Though he still couldn't breathe, at least his face wasn't submerged anymore. A ragged gasp came from in front of him, and Liess's grip on his neck twitched, then finally let go.

He gasped, his hands going to his throat, massaging it, and hauling in a breath of the air in his small bubble. The air wouldn't last long and shrank with each breath, but he could replenish the air as long as his strength would allow. He just wasn't sure how long he could keep it up, the pull on his magic more taxing the longer he had to create air from nothing.

"Dev?" Ziggy demanded from somewhere behind him, the sound echoing strangely through the air bubble and the water between them.

The pitch-black house was now completely filled with water, so they should be able to open the door. He reached out blindly, groping for Ziggy's arm. He found her shoulder and grabbed it. "Try the door now," he said, his voice hoarse.

Liess had remained silent, and the only reason he knew her general location was by sensing the air bubble around her. All three air bubbles were growing smaller with each breath. He pushed life back into the bubbles, replenishing their air. As Ziggy continued to fiddle with the door, Dev snaked a hand out to grab Liess's arm. She jolted but, thankfully, didn't gut him.

"I can take that away again," he told her, his voice coming out eerie and hollow even to his own ears. A strange emptiness settled over him as he spoke into the watery darkness. "You think I'm weak? I control the very air you breathe. I don't need a weapon to make me stronger."

As soon as he said the words, a comforting warmth stole over his center, and he felt his air bubble grow larger even though he hadn't done anything to it. He took another reassuring breath of air and went on. "I don't want to kill you Liess, but if you won't bloody leave me alone, I will."

Liess didn't say anything, only continued breathing the air he gave her.

"Ziggy, what in the pits of Malhela is going on with that door?" he demanded.

"I don't know!" she groaned, and the sound of a futile kick

against wood reverberated through the watery house. "It's like the boat is still stuck fast against it, but there's no current to hold it down! Would Perrin and Fenra have done this?"

"No. No, and I'm worried that was Fenra earlier, making that sound. We need to find a way out of here."

"Get back," came Liess's voice. "Both of you—unless you want to feel the swing of my axe."

Dev quickly swam backward, moving away from the door. He'd never been afraid of water, but swimming in complete blackness filled his mind with all manner of horrible things that could be in here with them. If the water could get in through those missing planks, what else could? Could a tagor rip more planks off to get to them?

He maneuvered closer to where Ziggy had retreated and put a hand on her arm again. He pushed more air into all their air bubbles, beginning to feel the strain as he let his limbs float weightlessly around him. It was one thing to manipulate the air around him but creating it from scratch meant pulling directly on his own energy. His grip on Ziggy's arm tightened as his head swam, dizziness threatening to overwhelm him.

Thunk.

Muttered curses came from Liess. "Hope you briigards moved back enough," she grunted—then *slam*.

The sound of cracking wood echoed through the water, and Liess swung again. More splintering followed, louder now, as she tore chunks of wood from the doorframe. "What is this cottage bloody made of?" she muttered. Dev gave her more air, then his hand on Ziggy's arm went limp.

The next thing he knew, Ziggy was pulling him through a jagged hole in the house—the remains of the door. He blinked, the dim pre-dawn light of the *solanse* coloring the murky water enough for him to see the remains of Perrin's raft stuck fast to the front of the lost house as though bolted there with jagged hack marks from Liess's axe creating an opening.

His face broke the surface of the salt swamps, his air bubble bursting as his magic released, flooding his mouth with briny water. He scrambled for footing as Ziggy dragged him along, finally finding the slimy steps leading up to the bank and getting his feet beneath him. At last, the three of them threw themselves on the soggy bank, gasping for breath in the thick air of the solanse.

Then Dev noticed the arrow pointed at him.

It was Perrin's bow, but the one wielding it was Midruna. She stood on the next bank over, Fenra and Perrin at her feet.

Dev hauled himself up to his feet. Midruna fired her arrow, but Dev threw it aside with a burst of amethyst wind. He stumbled a little, but it was much easier to move the existing air, even with his energy depleted. Dev continued on, sloshing across the ankle-deep water between the two soggy islands and gathering air at his fingertips.

"Dev…" Ziggy began.

He ignored her. He would handle this.

The mage stepped back but held her chin high even as Dev brought his condensed wind to wrap in a thick bind around her torso, knocking the bow from her hands and pinning her arms to her side.

"What happened to Fenra and Perrin?" he demanded. Their bodies lay on the ground behind her, and Dev couldn't tell if they were alive. He was *sure* that howl earlier had been Fenra's. "What did you do?"

She glared at him.

He pulled on the bonds around her, squeezing and drawing his dagger from his sopping wet clothes. "*What did you do?*"

Midruna smirked, unnerving him. "You are just like them. The silverswords. Aligning yourself with them. Of course, you were groomed to be one, I guess."

Dev opened his mouth, but it was Liess who spoke. "Aligning with silverswords, eh?" she sneered. "If I recall, you had no problem with that earlier last night."

Midruna pursed her lips and narrowed her eyes at Liess. "As if I had a choice."

"You gave up the location of the safehouse easily enough," Liess said.

Ziggy sloshed over to the island toward Midruna. "*You're* the reason this bloodsucking briigard got onto the boat—"

"Watch who you call a briigard, Ashbrok. I just got you out of that watery grave."

"Actually, I believe Dev was the one who saved us from the grave—"

"Enough," Dev said. He brought his dagger under Midruna's chin and tipped her head up. "What did you do to Perrin and Fenra?" He pressed the dagger in, drawing blood. He almost didn't care that she'd given information to Liess or tried to drown them—but if anything had happened to Perrin...

Midruna sniffed at the pain, but her eyes darted toward the water down where the lost house sat.

Then something moved in the water—something large. Dev whirled around to face it. When he saw the jagged remains of the boat hurtling at him, saltwater sloughing off it as it soared straight out of the water toward him and Ziggy, he yanked at the air around him, shoving it at the oncoming craft and redirecting it to soar over their heads. It crashed into the next island with a wet thud, and Dev turned to stare at Midruna.

"Wood mage?" he guessed, sending a thick tendril of air to her clamp down her fingertips—how he assumed she'd controlled the raft. Midruna raised her eyebrows in acknowledgment.

Ziggy crouched over Perrin and Fenra. "They're alive—well, Perrin is. Fenra... I do see air moving around her leaves—does that mean she's breathing?"

Dev continued staring at Midruna. "Why?" he asked quietly. "I thought you wanted a mage on the throne."

Her jaw gritted, she said, "We did. What I said earlier was true. But that one over there"—she jerked her head toward Liess—"hunted me through the salt swamps to get the safehouse location out of me. You're supposed to be the king, but you're working with silverswords. You're working with them."

"Not all silverswords are with Rhivven."

"They're taking mages!"

"Who is?"

"The silverswords," Midruna hissed. "I saw one of them take a mage from the Carriage House. So I left! And here you are, working right beside them. Friends with one of them!"

"Not everyone who takes the silver is against you," Dev said wearily.

"They're not human anymore. You can't trust any of them. I thought you were different." She spat on the ground at his feet.

"So your solution was to drown all of us," Ziggy sneered, "including the rightful king of Tytan, who is a mage."

She didn't answer. Of course, the price on Dev's head would be enough to set her up for a life of luxury in Tysaine.

"I'm only working with *one* silversword here, anyway," he explained, cocking his head in Ziggy's direction. "Liess Astor, if you didn't realize, is trying to kill me."

"She knew who I was," Midruna said, as if that were a valid defense.

Dev shook his head and turned away. "This isn't helpful," he muttered to Ziggy, who was still crouching down over his friends' bodies. Fenra had no skin to check, as she was covered in bark, but her long leaves were fluttering in the air that seemed to be coming off of her. She had a pained look on her face. Dev wondered just how much a wood mage could affect a dryad. He knew dryads were vastly different from the lifeless planks of "deadwood"—as they called it—yet they were related to living trees.

Perrin was breathing, but blood streamed from one of his temples. Dev shook the boy's shoulder. "Perrin? Perrin."

The boy's lashes fluttered, and he turned his head, muttering something unintelligible. Then he jerked upright, one hand going to his bloody temple, and stared at Dev in shock.

"It's all right," Dev said, putting his hands on the boy's shoulders, "No, no, lie back down."

It was becoming increasingly light out, and the sun chose that moment to break through the verdant green expanse of the salt swamps. Dev's gaze went east to meet the sun's rays and locked eyes with a lurking tagor twenty paces off, just before the creature slid underwater and disappeared. How long it had been watching them was anyone's guess.

The boat was ruined. Now they knew why the craft had been stuck fast in front of the door, and why one of the steps into the basement had moved, throwing Ziggy down the stairs—Midruna.

The wood mage had been unceremoniously tossed onto the mud, her arms and fingers still bound. She wasn't physically as strong as Liess, so the drain of maintaining the bonds was far lesser this time, or perhaps Dev's limits had expanded.

As the sun rose, Ziggy checked Perrin for more injuries but found only the one at his temple. She helped him sit up and take a sip of water from his flask.

The longer Fenra stayed unconscious, the more worry seeped into Dev. Had Midruna done permanent damage to the dryad? It would break Vilvan's heart to learn that anything had happened to Fenra. And Dev wouldn't let that happen.

He kicked the remains of the boat and walked over to the wood mage, who looked up at him uninterestedly.

"What did you do to Fenra?"

Midruna shrugged as best she could within her bonds.

"I'm done playing games," Dev muttered. He sucked in a breath, ready to pull the air from around Midruna's face. She deserved it after trying to drown them for no good reason.

But then a flash of Shad's face—constricted as Dev choked the air out of his lungs—pervaded his mind. It had been one thing to deprive Liess of air when she was trying to murder him amid their near-drowning. But out of spite? Torture? No. That wasn't him.

The woman looked up at him, no hint of regret on her face for what she'd done. She'd fled the Carriage House when other mages started disappearing—likely taken and killed by the 'swords. Then Liess had tracked her down and forced her to divulge the secret of the safehouse. Was it her fault for wanting to flee Tytan? For getting caught up with the silverswords and a fugitive king?

He dropped the air. He wasn't a killer, even if every word she said was a lie. He wasn't a silversword. And he didn't need weapons or even magic to make him stronger.

Reaching down, he yanked her to her feet and pushed her forward. "You're coming with us as far as Verindas."

"Dev, *what* are you doing?" Ziggy said. "We already have enough deadweight that wants to kill us." She rolled her eyes at Liess.

But Dev was looking at Perrin, who was watching him closely. Perrin nodded. If Dev wanted to be the king of Tytan, he couldn't be like the silverswords—killing to get what he wanted.

"She can find her own way from there."

"And what about us? She'll tell the silverswords where we've gone—that you're here in Tytan."

"No, she won't."

"How can you be sure?" Ziggy demanded.

"She needs to get out of Tytan. I'm sure she knows the silverswords won't believe a mage on the run telling tall tales about a Verrence in the swamps. They'll cart her back to the Carriage House."

Midruna glared at him, her eyes wide as the idea sank in.

Liess swaggered over to him, and he sighed. "Liess," he said in warning, holding up a hand.

"I'm not going to kill you," she snarled. "Unfortunately, thanks to what this little kirich did, we might be even now."

LIESS

Devryn raised his eyebrows, and Liess very slowly slid her axe into its proper place in her sheath, letting the leather flap settle over the blade. She ran her thumb along the leather guard, the motion soothing her inner turmoil.

After nearly drowning in that cursed underwater house, she was beyond ready to get out of the salt swamps; even the thick air choked her with too much humidity. She was sticky with salt, her lungs tight from Devryn trying to kill her, and there was no way on Morgha's green earth she could return to Rayva without the missing prince.

Except the briigard had just saved her life.

She swallowed, thinking of her encounter with King Rhivven in the throne room. She could either return a queen or a corpse. The choice should be obvious.

The wood mage shifted from where she'd been tossed to the ground, and Liess's gaze just barely caught the subtle movement of Midruna's hands—though her fingers were bound together, she moved them as a whole, her nose carving an upward line as she tilted her head.

Every stick on the ground—every splinter of the broken boat—rose into the air. All pointed at the mage's foes, pieces chipping off to sharpen into stakes.

In the second it took for the mage to command and aim her pikes, Liess had unsheathed her axe and swung it in a steady arc from the mage's left shoulder to her opposite hip. Midruna softened as the wound darkened. In these moments of clarity, it was as if time slowed and everything went quiet. She didn't even hear Midruna's head hit the wet ground as the mage fell, dead. The pikes, frozen in the air, all dropped without fanfare.

Then everything became fast and loud again, and everyone was shouting.

"What in the blessed name of the Bard did you do that for?" Ziggrune demanded, rounding on her. Devryn let out a shout of surprise and leapt back from the dead body.

Liess straightened, rolling her shoulders in agitation. "You saw the stakes, did you not? She was going to kill us all."

Devryn stared at the mage on the ground, and suddenly the woman's arms went limp as he let go of the air binding them. Liess had been surprised when he'd tried that on *her*. She didn't think the mages learned anything like that at the Carriage House, particularly not the spoiled prince.

He was definitely not the pompous prince he once was, parading around the Rayvan Palace in the days before Shadryn died and everyone in Tytan had discovered the truth about Queen Eileigh's blood. Then the briigard had been shipped off to the Carriage House, and King Haemond had the nerve to tell the enclave that a mage would be good for the throne.

Silverswords had ruled Tytan for two hundred years. And that was how it should be—the kingdom united under strength. And she would rise upon that throne at Rhivven's side. The idea filled her with a hot mix of elation and—she would never admit it aloud—terror at the idea of becoming Rhivven's queen. Of course, he probably only wanted her for the duty of providing heirs, but to be his wife and obey his every command... She shivered. She'd been under his command at the enclave and on the battlefront at Viren, but this would be an entirely different battlefront.

Was that really what she wanted?

She froze. Of course it was. Rhivven was her king, the strongest silversword on the continent. She would do whatever he ordered.

The only problem was the spoiled prince she'd been sent to retrieve was actually a virtuous briigard who'd saved her life—after successfully threatening it anyway.

The boy—Perrin—was stirring. Liess crossed her arms, surveying him and the others and calculating her chances of capturing Devryn now.

He was more powerful than she'd originally thought, and it was becoming clear they were evenly matched, particularly with Ziggrune on his side. She rubbed her finger along the sheathed blade of the axe and turned to face the prince.

"We're more than even now. Get me out of this gods-forsaken swamp, and I'll leave—"

Ziggrune took a step closer, hand on her sword.

"—I'll leave you alone *for now*," Liess continued. "You can't really expect me to give up, can you?" They weren't stupid. She knew they would see through her if she pretended to be a weak-bellied coward and give up her quest to retrieve Devryn. The idiot was heading for Rayva, anyway. The prince and his friends had grossly overestimated the soundproofing in the shack's basement, and she'd heard every word.

Liess raised an eyebrow at the prince, daring him to challenge her.

Devryn studied her face. "You carry the dryad, then."

DEV

Dev walked close to Perrin, afraid the boy might have something wrong with his head, after being unconscious for so long. But Perrin sloshed through the shallow water around the muddy islands just fine, an arrow nocked at his bow, and his eyes alert.

Fenra, however, was still unconscious in the arms of Liess Astor.

Dev didn't trust the silversword for a moment, even if he had saved her life—but having her carry Fenra occupied her arms while they trudged through the salt swamps.

"Wait, this can't be right," Liess said, glancing at the afternoon sun. "We're heading south."

"And?" Dev said, narrowing his eyes at her.

"And I thought we were getting out of this swamp," she all but growled.

"The Notch is south," he said simply. "But we're not heading there."

"Where *are* we headed?"

Dev let the smirk he'd been holding in draw up the corner of his lips. "To the de Wald gathering. We have to do something about Fenra, so we're taking her to her family."

He and Perrin had discussed it in near-silent whispers before setting off. Dev had originally wanted to head to the Resbrok manor—dreaming of soft beds and feather pillows, or at the very least, dry feet—but the reality was, only the dryads would know how to heal Fenra or figure out what was wrong with her. As much as he wanted to get to Rayva in time for the tournament, Fenra had protected them, preventing the waters of the salt swamp from drowning them, until she'd been struck down by Midruna. It was Dev's fault the dryad was injured—or sick; he still had no idea what was wrong with her.

So he'd followed Perrin's lead south. Now that Liess knew where they were going, he let her draw ahead to the front, where they could all keep an eye on her.

"El took me there once," Perrin said, nodding ahead. "It's maybe another hour by foot."

Dev nodded. "What's one more hour?" he said breezily. "How is Fenra's brother doing anyway?"

Somewhere between almost killing Liess, then saving everyone's life with his air magic, the idea of Welding with the Sword of Morin had lost its dangerous appeal. He felt his own magic growing stronger the more he used it. He'd never thought he could hold a silversword like Liess with just air before. But he could still get the sword for the dwarves like he'd promised—if they made it in time.

"He wanted to help with the refugees, but the elders wouldn't let him leave the family gathering. We'll get you up to Rayva, though, Dev," Perrin promised. "King Dev, I mean. Sorry."

Reaching a hand to lightly ruffle the boy's short hair, he said, "No 'king' here."

Perrin huffed. "You're more a king than *he'll* ever be," he said, and Dev couldn't help but picture Rhivven sitting on his father's throne, his knees spread wide as he leered down from the dais.

"Who else would tromp across the salt swamps to heal a dryad in his protection?"

The side of Dev's mouth went up in a half-smile. "Thanks, Perrin."

Low and tangly viragrove trees covered in Andisia moss soon gave way to the more stately cypress trees, their knees poking out of the swamp water around them. Ahead, Dev saw a small lake, and his breath caught in his throat when they emerged at the edge. Massive trees lined the shore, some resembling willows and others cypress or oak—the dryad elders, from what Perrin had told him. The power emanating from them seeped into his skin—almost like the feeling of the Gold Wood.

"So this is a dryad gathering."

A nearby tree groaned as if moving in a stiff wind. Dev stood up straighter. Several figures down the shore began moving toward the small party, and Perrin raised his hand in greeting.

A young dryad bounded toward them, short leaves on his head and a bright look in his green eyes. "Perrin! It's great to see you, I—" He stopped short, his gaze landing on Fenra.

"We don't know what happened to her, El," Perrin said. "A wood mage attacked us. She did something to Fenra."

"A wood mage?" El repeated, wrinkling the bark alongside his nose. A burst of air emanated from him as he drew closer to the dryad in Liess's arms. Dev put his hand on his dagger, eyes on the silversword.

Liess had been suspiciously compliant as they headed south. He knew all she wanted was to bring him back to Rayva and deliver him to Rhivven—but by the Bard's luck, that was where he wanted to go anyway. Maybe he could use that to his advantage.

Other young dryads had joined them, and Dev lost himself for a moment of wonder at the sight of the toddler-sized dryads, awkward limbs tripping over their own feet and the exposed roots of their elders every other step. Their tiny leaves were tangled, their green or yellow eyes wide, and the youngest held a sort of blanket knit from Andisia moss.

El was speaking, motioning for them to follow him along the shore—which was no longer muddy earth, but a patchwork of roots and cedar knees. "Watch out for Elder Elizareth's knees, Minna!" El hissed at the youngest dryad toddler, who promptly tripped—too busy watching a passing treefrog instead of her feet. Two other dryad children rushed over to help her out of the calf-deep water and placed her back up on the roots.

Ziggy shot an incredulous glance at Dev, and he shrugged, smiling. If the Bard had told him this particular stop would be in Dev's tale, he would have laughed in his face. Dryad toddlers?

At least El didn't seem too concerned about Fenra. "Elder Sprate will be able to help her," he was saying. "He only recently put down his roots. He spent his *voixage* learning about magic and botany in Tirnalore. I hope to go there myself on my *voixage*. Of course, I don't *just* want to learn about botany. And I don't see myself staying in Tirnalore the entire fifty years. I've already got about twenty places in the chart I've been making for once I leave the *solanse*, and with the money Fenra sends me..."

Dev's attention flagged as El listed all the places around the Svoran continent he wanted to visit. He gazed up at the elder dryad trees, the majority of them stationary, with the exception of the willows who swayed in the occasional breeze, and a few here and there that seemed able to move their limbs more than a tree should—he supposed the more mobile ones were those who had put down roots more recently.

They picked their way across the woven root path, and Dev wondered if the elders could feel their footsteps.

Eventually, as El was describing the places on the Tytan coast he'd visit all the way up to Rokhold, their ungainly procession drew to a halt. Little Minna had lost her footing again and was saved from falling in the now waist-high water by a nearby tree—which lashed out a branch with a vaguely hand-shaped tip. The tree groaned and turned in their direction. Twice as tall as any of the humans, its face shifted toward them, its short leaves rustling in an unseen breeze. "What's this, Elfrar? Humans?" the tree said slowly in a sepulchral voice.

El bobbed his head. "Yes, Elder Sprate. They brought Fenra—she was attacked by a wood mage."

Sprate twisted toward them with a groan, his roots straining slightly in the muddy soil at his feet. "Place her here," he said, patting the ground in front of him.

Liess, an unreadable expression on her face, trudged forward and deposited Fenra by Sprate's roots. Then, much to Dev's concern, the silversword sidled up next to him.

Ziggy came between them inhumanly fast, missing nothing. "Try anything and you're dead," she whispered.

Liess scoffed as if offended. "I merely wanted to talk to the prince, Ziggrune. Relax."

Ziggy rolled her eyes but remained where she was, one hand on her sword hilt.

"Well?" Dev said out of the corner of his mouth, watching the dryad inspect Fenra. Sprate had leaned over and was running his bark-covered hands over Fenra's limbs. His eyes glowed yellow, and a gentle glow emanated from the center of his trunk. He groaned idly while he inspected the girl.

"*Well*, how long are we going to be here?" Liess asked, gesturing around the dryad gathering.

"As long as we have to be," Dev said, crossing his arms.

Ziggy made a *hmm* of surprise from behind him. "You don't want to get to..." she trailed off meaningfully.

Dev shrugged. "It's not as urgent as I thought it was," Dev said softly. To his surprise, Ziggy gave him a hearty pat on his shoulder, and heat rushed to his face. He watched a group of tagors on the other side of the lake catching the last rays of sunlight. The largest stretched its leathery wings, then slipped into the water.

Sprate straightened up, and everyone looked at him. His gnarled face twisted into a reassuring smile. "She'll live. I've done what I can to balance her humors. What she needs most now is rest."

Relief cascaded over Dev, and he smiled. Perrin rushed over to the dryad and took her willowy fingers in his.

"What happened to her?" Perrin asked Sprate.

Sprate groaned as he lifted his hands away from his sides, until they pointed outward like branches again. "Wood mages mostly find their magic in deadwood, but with a certain amount of effort, they can affect living wood as well. This mage wasn't particularly skilled and only caused Fenra's rings great pain. The *solanse* will heal her."

As they watched the sun set through the trees, and the tagors sunning on the other side of the lake, a riot of orange shining through green, Dev, Ziggy, Liess, and the dryad children followed El off the roots and into the heart of the *solanse*, to a place where the ground was a little firmer. Dev thanked the Bard for the reprieve of soaked feet, even if it was temporary. He sent a gust of warm air into his shoes, attempting to dry them.

Ziggy cleared her throat and gave him a look. He smirked and sent some warm air her way as well. He knew it was working when she gave a hearty sigh.

El stopped at a curious clearing. In the back of Dev's mind, he'd been hoping for a nice warm fire and maybe a dwelling of some kind so they could rest for the night before traveling to Rayva, but as he took in the clearing, he realized the dryads needed none of those things. The branches of nearby elder trees stretched overhead, forming a roof of overlapping leaves that made any dwelling unnecessary. The dryad children rushed to play on the boulders littering the clearing, which acted as a kind of playground for them to stretch their limbs. The youngest, Minna, took her blanket and cuddled up in the roots of a nearby elder, watching the others play.

Keeping a watchful gaze on Liess, Dev sidled up to Perrin, Ziggy, and El.

The dryad let out a gust of fresh air from his leaves and told them, "You can stay here for the night. The elders agreed, since you helped Fenra by bringing her here."

"Oh?" Dev said, looking around. "When did they agree on that?"

A nearby tree groaned idly, and a voice entered his head—*Stay the night, but do not linger here. We cannot tolerate the song of those weapons for long.* The voice was vaguely feminine, with an ethereal depth like it came from the *solanse* itself.

Dev gave a curious glance at Ziggy's and Liess's weapons, knowing full well the elder was referring to them. Ziggy had also mentioned being able to hear silversword weapons. Having grown up surrounded by members of the enclave, Dev knew they didn't all have that ability, but she was more observant than most people he knew, and the silversword ritual enhanced innate abilities.

Not knowing exactly who he was speaking to, Dev simply thought the words, *Thank you for the shelter. We will be gone first thing in the morning.*

Another groan came from the tree as a breeze wove through the leaves above, and Dev took that for as much of a response as he was going to receive.

CHAPTER 22

ZIGGY

The dryad children slept standing in the northeastern corner of the clearing, huddled near each other and swaying gently like trees in a breeze. Each emitted the faintest yellow or green glow—much like the elder trees surrounding them. Ziggy paced the clearing, careful not to disturb anyone. Dev had woken her an hour ago to keep watch. She had been keeping a close eye on Liess, but this close to the lake, she also needed to watch for tagors. She doubted other humans would venture this far into the *solanse*—or into the middle of a dryad gathering—but she *was* traveling with the most wanted person in Rayva. The sweet fool. Ziggy would have killed Liess Astor half a dozen times by now if it weren't for him. And speaking of the bloodthirsty kirich...

Liess's prone form shifted, and the woman looked around the clearing, then ran a finger over her axe sheath. She only had an elbow lifting herself off the ground before Ziggy was standing over her—sword pressed across her throat to prevent her from rising, knees pinning down her arms to keep her from reaching her axe.

Liess growled at her.

Ziggy smiled in the darkness. "And here I was *just* thinking about killing you. Trying to sneak off, are you? Or did you think you could kill Dev on my watch?"

"Get off of me," Liess spat, silver eyes glinting.

Ziggy pressed the sword edge even closer. Mystic rang in her ears, a song of justice, of revenge. She clenched her jaw. She had Liess under her blade—how easily they could be rid of the increasingly obnoxious problem of Liess Astor.

Dev, Morgha bless him, was not cut out for killing, but that was one of the reasons she liked him. It was also why *she* was here. Her breath coming heavy, she said, "Dev thinks you're useful for some reason, but I don't. I've seen you in the enclave. I know you've been licking Rhivven's boots since your crossover, but the *king* doesn't actually trust you, does he? After you let us slip through your fingers at the Notch—well, I'm surprised you're even still alive."

A second of warning—a slant of silver-ringed eyes—was all the time Ziggy had before Liess lashed out, attempting to break free of her hold. *Apparently, I touched a nerve*, Ziggy thought with a grin. She held fast. She didn't know if it was from the comfortingly heavy air of the salt swamps or the rush of finally feeling like she had the upper hand, but adrenaline coursed through her veins, and she pressed her knees harder against Liess's limbs.

Liess tried to kick Ziggy but missed, which only brought Ziggy's sword higher up on her neck.

"So why shouldn't I kill you?" The ringing in her ears was growing louder. She heard a loud groan from one of the trees, and Ziggy suppressed a shudder.

Liess blinked. "Because your *Dev* there is heading to the tournament in Rayva, and I know Rhivven's plans for it."

"How could you possibly know that?" Ziggy demanded, narrowing her gaze.

"I overheard you in that sunken house."

"I thought the basement was soundproof."

Liess actually shrugged beneath Ziggy's blade. "Not as sound-proof—or as waterproof—as anyone thought, was it?"

"And what do you know of the tournament?"

"Why should I tell *you?*"

Ziggy knew the instant her blade drew blood; Mystic's blood-song rang true and even elicited a deep groan from several trees nearby. "Because I'm the one who's going to cut your throat in the next three seconds unless you give me a reason to keep you alive," she nearly growled.

Out of the corner of Ziggy's eye, she saw the dryads shift.

"The tournament is for the Sword of Morin—"

"Fantastic information, something we've heard is written in flyers across the continent."

"—and whoever wins it will be forced to Weld with it."

Ziggy flinched, Mystic's song becoming discordant. The trees around them groaned again, and this time, Dev called out, "What in the Bard's name is going on over—" She heard him come up behind her. "Ziggy what are you doing? The elders are—"

The breeze running through the treetops shifted to scour the ground, and between Dev's admonishment and a strange ethereal urge to retreat, Ziggy found her feet again and staggered back, pointing Mystic at Liess's throat.

"She was up to something," Ziggy told Dev.

"I was just going to relieve myself, if you must know," Liess ground out.

"Put your sword away," Dev said, clutching his head. "The elders are angry—they were hesitant about us staying under their boughs in the first place. They can feel your Welded weapons."

The arm holding Mystic went limp, and she stared down at Liess, who, to her credit, hadn't unsheathed her axe even after regaining use of her arms. Ziggy swallowed and slid Mystic back into her sheath with a metallic ring of finality.

The breeze settled down, and she became aware of cold sweat on the back of her neck. A tree groaned. The thick *solanse* air pressed against her more oppressively than ever; something had shifted. She took another step back from Liess.

Dev put a hand on her arm. "The elders—can't you hear them?"

Brows furrowed, Ziggy shook her head.

"Maybe they're only speaking to me," Dev muttered. "They want us to leave. Now."

Ziggy blinked, taking in the clearing once more. The dryad children remained where they stood, still swaying slightly in their sleep. The elder trees had calmed down, but Ziggy could sense something off about the air. She nodded. "I'm sorry. I thought she was up to something. She put a hand on her axe."

Dev pursed his lips and nodded, picking up the satchel he'd been using as a pillow, and going over to wake Perrin.

After they exchanged a few short words, Perrin rolled over and went back to sleep. Dev came back over shaking his head. "Perrin's going to stay and make sure Fenra's all right. I guess his *mazir* is all right with this kind of thing."

Dawn had yet to make its timid approach, so they set off by the light of the stars and the dim glow of the elder trees, bidding farewell to the gathering.

"Liess should walk in front," Ziggy said, her arms crossed. "She knows we're heading to Rayva. We might as well let her lead."

The silversword must have heard her, and she tiredly acquiesced, heading north by the stars. Dev was quiet, so Ziggy went on. "She told me about the tournament. The winner will be forced to Weld with the sword."

"Huh," Dev said pensively.

"So there's no point in you entering, right?"

They crossed a small stream that fed into the lake, and Ziggy mourned the loss of dry ground as the small mounds of mud that passed for islands became their path. Guilt at getting Dev ousted from the gathering prickled her. But if Liess had slit all their throats, neither of them would be walking out of here at all. The starlight grew brighter as they emerged from the thick foliage of the dryad gathering, allowing them to see more clearly.

"I'm still entering," Dev said.

"I thought you didn't want the sword anymore, you said—"

"I said it wasn't *as* important, but that doesn't mean it isn't important. Ziggy, if I get the sword, the chances they'll let me walk out of there alive would make the Bard laugh. Escaping a crossover is just another part of it. I just wish I had gotten more sleep," he grumbled.

"I'm sorry, Dev," Ziggy said. "I didn't know the elders—"

"It's not just about the elders asking us to leave. You know I don't want to kill Liess."

"I know."

"Would you have done it?"

Ziggy frowned, thinking about it. She remembered her sword ringing when it had drawn Liess's blood, how the energy zinged through her veins. No wonder people thought silversword weapons hungered for blood. A sigh escaped her. "I don't know. Maybe. But you know she's just trying to deliver you to Rayva, right?"

She practically felt him roll his eyes. "Of course I do, Ziggy." Liess, of course, could hear every word of their conversation— neither of them was stupid enough to think otherwise—and he pitched his voice even louder. "But we need to get to the capital for that, don't we? Eh, *Liess?*"

The silversword ahead let out a quiet snort and kept walking, charting their path north.

DEV

A cool gust of air slid down Dev's neck, jolting his senses awake. They'd been walking for at least a day, and he'd begun using his magic to help him stay alert. He didn't know how long it would take to get out of the *solanse*—and they'd lost their guides.

Luckily, Ziggy had grown up on an estate at the edge of the *solanse* and could help them avoid the most treacherous waterways. Dev had stopped talking to her as the night wore into day, though, his irritation growing. They'd had a safe place to sleep for the night, guarded by the dryad elders, even if there *was* an enemy silversword in their camp, yet Ziggy had to anger the elders by using her sword for violence.

He wouldn't forget the elders' voices in his head anytime soon —ethereal voices booming in his dreams, waking him from his slumber and telling him to make it stop. To leave the sacred place. To stop the blood from spilling.

But he wasn't irritated with Ziggy, he was irritated with himself.

It had been his idea to take Liess with them in the first place, thinking he could get information about Rhivven or the tournament out of her. She was close to Rhivven in the enclave. She likely knew a few details that could be useful. But he'd chosen not to torture her or kill her, and now they were stuck traveling with a silversword who wanted him dead or captured—and wasn't doing a convincing job of pretending otherwise. Dev hadn't bought her act for a moment that they were even, no matter what she'd said back at the lost house.

He set his jaw, sending another cool burst of amethyst air down his neck. He shivered. It was colder than he'd intended.

The memory of the elders' voices had echoed in his thoughts all day as they sloshed through the salt swamps.

Sacred place. Stop the blood.

Wasn't that what he was in Tytan to do?

Tytan had many sacred places. The Gold Wood, the Great Mountain, the *solanse*. All taken from their rightful owners, usurped by the crown.

He could think of one way to build an army against the silverswords and reclaim the Rayvan throne: return all the sacred places, starting with the dwarves and their Mountain. He was more certain than ever now that he didn't need the legendary sword for himself, but if he returned it to the dwarves, that would be the start of a revolution.

It was a start. And he could do it—he could reunite Tytan, bringing them against the very forces Dev had grown up intending to join: the silverswords, with the Butcher of Viren at their head.

Dev couldn't help but wonder how the tale of Devryn the Reuniter might go down in the Bard's tales.

Or if he didn't win, Devryn the Dead.

Dev could hardly believe his feet as they trod on dry land as the soft, grassy hills began to rise, leading them into the Virenish highlands.

Dev demanded they stop to bathe in the first stream they saw, earning a look from Ziggy.

"You haven't had enough water?" she asked, her eyes wide.

"I've had enough *salt water* in places I'd rather not, and I'd like to properly bathe before I grow any crustier." They stopped at one side of the stream, and Liess headed downstream. "Any idea where we are?" he muttered to Ziggy.

They were hidden from the surrounding farmland by a small copse of trees. Dev had been to the highlands before, but the last time he'd spent any proper time here, the countryside had been ablaze—he'd arrived with a contingent of mages to extinguish the fires after the silverswords declared victory.

Dev stepped into the deep stream first, stripping off his clothes unceremoniously. He'd shared a room with Ziggy back in Tirnalore and had long since lost all sense of discretion around her. He dipped his head beneath the surface, cool relief washing over him. When he came back up, he set to work rinsing his clothes. Fresh water coursing over his body had awakened him better than any burst of air.

"Somewhere near Holvdan maybe? I'm not very familiar with the highlands," Ziggy said. She stood on the bank watching Liess. "We can get some horses at least."

Dev rung out his tunic and tossed it onto a rock nearby, where he could dry it fully when he got out.

"Buy or steal?" Dev asked.

Ziggy shrugged. "Whichever."

He chuckled and, quite by accident, winked at the woman. She eyed him, missing nothing. "You know, my prince-king, some might take a wink from a completely naked man in the wrong way. If you know what I mean."

A mix between a scoff and a laugh rolled out of him. "Sorry. Didn't think I was your type anyway. I've seen the way you look at Evandahl."

She shrugged. "He's nice to look at, but I wouldn't want to get caught up in his schemes."

Dev gave her a mock pout. "And I'm not nice to look at?"

He was rewarded with a roll of silver eyes. "I like 'em with a few more years on them, as you *must* know, my prince-king, who knows *very well* that he's attractive from the way nearly everyone on the continent looks at him."

"That's all I wanted to hear," he said, grinning at her before dunking his head once more.

Properly clean and as close to happy as he'd been in quite some time—enemy silversword in his company downstream notwithstanding—Dev waded over to the edge and got out, Ziggy pointedly turning to look in the other direction as he dried his clothes and got dressed. Though the fabrics were a bit stiff, the dry, salt-free clothes felt like silk after wearing sandpaper for the last few days.

Ziggy stripped down and carefully set Mystic at the edge of the stream, the pommel facing her so she could easily draw it if needed.

He stood watch while she bathed, then set about drying her clothes as she lingered in the pool. They could both see Liess sulking by the edge of the stream in her damp clothes, fastidiously cleaning her axe.

"I know she's just trying to bring me to Rayva," Dev said, his voice low—though he had no delusion that Liess couldn't still hear him. "But we need to get there too."

"She's going to betray us."

"I know."

"So why in the name of the Bard's favorite quill is she still here? We don't have to kill her. We could just tie her up and leave her somewhere."

Dev shook his head with a sigh. "I don't know."

"Dev..."

He lowered his voice, hoping Liess wasn't eavesdropping. "I kind of grew up with her, you know? Back when I was a kid, before I met Fig at the Carriage House. The Lord of Southmarch sent her to Rayva every summer for training. We'd spar and play marstones with the other kids, get in trouble trespassing in the Verrence Armory. We were all going to crossover together, until... well, my brother."

She didn't seem convinced. "She's close to Rhivven," he added, somewhat defensively, even though he'd exhausted that excuse by this point.

"All the more reason to ditch her," Ziggy said, leaning her head back so that her blonde hair fanned around her in the water.

"Then we'll have no idea where she is or when she'll come for us. If we keep her with us, then..."

Ziggy lifted her head, water running from her hair. "Then we need to be prepared for *when* she betrays us. We're only getting closer to Rayva—she'd want to take you before we get into the city, I think."

Dev nodded. "We'll be prepared for it then."

"And you're still sure you want to go for the sword?" Ziggy inquired, getting out of the stream with absolutely no warning.

He raised an eyebrow at her in challenge. She plucked her clothes off the rock where he'd dried them and dressed unhurriedly, as if trying to make him uncomfortable.

"I'm sure," he said, unbothered. "I need to be in Tytan—not off chasing foreign allies. Wanting help from the Hollow Isles in the first place—that was my mistake. Sure, in Tirnalore we had a place to stay, and no one was trying to kill us—well, not much—but I don't think we got any closer to securing help from Evandahl and his mages. Like you said, the man's full of schemes.

"The dwarves, though—we've already made headway with them. If I can help win back their sword, they might trust me. Maybe even enough to fight if it comes to it. And you know

Rhivven isn't going to let the dwarves win the tournament. Otherwise, he would have just handed it over."

"And you think this is the best way to do it?"

Dev pinned her with a look. "Do you have a better idea? Fig is off trying to help Vaelor, who's probably—" His voice cracked, and he cleared his throat. He looked down, not meeting her eye. "Vaelor needs his sword fixed. Even I know he can't survive forever with that connection broken. And you—well, what do you think? I know you didn't have a choice in joining up with us, but you must have some opinion."

She crossed her arms, appraising him. "No, I didn't have a choice. But if you're asking, I think it's a good plan."

"Then why have you been questioning me this whole time?" he demanded, throwing his hands down.

"Because I wanted to make sure you were doing it for the right reasons. In fact, I think giving the sword to the dwarves is the most king-like thing you could do. I know I'm a silversword, but I'm not one of *them*. They think they can take and take and take. If your aim is to *give*, then I'm with you all the way. I just don't know how in the Bard's name you're going to get in and out of there with it without getting yourself killed."

A slow smile crept up on Dev's face. "I'll have you watching my back. That's all I need."

She punched him on the shoulder. "Ouch," he grumbled.

"Sorry," she muttered. "Thought I did that in a light, endearing way."

He scoffed, shifting his entire attention to Liess, who was attempting to wring out the clothes that hung limply from her body.

"Think I should?" Dev said, raising a palmful of amethyst colored air swirling around his fingers.

"Might keep her from killing you for another day."

"It might. She did seem to enjoy not dying back in the lost house."

He cleared his throat and walked over to Liess, holding his palm open. "Want a hand drying those?"

LIESS

Briigard, Liess thought, enjoying the feel of dry clothes on her skin more than she should as she walked. *Why in the Bard's holy name would he do such a thing for me?*

She followed Devryn and Ziggrune away from the stream as darkness fell. Devryn tossed Liess a heel of bread and a hunk of dried tagor meat. She despised the stuff, but it wasn't foreign to her. She'd grown up on the outskirts of the Virenish highlands, where the heathens often tried to pedal their wares to the proper Tytan nobles. Southmarch traded in timber, and her father would occasionally accept a few crates of dried tagor in barter for the lean winter months when food was scarce.

Liess had kept her mouth shut when they'd discussed where they were and which direction they'd go. She'd grown up in these hills, and the message she'd left by arranging stones in Mos Creek would point someone in her direction sooner or later. All the children at Southmarch were trained in woodcrafts from an early age —using them to locate their way home, survive for days on end in the salt swamps and highlands, and interpret and leave signals for others. The simple stack of stones placed just as she'd been taught would send a message to anyone else in the know that she was heading for Southmarch and needed assistance. She merely had to slow these briigards down long enough.

"You're veering west again, Liess. We're not idiots," Ziggrune intoned from behind a few hours later. Night had settled in, and the stars had come out.

Liess ran her thumb down her axe guard slowly as she corrected her path, listening to the forest around her. She knew exactly where she was going, but they had already entered Southmarch territory, and from the mutters of the idiots behind her, it was clear she was the only one who knew that fact. It was honestly too easy. She'd been a little concerned Ziggrune would know their direction, but it was obvious she wasn't familiar with the highlands, which made sense given the location of Ashbrok. But Devryn, on the other hand? She was disappointed in him. If he didn't know the geography of his own country well enough to realize where he was, he wasn't fit to be king.

She'd held up her end of the bargain, halting her ambitions of abducting Devryn while they were in the salt swamps. But now they were in the highlands, and Rhivven had given her this final chance.

Regardless of whether Devryn was a bleeding-heart idiot with the heart of a saint or not.

"I'm heading for Rayva, like you wanted," Liess called out tiredly.

Liess knew Ziggrune's exact position, because the woman's sword sang to her like white snow calling down moonlight—Mystic, she believed it was named. And because she knew exactly where Mystic was, Liess also knew the instant Ziggrune drew her weapon. The sound of sliding steel echoed through her core, and Liess whirled around in time for her axe to clash with Ziggrune's sword.

"You kirich," Ziggrune growled. "You're trying to lead us into Southmarch territory, aren't you?"

Trying? Liess thought with a wry twist of her mouth. *Already done, poor Ziggrune.* She felt a group of weapons drawing closer, and a grin bloomed across her face. "Oh, please. Don't tell me you'd be surprised by that?"

A low chuckle came from behind them as a man stepped onto the starlit path. Perfect timing. "You're already in Southmarch territory, Virenish heathen."

Liess recognized the weapons moving in, though most of their wielders were still invisible in the trees.

A purple wind whirled around Prince Devryn. Ziggrune turned, her sword aimed at Bjorn Conwell—the captain of the guard at Southmarch Keep. She'd recognize that grizzled beard and bald pate anywhere, not to mention the call of his weapon. He'd trained her since she could hold a practice sword—through the long winter months inside the keep, when she wasn't being shipped off to Rayva with the other noble brats.

The others, who Liess could feel lurking in the trees around them, stayed put, weapons at the ready. They called to her like wolves howling in the dark, the loudest voices belonging to the silverswords among them, anticipating the fight.

Devryn cursed everyone from the ancient dragonet god Drakioryn to Liess herself, all while gathering more amethyst wind about him. Ziggrune set her back to Devryn's as they prepared to stand off.

Liess huffed out a breath—then in an instant was nose to nose with Devryn, yanking a fistful of his tunic. "Did you really think I wouldn't *try?*" she whispered. "I'm disappointed in you."

Amethyst-colored wind swirled around them, though it wasn't strong enough to knock her off balance. She gazed into his face, but in her mind's eye, she saw only Rhivven's throne room. Sure, she'd played in the back of that room with Dev when they were children—but that was before everyone had found out he had the cursed blood of Old Svora. He wasn't fit to sit on that throne.

And she would return a queen.

The air swirled around her faster—and harder—somehow twisting around her neck.

When she tried to draw her axe, she found her whole torso had been wrapped in that infernal wind without her noticing. How could air, of all things, be so strong? Everyone knew air mages were too weak to do much more than snuff out a candle. Except, throughout this entire trip through Viren, she'd seen Devryn use air magic the likes of which she'd never heard of even in the Bard's legends.

She stared at the king who never was, her eyes bulging of their own accord as her air was cut off. A ribbon of that Bard's-cursed air wrapped around her neck, tightening...tightening. The briigard. But he didn't have it in him to snuff the life out of her, as she'd seen time and again these last few days.

She heard the clash of weapons around her, Ziggrune's sword singing as it sailed through the air and met with metal then blood.

Stars burst across Liess's vision, as she tried to meet Devryn's eyes. The air tightened again. She entertained the thought that maybe, just maybe, this time he'd slip over the edge of that moral quandary of killing her.

She fought like Corava herself before the Virenish goddess was chained and confined to her watery grave, but Liess's limbs were immobile like she was no more than human, tied with the strongest rope.

The stars went out one by one.

Devryn was a coward, a weak air mage. That was what she had always believed. Right?

She wouldn't let him be the one to end her. As she pulled her head back to slam her forehead against him, the night sky flickered then went dark.

I suppose I'll make as fine a corpse here as anywhere else.

DEV

They ran.

Dev pushed through the exhaustion. From their trek through Viren. From the heavy pull on his magic he'd had to use to subdue Liess.

Not just subdue… He'd ended her life.

Finally, after all his empty threats, he'd followed through. Maybe he was just as bad as the silverswords. But there hadn't been any other way. Right?

Ziggy pushed him on, her enhanced body probably not even flagging after what little sleep they'd had in the last couple of days. She elbowed him when his footsteps slowed and uttered little joking jabs at him when he stopped entirely to catch his breath. She'd dispatched a couple of their would-be captors in the confusion after he'd killed Liess, then yanked on Dev's arm so the two of them could flee.

Despite killing Liess, he didn't know how many silverswords or Southmarch guards might have followed.

Finally, after the stars slowly winked out over the hours they ran, and the sun was thinking about peeking over the horizon, they reached the Belta Valley and spotted the city of Rayva in the distance, the silhouette of the palace and the head of the Tesvier the Relentless statue high above the rest. A distant glow across the valley, the pre-dawn light muddling the details of the landscape.

He still didn't know how Liess's people had found them. Ziggy had unhelpfully pointed out that the silversword could have left markings of some kind as they entered Southmarch territory. They'd been fools—fools to pretend they trusted Liess, and bigger fools not to kill her the moment they'd come upon her.

No, *he* had been the fool. He was supposed to be the leader, but he hadn't even recognized the geography of his own gods-be-damned country. He was supposed to be strong. If only he'd let Ziggy kill the silversword the half dozen chances she'd had. If only he'd followed through on his threats. But no—because he'd grown up with Liess strutting through the castle in the summers, spent nights lurking about the palace with her and trading hypotheses on what the crossover rite would be like—only to have her show up on the day his father was killed and an attempt was made on Dev's own life.

What had he hoped he would get out of her? Some kind of aid? She'd shown him nothing but disdain. Nothing but loyalty to Rhivven's rule.

He couldn't pretend she hadn't deserved it. Not anymore. At least he'd finally followed through this last time, ending her for good. Despite their history, she'd sided with Rhivven, betraying the centuries-old line of Verrence kings to rule Tytan.

And yet some weak part of him had offered her kindness, hoping she might return it—only to be betrayed, just as Ziggy predicted.

A tagor will fight like a tagor—or so went the Virenish saying.

He furiously wiped a tear from the corner of his eye. Only the Bard knew whether it was for Liess—or for himself, for having killed her, strangling the very life from her. Not with his bare hands, but with his magic, which, because of Liess, had grown stronger as he learned to wield it in a way capable of containing a silversword.

He wiped away another furious tear and tried to push the thoughts from his mind.

They were ready to face Rayva, to return to the capital of his forebears, to take the smallest step toward reclaiming his throne. He couldn't stop now. He couldn't doubt his intentions or he'd doubt everything. Doubt would seep into his core like black ink, staining everything.

And part of him wondered if it had already begun to do so.

LIESS

Liess woke to a sickeningly familiar sight: the ceiling of the red sister's temple in Southmarch.

She'd found herself here a dozen or more times over the years, healed from one wound or another. But this time...she clutched at her throat and torso and grimaced. The briigard had practically strangled her to death. She thought he *had* strangled her to death. She didn't think he had it in him. Except she must have only passed out from the lack of air.

She pushed herself up, scrambling to get her feet beneath her. She was sitting on a cot in the back room of the fount, now perfectly healthy thanks to the ministrations of the red sister— who was nowhere to be seen. Judging by the light coming in through the temple windows, it was near dawn. Devryn and Ziggrune would be long gone by now. Devryn had escaped again, by some blessing of Morgha. Conwell and the others hadn't known who they'd be up against, only that Liess needed assistance. And Dev's magic was more powerful now than she'd ever imagined.

Before she could set off in search of Devryn and Ziggrune's trail, a curious sensation met her.

The sound of worn steel. The scent of a weapon—powerful and battle-scarred.

Rhivven.

She sprang to her feet just as he entered the room, Captain Djuren close behind, with Conwell trailing after them, his head down.

Liess froze, her stomach muscles seizing. Her sheathed axe lay on the cot, and she longed to take hold of it.

The ancient dwarven sword he'd had with him last time was gone—the prize of the upcoming tournament—but its presence still lingered on him, even now. His face was drawn in a sneer as he looked down on her, one hand on the hilt of his Welded weapon.

"Liess. I hope you are well." His gravelly voice was as dark as velvet.

"My king," she said, bowing her head. He was so close he'd left her no room to give a proper bow. Rhivven always seemed to know just how his presence affected her, invading her personal space as he did.

"I received word you were gravely injured, and that Devryn is once again in Tytan."

She swallowed. "Yes, Your Majesty." Her mind and stomach twisted together. Of course, if he knew that, then he also knew she had failed *again*. And yet, if she spilled everything she knew about Devryn, she had a feeling Rhivven would spill her insides to the floor.

So she remained silent in her failure. He rewarded her with a sharp blow to the face, which sent her flying back to the ground. She caught herself at the last moment, but he was faster. He picked her up by the shoulders and struck her again, giving her only a second to fall before picking her up again.

And then he was gone, and a sickly feeling shot through her very bones, as she blinked her rapidly swelling eyelids.

He was holding her axe. She had to fight every instinct to leap to her feet and snatch it from him—something she knew would only lead to more violence. She wouldn't put it past him to kill her with her own Welded weapon. Was this it, then? He had given her so many chances, and she had failed him time and again. If she revealed what she knew of the prince... He was going to the tournament. Rhivven could set a trap there.

She thought of what had happened in the cursed salt swamps, at the lost house...and how Dev had spared her life more times than was intelligent.

And yet the fear of Rhivven's rage if they failed to catch Dev at the tournament kept her lips sealed.

She raised a shaky knee. She'd rather die on her feet, and even if he beat her until she couldn't stand, then she'd die trying to remain upright.

He turned her axe over in his hands, and she winced—but he didn't stop her from getting to her feet. He deigned to let her.

"The dwarves are unsettled," he said with gravelly triumph, "with the Sword of Morin out in the open."

Her eyebrows lifted against her better judgement, and she winced as the bruises on her face made themselves known.

"You have once again failed to capture Devryn, little Liess," he said, pulling close to her ear. She was sure at any moment she'd feel her own weapon slicing through her throat. She swallowed, as if knowing the workings of said throat were numbered. At least she was on her feet.

"But he does have two centuries of Verrence kings in his blood. Djuren has convinced me to give you another chance."

Her gaze flicked over Rhivven's shoulder to where Djuren stood, his stony face revealing nothing. What was that briigard up to? He hated Liess; why had he offered a single word in her favor?

The sickly feeling of having her weapon held by another was doubled by a very real nausea. She would not get caught in Djuren's net, either. The briigard was up to something, had been since recovering the Sword of Morin from the Mountain. Why had he retrieved it in the first place? She still didn't know how he'd gotten his intel.

"I thank you, my king," was all she dared to say.

He surveyed her for an uncomfortable minute. "I've decided to give you a new task to prove yourself, since you seem incapable of this one. You will raise an army. The dwarves will not win the sword in the tournament. The briigards are stewing already, and when the sword is Welded to our newest silversword, the traitorous ones will be unable to stand quiet any longer. I expect my army to be ready when that happens."

"Of course, my king. Thank you."

"Leave us," Rhivven barked.

Djuren and Bjorn left with haste, knowing that the order had been directed at them.

Liess, who still hadn't ruled out the possibility that Rhivven might cut her down with her own blade despite his new order, stood ready.

He reached his left hand up to stroke her face, his thumb crushing one of the bruises—she didn't doubt he'd done it on purpose. He smelled of hot metal and cloves and the most dangerous energy in all of Tytan.

"I do not doubt that Djuren has his own reasons for speaking up for you," he growled in her ear. "And I need a silversword strong enough to stand beside me—the gods have cursed me with some affection for you after all. But that doesn't mean I won't kill you if you fail this time. I swear by Morgha's grace, this is your last chance."

Liess spent no time gathering supplies in Southmarch before hitting the road. She was used to roughing it and would acquire what she needed along the way.

Djuren had left before the king—traveling north, he'd told Bjorn.

Liess would go north too.

She left instructions with Bjorn to gather the Southmarch silverswords and meet her in the Belta Valley, where she would gather her army until they were needed to suppress the dwarves. But first, she had another task.

Cantering out of Southmarch on a borrowed mare, Liess followed Djuren's clumsy trail north. He'd always been a terrible rider—ever since she'd trained with him in Rayva. But he'd been a good opponent to sharpen her skills on after her crossover. Too bad he never seemed to get over being bested by her repeatedly once she'd mastered her Welded weapon, which had taken some getting used to. She'd had to work hard after her crossover to tune out the constant ringing of other people's weapons—and then learn to use the noise to her advantage.

It initially appeared as if he was heading to Holvdan, but by nightfall it was clear he had another purpose.

The Gold Wood.

Her instincts were right; the bloody briigard was up to something. Djuren should be by Rhivven's side in the capital, preparing for the tournament. It had been years since either of them had been assigned the Gold Wood patrol, and there was no other reason a silversword had business in the cursed place—which meant he was going to the Carriage House.

She dismounted just outside the glittering forest, the place bursting with the magic of Old Svora, and gave her mare a slap on the rear. The old girl would find her way back to Southmarch. Bjorn had trained all the beasts for decades—when you lived just outside the treacherous Virenish highlands, sending your mount home to get help wasn't a luxury; it was a necessity.

Wishing the Bard's-cursed trees didn't illuminate the night with their gilded glow, she entered the forest on foot, following the obvious trail. Djuren was making it far too easy.

She narrowed her eyes and slipped away from his path—just in case he had *wanted* her to follow him. Every few minutes she'd veer back and locate the path again, but it was clear that he was heading to the Carriage House.

Liess finally got close enough to sense his weapon and drew up short, careful not to enter his range of hearing—which, admittedly, was poor for a silversword. Crossing over only enhanced natural abilities or bestowed the strength of one's weapon; not even the arcane ritual could make someone observant who never listened in the first place.

The ornate Carriage House in sight, Liess put her back to a tree and glanced around the side. She couldn't see Djuren; the briigard was probably inside.

After a few minutes, incessantly running her thumb over her axe guard as she waited, she began to doubt her rash decision to follow him. She was supposed to be gathering an army for Rhivven. A shudder ran down her spine as she thought of the king's order. Her last chance. She couldn't fail again.

But she couldn't shake her suspicions about Djuren. The briigard had fought against every appointment she'd received in the enclave, never forgiving her for persistently wiping the floor with him during their training. At the time, she'd pitied him—his ego was obviously pathetic, still clinging to that after all this time. So *why* had he spoken up for her?

Over an hour later, she felt his sword move in a significant way. He was leaving, heading north once more. Another weapon accompanied him—this one a tiny thing, not Welded. It was small enough to be a dagger: sharp and concealed.

Liess's eyes darted between the Carriage House and the way south. She should get started on her task for Rhivven. She knew she should.

But she slipped around the tree and followed, relying on Djuren to not pick up on her footsteps through the soft auran leaves. Strange sounds and smells emanated from the Carriage House as Liess circumnavigated the place, its superfluous music and strange food assailing her keen senses. But the sense she focused on most was Djuren's weapon—and the little dagger. She suspected he'd left with another person—a mage, by any reason-able guess.

She slipped behind the wide trunk of an auran tree just as Djuren and a small figure came into view. At that moment, Liess felt the small dagger move. The mage made a pathetic attempt to escape, pressing the tiny weapon against a wall of steel.

Djuren easily discarded the dagger, tossing it into the leaves. While he was engaged, Liess dashed forward to hide behind another auran. Now close enough to hear them, she prayed to Morgha that she was still out of Djuren's hearing.

"—coming with me, you little kirich."

"No!" she shrieked.

"Don't be so ungrateful," Djuren growled. He muttered something indistinct, ending with, "—will make you an even more powerful water mage in Rokhold. That's his favorite kind."

"Let me go!" the mage screamed, pummeling useless fists against Djuren's armor. Djuren grabbed her hands and the mage screamed in agony, finally succumbing to stillness. Liess wouldn't be surprised if Djuren had broken her wrists with his powerful grip.

Liess's fingernails clawed the gilded bark of the tree, watching. What business did Djuren have with mages, and making them more powerful? In Rokhold, of all places, the far-off holding prac-tically abandoned.

The Bard be damned—and so was she if she neglected her orders from Rhivven much longer—but she was going to find out.

ECHOES OF SILVER

HALVARD'S PIT

CHAPTER 27

FIG

Fig inhaled the Gold Wood air, savoring the magic that coursed through her body stronger than ever. She stretched her legs again. She'd found a secluded spot at the edge of the wood and had been watching Green's Tavern for an hour now. There was no sign she'd been followed here—and no sign of any silverswords. Her belly grumbled again, and she got up.

Securing her hood, she walked swiftly out of the forbidden wood; the last thing she needed was to be arrested for trespassing on the "king's" land. Bidding goodbye to the amplified magic washing over her, she strode toward the tavern door without a backward glance at the glittering gold trees.

The early afternoon crowd was thin, and Fig caught the barkeep's attention quickly as she made for a secluded corner. The barkeep—Green himself—came over with half a smile on his weathered face. "Been a while since I seen you," he commented, idly taking a cloth from his apron and wiping her table.

Fig hummed her assent. "It—er—hasn't been safe for me,"

she said quietly. Only a few patrons sat on the other side of the tavern, but she didn't want her voice to carry.

"Oh, aye," Green said darkly.

His tavern, like all the others, had wanted notices plastered inside on the door. Dev's face was most prominent, but Fig and Vaelor's were a close second. Still, Fig trusted Green; he'd seen her and Bruna through some tough times and tough jobs. *I should have come here first looking for Conham*, she thought. But she hadn't wanted to leave Rayva without Vaelor.

"I'm looking for someone," she said quietly. "I don't suppose you know of Flourice Conham?"

Green shrugged. "Know of but haven't a clue much else about him."

Nodding, Fig asked, "Can you get word to Harryn for me, then? I had to leave Rayva unexpectedly, and he was tracking down Conham for me."

"I can."

"But—roundabout, eh? I can't be sure he didn't try to turn me in," she added.

The tavern door opened, and Green nodded once. "And a plate?"

"Yes," Fig said, practically melting at the mere idea. "Whatever you've got."

He touched his forehead briefly, then returned to his usual spot behind the bar. Minutes later, a serving girl brought her a loaded plate and a mug of beer. She dug into the hefty servings of roast shafra and root vegetables, barely registering what she was eating. She knew she shouldn't linger in public for too long, but perhaps she was a little punch-drunk on the effects of the Gold Wood. And the Bard knew she was *hungry* after the tumult of the last few days.

As more people started trickling in for an early dinner—Corava's Day was approaching, and darkness came quicker in the early autumn nights—Fig mopped up the juices on her plate with the remains of her bread, washing it down with the rest of her beer.

On her way out the door, she paid Green—not just for the

food, but a little extra for his time and secrecy. Once she was outside and the door had slammed shut behind her, she realized she had nowhere to go. She hadn't wanted to rent a room at Green's—it was far too public of a tavern—but she no longer had a home in Tytan to return to. She'd burned that to cinders along with Bruna's body.

The gold sifting down from the auran trees called to her, and she knew the only place she could go that was safe: the tower. But she wouldn't enter the Gold Wood here, not with more patrons arriving at the tavern by the minute.

So she headed north on the road circling the Gold Wood; all the while the Great Mountain loomed over her. She thought back to all the dwarves descending on Rayva, all hoping for a chance to win the Sword of Morin. Did they really think that Rhivven would just give it to them? There *had* to be a catch. Fig was certain that Rhivven was looking for someone to Weld with the famous dwarven sword. She shuddered at the very idea.

Speaking of the dwarves and their Mountain... Fig stopped in her tracks. There was a definite curl of smoke coming from somewhere in the vicinity of the Mountain. She thought she'd seen it days ago before they'd begun their trek along the Twist. She could even smell the smoke from here. But the question was—was it *on* the Mountain or *inside?*

After what was actually a pleasant walk through the Gold Wood, Fig found herself longing for one of the rope beds in the tower—even if she had to contend with Knoll's hammering. It was still early, but despite the added power of the Gold Wood, her feet were dragging, and she wanted nothing more than to lie down.

The tower was quiet when she reached the clearing, and she walked around the perimeter of the small valley twice, checking for anything strange.

When she pushed the tower door open, the hearth was unlit. Had Knoll moved on? Her heart began racing. She still needed him to fix Vaelor's sword.

Her eyes fell on the faint glow of dying coals in the raised hearth, and she realized many of Knoll's tools were still here. She carefully shut the tower door behind her, connecting with the flames in her core, ready should she need them. Had silverswords found the tower on one of their patrols? The 'swords were quite superstitious about the wood, considering their mistrust of mage magic, so they normally didn't deviate from their regular paths and the one road that went in and out.

The room was tidy, showing no sign of a struggle. The dry stone basin in the middle of the floor was the same. Mugs had been washed and set to dry on a windowsill, and Knoll's camp bed had been made up. She thought a few of his things might be missing, since the place looked a little emptier than before, but she couldn't be sure.

Carefully inspecting the room a little further, she had to wonder if he'd just gone out. The dwarf probably needed supplies or food every so often, she reasoned. The coals in the hearth were still red with a hefty crust of gray ash, so he hadn't been gone *that* long. She poked them with a log before putting a few pieces of kindling in and building the fire back up. There was a chill in the air, and the third floor of the tower would need as much heat from down here as it could get.

She nodded, resolving not to worry about Knoll. Surely, he'd left of his own accord, and after she'd been hunted, attacked, and on the run for over a month, Fig was just on edge. She heaved the heavy bolt over the door and climbed the stairs in search of a hammock bed to collapse on. If Knoll came back, she was sure he'd knock.

When she found the bed she'd slept in last time, she curled up into a ball, gazing out one of the windows at the darkening sky, feeling more alone than ever.

Avoiding the memory of Vaelor standing guard by the top of the stairs, his silver-ringed eyes flashing in her direction, her thoughts moved to the memory of Mairead sleeping in the cot beside her.

She wished she had a way of warning the girl about the red brothers and their crimes at Mar Nevan. Would their atrocities reach beyond the holy city? Fig shuddered. Mairead must have reached Thoan by now; it was the nearest town to Mar Nevan and its most frequented place of port. Fig resolved to send word in the morning to warn her. Perhaps Green could get a letter through the couriers.

Eventually she drifted off into an uneasy sleep, waking several times thinking she'd heard something. Once, fire sprung to her hands when she jolted awake at some non-existent threat. She listened for the better part of an hour before falling back asleep, heat burning in her core, amplified by the auran trees.

The next morning, despite feeling like she'd been in a fight with a tagor from all the tossing and turning and poor sleep, she quickly got dressed and set about hiding her things in her bed alcove, including Vaelor's sword. She held it in her hands and caressed the outside of the bag, clenching her jaw. Then she found a tarp and covered it. This would be the safest place to leave it until she'd rescued Vaelor. If something happened to her, the others would know to come here.

The tournament was tomorrow, and there would be more silverswords roaming the city. She couldn't risk anything happening to the sword while she tried to break into the palace. Vaelor should be arriving in Rayva any time now, and she had started to rely on the tournament as the distraction she needed to rescue him.

She set off for Green's Tavern once again. She knew it was unlikely that word had reached Harryn by now, and even less likely that Harryn had found Conham, but in any case, she needed food and could try to send a warning to Mairead.

Retracing her circuitous path from last night, she headed north toward the Mountain, where the road was quiet. Her stomach rumbled as she found the dirt path, and she stared up at the Mountain, searching for signs of life she thought she'd seen before. But there was nothing, only a rocky surface spattered with the only kinds of trees that could grow in the rocklands: scrubby bushes and evergreens.

She reached Green's without incident, and her mouth watered as soon as she opened the door. She'd had an early dinner last night, and two long walks since then. Green wasn't there, but Fig made requests of the bleary-eyed barmaid attending the counter and went to settle in at the secluded table she'd sat at yesterday, only...

A man was already sitting there, and he was looking directly at her. He was thin, with a well-groomed silver goatee and a hat covering one eye.

Unnerved, Fig turned her attention to a different table and sat down. She hadn't seen silver rings around the man's eye, but that didn't mean he wasn't dangerous. You didn't have to be a silversword to be cruel; just as not all silverswords were cruel and bloodthirsty.

She simply hadn't known that until meeting Vaelor.

Highly aware of her every move and wondering if the man was still staring at her, Fig waited for the breakfast the barmaid brought only a minute later. A steaming bowl of porridge and a plate of sausages distracted her briefly from the thought that she was being watched, and she tucked in heartily. When the barmaid returned with a huge mug of tea, Fig had all but forgotten about the man.

So when he dropped into the chair across from her a moment later, she almost spilled the tea down her front.

"Good morning," the man said.

Fig spluttered, trying to get control of her cup. "Bard's quills," she muttered, brushing a few spilled droplets off her tunic. She cursed herself for letting down her guard. What had she been thinking? First, she'd let that silversword surprise her at the safehouse, and now this? She had gotten too used to having other people around to watch her back.

"My apologies," the man said. She thought she saw a smirk behind his tidy beard and something mischievous in his eye—the one peeking out of the shadows of his hat.

Fig stood, pushing the chair away with the backs of her legs, a warning look in her eye.

"You might want to stay," he said, "if you want to hear what I have to tell you." He twirled a hand at the barmaid, who bustled back into the kitchen.

"What is it?" Fig demanded, not returning to her seat.

He gave her a pointed look with his one visible eye, then glanced at her vacated chair. Then the barmaid returned from the back kitchen, a tea tray in hand. As the girl set it on their table, Fig sat back down, feeling more curious than cautious. Something about the man—or perhaps her own exhaustion—made her walls lower, and whether that was a smart idea or not, she suddenly didn't care.

When they were alone again, he gestured to the pot and let her pour first. Fig obliged and filled both their cups, knowing that never in the Bard's age would Green allow anyone to poison his tavern's food or drink. It was a lighter tea blend than she'd been drinking, with what she suspected was a hint of floral fallondir, a flavor she remembered well from the Carriage House.

"So," Fig began as soon as they'd both had a sip, "who are you, and what information do you *think* I'm looking for?"

A coy smile turned up his lips and he chuckled. "Flourice told me you were a bit fiery, my dear, and clearly, my husband did not exaggerate."

FIG

"Your husband?" Fig repeated quietly. "I—well...I'm sorry I was curt, but..." She didn't know where to begin. *But I was just ousted from Rayva, the one place I need to be to rescue someone I might just lo—*

She cleared her throat, but he waved a hand as if waving away the curtness.

"Understood, my dear," he said. "I've seen the flyers. And we've all heard the rumors."

"I'm sorry, I don't know your name," Fig admitted, taking another sip of tea.

"Quite all right. Flourice's always been the popular one. I'm Torry."

"It's nice to meet you, Torry. Did Green find you, or—"

"A mutual acquaintance named Harryn, actually. He said you might come here."

"Oh, so the blighter *didn't* betray me to the silverswords, after all. That's good to hear."

Torry gave a polite snort and sampled one of the plain biscuits from the tea tray. "Flourice wanted to come personally, but it's not safe..."

She nodded but felt her hopes plummeting. "I don't want to put him or you in danger."

Torry gave her a wry smile and tipped his hat up slightly to reveal his other eye—what was left of it anyway. A scar crossed the place it should have been, and only scarred skin remained. "Us smaller folk are always in danger, aren't we? Those in power don't see us as equals—even though we'll all go to Morgha's arms just the same in the end, eh? *This* happened after our dear queen died, when we departed the crown's service. But Flourice and I have a way—you'll just have to come to him."

Repressing a gasp, all Fig could do was nod again. Torry seemed perfectly pleasant—after she realized he wasn't out to kill or betray her. He had an aristocratic air about him, from the way he sat up pin-straight to the way he sipped his tea, like someone who'd lived in the castle among royalty. Dev had been just like that when he arrived at the Carriage House.

"Tell me what I need to do," Fig said.

Torry frowned and appeared hesitant. "First, you must understand. When Queen Eileigh died, much of the joy left the castle, and so, we left too. King Haemond was furious, seeing the exodus of many of his wife's retinue as a betrayal. Our names were blackened, and quite fittingly, Flourice and I sought refuge in Black End with his kind. Things became even more dire for us when it was revealed that our dearly departed queen had the blood of a mage." He gave a little shiver, and Fig had to suppress one of her own as she thought of Shadryn.

"And with recent events," Torry went on, "Flourice had to—"

The tavern door banged open, and two dwarves entered. The sound brought Green from the back room, and he nodded to Fig before hassling the dwarves for mistreating his door.

"Had to what?" Fig hissed at Torry.

He shook his head. "Perhaps we should step outside. It's getting a little too crowded in here."

Fig agreed as she heard the door open again. She reached for her coin pouch, but Torry waggled a finger at her, dropping some coins onto her table and his vacated one.

Outside, Torry gestured to the road south, and Fig matched his purposeful stroll. She wasn't sure where he was going with his story but was invested enough to continue on with him. Close to the Gold Wood, she felt the flames burning strong in her core, ready if she should need them. In fact, she had to concentrate more on keeping them *in*. She would have no trouble fighting off Torry and anyone else if he betrayed her.

It was a little while before Torry spoke. "He's back at the Carriage House. He wants you to meet him there."

Fig drew in a sharp breath, inhaling the sweet scent of honey from the Gold Wood. Her gaze went to the aurans, knowing that deep in the forest lay the one place she'd sworn she'd never return to. The prison of gold and marble, where the crown kept mages under its thumb. And now, the bearer of the crown was even more bloodthirsty than Haemond...

"H-How?" was all she could manage.

"They welcomed him with open arms," Torry said with a shrug. "Despite not returning there once he'd ended his service with Queen Eileigh, they cleared his record with the crown. They've got him teaching now—and I can tell he rather enjoys it."

Brows furrowed, Fig slowed her footsteps. This section of road would meet up with the one that led into the forest, the only road to the Carriage House, and now she knew why he was leading them this way. "I can't," she said. "They've got posters plastered across Tytan with my face on it—I can't be seen *there* of all places." That wasn't the only reason, but it was the most logical argument against going. What she really needed was to find Vaelor.

Torry cocked his head. "Aren't you seeking Flourice's help to break into the palace? Isn't *that* the last place you should be?" he asked, a hint of snark in his tone.

Fig stared at him, her mouth open a little. "That's beside the point," she muttered, though she did stop walking and crossed her arms, rubbing sparks from the fingertips of one hand. Even though she'd spent the last night inside the Gold Wood, it was making her lightheaded. Or maybe it was the idea of going back to the Carriage House. She took a deep breath of the honey-scented air, extending her senses around her.

She didn't think Torry was leading her into a trap. Green had seemed familiar with him, and Fig really needed Conham's help to get inside the palace—the one place she was certain the silverswords would bring Vaelor. The tournament tomorrow would be the perfect distraction, but she was running out of time to figure out how to get inside and find him.

She glanced up and down the dirt road, stuffing down the horrible realization that this was near the place she'd been chased by three silverswords and rescued by Vaelor the night Dev had come to find her.

"You lived in the palace too, didn't you?" Fig asked him. Perhaps she could get the information she needed from Torry, instead of risking a return to the Carriage House.

He nodded. "Briefly. I was a tailor for dear Queen Eileigh—that's how I met Flourice."

"So you know your way around the palace too, right? My... friend was captured by the silverswords, and they'll be bringing him straight to Rhivven. I need to get to him before they..." She couldn't finish, but her hopes fell as she caught the look in Torry's eyes.

"I'm sorry, Fig," he said. "Flourice was there for twenty years. I only spent one year in the palace and hardly scratched the surface. I know where the dungeons are, of course—hard to miss —but your friend... I don't suppose he's the 'sword who helped Prince Devryn escape Tytan?"

Fig nodded solemnly.

"I thought that might be the case," he said. "Then Rhivven will put him somewhere special. King Haemond had a place for political prisoners, I know that much. And on the rare occasion a silversword was imprisoned, the enclave has a special dungeon deep inside the palace."

Fig nodded. "You were only in the palace a year?"

"Yes, it was quite hard to get past the fiber arts mages with my mundane skills, but they finally took me in the end."

"You're not a mage?" Fig's respect for the man's skills grew exponentially if he'd worked his way into the queen's service without magic.

Torry shook his head. "Gods no. But they've let me stay with Flourice in the quarters they've given him at the Carriage House. They only keep a close eye on the movements of the mages. They don't pay much attention to my comings and goings, which was why Flourice sent me to see you."

Fig put a hand over her mouth and chin in thought, gazing past the glittering gold that sifted down from the aurans and wondering how in the Bard's name she was going to break into the castle without any help. "Fine, I'll go."

Fig was glad she'd spent the previous night in the Gold Wood, preparing her again for the magic of the aurans, because when the Carriage House came into view, she still had to fight back the flames that attempted to burst from her hands. They traveled parallel to the dirt road she'd traveled dozens of times. Even though Torry assured her the silverswords posted at the Carriage House had left last night in preparation for the tournament, she wasn't reckless enough to walk down the road directly to the entrance.

Suddenly, the marble building loomed in the distance. Great columns framed the double front doors, with floor-to-ceiling mullioned windows covering most of the building's two-story facade. Various additions had been made over the years behind and beside the main structure, all done in marble with gold cornices at every juncture or corner. Fig's gaze was drawn unbidden to one of the additions to the right, the top corner window that looked south. Her heart clenched. That room had been her home for several long years, and she'd given it up for a chance for real freedom from the oppressive thumb of Dev's long family line of silversword kings. She shook her head, the absurdity of her and Dev's relationship always made her heart lighter. Dev was in no way like the rest of the Verrences, which was why she'd always believed he would make the perfect king.

Torry took her down a circuitous path around the gardens and led her in the back way. Hairs rose on the back of her neck as she wondered who might be watching them from the windows above. She hardly paid any attention to the beautiful gardens— there was almost always a mage in residence who helped them flourish, whether it was a water mage who simply kept the plants happy, a green mage who could influence the actual plants themselves, or even a traveling dryad. Or perhaps the plants simply thrived from the ambient magic of the forest.

It wasn't long until they reached one of the back entrances. Fig had used the door many times to sneak in and out of the Carriage House and meet Dev at their secret spot in the wood. Torry held it open for her, and she gave the aurans one last glance before heading inside.

Fig realized she was holding her breath as they walked down the back hallway, passed a few empty study rooms, and finally turned down the hallway that led to the private quarters. The idea that this might be a trap still weighed heavily on her, but her need to get information from Conham outweighed her fears. She hadn't heard anything from Emrah, and the second he got close enough to Rayva, he would catch her up on what was going on. She had to do all she could to prepare until then.

These quarters were reserved for the teachers and mages over a certain age—because the two categories were often one and the same, since most mages never left. *The registrar must be happy to have Flourice back*, Fig thought. It was the registrar's duty to keep track of all the mages in residence, and, more importantly to the crown: which mages left, where they were going, and why.

Of course, the registrar's staff would be keeping an eye on Flourice, a mage who'd been out of the Carriage House and royal service for several years. But luckily, the registrar's offices were on the second level of the Carriage House, located directly over the front entrance, looking down on both the door outside, and the main staircase inside. If Flourice ever chose to leave out the back and didn't come back, then he'd be branded a fugitive mage once more.

Torry stopped at one of the doors and pulled out a key. Fig looked up and down the hallway, but they had yet to encounter anyone so far. She soon found herself being led into their quarters and was glad to be behind closed doors before being discovered. It was beyond reckless to come into the Carriage House itself, but what else was she supposed to do?

A heavenly aroma stole over her, florals mixed with the heady scents of rich food, wine, and incense, so much that her head spun. She brushed sparks from her fingertips as she took in the large living space, which resembled something closer to a royal entertainment salon than a dorm room. Silk fabrics draped across the room, hanging down in curtains and sweeping high above from the ceiling beams. They were dyed in all manner of colors, blending seamlessly from one color to the next. Turquoise by the door where the fabric framed it like a curtain, then shifting to green and golden hues, rising to yellow at the apex of the ceiling, before sinking back to gold, then deepening to maroon. Draperies and lush fabrics filled the whole room. She had seen Conham's color work before, but this... It took her several minutes to realize they weren't alone in the beautiful room—so engrossed was she in the decorations.

Flourice Conham cleared his throat, offering her a small smirk from where he sat perched on a couch of gold brocade, one foot up on a matching footstool. He was a little stockier than his husband, with kind blue eyes. He held himself as poised as any member of court might. His right hand was curled protectively around a glass flute of orange juice—likely mixed with the bubbly spirit *vitale*—and his face morphed into an expression of delight.

"Fig, my dear," he said, lifting the vimosa at her in a salute of sorts. "I wasn't sure you'd come."

Torry had crossed the room while she had been distracted by the draperies and was mixing another vimosa. The *vitale* bottle's label was written in Pan Viddan—an authentic vintage only came from the Vitale region there. He tipped an empty glass in her direction, and she shook her head. She was already lightheaded from the rich incense and the feel of magic on her tongue, so thick here in the heart of the Gold Wood.

"Conham," she said, nodding. "Thank you for sending your husband. I was afraid Harryn had betrayed me, and we'd never get to meet."

Flourice chuckled and ran his other hand through his immaculately trimmed gray hair. "Harryn. He's a slippery sort, but he's no traitor."

Fig's shoulders stiffened at the word, the one branded on all the flyers with the drawing of her face.

"Relax, Fig," Conham said. "You're no traitor either. Come, sit. You look—er—tired."

She snorted quietly as she accepted the offer, perching herself on the burgundy couch opposite his. The pillows had a mesmerizing gold and black pattern around the edges that her gaze couldn't stop landing on. She *was* tired, though she suspected Conham had skirted around a less polite description of her haggard state. She'd caught a glimpse of her reflection in one of his ornately framed mirrors: dark circles under her eyes, her curly hair frizzy and tangled.

Conham leaned forward slightly, peering at her with his clear blue eyes. "We've pieced it together, Torry and I. We've still got people in Black End, of course. Heard all about how they tried to kill Dev. And Rhivven was *not* subtle in taking the country. But who can stand up against their coup?"

"Who indeed?" Fig said, sinking farther into the couch cushions than she would like. She was likely to fall asleep if she got any more comfortable. "We've been looking for allies, actually. One of our number was captured, and I know they'll be taking him to Rhivven."

The older mage nodded, finally setting down his vimosa glass, which he'd yet to take a sip of. "I'm afraid I don't hold all the answers about the castle"—her face fell, and he hurriedly went on

— "but I can tell you how to get in, and where they'll have put him, and that's a start. How you can get him out is another thing entirely. Who is it that they've taken?"

Her fingers ran along the stitching along the couch cushion without conscious thought. "A silversword. Vaelor. He's the one who saved Dev's life."

Conham nodded, and Torry came up behind him and put a hand on his husband's shoulder, taking a sip of his own vimosa. "There are ways in," Conham said. "And I can tell them to you, but first I want to tell you about an opportunity."

Fig sat up straighter. "What do you mean?"

"Fig," Conham said genially, his blue eyes boring into her own, "you've always been a good mage, helping people and the like." He shared a look with his husband, who tentatively smiled back.

What in the gods was he talking about? This didn't sound like a trap...did it? Bard's quills, she should get going.

"Well," Conham began hesitantly, "where better to help people than here, at the Carriage House?" The bottom dropped out of her stomach, and she bolted to her feet. The burgundy couch made an ugly noise as it scooted back an inch on the hard wood floor. Conham stood too, bumping into the coffee table and nearly toppling his untouched vimosa. "Now, Fig, I'm just trying to help you. You could—"

"I can't do *anything* from here," she seethed, already navigating her way around the plush furniture and through the curtains of fabric swooping about the place to section off areas of the room. "Nothing except the will of the crown, which, in case you forgot, is the Butcher of Viren!"

"Wait, please," Conham called. Torry muttered something Fig didn't hear. She'd nearly reached the door. Slowly, she turned to face them, her hand on the doorknob. She knew coming here was a bad idea. The Carriage House of all places. How had she let Torry convince her? She was a desperate idiot clutching at straws. She would find a way to rescue Vaelor herself.

"Fig," Conham said, "whatever the enclave thinks you've

done, well...if you come back to the Carriage House, you won't need to worry about that anymore."

She stared at him for a long moment, her brain refusing to work. Finally, she said, "What?" The single word came out ruder than she'd intended, but she felt he deserved it.

"I can't help but wonder if you were roped into helping Dev—you didn't seem the sort to get involved in such a thing after leaving the Carriage House. And now you're planning on breaking into the castle alone? To rescue a *silversword?*" He shook his head, pinching the bridge of his nose. "If you come back to stay at the Carriage House, the enclave can't touch you," he said slowly. "All will be forgiven, forgotten."

"I..." Her brain whirred as she took in the luxurious room, the draperies, the smell of rich food and drink, the Tysainian incense. "That's why you're here, why you're living like a palace lord, isn't it?"

Torry was carefully looking at the floor, but Conham stood up straighter. "We—"

"And you want me to abandon Dev, the rightful ruler of the Rayvan throne, and Vaelor—" Her voice cracked, and her vision blurred. She shook her head violently. "This place is a cage. The last thing I want to do is shut myself away, exchanging one boot on my neck for another."

She took a deep lungful of the rich, magic-heavy air and shook her head. "And you're wrong—even if the enclave absolved my crimes, like they appear to have absolved yours, they can still touch me here. Their hands touch everywhere, from the Mountain to the Notch and even our beautiful forest." She scoffed. "I don't care if you eat from their bloody hands in exchange for *this*, but I'll have no part in it."

"Bard strike it, Fig," Conham growled uncharacteristically. "Don't let your temperament turn down a good opportunity. It's not as if we've rolled over and let Rhivven have his way with us—you could still help Dev from inside the Carriage House. We're doing our best to stay on the *right* side of things—we, well, when a mage wants to get out of Tytan, we help point them in the right direction. We are *trying* to help you. And that's much easier when we have our ears to the ground in the middle of things, instead of on the run or cowering alone in a safehouse like we did in our days back in Black End."

Heat rising in her throat, Fig found her body frozen as her hand gripped the doorknob. She took in the luxurious living quarters and wondered if she could indeed aid Dev from in here —and if Conham was to be believed. She almost swayed at the thought of having her own home again, here in the Gold Wood...

But no, there was no way in the blackest pits of Malhela that she could place herself under Rhivven's rule. Because no matter what the registrar, the masters, or the headmaster said, it was the silversword king that ruled these halls. The king who ordered where the mages went, what they did, and what they were allowed to learn.

She shook her head and felt the sparks under her fingertips cool and die out. "I can't. I couldn't. Whether I could help Dev or not—*I need to rescue Vaelor.* And to be perfectly honest, I think my crimes are far past absolution." A weak chuckle escaped her.

Conham came closer, tentative, like he was approaching a skittish animal. "I am sorry. I hope you don't think less of us for—"

"Of course not," Fig said softly, her gaze flicking between the two men. "I do wish I could join you here. Maybe someday, when we have—" Her voice cracked.

Conham finished her thought, "A mage for a king?"

She nodded.

"Come back and sit down," Conham urged. "At least allow us to feed you."

Nerves jangling, she shook her head. "I can't. I'm sorry. I should really be going back."

"But what about the palace...?" Conham began.

"I'm sorry. I shouldn't have come here."

FIG

Fig held up a finger to Green, and he promptly brought over a pint.

She didn't regret leaving Flourice and Torry. After their proposal, she couldn't stomach staying there any longer. Flourice had looked like he had wanted to follow her, but his husband stopped him. She would have to figure out how to rescue Vaelor herself. As well-meaning as Flourice had been, she couldn't quite trust his intentions—and couldn't stay a second longer in that place.

So she'd decided to hang around Green's, where she might be able to glean some news of what was going on in Rayva with the tournament tomorrow.

Tomorrow. She had no plan to rescue Vaelor, no contacts inside Rayva besides Harryn. But she'd go anyway. She'd find a way.

A tankard appeared in front of her, froth spilling ever so

gently over the top. She tossed a coin to Green, and he nodded his thanks.

For the next couple of hours, the conversations around her divulged nothing she didn't already know. There was to be a tournament, and the ancient sword was the prize. The couple next to her discussed in great length the chances of their neighbor, who had pledged to enter. As they waxed on about Franchand's prowess at butchering cows and his high chances of defeating others if it came to feats of strength, Fig decided to take her leave. She slid another coin to Green as he walked by with a muttered thanks, then slipped out of the tavern and into the evening.

It would be a long walk back to the tower, but she headed north, taking the circuitous way, anyway. She followed the shadow of the Great Mountain silhouetted in the distance, a black mass in the ocean-colored sky.

Not ten minutes into her walk, she heard a sound that drove a spike of fear into her chest. The clank of armor—several sets. No. More than several. Too many to count. She slowed her footsteps, sending out her senses into the night: the heady glow of the Gold Wood to her right, and a thick coppery blanket to her left, coming from the direction of Arem. She couldn't tell by sound or sense how many there were, but she had no doubt that a large number of silverswords were moving south, heading right this way.

Her heart hammered, and she turned back the way she'd come, wondering just what in the Bard's broken quills a large contingent of 'swords was doing out here.

Green looked surprised when she pushed the tavern door open again. She slowed her steps and faked a drunken stumble as she approached the bartop. "Got a room for the night?" she slurred. No one who she'd been drinking next to previously seemed to notice, but she kept up the act all the way up the stairs until she'd shut herself safely into the room she'd rented.

She slammed her back against the door, sliding down and clutching her knees. 'Swords on the road, and she had no way to break into the palace in Rayva to rescue Vaelor, only the distraction of the tournament as cover. Surely the Bard was laughing as he wrote this tale.

The bed was comfortable, at least. She'd barely had her eyes shut for five minutes when something sent her flying out of bed and jamming her feet back into her boots, heart pounding like the very arms of Morgha were reaching for her.

What in Drakioryn's scaly hide are you doing at the tavern? the voice in her head demanded.

Emrah! she replied, blinking furiously as she shook off the call of sleep. *Wh—Where are you? Where's Vaelor?*

Moisture sprang to her eyes at her friend's voice in her mind. She stood and went to the window, wondering how close he was. It seemed like every time they parted, she was more thankful than ever to be reunited with him.

He's somewhere in the dungeons. He was unconscious when they brought him in, though, so I had to figure it out from outside the walls. I didn't want to find you until I knew they were putting him somewhere for good—

Oh, thank the mother— Fig began, but Emrah spoke over her.

Fig, they're going to get him killed. They're entering him into some tournament tomorrow.

Fig froze for a second. *The tournament? I was planning on using that as a distraction... But how will that get him killed?*

There's only one winner, Emrah told her. *That's what the red brother who accompanied the swords said. One winner, because it's a fight to the death.*

The ale in her stomach threatened to make a reappearance. *No. I can't let that happen.*

She reached down to lace up her boots, fumbling with the knots in the dark. She let out a groan and yanked the laces into order by feel.

Where are you? she asked Emrah. *Are you coming to the tavern?*

A huff of some kind slithered across her brain. *Hunting in the*

Gold Wood, was his reply, and she sat back on her bed. She could somehow feel the tiredness in his voice...and the hunger. She wasn't sure if she'd ever been able to feel anything other than the sound of his voice before, but perhaps this time, because it was so strong...

Good hunting, then, she replied. *Thank you, Emrah, for watching over him. I—You and I will leave for Rayva in the morning, then, aye?*

Aye, came his response.

She sighed heavily, leaving him to his hunting. The poor dragonet had been following Vaelor for days now; who knew how he'd been eating or resting in all that time. She could wait one night before storming the capital. Besides, it wasn't as if she had anywhere else to rest in that infernal city.

But there was no way in the darkest pits of Malhela that she was getting any sleep now. All she could think about was Vaelor being hauled into the dungeons below the castle and whatever the tournament would bring the next day.

A fight to the death. Surely, as a silversword, Vaelor would have an advantage over most of the contestants. But in what condition was he in? Fig didn't think for a second he'd gotten through the journey to Rayva unscathed, being in the care of the silverswords and a red brother.

She tossed and turned most of the night with her eyes open, her gaze unfocused as she tried to work out how she might rescue Vaelor from the tournament. She barely knew anything about the gods-cursed thing; she'd been so focused on getting into the castle.

Yet try as she might, she couldn't come up with a perfect plan that wouldn't involve getting her killed. As dawn began to hint at its approach, Fig lurched from the bed and put her boots back on once more. She couldn't take it anymore. Her stomach felt sick, her hair was tangled, and her fingers fumbled when she tried to corral it into a tail with a leather thong. She took leave of her room and made her way downstairs, giving the empty room a cursory glance before she departed. She couldn't eat, and even the delicious smells wafting from the back kitchen didn't tempt her.

Only when she approached the honey-scented Gold Wood, did the tension in her shoulders ease a little.

Fig was tempted to call Emrah, but she didn't want to wake the dragonet—wherever he was—so she checked and double-checked that she had all of her things, then turned toward Rayva. Emrah would catch up. Fig couldn't sit in the tavern any longer knowing that Vaelor was getting thrown into the tournament today.

Leaving without me, Svoran? a voice in her head drawled.

She felt his presence before the little dragonet swooped up from behind to land on her shoulder. Her hand went to his head as he bumped his snout into her cheek, and she closed her eyes. *It's good to see you, my friend. Thank you again for going with Vaelor. I owe you.*

He chittered, his little claws kneading her shoulder like a cat would. She smiled. "To Rayva, shall we? I've no friends there, well, maybe a few among the criminals, but I lost the safehouse I was supposed to stay at."

Sparks snorted from his nose as he chuckled, and she started walking.

And what of the red sister you left Mar Nevan with? Emrah asked.

Sent her home on a ship to Pan Vidda. I managed to do that, at least, before all Malhela broke loose. A silversword almost caught me outside the safehouse.

As she caught Emrah up on the unseen dwarf interference in the South Ninth district, her departure from Rayva, and her unnecessary and ill-conceived trip to the Carriage House, they joined the early morning travelers flocking to Rayva. Emrah tucked himself into the crook of her neck and shoulder, hiding in the shadows of her hood as he filled her in on his journey south. Djuren had only stayed with them as far as Thoan, when he'd had received an urgent message from Rhivven and left the red brother in charge of his contingent to bring Vaelor south. She could sense Emrah skipping over some things, but Vaelor was alive, and that was all she needed to know.

When they came upon a slow-moving wagon heading in the same direction, Fig picked up her pace, easily passing the gaggle of children packed in the back among sacks of produce. The two parents on the driver's bench chatted happily as though on a holiday.

"Velga's going to enter, did you hear? Guess her ankle healed up enough to compete, eh? That'll be a wonder to see."

"Oh, aye. Though I'm less interested in watching as I am in selling off these rutabagas before the end of the season. You can go to Halvard's Pit with the boys, and I'll stay at the stall..."

Halvard's Pit, she repeated to Emrah. *I once saw a man fight a direboar in the arena for sport.*

Emrah let out an audible snort, and as Fig had only just passed the farmers on the wagon, she coughed loudly to cover it.

What were you doing watching that? Emrah demanded.

Fig sighed, shaking her head. *I was a 'guest of the prince,' back when Dev and I were together... I don't think he wanted to watch it alone. It was gruesome.*

And did the direboar win?

It was...terribly close. Someone in the enclave had thought it was a good idea when they found the beast roving outside Rayva. I never learned what that poor briigard fighting the beast did to anger the enclave.

The closer they drew to the gate, the more travelers they passed. There was an air of festivity, with children skipping along the side of the road and adults conversing jovially with one another. The only other travelers not partaking in the lively conversations were the few dwarves she passed. Unsurprisingly, they wore dour expressions and marched to Rayva as if on their way to a funeral rite.

After everything Fig, Dev, and the others had gone through with the Feijowa clan, and the lengths the Feijowa had gone to over a mere suspicion that Emrah had stolen the sword, she couldn't believe Rhivven was actually going to give the dwarven sword to just anyone. The dwarves had been unsettled ever since word got out about the Sword of Morin. Those loitering on the streets of Rayva on her previous trip. The one who attacked a silversword to save Fig outside the safehouse. It was all over the sword.

You know it's for the Sword of Morin, right? she asked Emrah. *The prize for the tournament?*

Aye, Emrah replied. *The dwarves look mighty unpleased already. How many do you think will enter the tournament?*

Fig stared up at the towers and pitched roofs of Rayva jutting up into the morning sky. From here, the helmet of Tesvier the Relentless was just visible past the gate towers, which were rapidly approaching. Fig was certain the dwarves would put in a good showing of tournament entries in an attempt to win back their sword. She knew better than to discount the importance of a single sword—or the lengths some might go to obtain this one.

But as far as she knew, the deadly outcome of the tournament was not yet public knowledge. How many would die for the sword? She wouldn't let Vaelor be one of their number, and she now knew what she was going to do.

To her surprise, the same guard who had spoken to her the other day was back at his post and seemed to recognize her clothing, which she had yet to wash. Luckily, that fact wasn't outwardly evident to anyone but her—and probably Emrah.

"You made it back for the tournament, I see," the guard said, looking her over along with the rest of the incoming traffic.

Fig nodded, keeping her face hidden. "Of course. Wouldn't miss it."

LIESS

"Belta Valley?" Shipman asked, rubbing his stubbled chin as they walked down the tiny Ghorvost port.

"You're to report there immediately," Liess told him. "Lieutenant Conwell is awaiting your presence." It was a lie, but Bjorn Conwell *was* in the Belta Valley with the beginnings of Liess's army, and if she didn't send any other silverswords there, Rhivven would know she wasn't doing her job.

She'd given Djuren a head start with his captive mage, but since she knew where he was headed, she'd stopped in Ghorvost for provisions and to work on her task.

"How many others are here in Ghorvost?" she inquired, eager to get going. Though she didn't need to be in Rayva for the tournament, she knew Rhivven would want her army ready for the fallout afterward.

"Ten," he reported.

"Send ten, then," she said, turning away. She'd already packed everything she needed in the saddlebags of her newly acquired horse—the Southmarch name made up for her meagre coin—and was eager to pick up Djuren's trail again. Even if she didn't find him in Rokhold, she could try to find out what he was up to. There wasn't much to search up there, and she was running out of time.

"Ten, my lady?" Shipman barked.

"You can be one of them—or not. But King Rhivven is gathering an army, and this is not a request."

Shipman swallowed, eyeing the tavern at the corner of the port. By the smell of ale on his breath and his ruddy nose, she was certain he enjoyed certain comforts of a quiet life in this pathetic port town, and was therefore unsurprised when he said, "I'll remain here to keep order."

"Very well." What did she care? She turned and strode toward the tavern, where her horse was tied. "Do it now, then!" she barked over her shoulder.

Shipman hurried back the way they'd come, and she nodded to herself. Ten more for the ranks. She didn't think she'd have time to stop in Arem before hastening on to Rokhold, which would be an arduous ride to begin with.

A call from an incoming fishing boat drew her attention and she turned.

Unless she didn't have to ride...

"We're nearly there, my lady," the old captain said, gnarled fingers wringing together before him.

"Good," Liess said, staring out at the rocky shore.

"Will you..." the captain began in his dusty voice.

"Not yet," she said, glancing at the boy tied up at the bow. "I will require your services on my return, of course. I'm sure your grandson understands."

The wiry youth glared at her, a rope between his teeth halting the insults he clearly longed to throw at her.

The old captain nodded, his bald pate flashing in the light of the setting sun, and he steered them so they landed just out of sight of Rokhold. The boat rocked to a gentle halt as the captain dropped anchor, staring at her with wide eyes.

She'd once known a silversword who grew up in Rokhold, but the territory was so remote, it was barely worth the ink it took to mark it upon a map. Once, it had flourished with trade from the Hollow Isles, which trickled down the coast with specialty weapons from Kildaria and richly woven shafra fabrics, but that had ended with the blockade to the Isles, killing Rokhold's economy—or so she'd been taught. All that they had now were the rocks they stood on.

After tying up the captain and securing him on the opposite end of the boat, so he and his grandson couldn't attempt an escape together, she leapt off the rail of the small fishing ship, hand on her axe guard.

"Wet feet again," she muttered, tromping through the shallow water to shore.

Hoping she'd made up some time to catch Djuren, she approached the territory just as darkness fell.

By now, her feet were still damp but dry enough that water wasn't squelching in her boots with every step. She'd followed the scent of wood smoke to find a small, run-down castle with candle-light flickering in half the lower windows.

She darted into the shadow of a stone retaining wall just under the castle and tried to listen. She could feel several weapons inside, one of which was Djuren's.

"Got you, you briigard," she muttered. She bit her lip, thinking. She couldn't hear anything going on through the thick castle walls, but there was the call of a weapon she'd never felt before that had a cold ring to it.

If she got caught lurking here, she might have to explain what she was doing, but she did have an actual reason to be tramping across the continent. With a sly smile, she stepped out of the shadow of the retaining wall and headed for the door, hoping to the gods that Djuren would answer it himself—if only to see the look on his sour face.

She raised a fist and beat upon the rough wood.

Voices halted—one unmistakably suppressing a sob—and feet came pounding toward the door.

Just as she'd hoped, the briigard himself wrenched the door open.

"Djuren?" she said, feigning surprise. "What in the Bard's name are you doing all the way up here?"

He wrinkled his face—his broken nose hadn't been set properly and rendered it more crooked than before—and stared at her. "I could ask you the same, Liess," he said slowly.

"You know why I'm here," she said, trying to push past him and enter the small castle.

He put out an arm, and she drew up, pinning him with a look.

"Gathering my army?" she reminded him. "That was your idea, wasn't it? I want to speak to the noble here. Assuming there is one?"

Djuren glared at her and lowered his arm. "Fine."

She didn't press him as to what he was doing here but strolled in nonetheless. The smell of blood hit her as soon as she walked in, and she ran a thumb over her axe guard.

"Well? Who runs this place?" she asked as he shut the door.

"That would be me," a man said, coming out of a room leading off the foyer. As he shut the door behind him, she realized who he looked like... Devryn Verrence? No, by all the gods. It was *Shadryn* gods-forsaken Verrence. She would recognize that face anywhere. He was older, and his visage was framed in sorrow and shadows. *How?*

She swallowed. "Well met, sir," she said, keeping her voice calm. The dead prince carried a spear—the strangely cold weapon she'd sensed from outside. But it was...impossible. He was Welded with it—a mage. That also explained the black ice encasing the spear tip.

Running her thumb over her axe guard once more, she opened her mouth to speak. This deceit was much deeper than simply catching Djuren in an act of wrongdoing. Shadryn Verrence was supposed to be *dead*.

"My lord, I've come seeking silverswords," she went on, feigning ignorance. It was a lame response, she knew, but she wasn't about to indicate that she knew who he was. She kept her breathing and heart rate as steady as she could.

"Liess is gathering an army for King Rhivven," Djuren elaborated, watching her with keen eyes. She gave him a characteristically nasty look.

"As I was about to say."

Shadryn strolled away from the doorframe, his mannerisms so like his brother's with his confident swagger, except one thing—an almost imperceptible trail of black frost followed each footstep, only to disappear seconds after he'd stepped. Liess knew without a doubt the room he'd come from was where the smell of blood emanated. It dawned on her then that she'd heard a woman sobbing before.

"There are no silverswords here," he said cooly, "Except Djuren, of course. You've come a long way for nothing."

"It appears so," Liess said, regretting her hasty decision to storm the castle. She'd never thought—not in a million of the Bard's stories—that she would run into the dead prince. Her gaze flicked toward his spear, which any silversword could tell was a Welded weapon. How was it possible? She wasn't about to recruit *him*, though. "Well, I do have an army to gather, and if there are none here—"

"Wait," Shadryn drawled. "Stay. We'd like to offer what hospitality we can to a member of the king's service, before you set back on the road."

The king who'd been responsible for killing Haemond *Verrence*.

Liess grit her teeth. "I should really—"

"I insist," Shadryn said, coming closer and taking hold of her arm. His grip was freezing. She had no choice but to let him lead her into another room, this one set with a few chairs, small tables, and little else; the furniture looked like it had been part of the castle for a dragon's age. Liess sat in a hard wooden chair and pressed her knees together. After a few minutes, a servant brought a tray with biscuits and tea. Shadryn sat and poured cups for everyone, but Djuren perched on another hard wooden chair in the corner and raised his hand to decline. Liess sniffed her cup of tea, and her eyebrows shot up. It wasn't the kind of backwater tea she'd been expecting.

"You appear surprised at our selection, Miss...?"

"Astor. Liess Astor, my lord."

"Oh, I'm not a lord here," he said, waving a hand before taking a sip of his own tea. "Merely a caretaker."

"I see," Liess said. "The tea smells wonderful, thank you." She took a sip and burned her tongue, but she was eager to finish it and take her leave.

"It's Tysainian. I've grown fond of a particular blend from there."

Liess and Shadryn sipped their tea slowly, while Djuren sat in the corner with his arms crossed. Finally, when the contents of her cup were at an acceptable level for her to make her excuses, she set it down on the saucer and opened her mouth to speak.

At that moment, a sob came from the other room—the one Shadryn had emerged from earlier, which reeked of blood.

"Take care of that, will you?" Shadryn said.

Djuren stood, then quickly disappeared from the room without a glance at Liess.

Shadryn had propped his ice spear against his chair when he'd sat, and he now took it up again. His *Welded* weapon. But the rumors—including those she'd heard from Prince Devryn's very lips before they'd carted him off to the Carriage House—all said Shadryn had been born a mage. And it was true; where else was that frost coming from?

"Don't think I didn't recognize you, Liess Astor," Shadryn said quietly, and suddenly his spear was at her throat. "And I don't believe for a moment you didn't recognize me."

She held her breath. She'd dealt with men like this all her life. Her father. Rhivven. She knew how to deal with him. She sat still and lowered her gaze to his weapon, her heart thumping in her chest.

"You ran in my brother's circles every summer since he was six. He sent you here, didn't he?" He asked the last part so quietly, had she only had mundane human hearing, she would've missed it.

She bristled. "Of course not. I'm trying to capture that briigard."

Shadryn chuckled, pulling the spear tip a hand span away, while still pointing it at her throat. "Oh, I like you. You're nothing like Djuren. He does what he's told, though. What really led you here to Rokhold?"

Liess stared at him, knowing the situation hadn't changed a lick despite his apparent ease. She didn't mind being honest in this case—it might be the only thing that got her out of here alive. "Well, *Djuren*, my lord, to be quite honest. He left a rather sloppy trail. And I thought he was up to something."

Shadryn rolled his eyes. "That briigard. But I can't punish him after all the good work he's done for me. But you...you're a bit of a problem, aren't you?"

"In what way?" she said, using all her restraint to keep her voice level. "I came seeking silverswords, and I found none."

"But of course. Except you found something else. *Someone* else."

Liess shook her head, but his raised spear stopped her. The chill from the ice sent a shiver down her spine.

"I don't think I'm someone you're likely to forget."

"Then what do you want me to do?" she whispered.

He lowered the spear again and gave her a tight-lipped smile, surveying her with his head tilted back. She could see strange black veins in his neck when he leaned back, which had been hidden by the shadows until now.

"You're gathering an army, did you say?" he asked.

She nodded. "Yes. To quell any uprising from the dwarves,"

she admitted, her stomach muscles tight. The problem with Shadryn Verrence was that she had no knowledge of what made the briigard tick. Rhivven, she knew like the back of her own axe. She knew when to stay silent, and when to divulge what he wanted to hear.

Shadryn was nodding, though. "Good. I want you to go do that."

Liess's shoulders dropped suddenly. "Pardon?" With a sharp crack, black ice protruded from the floor, freezing her in place quite literally. Shards pointed straight at her throat, inching closer. She was surrounded by spikes of ice—completely trapped.

Shadryn leaned in close. "I want you to do what King Rhivven has asked and amass his army."

"I—I will."

"Good girl," he said. "You know...Djuren's told me about you. Your rise in the enclave over the years. Your close relationship with Rhivven—"

A scream came from the other room, and Shadryn pulled away.

The door burst open, and the scent of blood overwhelmed Liess's senses.

Shadryn had the courtesy to let go of the ice surrounding Liess, and she put a hand on her axe as he stood and went to the hallway.

Against her better judgement, Liess followed.

A girl of about twenty stood in the foyer, her clothes a bloody mess. She looked like she'd been stabbed—and by the gods, she had been, right in the heart. A large, recently healed scar poked through the slash in her bloody tunic. Black lined the veins around the scar, just as it did her wrists and neck. She staggered away from Djuren, who pursued her.

"Leave me—alone!" she yelled.

Everything stopped.

Liess couldn't move. Her body wouldn't let her. But it wasn't the ice from Shadryn, it was something else. Like her own blood had betrayed her.

Djuren and Shadryn appeared just as stricken.

Shadryn shook it off somehow, bringing his hands together in a clap. "Well done, Morandra! Now scurry off and get cleaned up. You're quite indecent for our guest."

Morandra stared at Shadryn incredulously. Shadryn merely waved his hand at Djuren, seeming to free him from the restraint, and Djuren—surprisingly gentle—tried to guide Morandra back into the room. The girl looked shaken and stared at her blackened fingers in wonder.

Liess thought she spied the whisper of a red cloak inside the room before the door shut, leaving her and Shadryn alone in the foyer, with Liess still unable to move her body.

"Marvelous, isn't it?" Shadryn asked, pacing around her. "It doesn't always take, you see, but for those who survive, well, their powers rival the gods."

Since Liess couldn't move or respond, she waited.

"My dear Liess Astor. I've told you what I want you to do, and it won't go against your dear Rhivven's orders. But I want this—this place and everything you've seen here—to remain between us. I think you can understand that. Because, well, little Morandra there is still getting control of her skills and seems quite natural at manipulating blood. I don't think I need to tell you what will happen if you open your mouth."

His circuitous stroll around her ended as he stood before her, leaning casually on his spear. With a wave of his other hand, he released the tightness in her blood.

She nodded.

"Good girl."

Back on the boat, Liess untied the captain and his grandson without a word.

The youth looked like he wanted to pick a fight with Liess,

but the captain made haste to get the vessel back on the water, while giving orders to his grandson. The stars were bright. They would have no trouble getting back to Ghorvost tonight, from where she would ride like a dragonet on the wind to Arem to continue gathering soldiers.

If she never saw Shadryn Verrence again, it would be too soon.

FIG

A lute played while Fig made her way through the streets surrounding Halvard's Pit. Tents and tables were set up anywhere vendors could find space, hawking their wares to passersby. Fig smelled roast chestnuts, and her mouth watered, but her stomach was making it clear that if she sent anything down there, it would find its way back up.

First, we need to find out if they've moved Vaelor to the pit, she told Emrah. She had some other ideas but wasn't yet ready to voice them.

Where would they put him? Emrah asked as Fig weaved her way through the crowd.

I'm not sure, she replied, studying the arena as she began to circle the immense structure. Arguably taller than even the Tesvier statue on the other side of the city, Halvard's Pit was a behemoth of stone. Columns and interwoven carvings lined the outside of the arena, and on the ground level, dozens of tunnels led straight to the sand—tunnels the competitors would enter through. The poor could watch through the bars when they closed the gates.

They passed one of the public entrances, a grand staircase that led up to the spectator levels. Massive stone braziers had already been lit all around the outside of the arena, announcing the fight to come.

There've got to be some holding chambers underneath would be my guess, Fig thought to Emrah.

Get me close to one of those tunnels, and I'll go look.

What? And risk you being seen?

Emrah snorted aloud, and she sighed.

Fig continued walking around the arena, glancing in each of the tunnels as they passed. *Look,* she told him, *there's a pattern. Seven tunnels, then a wall of stone just as wide, and then the tunnels start up again.*

She walked closer to the tunnels with what she hoped was an air of someone admiring the architecture of Halvard's Pit and anticipating the fight to come. A flock of children descended on a vendor selling apples coated in caramel, and Fig was confident no one was paying attention to her.

When she stood directly in front of one of the tunnels, staring down the dark stone pathway, Emrah took off from her shoulder, heading for the square of bright light at the other end.

As soon as he disappeared into the arena, he reported back. *You're right, the sections that look blocked from the outside are staircases that lead down. There're bars, but I can slip through.*

Don't—

Too late, Svoran.

You're going to need to keep talking to me then, so I know you're all right.

Missed me while I was gone, didn't you?

Fig's face flushed. *Of course I did, you little—Just be careful, will you?*

Yes, Mother.

Fig crossed her arms and wandered away from the tunnel entrance, on edge. She stared at the apple vendor and forced herself to buy a perfectly plain apple, which she thought she might be able to stomach. The caramel-coated ones made her mouth water, but she didn't think she could handle that much sugar with her insides in such turmoil.

Anything? she asked him, accepting an apple from the farmer and resuming her stroll around the arena. She'd come back for Emrah when it was time. She didn't want to be caught loitering anywhere for too long.

A very long curved corridor. I suspect it runs around the entire circle of the arena. Some empty rooms so far, and I think I see a fount up ahead by the next staircase.

That makes sense, if they deign to heal fighters in a normal tournament. Anyone else down there?

Just some—ah, silverswords ahead.

Fig resisted the urge to yell into Emrah's mind to get out of there, to get away from them. But she didn't want to distract him, and she knew he was smart. She had to remind herself that he'd gotten along just fine without her before they'd met.

She kept walking, taking the occasional bite of her apple. It was crunchy and sweet, the best apple she'd had in months; the farmers had clearly brought their best stock for the occasion.

Fig wondered at the Tytanians' acceptance of Rhivven as a ruler. For people like the farmers and tradesmen, did it just look like another bloody silversword on the throne? Or did they know it was useless to fight back against a tyrant such as the Butcher of Viren?

Did anyone even bother to mourn the downfall of House Verrence and the promise of Dev as king?

Finally, she turned back around to make for the tunnel she'd sent Emrah down. She tossed her apple core into one of the large braziers outside the arena, and brushed sparks from her fingertips nervously. Finally, she couldn't take it anymore. *Emrah?* she demanded.

Oh, Fig, right! Sorry. I found Vaelor and was so busy speaking to him that I—

You found him? She nearly shouted the words aloud.

He's in a cell down here, there's a pair of silverswords at his door, but I can talk to him from here.

Thank the gods, she said. *Is he all right?*

A long pause, during which her stomach somersaulted while her brain tried to reassure her that Emrah was talking to Vaelor.

He looks fine, Emrah said, though she thought she could detect a note of not-fineness in his tone. She didn't press it. He was alive.

And he knows all about the tournament?

Aye. And from the look in his eyes, he wants you as far away from the arena and Rayva as possible.

Fig scoffed. *By the Bard, does he think I can just sit around at the tower and wait to hear about how everyone in the tournament was slaughtered—including him?*

Of course not, Emrah said, his voice a little sad.

She took in a deep breath. *Of course he doesn't,* she replied. *Tell him I will find a way. Tell him I—* Her chest constricted, and she cut off the words tumbling from her conscious thought.

Emrah didn't reply, and Fig could only imagine what the little dragonet was saying to Vaelor. Her face warmed, and she crossed her arms, turning to gaze up at the great arena. The sound of a harp struck up nearby, a merry tune filling the street.

The sharp scent of copper assailed her nose before the sound of clanking armor reached her ears, and she turned away from the group of silverswords marching down the street.

Emrah, I think we should go, she said, holding her breath. The silverswords kept marching, then paused on the next block. Fig heard shouting and glanced out of the corner of her eye to see the 'swords dragging a dwarf from the lintel of a nearby building. All he'd been doing was sitting there, watching the arena.

Now, Emrah.

A chirp from the tunnel caused her to turn just in time to get a face full of dragonet wing as Emrah clambered onto her shoulder. She quickly fixed her hood and turned away from the silverswords, Emrah's scaly weight comforting her.

Well? How is he really? she asked him.

He shifted a little on her shoulder. *A little bloody, but nothing broken.*

Fig sniffed. *Suppose it could be worse.* She picked up her pace.

Where are we headed? Emrah asked, claws digging in a little harder.

To the lists. I'm entering this gods-forsaken tournament.

No scale-rotting way, Emrah's words clawed through her mind. *You're not actually going to...*

Around the other side of the main spectator entrance, Fig found the wooden gazebo which had clearly been constructed for this very purpose. A woman with a scowl stood at a counter, lording over a large open book. A burly dwarf at the head of the line was registering herself, lifting her arm high to write in the book.

They had hours before sundown when the tournament would begin, and despite Emrah's increasingly curse-ridden admonishments and claws digging into her shoulder, she got in the back of the line and waited.

After all the tossing and turning last night, all the attempts to think through a solution to save Vaelor—well, the one solution had been so obviously staring her in the face she hadn't even considered it...

Because, by all accounts, it was insane.

A fight to the death, Fig, Emrah hissed in her brain. *Don't kill yourself to save Vaelor. He can fight.*

Yes, but can he fight his way out of this? she asked, her gaze going around to the dozens of men and dwarves loitering around the lists. *Vaelor saved me at Nithe—broke his sword in the process. I owe him—*

Not your life! Emrah argued. *You can't save him if you're dead! And the second you use fire magic, the silverswords will kill you!*

Fig's gaze unwittingly flicked to the two sheafs of paper nailed unceremoniously to the front board of the registration galley: *No mages* and *No silverswords*.

She was a little surprised Rhivven hadn't barred dwarves from entering as well, but he must have his reasons.

It was finally her turn at the book. She stepped forward after a woman before her trundled off, smelling of ale and walking with a slight hitch in her gait. Fig sincerely hoped the woman had only been asking questions and not entering the tournament herself.

"Name and occupation," the keeper of the lists barked, pointing at the large book. "You can write, can't ye?"

Fig nodded and picked up the quill, drawing in a steadying breath. Emrah's claws were digging into her shoulder, and she wouldn't be surprised if her whole shoulder and neck was scratched and bloodied later—if she wasn't lying dead in the sand of Halvard's Pit like that bloody direboar and had a chance to inspect them later.

She had to stuff her left hand into her pocket and clench her fist around some sparks, so she wouldn't singe the woman's quill. She quickly scratched the first name that came to her mind on the line. *Avelina... Fair.*

Occupation... Her mind went completely blank. The woman standing there was staring at her as if she were daft.

Blacksmith. Out of the corner of her eye, she could see the woman narrowing her gaze as Fig wrote the word.

So she added *'s Apprentice*, and the woman nodded. "Fine. Enter in the tunnels before sundown. Bring ONE favored weapon for the combat portion, and don't be late."

"Got it," Fig said, turning away.

Combat portion, my rear, she thought to herself. *The entire thing will be combat.*

You daft Svoran, Emrah said, but this time she could hear the sadness in his voice.

An hour later, Fig found herself alone in one of the stone tunnels. She had a sneaking suspicion it was the one she'd been lurking around earlier. The registrars had harried the entrants who showed up to one per tunnel. Fig's hands were shaking, and she forced them into fists by her sides.

Behind her lay the streets of Rayva, the crowds thronging through the main entrance to the arena stands. Some wore crow masks for the holiday, others were draped in black garlands, but the prevailing attitude was one of excitement for the upcoming tournament. Before her lay the sands of the pit, a cacophony of sound coming from the seated spectators.

You don't have to do this, Fig, Emrah said quietly in her mind. He clung to her shoulder. *There's got to be another way to get him out.*

Fig sighed. *I'm doing this. He'd do it for me.*

A loud *clank* sounded behind her. She whipped her head around to see an iron gate lowering, closing her off from the street.

That was it, then.

Her heart hammered in her chest and her stomach seized. She wondered if the apple she'd eaten earlier was going to make a reappearance.

Emrah, can you speak to Vaelor? she asked, an edge of panic seeping into her.

No, you daft Svoran, he replied, with only a shadow of the usual snark. *I can only do that with* you *at a distance. You know that.*

Fig swallowed, her breath coming fast now. She needed to maintain her calm, or she would be useless in the pit. She didn't know how many competitors there would be, but she would fight them all. She just had to get to him.

She stared ahead, looking at the sand, thinking of all the blood that would be spilled there soon enough.

The blood...

Hey, Emrah? she asked, her thoughts racing as fast as her nerves. *When I talked to the head priestess at Mar Nevan, she said something about our bond being incomplete. And I've been thinking...*

She huffed and swallowed a lump in her throat. She put a hand up to cover his claws with her fingers and said aloud, "I don't know if I—I don't know if I'm going to make it out of this —" Her voice cracked. "And, well, I want to complete the bond, if we can. I've been thinking about when we first met... Do you remember that you bit me—and then, later, you burned me?"

Emrah tensed on her shoulder, his spine arcing. *The bite was an accident!* he said defensively. *And I had to burn you because you were bleeding out—*

Fig gave a watery chuckle, her eyes glossing over with unshed tears. *No, no, it's fine,* she thought to him. She no longer trusted her voice to remain calm. *But I was thinking—blood and fire. You took some of my blood, and I took some of your fire. What if we're missing the rest?*

Svoran, if you really wanted to bite me, you could have just said so.

"Emrah!" Laughter burst from her. *I'm serious. I want to finish the bond before it's too late.*

Well, when you say it all serious like that, how am I supposed to say no? Of course, Fig.

She glanced into the arena, but couldn't see any activity there, and no one was on the streets except a few vendors who couldn't be convinced to leave the promise of sales. Fig didn't see anyone watching them, so she crouched down by the wall in the most shadowy part of the tunnel, and Emrah got down on the floor before her.

Without talking about it further, he reached a claw to his back flank and nicked himself between scales. Sparks spilled from his jaw as he hissed at the pain, and Fig frowned. "Oh, Emrah."

It's nothing. Here. He was offering her a tiny bloody claw. With a finger, she got some of his blood and put it to her mouth. As quickly as it passed her lips, she swallowed, not wanting to prolong the strange idea of the ritual. She wasn't even sure it would work.

And now... she thought.

Burn it, Emrah suggested, his golden eyes glinting at her in the darkness.

Are you sure?

Sure as fire burns.

She closed her eyes for a moment and reached into her core, connecting to her flames and summoning the gentlest burst she possibly could. Bringing her burning finger to his wound, she made sure she didn't maintain the fire any longer than necessary. Her gut clenched at the sight of it—the idea of intentionally hurting Emrah. But he didn't even flinch.

She sank back onto her heels, waiting. Mother Savidah could have been lying, and Fig was just guessing about the blood and fire.

Something hot roared through her core, so quickly she leapt to her feet looking around in wonder.

Um, Fig? Emrah said, still crouching on the floor. *What was that?*

You felt it too? she said, her heart leaping, but now there was an odd feeling of pressure building in her. *Maybe this wasn't such a good idea.*

I think it worked! Emrah said. *Something feels d—*

A cymbal crashed from the arena, and at that moment, the gate before her began to lower. It was time.

FIG

All of Fig's insides felt like they were suddenly on fire.

She stumbled over the gate as it sank into the sandy ground and found herself positioned in the arena between two other competitors, both staring around just as wildly as her. She swayed. It hurt to breathe, hurt to think. Everything *burned*. It was all Fig could do to keep herself upright. *Emrah?* she cried in her thoughts. *Am I...on fire?* Somehow she knew he was still in the tunnel behind her, a glowing green ember in her mind's eye. Her hands groped about her torso, feeling for a burn that wasn't there. It felt like all the blood had drained from her face.

A mental groan replied in her thoughts; he was experiencing the same thing. Something was wrong.

What had she been thinking, attempting to complete their bond just before the tournament?

She brought her gaze down to her hands, which were, surprisingly, not aflame. She figured there would have been outbursts from the other competitors or the massive crowd if anything like that had happened. So only her insides were burning, then. Taking calming breaths to work around the pain searing through, she tried to get her wits about her.

What looked like a hundred fighters from all across Tytan stood spaced around the pit. She couldn't place which was Vaelor out of the half dozen taller forms in the arena. The majority of the competitors were dwarves, and the one next to Fig carried a great double-sided axe. Most stood straight-backed, awaiting the royal order while the assembled crowd cheered.

Panting and sweating, she turned her gaze to the royal canopy. She didn't recognize any of those surrounding Rhivven, though even from here she could tell from their stances that they were all silverswords. At the slightest raise of Rhivven's fingers, the cymbals crashed again, echoing through the pit and silencing the crowd.

Rhivven didn't need to stand in order to call attention to himself. He shifted his legs in the slightest and picked up a sword that leaned against his throne.

Heart racing, Fig tried to focus on him, but her vision was blurring. What had she done to herself? She was already risking everything by putting herself in this tournament. How could she stay alive long enough to rescue Vaelor when her *whole body* was on fire? She flexed her fingers, her breath shallow.

"People of Tytan," Rhivven announced, his gravelly voice echoing though the arena. "I hold in my hands a powerful sword, the likes of which hasn't been seen in a dragon's age. One competitor today will leave with this sword—bound to them for life, in service of the enclave which grants them that power."

There was an uproar from the dwarves—deep voices raised in anger and confusion.

Rhivven beckoned with his other hand, and two figures in red stepped forward.

The red sisters had their hoods up. One pushed a small cart that held a large basin of water with a wooden dipper balanced across the top. Her face was indiscernible from here.

Fig was still having trouble breathing and staggered back a

step closer to the tunnel she'd come from. But the gate had closed, and she was trapped on the sand within Halvard's Pit, the crowd roaring down on her...her vision still blurry.

She couldn't focus on the other competitors—gods, she could barely stand.

"Only one of you will be leaving this arena," Rhivven's voice ground at her ears. Whispers wove through the crowded arena, growing in what she could only interpret as excitement. The dwarves had grown silent. "Whichever one of you gets *and keeps* the sword—for the glory of Tytan! Begin!" With an inhuman burst of strength, he tossed the sword onto the sand, somewhat near the center.

Fig blinked, her vision still hazy. A few of the other competitors cautiously advanced on the sword, glancing around as if uncertain they had heard right. *Only one of you will be leaving this arena.*

Clenching her hands into fists, Fig took a steadying breath. *Not if I can help it.*

She staggered forward. She had to get it together. For Vaelor.

A dwarf on the other side of the arena made a run for it, stocky legs sprinting toward the Sword of Morin, until the woman next to him bolted into his path, whipping out her sword as she collided with him.

Then all Malhela broke loose.

The rest of the competitors surged into motion, clearly realizing that this would, indeed, be a fight to the death.

I have to find Vaelor. Everyone else is going for the sword. Emrah, can you fly?

A somewhat-positive groan echoed in her mind, and she nodded. She could barely walk from the pain, but the fiery heat surging through her seemed to be lessening—or she was getting used to it; she wasn't sure which. Her vision was still poor, and she hoped to the Bard it wasn't permanent.

One of her neighbors lurched toward her at that moment, a slight limp evident. Fig's eyes widened in horror as she realized it was the woman she'd seeing registering earlier. Fig dodged to the other side and aimed a kick at the woman's middle, sending her staggering back. A dwarf with a thick ginger beard surged into view, hammer swinging straight at Fig. She rolled across the sand, throwing her aching body out of the way.

The hammer caught the woman with a limp and Fig scrambled away, fingers slipping through sand, her heart thundering in her chest as she got to her feet. Her vision flared and went completely out.

Emrah! she screamed in her mind. *I can't see—I can't—*

Her vision burst back, but everything glowed gold down in the little sand pit from her high vantage point. Pulses of light marked the humans and dwarves from this height, one of the smaller bodies glowing the brightest gold among them. Her heart filled with warmth at the sight of it.

Fig? Fig? What are you—seeing this? Watch out!

As if a bucket of cold water had been splashed over her face, Fig was ripped from the warm golden vision. What in the name of the Bard...?

The dwarf with the hammer was coming straight for her—which she had somehow seen from above—and she ducked and rolled to the side again, sweeping her legs in an arc to bring him to the ground. Fig sprinted away, her vision now clear and back to normal. Even the burning inside was simmering in a more tolerable heat.

Fig, Emrah said. *Were you...seeing through my eyes?*

I...I think I was! she told him, swallowing a lump in her throat as she ran through the sand, searching for Vaelor. She found strength rising in every place the burning inside her had scoured, and a surge of the sweetest adrenaline shot through her. Now the fire in her veins fueled her, pushing her across the arena, kicking up sand in her wake.

Everyone in the arena was engaged in combat except her. She gave the sword a wide berth so no one would think she was going for it, and thankfully, no one challenged her.

Find Vaelor, she implored.

I'm working on it, Emrah assured her.

She could feel exactly where Emrah soared above her, and somehow, she knew their bond was complete—born in the burning flames, sealed when she'd seen the arena through Emrah's eyes, and now alive in the fiery adrenaline coursing through her. She raced on, dodging between the fights that had broken out across the arena. Already a handful lay dead, and Fig had to check those fighters and assure herself none was a big Viren with long hair.

He's here, Emrah called. *Just here!*

She didn't need him to tell her where, just ran, somehow knowing where Emrah meant. She saw his hair swing as Vaelor whirled to block a dwarf's blow, the double-sided axe colliding with Vaelor's borrowed blade. Fig winced as Vaelor almost buckled under the blow, weakened from his journey from Mar Nevan, but she was almost to him, almost—

She'd been keeping the Sword of Morin in the corner of her eye, so when a scuffle by the sword broke out, she slowed to look. A fighter draped in a dark hood—one that blocked his vision so that he'd nearly missed the hammer swinging for his head. Then he ducked, and the wielder of the hammer was blown off his feet by a gust of wind—tinged purple.

No. By all the gods, no.

The man scooped up the sword, holding it high in triumph.

The crowd roared, and every fighter in the arena turned their attention to the man at the center. Fig's insides burned in a whole different way. No. How could Dev *possibly* be here?

He flung his hood back, sword held high.

A lone woman's voice from the crowd called, "Long live King Devryn!"

FIG

Fig cursed, her attention split between Vaelor and Dev. The briigard was supposed to be safe in Tirnalore for the Bard's sake!

Amid the crowd's cheers and shouts of surprise, Fig ran full tilt toward Vaelor. The other fighters had temporarily frozen, thrown off by the appearance of their lost heir, but Fig was sure that the glory of the sword would soon call to them again, even if it was currently held by their lost prince. The fact remained that they were all still trapped in the pit, while King Rhivven Reynolt and his cronies stood above.

The dwarf fighting Vaelor had stumbled back a few feet and was staring dumbstruck at Dev. He had a wary look in his eyes, and sure enough, he began advancing on Dev. Vaelor followed the dwarf. Fig picked up her pace, strength flooding her legs, and she caught up with him, grabbing his arm.

"Vaelor!" she cried.

He turned, sword raised, but when his eyes met hers, he practically went limp. "Goldfire? What are you doing here?" His eyes darkened. "No, no, no. You can't be here."

"Neither can you," she insisted.

"When Emrah told me you were near the arena…"

"I had to," she said.

Vaelor grabbed her by the arm. "Dev…"

"I don't know how in the Bard's broken quills he got here, but it's—"

"Time to leave," he finished.

"All of us."

If it had been anyone else in the arena who'd picked up the sword, she and Vaelor would have had the perfect distraction to attempt an escape. Unfortunately, they now had to get to Dev as well—and he was at the center of attention, in front of thousands of bloodthirsty spectators.

Two dwarves had shaken off their shock of finding the missing Verrence in the middle of the pit and were now only a dozen paces from Dev. The other combatants appeared on the verge of joining them, having halted their various scuffles throughout the arena. Fig and Vaelor ran to the center. Fig's insides still burned a little, but she used that feeling to stoke the flames at her core, ready to fight.

Dev blasted the two dwarves with his full powers, amethyst-colored wind spiraling from him, kicking up sand into a purple whirlwind around himself. Fig shielded her eyes.

A group of human fighters—who seemed to have formed an alliance against the lost prince—advanced, their swords and maces raised.

Dev was fully exposed, and Fig was already a fugitive—so she didn't hesitate to summon her flames. They'd been begging for release ever since she'd stumbled from the tunnel with her fresh bond with Emrah. So when she hurled a burst of gold fire at the mace-wielding man nearest to Dev, the flames were ten times more powerful than she expected.

The whirlwind Dev had swirling around himself—already a powerful exhibition of magic she hadn't known Dev was capable of—picked up the flames, and gold fire intertwined with the amethyst wind. The sandstorm surged with Dev's power, moving out to strike the others advancing on him.

Cries of pain rang out from inside the whirlwind, which had turned from sand into shards of glass.

"Dev!" she cried, holding her hands out, sparks dripping heavily onto the sand.

He's all right, came a voice in her head. Emrah, still circling the arena. *That was some fireball, Fig!*

I didn't mean to—

Her thoughts shut down as the glass shards dropped, and Dev released his magic. He stood dumbstruck in the sand, still holding the Sword of Morin. The two fighters who'd gotten hit with the whirlwind lay in the sand.

"Fig? What in Drakioryn's ba—" He shook his head. "*Vaelor?*" Then the moment was ruined by half a dozen fighters charging toward them. Fig and Vaelor drew close to Dev, and the three put their backs to each other, facing outward. Fig could feel the agitation coming from Emrah.

Dev lifted his hands.

The glass shards rose once more, this time pointing outward in a fast-moving swirl of broken glass.

"I don't know how either of you got in here," Dev said, "but did anyone have a plan to get out?"

Vaelor made a low sound of disagreement, and Fig shrugged, flames dripping idly from her hands, careful to keep them under control. She looked down at the sand before her and up at the stands—through the wall of circling glass shards. She hadn't known Dev had this kind of power—sure, he could fight using bursts of magic, but the strength it took to hold this kind of massive whirlwind and the control of holding the glass shards...

"I...might have an idea," Fig hedged.

A dwarf woman chose that moment to brave the glass shards, trying to knock them aside with her sword to get to them.

Dev focused his energy on shifting more shards the dwarf's

way, but the gap it left on the other side was too inviting—a set of dwarves was now coming in that direction.

"Dev, just give the dwarves the sword!" Fig said, realizing the simplicity of it. "You don't need it!"

"I—I have a plan for it. And they'd never get out with it alive," Dev said tersely, his attention focused on the purple haze around him holding the shards. "What was that about you having an idea?"

"Right," she said. "It's just that it's…"

"Get on with it!" Dev insisted. Through the whirlwind, they could see the remaining human fighters advancing, the pull of the glory Rhivven had promised giving them courage. Fig understood why the dwarves wanted the ancestral sword, but the others…

Quit stalling, Fig, and just do it! Emrah told her.

You don't even know what I'm going to do!

Somehow I do, Svoran. And it'll work. Just do it.

She couldn't say no to that. "All right, Dev, when I tell you, get ready—"

She hissed in a breath through her nose and connected with her inner flames, which felt like the gods had turned volcanic. As she exhaled, she pushed the flames down at the large area of sand before her, which boiled into a massive pool of molten glass in mere seconds. The three of them leapt back from the red-hot pool they now stood beside. A few other fighters also had to leap out of the way, rolling on the sand to avoid it.

"Now, Dev!" She pointed to a break in the stadium's architecture that revealed the main entrance into the arena.

The glass shards from the makeshift shield dropped around them, clinking together as a burst of amethyst wind surged into the pool of glass and pushed. Dev planted his feet and shoved his magic upward, forming the molten glass into a massive arc that led out of the arena—and right through its front doors.

Wind whipped around Dev as he shoved more magic into the massive glass arch—the bridge arched up from the sand and cooled swiftly with the force of his winds. Without discussion, the three of them leapt toward it, Dev still holding the Sword of Morin. Vaelor came up behind Fig and raised his sword at the rest of the fighters in the arena—because dwarf or human, they seemed to realize that Dev really was escaping with the sword. Fig didn't understand why he wouldn't just give it to the nearest dwarf, but she'd have to trust he had a plan for that as well. Out of the corner of her eye, she saw a commotion near Rhivven, glints of silversword armor approaching the rails as if they might leap down to the sand and finally intervene.

As Fig and the others rushed toward the glass arch and reached the place where it rose out of the smooth glass pool, Fig panicked; there was no way they could run up this slippery surface—

A gust of wind blew from behind, giving the three of them a lift. She screamed, arms pinwheeling as her feet slid along the glass arch until the cooled glass wave evened out.

Fig fell onto her rear as she slid along the arch, crossing the spectator level of the arena alongside the other two. A muscular blonde-haired woman dashed toward them, and Fig worried for a second it might be one of Rhivven's silverswords, until she saw the woman was unarmored and familiar.

Ziggy leapt onto the glass arch behind them, and Dev's wind hurried them all along. Fig was screaming again—though whether in elation or terror, she wasn't really sure—as they slid down the massive glass slide and out of the arena. Dev had pushed the last of the molten glass over the stairs that descended to the street, which they were quickly approaching. Finally, she skidded across the cooled puddle of glass and sprang to her feet on the stone pavers in front of Halvard's Pit.

She swayed and stumbled drunkenly as the adrenaline raced out of her system, then came to a stop, staring up at the massive glass arch before them.

"Gods, Fig!" Dev screamed, landing gracefully as he used a wisp of wind to right himself. "I didn't know you could burn like that!"

Fig's heart hammered in her chest, and she flung her arms

around Dev. "I didn't know you could do that, either. What in the Bard's name are you even doing here?"

Vaelor joined them as Fig and Dev broke apart—followed by Ziggy.

"Ah, there she is," Dev said, raising the Sword of Morin at her in greeting. "I told you it would all work out."

Ziggy's descent was anything but graceful, considering that she'd launched herself onto it from the spectator level. Dev straightened her out with a wisp of wind and helped her to her feet once she reached them.

"We need to go," Vaelor said.

"I think they might have noticed your escape," Ziggy said, putting a hand on her sword hilt.

"How much time do you think we have to get out of Rayva?" Dev asked.

The clang of metal gates echoed through the arena. In the flickering light of the braziers, they could see the gates of the tunnels opening again and the remaining fighters being freed from the pit. At least the dwarves and the other fighters would get out safely. Rhivven had probably ordered them to track down Dev and the sword, though.

"None. Go!" she cried. The four of them took off into the darkening city, Emrah sailing overhead.

Her heart thundered, and suddenly her vision grew bleary again. *Oh gods, not again.*

Then everything was golden, and she was looking down at four pulses of light moving through Rayva's streets. One pulse was a bright gold color. The large one next to it was silver with pulsing flickers of red. She flapped her wings again and—

Fig pulled her sight back to her own body, which had somehow continued running despite... *Emrah, was I...?*

Indeed, you were.

Gods, it was like I was you—flying! And seeing everything—

It's like you were in here with me when that happened.

Well, maybe now's not the best time to figure all that out. I'm just glad I can see—I thought I'd gone blind in the arena—or mad, maybe. For now, can you be our guide out of the city?

Do tagors have teeth?

Fig snickered and raced on, relaying the directions as Emrah guided them from above to avoid any silverswords. Despite the adrenaline still coursing through her veins, making her nearly delirious while also being the sole thing keeping her upright at this point—her heart soared. She had completed her bond with Emrah, a strange but comforting feeling that had more than doubled her magic, and the Bard knew what else. Above all, she had rescued Vaelor; the heavy weight of his absence was finally lifting. And the fact that Dev and Ziggy had both been here had to be a blessing from the gods, because things finally seemed to be going her way.

But she knew that like Morgha's two sides—life and death— her luck would eventually swing back in the other direction.

And this time, she would be ready.

MAIREAD

Mairead adjusted her gloves, pulling the leather tight to meet the tips of her fingers. Derrin had gone inside Arem's only tavern to inquire about a room they weren't actually going to rent, while she and Uncle Howarth loitered with Folly behind the barn where they'd parked Derrin's cart. They couldn't have left Folly behind if they'd wanted to, the happy golden dog had trailed the three of them as they had made their preparations to leave Thoan, hopping into the cart before anyone else.

She leaned her head against the side of the cart, letting her heavy eyelids fall shut in the safety of her new cloak's black hood. Derrin had a strange assortment of things in his cart, intended to aid her initial flight from Thoan. Between that and the curiosity he'd shown about Dev's escape from Tytan, she couldn't help but wonder exactly what else he did besides run his family's print shop.

He'd provided them all with changes of clothes, and Mairead took the cloak with the biggest hood to hide the new tattoos that ran down the left side of her face. Mother Savidah may have helped her by giving her a means of identifying Morgha's magic, but the marks were even more troublesome to hide than the tattoos on her hands. On their journey here, she'd studied the scroll that Mother Savidah had sent her, but the runes it was written in were indecipherable—at least to her.

The tavern door opened and closed, and Mairead tensed, opening her eyes and pulling her head away from the weathered wood. Folly let out a little *whuff*. But it was just Derrin heading toward them, hands in his pockets. He shook his head.

Mairead's hopes plummeted. Of course they weren't here. It had been over a week since Fig and Vaelor had set off down the Twist, and could still be in Mar Nevan for all she knew—either held against their will or still working out the problem with Vaelor's sword—and there was no way Mairead could follow them there.

She inhaled sharply through her nose, and said, "Well, that's too bad. I have one other idea of where we can check." She hadn't yet told Derrin about the tower, even though that had been the first place she'd wanted to run and hide after killing the red brother back in Thoan.

Her uncle gave her a sad smile. "We should probably stay here for the day. You look exhausted."

Mairead shook her head. "No," she said sharply. "Sorry, it's just..." She lowered her voice, her hands shaking a little. "The other red brothers from Thoan... Well, I think they're on the move."

Uncle Howarth matched her tone, "Why do you say that?"

She raised a shaking finger to tap under her left eye, and her uncle nodded. He might have spent his whole life as a goat farmer and soap maker, but he was one of the most observant people she knew.

"Lead on, then," he told her.

"We should leave the cart here," she told Derrin.

He spluttered, "W-What? Why?"

"We won't be able to take it the whole way, and abandoning it anywhere else will look suspicious."

She thought he might argue more, but he began gathering his things out of the back, and she did the same. Folly hopped out and stuck his wet nose in her hand; she gave him a pat on the head.

"What is it you do, anyway, Derrin?" she asked him a few minutes later as they began walking east on the Mountain Road. "You seemed rather interested in the story about Dev last night."

He shrugged. "Well, he was the crown prince until recently. It's not like I can pretend the Butcher of Viren actually earned the throne."

Mairead turned and arched an eyebrow at him.

He let out a soft snort. "I happen to have some acquaintances who still support House Verrence, is all."

She let it drop. If he was on the side of House Verrence and her uncle vouched for him, she believed she could trust him. Except...

"You know, you could have taken your cart and gone back home. The red brothers had business at my family's house, not yours. You wouldn't have been linked to the death at all."

He didn't speak for a long time, then finally turned to look her full in the face, peering under her hood. "The people I mentioned, they're not just acquaintances, Mairead. It wasn't only mages who wanted to see Devryn on the throne. We've been working to support his cause from within Tytan, but it's been difficult—"

"Then why aren't you going back to Thoan? I assume you have some kind of network there...?"

"Well, because of *you*, Mairead. You knew Devryn. You would help us put him back on the throne, wouldn't you? Can you get me in contact with him?"

She stopped walking, turning to face him, her eyes narrowed. "How do I know you're not just trying to get Rhivven's reward?" She still hadn't forgiven him for wanting to abandon her uncle.

Derrin shut down, his eyes darkening as the hopeful expression slid off his face. Mairead tried not to feel guilty; she'd seen that look before. Despair. He turned his back toward her and faced the Mountain.

Uncle Howarth put a hand on her shoulder and led her a few paces away. "I wouldn't expect you to know, Mairy," he said quietly, "but Derrin's parents were killed by silverswords right after the coup. They were in Rayva printing stories that weren't the right "angle" that Rhivven wanted..."

"Oh," she said, her face burning. She closed her eyes and said a silent prayer for them.

"It's fine," Derrin said, his back still turned but evidently overhearing. "You didn't know."

"I'm so sorry, Derrin." She thought back to the warm kitchen at Derrin's house; more than once, she'd tumbled inside on Derrin's heels to steal a cooling bread roll from the table with her playmate. The blue apron his mother always wore, covered in flour. Derrin's father's apron, always covered in ink, hanging on a peg by the door.

Mairead blinked away the pricking in her eyes and said, "If I could contact Dev, I would, but we'd need a dragonet to do that. The last I knew, he was safe in Tirnalore. But there's a place we all know—a safe place—that if any of them were to go to, it'd be there..." She waved her hand toward the Gold Wood to the south. Derrin's eyes widened, and her uncle huffed in surprise, but if either of them had any reservation about entering the forbidden woods, they kept it to themselves.

"Are...are you quite sure you know where you're going?" Derrin ventured several hours later.

Mairead was sweating, her hood off and her gloves stuffed in her pockets. Deep in the Gold Wood, she wasn't worried about anyone seeing her tattoos—if the silverswords found them tres-passing here, they could kill them on sight for their very presence, so what did it matter?

Mairead didn't answer him—just kept trudging on. She knew

the tower had to be close by. But when she'd left with Fig and Vaelor, she hadn't really intended on returning by herself, so she hadn't taken much notice of the way.

Derrin had taken to walking in front, brandishing a small club he'd taken from the cart. Folly bounded ahead, taking in all the new scents with his nose pressed to the ground. The golden leaves glinted in the late afternoon light, which imbued Mairead with a sense of peace. If only she could find the Bard's-cursed tower.

She glanced north again and could no longer see the two red dots in the distance—thank Mother Morgha! Before they'd ventured south into the Gold Wood, she was certain the red brothers had moved closer to Arem, though it was hard to tell. They certainly weren't in Thoan anymore.

Could the red brothers see her like she saw them?

She shivered, and persevered onward, somehow knowing that once she found the tower, everything would be all right.

Her uncle stumbled, then caught himself on a tree.

"Uncle Howarth!" she cried, running over to him, guilt immediately flooding her chest. "I'm so sorry. I shouldn't have made you walk this far."

"It's all right, Mairy," he said. "But perhaps you two should go on and look for this tower without me."

"I don't think that's necessary," a voice came from somewhere behind them. "I know exactly where it is."

Mairead whirled around to spot not just one newcomer, but an entire group of people ambling toward them. Fig led the party with a huge grin on her face, with Emrah swooping overhead. Vaelor walked with a distinct limp and held Ziggy's arm for support, although the silversword woman gave no indication that Vaelor's weight was any trouble.

Derrin made a strangled noise of surprise as he came up behind Mairead. And she could see why.

Dev trudged behind the group looking more like a king than ever. An easy confidence flowed from his tousled brown hair to the sword strapped to his hip—despite a black eye and a torn shirt.

"Mairead," Dev called. "I like the new look, love."

FIG

Fig stepped over the threshold of the tower feeling like the Bard was smiling down upon her. Emrah, now a glowing ember in her consciousness, flitted over her head and circled up the stairs, clearly eager to inspect his home.

One thing, however, was not going her way: Knoll was no longer there. And this time, even his tools were gone. The ground floor of the tower was empty; only the powdery ghosts of coals remained in the hearth. Her buoyed spirits punctured a little, but as Mairead came in behind her, Fig hitched her smile back up. She wasn't sure how they would fix Vaelor's sword without a trustworthy blacksmith, but she'd worry about that tomorrow. Today, she was home with her friends.

The rest of the party filtered into the tower, forcing everyone to move upstairs. The two men who'd come with Mairead made themselves at home on the second level, where a few of the beds had been charred, while Fig and the rest headed to the top floor.

Her eyes were immediately drawn to the ceiling where Emrah had embedded gemstones over the years.

"Just like old times, eh, Fig?" Dev said, flopping down onto the bed he'd slept in the first time Emrah had brought them here.

"I don't know about 'old' times, but sure. I mean, I was just here the other day."

Mairead claimed a rope bed, and Ziggy tossed her and Dev's bags onto one of the top bunks before heading back downstairs, muttering something about checking the perimeter.

Vaelor had come up last and stood gazing out one of the wide windows. She felt like she'd barely gotten to really see him since rescuing him from the arena, and he looked like he'd been dragged through the darkest pits of Malhela and back. Bruises and scrapes marred his face, and his clothes were torn and bloody. But she knew it wasn't just from the arena; his time with the silverswords had clearly not been pleasant. She pulled the sword bag out from under the bed and walked over to hand it to him.

He turned to look into her face, and her heart nearly cracked. The ring around his eyes was bloody—not just the silver ring turned red, but flecks of blood encircling it, and she somehow knew it wasn't from an injury. She held the bag out to him, fists clenched, knuckles white.

"You keep it, goldfire," he said, touching her arm. "You've kept it safe this long."

Fig swallowed and turned away. Mother Savidah had said the magic would fade. How much longer did Vaelor have? She took a deep breath, schooling her shaky emotions, and went over to sit beside Mairead. The red sister looked up in surprise, and Fig was startled again by her new facial tattoos, which she'd only glimpsed briefly in the Gold Wood. "We need to fix Vaelor's sword—soon. Mother Savidah gave me some ideas, and I think we'll need your help too."

"M...Mother Savidah?" Mairead asked. "You spoke to the holy mother? But...what of Avelina?"

Fig gave her half a smile. "We've got a lot to catch up on. And the hearth is free, eh? Let's talk over dinner."

The seven of them and Emrah crammed onto the first floor of the tower, basking in the warmth of the hearth. Mairead's dog Folly had fallen asleep on the second floor. Mairead's uncle Howarth sat on a stool, with his friend Derrin on the floor beside him, one knee drawn to his chest. Dev and Ziggy sat on the stairs, their legs hanging over the sides. Ziggy would leave every so often to patrol around the tower. The first time Ziggy went out, Vaelor attempted to assist with the watch valiantly, but Mairead put her foot down.

"I'm all out of holy water," she reminded him. "And some of those wounds look pretty bad. We'll need to find some soon before you get blood poisoning."

"And not just for that. I think we'll need it for fixing his sword, as well," Fig added. Vaelor, sitting on his stool next to Fig, merely nodded. She wanted to lean into him, to bask deeper into his presence, but his injuries were hard to ignore, so she simply ran her hand gently over his knee. Her heart soared when she saw the corner of his mouth turn up in a smile.

The scent of roast vorse eagle filled the tower, and the party shared what stores of food they had. Fig hadn't been formally introduced to Howarth or Derrin, but the red sister had assured Fig privately that they were trustworthy. Derrin eventually sidled up to Dev, and the two of them got to talking in hushed voices in the corner.

After Fig finished eating, a warm sense of peace stealing over her, she elbowed Mairead jovially in the side. "So, you've traveled the Twist *how* many times? We barely made it through once!"

A wide grin spread across the girl's face, and Fig studied the new tattoo. Mairead had caught her up while they settled in earlier, and Fig wasn't surprised to hear Mother Savidah had orchestrated such a thing. Fig shuddered to think of Mairead fighting off a red brother on her own, but here she was, alive, and somehow happy. She had a different air to her, or perhaps it was the tattoo that made Fig perceive her differently.

"We need to get some holy water," Fig said to her under her breath.

Mairead nodded. "I know. I can tell something is fading in Vaelor... I don't know how to explain it. But how will we fix the sword? Can we just have any blacksmith do it?"

Fig twisted her lip to bite a corner of it. She thought back to when she was sailing over the city streets, looking through Emrah's eyes—the silver glow running next to Fig had red flickers in it. "I don't know. I have a feeling that fixing this won't be as simple as mending the sword and tossing some blood and water on it. So probably not."

Vaelor snorted. His eyes were closed, and his head leaned against the wall, but he was clearly listening.

Mairead sputtered. "*Tossing* some blood and water—" She scoffed. "I don't even have the energy to tell you off for that one. And what is Dev doing here? I thought he was staying in Tirnalore?" Mairead cocked her head toward him.

Ziggy came back in from her latest patrol, joining Dev and Derrin's conversation with ease.

"*That* is a very good question," Fig said slowly. "Dev!"

The heir to the throne lifted his head from his conversation with Derrin like a kid caught talking in class. "Yes?"

"What in the name of the Bard are you even doing in Tytan?"

The whole room quieted. Fig hadn't had a chance to ask as they'd fled Rayva, only slowing their arduous pace when they reached the golden boughs of the Gold Wood, and discovering Mairead shortly after.

He ran a hand through his already casually messy hair, then gripped the hilt of the new sword. "I heard of the competition for this sword, and—"

"And he left his safe haven in Tirnalore for a chance at the relic," Ziggy interrupted, taking a swig of Knoll's ale that they'd opened.

Dev gave her a look. "Well, yes. And I got it, so all the Bard's luck to me, eh?"

Fig gave an exasperated sigh, but she had been impressed by Dev in Halvard's Pit. She'd never seen his magic so strong, and nowhere near the amplification of the Gold Wood. That glass wave between the two of them had been the most impressive magic she'd seen since...well...Shadryn on the Isle of Nithe. Her insides went cold at the memory.

Dev went on. "And Derrin tells me here that there's a resistance in Tytan, who've been trying to work against Rhivven." Dev looked pleased with himself, as if he'd done all the work. Derrin ducked his head with a small smile.

"So you're not going back to the Fienn Da," Fig guessed. Beside her, Vaelor sighed, still leaning his back against the wall.

Dev shook his head. "No. I'm done running and hiding. I've got the Sword of Morin, and a plan to make allies of the dwarves. But first we need to get Vaelor fixed up. Where can we get some holy water?"

No one even tried to suggest that they just bring him to a fount. But he was in rough shape—not only suffering from the lack of connection to his sword but from a myriad of injuries. Mairead had dressed them as best she could, but some had been festering for days. Fig's chest constricted as the room quieted. She reached beside her to pat his knee once more, one of the safest places to touch him right now.

"I...think..." Mairead said haltingly, "we'll need to steal some from the nearest fount. Arem, maybe. Or Ghorvost might be safer." Her eyes darkened as she looked nervously northwest. She had changed so much since Fig and Vaelor had left her on their journey to the Twist. Had that only been a week ago? The girl was suggesting stealing from a fount—timid, caring Mairead, in her black cloak and red face tattoos.

"Why would Ghorvost be safer?" Fig asked, shifting in her seat uncomfortably. She avoided the village if she could; her friend Bruna had been from there, and they had a mutual acquaintance named Chamille who had more often than not wanted Bruna dead over the years. Fig, by proxy, hadn't wanted to tangle with the woman, a crystal mage who liked to dip her gemmed fingertips into politics, and often didn't bat a crystal-laden eyelash if one of her number got killed doing her work.

Mairead looked northwest again, as if seeing something Fig

couldn't. "I'm worried that the red brothers followed us out of Thoan and went to Arem."

"Well, they could be checking Ghorvost next, or Rayva," Fig reasoned.

"They're still in Arem," Mairead said quietly in a ghostly voice.

"H-How do you know?"

Mairead tapped under her left eye. "I can see them. In the distance. They're just two red dots—usually together to make one bigger glowing dot. But I tracked them the whole way after leaving Thoan. They're in Arem, probably going over Derrin's cart and talking to the tavernkeeper."

Derrin spluttered into his ale but didn't say anything.

"Ghorvost it is then," Fig said. Mairead's red dots sounded an awful lot like how she and Emrah could sense each other now that they were properly bonded. "That's the closest?"

"Unless you want to go back to Rayva."

Fig shook her head violently. "If the Bard never sees me in Rayva for the rest of my days, I'll be happy. Although, now I wish I'd actually stolen that holy water shipment me and Avelina were escorting..."

Mairead scoffed, demanding the full tale. After Fig recounted it, silence descended on them once more, as everyone contemplated how much easier everything would be with two full barrels of holy water.

"But what about his sword?" Dev said, nodding at Vaelor.

The silversword's eyes fluttered, and it looked like he was about to fall asleep until Dev spoke. His bloody eyes opened, and he tensed, gazing right at Fig; she gave him a reassuring smile, even though the inside of her chest was aching.

"The sword..." Fig began. "I have it here. I believe we need holy water—and of course, blood—once the sword is mended. There was a dwarf here a little while ago, a blacksmith, but he's gone now. He even took his tools."

Good, Emrah said. *Can't believe the Feijowa said he could stay here.*

Fig smiled at the dragonet, perched on the stairs above Ziggy. Her chest swelled with joy just looking at him. When her vision began to blur, she shook her head to clear it.

You really need to stop doing that, Emrah said to just her.

She ducked her head, cheeks warming. *Sorry.*

It's all right, Svoran. I agreed to complete the bond. I just meant you need to stop doing it by accident—it'll get you into trouble when you're not seeing through your own eyes. You're lucky you didn't fall on your face when you were running from the pit.

Well, maybe when we get two seconds when we're not about to die—or someone else is—where we can test it out more. Do you think you can see through mine too?

Sparks snorted from Emrah's nostrils, and everyone else looked at him.

Neither offered an explanation, and Fig smirked into her mug of ale.

Vaelor looked like he was about to fall asleep again. Fig wasn't surprised after the ordeal he'd been through. She got Ziggy's help getting him up to one of the beds on the third floor, Mairead trailing closely behind. The silversword carried Vaelor up the two flights of stairs as easily as a sack of apples, then left to hold watch down on the ground floor. It sounded like Howarth followed them, but made himself at home on the second floor, meanwhile Dev and Derrin's quiet conversation continued where they sat.

Once Vaelor was settled in one of the rope beds, Mairead checked him over once more, using some water and clean cloths from her satchel to go over his wounds again.

"He needs a healing," Mairead whispered when she was finished. "It can wait, but not too long."

Fig tapped her fingers on her thigh, careful not to release sparks. Her skin buzzed with the magic of the Gold Wood. She'd worried about losing control when they'd entered the Gold Wood, but now that the bond formation had calmed down, her control was stronger than ever before.

"Good," she said. "Because I don't think I have the energy to rob a fount tonight."

Mairead snorted, then looked closer at Fig. "Are you serious?"

"I was thinking about it. But I haven't slept much lately. Had a rough night in a tavern last night, after I learned the specifics about that tournament..."

"Well, your ropes are ready, my lady," Mairead said, gesturing to the alcove Fig had chosen.

She chuckled. "You know, I'm getting used to them."

"Unfortunately, so am I."

CHAPTER 36

FIG

Halvard's Pit was filled with smoke with Fig at the center of a tornado of flames of her own doing. She coughed, choking on the acrid smoke.

Smoke.

She lurched up out of her dream, managing to not get tangled in the rope bed for once. Only the smoke was *here*—in the tower.

Barking. A shout from downstairs sounded—pained.

Vaelor and Mairead were still asleep. Mairead was closest, so Fig dashed over and shook her, shouting, "Wake up!" then rushed to Vaelor, doing the same. Both responded quickly, though Vaelor took longer to get to his feet. Dev apparently hadn't found his way upstairs last night, as his bed looked untouched. Another shout came from downstairs, and Fig darted toward the staircase, leaving Mairead to help Vaelor.

Emrah? she demanded.

Gold flickered over her vision as she dropped into his sight—

he was in the Gold Wood and could see the plume of smoke rising from the tower in the pre-dawn light.

I'm on my way, he told her.

She put a hand on the tower wall as she ran down the circular stairs, the texture vibrating against her fingertips as sparks surged out. The second floor was empty, but that wasn't necessarily a good thing. Where was Dev? And Ziggy?

Her answer came as soon as she spilled onto the ground floor. She could see the purple wind and flash of steel fighting off two figures in the semi-darkness. Flames licked at the tower door, eating away at the wooden ceiling and the few furnishings. Howarth tended to Derrin by the far wall; he seemed to have been badly burned, but they couldn't escape through the flaming doorway. Folly was sniffing Derrin's shoulder, ears back and tail down as he whined.

Fig stared at the flames, hatred burning in her core. How dare they? Emrah's home! Her home too, she had come to think of it.

She ran a hand through the air like she was snatching the flames away, connecting to them and putting them out. But the flames seemed to jump right back into existence as soon as she made to join Dev and Ziggy outside. She snatched the air again, pulling harder this time, willing them to go out. They flickered out, then came right back, again licking at the ceiling.

She heard Mairead on the stairs behind her, struggling to assist Vaelor, so she moved out of the way.

She needed to stop the fires—or get out the door and join the fight—otherwise, all five of them would burn to death. She dimly registered the fact that Vaelor hardly seemed strong enough to walk; Mairead practically stumbled down the stairs with the heavy Viren.

She focused on the door. The flames continued to flicker back to life every single time she tried to put them out.

Emrah, I need help! The flames won't go out, I can't even—

"Fig!" Mairead called as she finally deposited Vaelor beside Derrin. "It's the red brothers! They must have followed me here."

Fig looked out through the tendrils of fire in the doorway. Dev was on the ground, two figures standing over him, and Ziggy was nowhere in sight.

The door itself had been forced from the frame and lay burning in the grass just outside, blocking the way. Flames wreathed the door and frame, forming a barrier of fire.

She charged forward, flames be damned, using a drop of energy right as she met them to ask them not to burn her. She held her breath and leapt.

It worked, mostly.

Scalded, she landed just past the burning door. These flames were like nothing she'd ever dealt with before, and she'd seen her fair share.

Sparks dripped heavy from her fingers as she faced the two red brothers, who signed with those intricate hand movements above Dev's prone figure. Dev's eyes were open, but he seemed unable to move. Ziggy had also fallen somewhere in the grass a few feet away behind the red brothers, and Fig couldn't tell if she was alive or dead.

Fig shot gold flames at the red brothers, a massive column of fire fueled by the magic of the Gold Wood and her newly solidified connection to Emrah. But she didn't stick around to see if the flames had struck their target. She rolled in the dewy grass to the other side of Dev, and slapped her hand down on the ground, connecting with her core flames and completing the spell she'd taught herself during those long hours in Tirnalore so long ago. A roaring circle of golden flames erupted from the grass around the red brothers. Her connection was strong—stronger than ever. The wall of golden flames roared, soaring high above their heads. On the other side of the curtain of flames, the two men shifted, their red tunics flapping from the sudden change in the air around them. Their gestures also changed, and all too quickly, her fire circle began to weaken. The flames dropped, sinking slowly toward the ground.

"No," she growled. Fig yanked on Dev's shoulder, urging him

farther away while the flame barrier still afforded them some protection.

Mairead leapt through the flaming doorway, landing a few feet from Fig. The girl's tattoos were glowing, and she held what appeared to be a butcher's knife, her black cloak fluttering around her.

The fire circle dropped with a final gesture.

Fig's eyes widened as Mairead lunged at one of the red brothers, ducking under the wide-arced kick he sent flying her way, accompanied by a hand gesture. Fig didn't know what kind of magic the red brothers wielded, but it was clearly blessed by their goddess's other face, the face of death.

Mairead ducked and wove between their magic with a precision and expertise Fig had never seen before, slashing with her butcher knife and somehow interpreting the red brothers' movements before they made them.

Dev began to stir. Fig helped him up, and he drew the Sword of Morin with a ring that echoed through the small clearing.

Fig took the opportunity to scramble back to the door, her hands reaching for the flames already there. Vaelor was still inside with Howarth, Derrin, and Folly.

Fig! Emrah called, and the glowing ember in her consciousness flooded her peripheral vision just before the dragonet landed on her shoulder. A surge of flames scoured her core, her already overpowered energy doubling.

Emrah, can you help me put them out? They've used some kind of magic on them; they won't go out!

I've never put out fires before, but let's give it a try!

He stretched his wings from his perch on her shoulder, and she put all her energy into snuffing out the flames. Both hands outstretched, she *yanked*, her chest pulsing with a new energy now that Emrah sat on her shoulder.

It was enough to pull the flames away from the doorway—for how long, she didn't know. Emrah leapt from her shoulder as she jumped over the charred wooden door and fell to the floor beside

Vaelor. He sat slumped against the side of the staircase beside Derrin, eyelids fluttering as he drifted in and out of consciousness.

"Vaelor? Vaelor!"

She grabbed his shoulders, and he focused his gaze on her.

"Goldfire," he whispered, clutching a wound at his ribs.

Fig cursed herself for not stealing holy water from a fount last night. He was clearly in a bad way; she just didn't know if it was from his waning connection to his broken sword, a result of the beatings he'd taken while in the silverswords' custody, or both.

Her vision blurred, and she thought for a moment she was looking through Emrah's eyes again, but then she dashed her palms across the tears forming in her eyes. "Vaelor! We have to get you out of here!"

Howarth had done his best to get Derrin on his feet, but clearly, the older man couldn't give her a hand with the big Viren. Folly was cowering on the floor, head on his paws, and whimpering.

The flames at the doorframe and fallen door were already rekindling, bursting back into life around the charred edges.

"Gods!" she cursed. "Hurry!" she called to Howarth.

I wish I could help you, Svoran, Emrah said from outside somewhere. *You need that other silversword to carry him. Where'd she get to?*

Ziggy! She's—fallen—the last I saw her, she was in the grass—

She could feel Emrah swoop away, muttering curses to the red brothers, to Drakioryn, to all the gods that ever were.

"Come on, Vaelor. Time to go." She put his arm around her and shoved her shoulder under his armpit, groaning and pushing with her legs. "Bard's *quills*, you're heavy."

"*Goldfire...*"

She staggered under his weight, inching her way to the door with the man in tow. He seemed to come to himself a little and shuffled his feet under him. Thanking the gods for whatever small help she could get, Fig connected with her inner fire and reached out to the flames licking the doorframe, asking them not to burn her or Vaelor. But their progress was slow, and she yelped as she earned a few burns, focusing more on shielding Vaelor than herself.

Confident that he had his footing while she guarded them from the flames, she didn't realize she'd been letting him walk on his own until he stumbled and fell to his knees, collapsing into the grass.

"Vaelor!" Fig threw herself onto the ground beside him, rolling him onto his side to look at him.

"Fig! Here!" Mairead dashed over, fumbling with something in her hands.

Fig looked up, dumbstruck. The two red brothers were dead, lying in pools of blood in the grass. Mairead had discarded her bloody butcher knife inches from Fig's knees, and the girl had some kind of flask in her hand she was working to uncork.

"Holy water," Mairead explained, "from the brothers."

Drakioryn's claws, Emrah remarked in awe, fluttering over to land on Fig's shoulder, his closeness like a warm blanket draped across her shoulders.

Fig reached up to cup Emrah's head, focusing on Vaelor's face as Mairead worked. Vaelor's eyebrows were furrowed, and his forehead damp with sweat. When she wiped her hand across it, she found his skin as hot as the flames they'd just walked through, even though the heat shouldn't have touched him.

Mairead was muttering something, pouring water on the worst of his wounds, and eventually she gave Fig a gentle nudge to back up, which she did, retreating still on her knees, clutching one of Emrah's claws.

A hand grasped her other shoulder, and Fig jumped, turning to find Dev and Ziggy standing burned and bedraggled by the tower, which was still aflame. The unkillable flames by the doorway licked the ceiling leading to the second floor, even though the red brothers were dead.

The tears that had threatened earlier broke loose. They had already lost so much.

Dev's arms went around her as he knelt beside her, and Fig swayed back as she watched the tower burn. Ziggy's hair was singed, but the silversword's attention was on something behind Fig.

She pulled away from Dev and twisted to see Vaelor propping himself up on one elbow and coughing—his skin now glowing compared to the pallor that had settled over him in the past few days.

Bloody silver eyes met her gaze. "Goldfire."

FIG

The tower still burned.

Dev squeezed her shoulder as Fig stumbled away to where Vaelor lay in the grass. Kneeling next to him, Mairead wiped her bloody hands on her black cloak, picked up the butcher's knife, and ran it through the grass to get the blood off. "The infection was worse than I thought," Mairead whispered, looking haunted at her misjudgment. "But it's all right now."

Fig hesitated a moment, unsure where it was safe to touch Vaelor's skin, but she *needed* to touch some part of him. She ran her thumb down his face from his temple down his jaw. He closed his eyes briefly at the touch, and his hand fumbled in the grass to find hers. She quickly grasped his fingers so he wasn't searching long. "Vaelor," she breathed. "Are you... Are you all right?"

He swallowed, his throat bobbing. "I... I think so." He'd looked as pale as a corpse when she dragged him from the tower, but he'd regained some of his color after Mairead's healing. The nasty wound on his arm was completely healed, along with many of the others. He still had a few bruises and ash in some places, but he was alive. She nodded, giving his hand a squeeze before bringing her attention back to the tower.

"Mairead," Fig said, "the fires...they won't go out. Do you have any idea what they might have done?" She gave a half glance toward the red brothers who lay dead in the grass. Fig had thought killing the brothers would have ended their spell, but the flames seemed to have a mind of their own.

Mairead shuddered, staring at the burning tower. The second floor would collapse if the fire was allowed to rage much longer. Fig stood and headed to the door. She could stop it for a few seconds at a time, slowing the damage until they figured it out.

Emrah had gone off to survey the woods directly around the tower, but as soon as he returned to her shoulder, she gave it another try, connecting with her inner flames and snuffing the ones eating away at their home.

The flames died out, and a sickly terror settled over her as she took in the extent of the damage. The fires had eaten through more of the ceiling than she'd thought; a gaping hole exposed the second floor, its edges mottled with black ash. The corner of a bed alcove was visible, the heavy frame sagging through the small hole. The doorframe looked ready to collapse, though the stones around it seemed stable even without the wooden frame for support. The tower door, flat in the grass, had been almost completely burned—Fig considered it a lost cause. It was the rest of the tower that needed saving now.

With sickening red sparks, the flames on the ceiling and what was left of the wooden doorframe flickered back to life. It had only been a few seconds.

"Agh," she groaned, slamming a sparking fist down on her thigh.

Dev came over and covered the flames in his amethyst wind, starving them from the air they needed. They went out again.

And everyone waited.

Fig wasn't surprised when they sparked back to life a few seconds later. They devoured the already unwanted hole in the ceiling and continued licking the corner of the bed alcove, feeding on the ancient wood and spreading farther along the ceiling.

Fig reached out a desperate hand and yanked the flames back, hard. Now she was sweating.

Drakioryn's scaly backside, Emrah cursed. *Those briigards. This is worse than when the Feijowa attacked.*

"Dev and I can keep putting it out," Fig insisted, earning a nod from Dev, who rallied purple air to his cause.

Not forever, Emrah said.

Fig put her fingers over his claws that gripped her shoulder.

I'm sorry, my friend. Her eyes stung.

"I may have an idea," Mairead said, coming to stand beside the two mages as the flames returned to devour once more.

"By all means," Dev replied.

"If the red brothers found us here—able to follow at that distance—it means they could see *me*, like how I could see them in the distance. So if I have some powers like the red brothers..." She popped open the cork on the bottle of holy water and dipped her finger in it, tracing a complicated symbol in the air and gesturing with her hand as if pushing it toward the flaming tower.

Fig swallowed the lump in her throat, watching the flames. She didn't know what Mairead had done but prayed to the gods —from Mother Morgha to the Bard himself—that it would work. She even tossed a prayer to Drakioryn for good measure.

A creak and a groan sounded from the second floor, and the bed alcove shifted farther into the enlarged hole. Everyone tensed, waiting for the floor to give out. But by some grace of Morgha, the flames began to sink into the wood and the walls, disappearing like they were returning to wherever they had come from. Eventually, none remained; only the charred wood was left behind.

They waited. And waited. Nobody moved. Ziggy came over and clapped a hand on Dev's back, and even Derrin and Howarth ambled over to watch. But no further sparks ignited, and no flames returned. They seemed finally—truly—doused.

Fig threw her arms around Mairead, Emrah's wings fluttering in both their hair.

"Ow!" Fig exclaimed, laughing through tears, and reaching to help Emrah untangle himself from her hair.

You gotta warn me, Svoran! Emrah complained as he lurched away, starting a lap around the tower to no doubt inspect the damage.

Sorry, she told him, but she was smiling at Mairead.

As soon as the fires were out, Ziggy dragged the bodies of the dead red brothers into a thicket of whorlthorn bushes at the edge of the clearing, vowing to bury them out of sight.

"It's all my fault," Mairead told Fig as everyone agreed to move away from the tower and into the safety of the trees, to the opposite side of the clearing where Ziggy had put the bodies. "They must have been able to see me like I could see them. I led them right to the tower."

"How were you supposed to know?" Fig asked, shaking her head and putting a hand on the girl's arm. "The new tattoos suit you, you know."

Mairead ducked her head, staring at her feet as the bottom of her cloak brushed the dew-drenched grass.

Fig got Vaelor settled comfortably against a tree while Howarth and Derrin hobbled over, Mairead close at their heels inspecting the damage. Vaelor was still a little pale, his eyes bloodshot. Mairead had healed his body, but the connection to his broken sword was still destroying him.

When Fig turned to retrieve Vaelor's sword from the tower, his hand had shot out faster than she was expecting to caress her wrist. "I'll be back soon. I need to protect your sword, right?" She nodded to where they could both see the tower with a watery smile.

How much longer did he have?

She caught Mairead's attention after the girl finished checking

Derrin, and the two women headed into the clearing toward the tower.

"We need to do something for Vaelor," Fig insisted quietly.

Mairead nodded. "The wounds are healed," she assured Fig. "But the rest is...more complicated."

Fig nodded. "I suppose we should rescue our things first. I need to get his sword—I shouldn't have left it in there."

"We'll figure out something."

Fig was certain there was an answer somewhere, but only the Bard knew if they would find it in time.

Emrah's presence flared in her mind before she saw him swoop overhead, and she asked him, *Where are you headed?*

Patrol again, he said. *Who knows if anyone saw all that smoke, eh? I'll veer toward the road leading to the Carriage House in case there's a patrol nearby.*

Aye. Be safe, will you?

As long as you are.

Lifting their shirtfronts over their noses, the two women stepped gingerly over the burned threshold and surveyed the damage. The ground floor reeked of smoke, and the ceiling looked none too secure. The bed alcove still threatened to fall through the charred hole—or, by the gods, the whole floor might collapse under the weight—so Fig dashed as fast as she could for the stone stairs, which hugged the wall. Mairead swiftly followed, and the two of them ascended to the second level, where, of course, they could see the other side of the hole. The bed alcoves were heavy, and the entire floor would need to be replaced. The whole thing could collapse any minute.

Fig shook her head and continued to the top, eager to grab Vaelor's sword and get out.

They collected as much as they could, hands full with Mairead and Fig's bags, Vaelor's sword, and Ziggy's and Dev's things. "We'll have to make another trip for your friends' things," Fig said on their way down. They ran from the safety of the stairs to the doorway, passing under the unstable ceiling for a few precious seconds. . But as they emerged into the dawn light, Fig dropped her tunic from covering her mouth, inhaling the honey-sweet air tinged with the scent of charred wood.

You shouldn't have gone in there, Emrah said, winging over to Fig's shoulder and bumping her neck with his head. *When that collapses...*

It's fine, Fig said. *Just one more trip.*

How'd it go? Fig asked Emrah.

Fig and Mairead carried all the bags over to the group by the trees as Fig had her silent conversation with Emrah, though Fig tarried as she chose her thoughts.

Fine, he replied. *No silversword patrols as far as I flew—which was far. No one on the road to the Carriage House either. But to the west... You know that tavern?*

Green's? Why is it always that *tavern?*

Sure. That one. A large group was gathered there. I was worried they'd seen the smoke and were coming for the tower... But it was dwarves. *A lot of them. And they didn't look too happy.*

Ah, well, I'm not surprised. The missing heir returned and stole their sword. They're not coming here, *are they?*

Sparks snorted from Emrah's nostrils. *They headed north—as soon as I saw, I winged it back here.*

North? In broad daylight?

There was only one thing of great importance that the dwarves would gather over, particularly after having an ancient dwarven artifact stolen from them. The Mountain.

Mairead had already dropped off her bags, and Fig turned to eye the tower again.

Do you really need that stuff? Emrah said, nudging her again. She picked up the pace, eager to drop off the bags.

We don't have much left, she said simply. *None of us.*

I have you, and I'd like to keep you alive.

She smiled, rubbing her hand on his head, and giving him the tiniest shrug to get going. *I'll be fine,* she assured him.

You better.

Yes, mother.

Fig carefully handed Vaelor his sword bag, and Ziggy took the other bags off her hands to distribute them. Then Fig made her way back over to Mairead, who was already standing before the tower, hands on her hips. Mairead gave her a look, then the two of them covered their noses again and dashed across the ground floor for the safety of the stairs. Fig only breathed easy when she'd crested the top of the second floor, rising above the damage.

"We need a blacksmith to fix his sword," Mairead said, continuing their conversation from earlier. "We've got holy water now; the brothers always carry it on them. I just never thought..."

Fig bit the inside of her lip, thinking back to Mairead with the bloody butcher knife. "I'm sorry you had to do that."

Mairead shrugged. They stopped at the second floor, where Derrin and Howarth had slept—or intended on sleeping, in Derrin's case. Apparently he'd stayed up late with Dev and Ziggy on the ground floor. Fig guessed they'd all dozed off before the red brother's attack.

She tried to locate Derrin and Howarth's bags by sight before deciding what to do about them. Finally, Mairead spotted what might have once been bags—burned remains scattered beneath the damaged bed alcove.

"I'd thought we could have gotten Dev in here to whisk them closer," Fig said idly, shaking her head.

"They'll understand," Mairead said.

Fig nodded, turning to go. Then she put a soft hand on Mairead's shoulder. "How were you able to fight them?" she asked, unable to stop the words.

Mairead looked around the tower, perhaps avoiding Fig's gaze. "I can see their sigils. So I can see what magic they're drawing from and what they're about to do. I don't know, it just made sense to me, so I was able to get in there and fight them."

"They're drawing sigils in the air?"

Mairead nodded. "Essentially. Some of them require certain fingers to do certain strokes, and there's more to it that I don't really know." She shrugged, looking wistful.

"That would explain all those gestures," Fig said.

"I didn't realize I could use the sigil magic myself. There's a lot about the holy water I still don't know. I had no idea it could bless me with such magic."

Fig nodded. "Well, we have the holy water for Vaelor now anyway.

"At least we didn't have to steal any from an innocent sister's fount." She shuddered. "Failing to protect the holy water is something that could easily get you removed from the sisterhood."

"I just wish I knew what had happened to Knoll," Fig said as they headed back down. "Wait, Emrah said a large group of dwarves was heading north. Maybe he's with them!"

"What are the dwarves up to?" Mairead asked.

"I don't know," Fig said. "But I doubt it's safe. The silverswords were keeping a close eye on the dwarves in Rayva leading up to the tournament—they had to know that giving away the Sword of Morin was going to be a problem, so there're more patrols and silversword presence everywhere. And now the whole situation's even worse with Dev appearing."

Mairead nodded. "Nothing's safe anymore," she said, her normally cheerful voice a monotone. Fig felt a pang of sadness at the change.

They reached the bottom of the stairs, met each other's gaze, and raced across the ground to the doorway.

When they were outside, Fig bumped into Mairead's shoulder gently and said, "Maybe someday it will be again. We just have to get Dev on the throne, eh?"

Fig spotted the ember in her consciousness—Emrah was sailing between the aurans—while they walked over to the group.

"I've been thinking about that," Mairead said. "Derrin works with some kind of resistance of people who oppose Rhivven."

"No wonder he sidled up to Dev last night," Fig said.

"I don't think taking that sword is going to help with the dwarf situation," Mairead said. "Remember after Nova Istra?"

"I'll never forget Nova Istra," Fig muttered. "The Feijowa were furious when they thought Emrah had stolen it. I just don't know why Dev took it upon himself to enter that tournament for a sword the dwarves might have won for themselves. Except..." A powerful sword, for a powerful mage...

Her strides grew faster as she marched toward the group, toward Dev.

He looked up from the tree he was leaning against, the Sword of Morin strapped to his hip.

"What is your plan for that sword?" Fig demanded. "You're giving it back to the dwarves, right?"

Dev balked at her, blinking a few times. The way he opened and closed his mouth made Fig narrow her eyes in suspicion. Why *would* Dev take it from the dwarves, right in front of them?

"Tell me, Dev," she said slowly, "why *exactly* did you leave the safety of Tirnalore, where you were gathering mage allies and funds, to sneak back into the country where every silversword is looking for you?"

He stuck out his chin and stood slowly, facing her down. "To claim the sword. I told you."

"But for what purpose?" He hesitated a second too long. "I knew it. You weren't seriously considering Welding with it..." Her voice was deathly low. "You were, weren't you?"

She saw his throat bob up and down as he swallowed.

Mairead stifled a gasp. "No, Dev!" The girl's voice was surprisingly strong. She'd been the one to administer Afrith's crossover; they had seen what could happen when a mage attempted the ritual. "It would kill you."

"I know. And I'm not going to," he said softly. Fig's ire flickered out completely.

He was scared.

"I..." Dev began. Everyone was looking at him, but he turned to address Ziggy. "I won't lie that it inspired my initial motivation for retrieving the sword. But I've come to my senses. I thought—I thought it would make me stronger. Strong enough to fight Shadryn. To reclaim the throne. To keep my friends from getting hurt in the process."

A deep voice from below chimed in, "Being stronger isn't always the solution." Vaelor's bloody gaze met his.

Dev put his hand on the sword hilt, nodding. "I know, my friend. I know that now."

Silence descended on them like the gold glittering down from the aurans. Fig stared at the tower, her gaze locking on the charred opening where the door had once stood.

"What will you do with it?" Vaelor asked Dev, nodding at the sword.

"I plan to give it back to the dwarves."

"Good," a voice said. "Because they're planning to kill you for it otherwise." Knoll strolled into the clearing, his hammer slung casually over one shoulder.

CHAPTER 38

FIG

"Knoll!" Fig shouted, relief surging through her.

The dwarf slung his hammer down from his shoulder, but he didn't put it away. "Everyone's looking for you," he said in his impossibly low voice. "From the Sylvans to the Feijowa clans. They're well riled up after the stunt you pulled in Halvard's Pit."

Then why are they heading for the Mountain? Emrah's voice chimed in. He was dripping sparks as he sailed over and landed on Fig's shoulder. *And how did I not see you coming?*

Knoll's braided beard twitched, and Fig thought he might be hiding a smirk beneath it. "Never you mind, dragonet. Although, you'd better hurry if you want to catch the gathering and return what's rightfully ours."

"Can't we just give it to you?" Fig asked, glancing between Dev and Knoll. Dev shook his head.

Knoll took a step back. "No, no, no. I'm not worthy to hold the Sword of Morin."

Fig's brows furrowed. "But you *can* help us fix a silversword weapon, right? You said so before."

Knoll ran a hand down his beard and surveyed everyone assembled, then finally put his hammer in the thick strap at his belt. "I could, but I don't know anything about..." He gestured vaguely at Vaelor, who was still slumped against the tree, following the conversation silently.

"We'll figure that part out," Mairead said, coming up beside Fig and hooking her arm.

Fig's lip trembled, and she squeezed Mairead's arm in return.

"Let me see it, then. It—er—doesn't look like we have much time," he said quietly.

Hands shaking, Fig fumbled with the flap on the bag that contained Vaelor's sword, the only thing linking him to life. She knelt on the ground and pulled out the pieces one by one, arranging them just as she had at the tavern in Rayva.

Knoll knelt beside her and silently ran a hand over them without touching the metal. With a groan and some audible popping of joints, he got back to his feet and tugged on his braids. "Something's waning in the sword, I'm afraid. I think... You'll need something stronger to temper the cracks so we can bring it back to life. Kind of like...over in Pan Vidda, they have a way of mending pottery. They fill the cracks with gold, making the broken pieces stronger, and in that case, filled with beauty. If we only had a stronger metal..."

Something tightened in Fig's throat like she had the hands of Morgha choking the life out of her. Vaelor's sword was dead... dying...? Of course, that made sense, it was in a dozen pieces. But hearing the words come from Knoll in this way...

"Something stronger?" Ziggy asked. "Like what?"

"Bloodril," Dev said, hefting the Sword of Morin. "Bloodril is the strongest metal, isn't it?"

Knoll shook his head. "Of course. But the clans wouldn't let just anyone have bloodril. And there's only one forge powerful enough to temper it."

"And where's that?" Fig asked, already knowing.

"The Mountain."

"Then that's where we're going," Fig said. "Dev needs to present the sword to the clans, and that's where they're headed. Maybe we can bargain with them for some bloodril to fix Vaelor's sword."

Knoll raised a bushy eyebrow.

"Will you come with us?" she asked him. "Will you try to fix his sword?"

"Oh, aye. I said I would. I've waited all my life to work the dragonhead forge. I'm not about to turn it down now, even if all the silverswords slit our throats after."

With that pleasant image in their heads, they readied to go, gathering what little they needed to take. Vaelor was able to walk, but a certain listlessness made Ziggy walk next to him and offer him her arm. They all made their way north, with the exception of Howarth, who insisted on remaining behind with Folly to watch over the tower. Mairead threw her arms around both her uncle and Folly before they set off, tears glittering in her eyes. She'd tried to convince him to go to Green's Tavern, but Derrin shook his head, insisting everywhere was dangerous for them now. Howarth had assured her Folly would alert him of anyone approaching while he camped in the wood.

Derrin walked beside Dev, as if he'd wanted nothing more than to follow Dev across Tytan if he could. Dev seemed to have that effect on everyone. Mairead kept an eye on Derrin, but his wounds seemed safe enough to delay a major healing for now.

Emrah sailed over their heads as the midday sun peeked through the aurans, gold light glinting all around them. Fig soaked in the magic of the wood, watching the glitter sift from the leaves. Every time she walked through here, she wondered if it would be her last.

Entering the Mountain might truly be the last thing she ever did—the dwarves' anger and the manner in which they were storming the Mountain were sure to draw silversword attention. But if there was a chance they could ally with the dwarves and fix Vaelor's sword, then she would take it.

Even though they were walking toward certain death—be it at the end of a silversword blade or a dwarven one. She slipped her hand around Vaelor's arm as they walked.

"Hey, goldfire," he said quietly.

"Hey yourself, Vae."

A small smile graced his lips. "I knew I should have never let you meet my *mazir* and hear that."

She smiled back sadly. Words of reassurance swirled in her throat, but she couldn't bring herself to say any of them.

We're going to fix this.

You'll be all right.

She couldn't guarantee any of that. So she continued walking beside him, the only reassurance she could offer—just *being there*.

Before leaving the Gold Wood, they paused briefly to share their remaining rations. The morning had not been kind to them, but Fig was finally beginning to feel alert and hungry.

Maybe now's a good time to try that experiment, Emrah told her. *Nobody's tried to kill us for a good three hours straight!*

Fig burst out laughing, and Derrin looked at her.

"Sorry," she muttered, waving vaguely at Emrah.

"Yes, you'll have to get used to that," Dev told Derrin. "Fig's got a *special* connection with Emrah."

Ziggy shared Dev's mocking grin.

Fig's stomach flipped, and she blurted out, "We, uh, completed the familiar bond. I forgot to tell you. I figured it out."

"You completed it? I thought you'd already bonded with him." Dev's eyes grew curious, and he looked her over as if checking for horns and scales.

"When we went to Mar Nevan, Mother Savidah told me it wasn't complete, and after that, I got an idea. It was blood and fire that we both needed to exchange. We'd only done half of the ritual when we first met. Now it's complete, I'm sure of it."

"When did this happen?"

Ziggy, too, looked interested. Fig remembered vividly telling them in that Fienn-Da safehouse back in Tirnalore about the bond, when she knew nothing about it. Not that she knew much more now, only that they'd certainly done *something*.

"Erm...right before Halvard's Pit."

Dev scoffed incredulously. "Only you, Fig. No wonder your flames were so..." He gestured wildly with his hand.

"I know," she said, gaze flicking up at Emrah. "But it worked out."

"I thought you were having a heart attack when you came out of your tunnel."

"You saw me in the arena?"

"Well, I didn't realize it was *you* until after I got the sword. Didn't think there was any way in all the Bard's stories *you'd* be in the pit."

"I could have said the same about you."

"Well, care to share the joke with the rest of us?" Dev said, nodding up at Emrah.

"Oh," Fig said, heat rushing to her face. "There's...I can... Apparently, I can see through Emrah's eyes now."

Ziggy let out a low whistle.

Fig glanced at Vaelor out of the corner of her eyes and could see him looking back at her.

"It...er...happened a few times in the pit, when I didn't realize what had happened. We wanted to try and see if it went the other way."

"Things are always better both ways," Dev said with a rakish wink, and an elbow into Derrin's side—who coughed incredulously. "Give it a try, why don't you?"

Fig ignored Dev's innuendo and sent a questioning feeling to Emrah. He let out a chirp in response. She had begun to notice feelings passing between them in addition to thoughts and words.

Ready, Svoran?

Ready.

She paid more attention to their surroundings than ever, studying the widely spaced aurans and wondering how close they were to the Mountain. Suddenly a green sheen slipped over her eyesight, but far from ruining her vision, it sharpened it. She could see the Mountain clearly in the far distance through the trees. Her new vision revealed details of shrubs and rocks at an impossible distance. Colors were more vibrant; light and shadow more contrasted.

"Emrah! You can really see this far?" Fig gasped.

A snort from above was her answer.

I hope I don't make your vision worse when I'm in your head, she told him privately.

Not at all. It just makes everything sort of gold.

She smiled. *I'm seeing in green. Can you still see out of your own eyes when you slip into mine?*

Of course, how do you think I didn't fall out of the sky? It's…a bit odd though, telling both apart.

Hmm, she thought at him. *Your view usually takes over my whole vision. I wonder if I can work on that.*

A chirp and a wing-snap came in response.

While Fig filled in the others on her new power, and they all readied to set off again, the dragonet soared away to scout out the Mountain. Fig knew he'd been inside it before, in a failed attempt to retrieve the Sword of Morin for the Feijowa clan, but she wasn't entirely sure humans would fit through the same passageways Emrah had been able to enter. Still, the dwarf gathering must have a way in somewhere.

Fig glanced at Knoll. He'd kept to himself since the trip from the tower, but now he leaned against a tree, gazing north. "How come you went back to the tower? You didn't want to go to the Mountain with the others?"

"I thought the prince might have gone there with the sword," he said. "I've seen your faces plastered over Tytan together; figured he'd come find you if you were still there."

"And you didn't tell anyone about the tower, did you?" Warmth filled Fig's chest.

He grunted. "Not my place to tell. The Feijowa owed me a favor. I just needed a hearth to borrow."

"Are you not in the Feijowa clan yourself?"

Knoll shook his head. "No clan."

"Oh. Do you know how to get in the Mountain?"

Another shake of his head.

A smile pulled up the corner of Fig's mouth. Knoll had given up going with the dwarf gathering to storm the Mountain, just to go back to the tower, to...what, warn them? Her smile bloomed larger, and Knoll's beard twitched. She wondered whether he was smiling too or frowning in annoyance. She didn't want to press him any further, but felt like they'd gained another ally, finally.

Without warning, Fig's vision went green.

Um, hello Emrah?

Fig! I've found the dwarves, but they've almost disappeared into the Mountain. I can lead you to the entrance, but I'd like to follow them inside.

Really? Wait, are you sure that's safe? Fig glanced around the group in panic, her enhanced vision making her nerves jangle even more. "We have to go. Now," she announced aloud.

Emrah ignored her worries, and for a brief moment, Fig attempted to look through his eyes to see what he was up to, but she wasn't quite able to do that at will just yet. The ability had come and gone during moments of high stress in the pit, which was not ideal.

Ziggy helped Vaelor stand, while everyone else scrambled to their feet. Fig was already marching toward the direction Emrah had disappeared. With his vision, she could see an incredible distance. Scrubby bushes stubbled over the mountainside, and crags and outcroppings zig-zagged across its surface, shaded by the occasional evergreen, but Fig couldn't see any way to get inside.

Are you sure you should go in there alone? she asked him. *Can you tell them to wait for us?*

I think it's best if I remain hidden—considering my history with the Feijowa, he said. *Now hurry up.*

They emerged from the Gold Wood and headed straight for the Mountain, Emrah sending directions to Fig as he recognized the terrain.

No, go up that incline there!

We can't, Emrah, it's too steep, she told him, exasperated. *We have to walk on two legs, you know. I can't just fly up there.*

No, I suppose you can't, he said.

She guided the others around a gentler set of rocks to reach the spot Emrah wanted them to go. Half an hour passed, and Emrah continued to check in to correct her path, the green tint flickering in and out as he dropped in to check on her. She wished she could drop into his vision to make sure he was all right himself, but she didn't think trying to learn how to do that was a good idea while on such steep terrain.

Vaelor and Mairead remained close behind her, while Dev and Derrin chatted at the back of the group. Ziggy walked carefully behind Vaelor, probably keeping an eye on her old friend from behind to make sure he didn't collapse. That's what Fig worried about, anyway. Every time she glanced back, he looked paler than ever, the circles around his eyes growing darker.

She prayed to the Bard the answer to Vaelor's sword lay inside this Mountain, or he might never leave it.

Finally, in a thick patch of evergreens, Fig found what must be an entrance to the Mountain.

Are you sure the dwarves went in here? she asked Emrah. She studied it. There were no footprints in the chalky soil, and the passage—framed by a few beams leaning against each other set in the mountainside—looked caved in.

Her vision flickered green again.

Drakioryn's bollocks, I thought they were up to something back there. I swooped in during a gap, some of them were still outside, fiddling with something. That's the place though.

"This it?" Ziggy said, swaggering over.

"Just the 'sword for the job," Fig said, grinning. "They went in this way, then collapsed it to keep anyone from following."

Ziggy cracked her knuckles and got to work.

Fig pulled Vaelor away when he went over to help, giving him a stern look. "Your job is to rest."

He gave her a bloodshot look, but Fig could see the sadness mixed with defiance.

She lowered her voice, putting a hand on his arm and leaning closer to speak into his ear. "You can't do everything. You need to rest. I'm trying to take care of you." She didn't voice the rest that went on in her head. *You're barely tethered to life right now. You won't be of use to anyone if you're dead.*

"Fine, goldfire." He spoke in a low tone by her ear. "But when I'm healed, I'm going to take care of you."

Fig shivered and pulled away, her face flaming. It grew hotter when she caught Dev's sly look as she turned back to watch Ziggy pulling stones from the blocked passage.

Ziggy grunted, squatting down to grab a large boulder and hefting it aside with a yell.

"Gods, Ziggy, that's amazing," Dev said, coming up on Fig's other side.

"If you're coming onto me," Ziggy said, panting, "now's not the time, my prince-king. At least I have my clothes on this time."

A snort ripped from Dev, and he burst into laughter. Fig met Mairead's eyes and gave the girl an incredulous look. Dev and Ziggy?

"Oh, please," Dev went on, seeming to notice the odd looks. "It was innocent. And I wasn't coming onto you just now, either. Your strength is merely a magnificent thing to behold."

"Riiight," Fig said, brows furrowed. "This collapse wasn't going to stop the silverswords long. Probably just a ruse, right?"

Knoll cleared his throat, finally weighing in. "The dwarves have ground shakers in their company. Ferrinwright clan is full of them."

"Ground shakers?" Mairead asked.

The dwarf shrugged. "Those who can shake the ground. 'S what I call them."

Fig had begun to wonder where Knoll came from, if he wasn't part of a clan here in Tytan.

"I saw something like that in Rayva when I had to escape the safehouse," she explained. "I've never seen anything like it. We were in a dwarf neighborhood, and someone caused a distraction, making the ground roll like waves. Knocked the silversword clean over."

"Aye, that'll be them," Knoll agreed.

They stared at the opening Ziggy was still working to clear. She'd moved enough for them to get through two times over by now, but more stones collapsed every time she got enough clear. "These...Bards-damned...rocks...there! Finally!"

Emrah? Fig called in her mind. *We've broken through.*

"And just in time too," Dev said in a dark voice.

Fig turned to see what he was staring at—south, toward the Mountain Road. A river of unmistakable silver glinted in the sunlight, clearly visible even to her mundane human eyes.

PART

IV

BONES OF THE EARTH

MAIREAD

"Oh, gods," Mairead said, the bottom dropping out of her stomach. Not only could she see the silversword army approaching—a stream of wickedly-glinting armor flowing north —but there was a blotchy red glow farther down the road. "They've got a red brother with them—at least one."

Fig clutched Mairead's hand. "We'd better get in then, eh?"

Mairead nodded, swallowing. There was no way she could abandon her friends now. It'd been written in the Bard's scrolls the minute those three had stumbled into Mairead's fount in Nova Istra. Mairead had been a fool to think she could leave them to their fates when she'd tried to return home to Thoan. No, she had to see this through to the end. Especially now.

She touched the bottle of holy water hanging from a strap at her belt in reassurance before awkwardly crawling through the opening. She scraped her head on the rough ceiling, then stopped to fix her hood, pulling her tunic over her mouth against the dusty passageway. Vaelor followed next at Fig's insistence, then

Dev scrambled in. Knoll made his way over the stones at the entrance with surprising agility, joining them in the tunnel as if he made this trip every day.

Outside, Ziggy and Fig were discussing how best to close it off.

"I have an idea," Dev chimed in, jostling Mairead's elbow. The three of them were huddled at the end, while Knoll strolled farther inside the tunnel. "Fig, that looks sandy enough out there. What if you heat it up, and we make a glass blockade?"

Fig frowned. "Maybe, but then they'd know for sure you and I were in here."

"Hmm, true," he said. "Ziggy? Feel like moving some more rocks?"

"I thought you'd never ask."

Fig crawled inside, and Ziggy began shifting the rocks outside again, so she could pull them closer once she was inside.

"Wait, where's Derrin?" Mairead asked, trying to peer past Fig.

He wandered into view, wringing his hands together and looking like he'd seen a ghost. "I-I'm sorry, I just don't think I can go *in*... What if we never...uh..."

Mairead crossed her arms, not really surprised. She'd been trying not to think about it herself—about never seeing daylight again, about being entombed here while the silversword army lay siege or stormed the Mountain. She shook her head. No, if the dwarves had come in here, they must have had a plan to escape or fight back against the 'swords. Once Vaelor was taken care of, surely they'd figure out what to do.

"Actually," Dev said, "I've got a different job for you, Derrin. Your family runs a printing press, correct? Well, I think everyone in Tytan should hear the tale of how I won the Sword of Morin back from Rhivven and braved the Mountain to return it to its rightful owners, the dwarves."

Derrin balked at him, looking at Dev as if the task were too good to be true. "I-I could do that, of course. I might have to move the press to another village, though..."

"Great, now get out of here, and keep an ear out—"

"Like if we all get killed in this Mountain," Ziggy said with a grunt as she tossed another rock. "Be sure to write the most *brilliantly* embellished tales. Those really do work best when the hero is dead."

Dev snorted. "Gods, I hope I don't have to be dead to make a difference. Now, go!" he urged Derrin.

Mairead shared a look with her childhood friend and nodded. Derrin bobbed his head and disappeared from view. Dev leaned out the opening and worked some barely visible air magic to confuse the tracks in the area, then Ziggy got back to work shifting stones.

Fig paced, clearly eager to get going. To help ease her worries, Mairead moved over to examine Vaelor again. He let her poke about, laying hands on him. She'd been keeping a close eye on him, but it was clear that nothing was medically wrong with his body—nothing needed healing, since she'd treated his wounds and infection, except...

He twitched away, then shook his head. She pulled her hands away. There was blood on her fingertips. She'd been prodding near his heart, where she'd once felt a horrendous scar—left from his crossover, the wound that had killed him. Now that scar was bleeding.

Mairead pressed her lips tight and swallowed a lump in her throat. Eyes still locked on his, she nodded. She wouldn't tell anyone. It was a tenet of her oath as a Sister of Morgha—the importance of her patient's privacy. She wiped her fingers on the back of her black cloak.

Guilt burned in her stomach when she glanced at Fig. Although Mairead was no longer a true Sister of Morgha, she had taken the oaths when she'd received her tattoos, and she still took them seriously.

When only a sliver of light remained at the entrance, Mairead took a moment to savor the sight of the sky—until Ziggy shifted more rocks in front of it, sealing them inside.

Fig didn't miss a beat and summoned a ball of gold flames to float above her hand. All Mairead could see outside the touch of gold firelight was a single red glow to the south.

Following Fig's directions from Emrah—with Knoll taking the lead—they began their journey into the Mountain.

"This must be a maintenance shaft of some kind?" Dev inquired.

"Seems like," Knoll grunted, running his fingers along the rough walls in admiration.

Mairead felt like she was intruding on a private moment; the dwarf's ancestors had been exiled from their home decades ago, and for what? The kings had never done anything with the Mountain, unlike the Gold Wood, which had given the mages a place to train. Mairead's gaze landed on Dev, and she longed to ask him what he knew. Surely as the crown prince—up until recently, at least—he would know why.

But a quiet hush—decades deep in silence—had settled over them, and she refused to break it. The tunnel stayed the same for the next twenty minutes, while Mairead kept glancing back at the red glow behind her.

Finally, when she could hold her thoughts in no longer, she remarked quietly, "I'm surprised the dwarves decided to gather and march on the Mountain in broad daylight. If they'd just waited until dark..."

"Oh, I think they wanted the 'swords to know," Dev said easily.

Fig hummed. "After you showed them up in Halvard's Pit, you think they wanted to take a stand of their own?"

"Sure. Is that right, Knoll?" Dev asked.

Knoll, taciturn as ever, just grunted.

"But why are the red brothers working with the silver-swords?" Mairead wondered aloud.

"Let's just hope they don't try setting the Mountain on fire like they did the tower," Ziggy said. "But you can put it out, right Mairead?"

Mairead gave a nervous smile, her attention on her feet. The stone floor was smooth, but worn from ages of footsteps, not from a chisel or hammer. She was beginning to worry about another confrontation with a Brother of Morgha. At first, she'd been terrified of them; now she'd killed three. At this point, she was more concerned for her mortal soul.

But she'd done it to protect her uncle—and then her friends. Surely Morgha would still take her into her arms, and not cast her into the deepest pits of Malhela for killing her own brothers in worship?

She huffed. She wished she knew more about the runes the brothers used. The knowledge could help her defend herself and her friends better, instead of killing people outright. At Mar Nevan, she'd only been taught a specific set of runes, those needed to perform a crossover, which were drawn in holy water and blood on the weapon. But between the archives and carvings in the frames of holy artwork throughout the temple in Mar Nevan, she'd seen hundreds of others. Those tattooed on Mother Savidah's face alone could probably fill an entire book. She felt another pang of loss as she thought of how Sister Avelina had been ousted from her precious archives; she was glad that Fig had managed to help her escape Tytan, at least.

That brought her back to the question of Mother Savidah. She'd not only given Mairead an incredible power—though disfigured her, stripping away any scrap of anonymity—but she'd helped Fig discover the truth about her bond with Emrah, and clues about fixing Vaelor's sword. Mairead wished she could go to the mother's chambers and beg forgiveness for the killing she had been forced to do, but more than that, she wanted answers. And not the veiled kind.

Everyone stopped walking when Fig held out an arm in a silent command to halt. Knoll had already gone ahead, sure of his footing even in the dark. Fig gave her ball of flame more power, then gently pushed it upward, letting it float high overhead.

Mairead's mouth opened in awe.

They stood at the edge of a boundless cavern, where a dozen soaring arches pierced through the dark void, meeting at an equally massive ornate tower in the middle. This would have been a feat even at the center of Rayva—but here in the Mountain, Mairead somehow knew it had been carved from the stone itself.

Fig lit another fire orb—the first one was floating too high to shed light on their path anymore. They had emerged at the edge of one of the bridges arching across the cavern. Knoll was already a dozen paces ahead, hands on his hips as he admired the expanse around them. The bridge was maybe twenty span wide, with low railings made of stone.

Mairead blinked back sudden tears. She was hit with an overwhelming sense of awe, something she hadn't felt since visiting the holy pool at the temple of Mar Nevan. It was incredible—the vastness, the craftsmanship. Even after decades, barely a stone was out of place. In the dim firelight, she couldn't even make out the other sides of the cavern, wreathed in dusty shadows.

The silence hit hard. Without realizing it, Mairead had made her breaths shallow. She was afraid to speak, but one question that she couldn't stop boiled to the top: "Where did the dwarves go?" Her voice came out as a near-silent whisper, but she was sure everyone heard.

Dev gave a thoughtful *hmm*.

"Emrah says they're in another cavern—he's on his way back now," Fig whispered. "We need to go this way and get onto that bridge going into that arched tunnel." Fig pointed as she gave the directions.

Knoll nodded, leading them forward. Six pairs of footsteps echoed like drums in the thick silence of the cavern.

"There's more than one of these caverns?" Mairead whispered, catching up to Knoll.

He grunted. "Oh, aye. Six—one for each of the gods, of course. This one's Baldwyn's." He gestured at the tower for some reason.

"Six?" Mairead demanded, eyes wide.

"Then it can't just be...this one Mountain, can it?" Dev asked.

"'Course not," Knoll mumbled.

Dev glanced at Mairead; he appeared as inquisitive as she was. But it wasn't just Knoll she wanted answers from.

"How come your ancestors…" Mairead began, then winced. Dev was her friend, and they had been through a lot together—from the salt swamps to the bloody cobblestones in Nithe—but he was still the heir to the Rayvan throne, with two hundred years of Verrence silversword ancestors behind him.

"Claimed the Mountain?" Dev finished for her, a ghost of a smile playing at his lips.

The silence pressed around them all, except for the beats of their footsteps. It seemed Mairead wasn't the only one who wanted to hear the answer.

"The Bard only knows," Dev admitted.

They were halfway across the bridge now, the tower in the center looming above them. A dozen bridges pierced the cavern, all converging at the tower, which displayed arched windows and doorways. Their path led into one such doorway, swathed in darkness.

Everyone froze at a familiar sound, the flapping of leather wings. The sound was amplified ten-fold in the empty cavern.

"Emrah," Fig said gleefully, pointing.

The green and gold dragonet was flapping toward them from one of the tunnels, sparks of gold sifting gently down from his claws as he rose to meet them.

Mairead broke into a grin watching the dragonet reunite with Fig. The strengthening of the bond was evident. The two of them gave off an almost imperceptible pearlescent glow when they were in close proximity. She had noticed it back at the tower, and from what she'd heard about everything that had happened at Halvard's Pit, Fig's fire magic had more than doubled.

"Welcome back," Mairead told him.

Emrah perched in his usual position on Fig's shoulder and chirped a greeting.

The dwarves are gathered in a chamber in the next cavern. It seems like they're going to stay there a while. They've got a lot prepared—even looks like they'd brought gear in beforehand.

"Right," Fig said, trudging ahead. "Let's go."

It had seemed like they were getting closer to the tower in the center, but the distance was deceiving; they still had a long way to go.

Mairead fell back in step with Dev. "You really don't know?" she pried, not ready to drop their conversation from before.

He shook his head, giving an exasperated sigh. "I wish I did. It's not as if the accounts are in the Hall of Records in Rayva."

"What about the Verrence library?" Fig asked.

"You think I didn't check there? Of course I did. Since the age of four I was pawing at the books in the palace. And when I found out I'd be king, well, I wanted to do everything I could to understand why Tytan was the way it is. Why mages are no longer allowed to live freely in the Gold Wood. Why dwarves are forbidden from inhabiting the Mountain." He sighed.

"I found records of the close-knit mage villages in the Gold Wood but always assumed King Bailemor had wanted to help the mages hone their powers by giving them the Carriage House and help protect the auran trees from extinction by disbanding the villages. But the dwarves..." He trailed off.

"The records in Pan Vidda are a little better on that subject," Knoll broke in.

"Is that so?" Dev asked slowly.

"Aye, it is. There were rumors of something dangerous in the Mountain, something that would destroy Tytan—the very way of life for the entire continent, even."

Dark silence seemed to press down even harder, the scent of centuries-old dust rising up and catching in Mairead's throat. *Something that would destroy Tytan?* Mairead's pulse set to racing, and just as she was about to question Knoll as to why he couldn't have brought that up *before* they entered the Mountain, there came a screeching roar, and the inky blackness of the approaching archway lit up with a massive burst of flame coming right for them.

Drakioryn's rising! Emrah shouted.

Mairead stumbled back, grabbing onto Dev in her haste.

"A dragon?" Fig shrieked.

Ziggy drew her sword and dashed up to the front faster than anyone could see. Knoll pulled out his hammer.

The fire burst died out, and Mairead stepped back even farther. Dwarf politics, silverswords, and red brothers trying to kill her she could deal with, but a dragon?

A dark shape emerged from the arched doorway, two glowing red orbs facing them.

Mairead grabbed the flask of holy water at her belt, ready to douse her fingers. She'd realized at the tower—in order to use sigil hand magic—she needed holy water on her fingertips. Just as she was fumbling with the cork, the red embers moved wildly—one to the side, and the other upward, very *unlike* eyes. Then, a cacophony of voices burst in her head.

Kill the two-leggers!

How did they get in?

They've another dragon with them!

Then finally—*Oy, oy!* Emrah's voice called as he rose into the air and let out a burst of orange sparks. *What in Drakioryn's scaly backside is going on here?*

"Dragonets?" Fig asked quietly. "More of them?"

We're dragons, *two-legger,* one snarled.

There's something odd about that one, another said, eyeing Fig as it circled closer, talons out.

She quickly lit another ball of flame—brighter this time—and tossed it above their heads. It illuminated a gathering of dragonets, all bunched together and hovering in the entrance of the doorway, scales glinting in a rainbow of muted colors. Neither Ziggy nor Knoll lowered their weapons. Mairead was surprised Fig hadn't called any other flames, but maybe showing restraint with fire around the dragonets was a good idea.

Who are you lot? Emrah challenged.

The dragonets shifted. A few perched on the railings on either side, sparks dripping from their claws; others disappeared back into the tower. A small group hovered in the doorway, blocking their way. A bronze-scaled dragonet darted forward: their apparent leader.

You first, the bronze one spat. *What are you doing trespassing here? This is our Mountain.*

"Oh gods," Dev muttered silently beside Mairead.

Emrah bobbed in the air above Fig. *As far as we know, this is the dwarves' Mountain, and we followed them inside.* He jabbed a wing in the direction of the tunnel the dwarves must have taken.

And who are you, Outsider? Bronze-scales demanded. *Bonded with a Svoran of all things?*

I am Emrah, and Fig is my human.

Mairead had to smile at the pride in Emrah's voice. She wondered if the completed bond had also helped Fig with her restraint—the mage had an unsurprisingly fiery temper when confronted.

Emrah continued. *The rest follow the true king of Tytan, Devryn Verrence, and we're trying to aid the dwarves—*

The ones who would claim our *Mountain?* Bronze-scales growled. Orangish sparks dripped from his snout, and it looked like his belly had coals in it as it glowed like a miniature forge.

Stop, stop! Emrah said. *My guess is the dwarves belong here just as much as you do. Your kind has simply kept living in these caverns after the dwarves were banished.*

Bronze-scales bobbed in the air briefly, his belly-fire going out. Mairead eyed the dragonet perched on the rail nearest her—a blue and silver one that was staring straight at Mairead as if she were planning to roast her.

These halls have been ours for generations.

I didn't realize there were more of us here... Emrah said, a strange note in his voice.

Mairead had never seen another dragonet. She'd always imagined Emrah had a network of friends they didn't know about, but from his expression as he scanned the gathering of dragonets, it seemed this was the first time he'd seen any in a long time.

Fig broke the silence. "Our friend here is hurt, and we need to get to the dragonhead forge. I don't suppose you know where that is?"

Bronze-scales faltered. *We don't visit that place. And I don't see how a forge can fix a man.*

He's no man, Furvin, don't you see his eyes? a dragonet chimed in.

He's a sivrin*! Metal blooded!*

I can smell it. And on the woman too!

Enough, Furvin—the bronze dragonet—said, letting out a burst of sparks.

Fig clasped her hands together before her. "Please, we just need to pass through the Mountain. We're not here to take it from you."

But those you seek to aid will, Furvin said.

"It belongs to the dwarves," Knoll intoned, finally making his voice heard.

Furvin glared down his bronze-scaled snout at Knoll. *The dwarves left generations ago.*

Dev cleared his throat, addressing Furvin, "Look, I know your kind have guarded and kept the Mountain all this time. But the dwarf numbers aren't that high. I think there's enough room here for all of you. And we don't have all the time in the Bard's scrolls, either, I'm afraid. There's an army on its way here. Silverswords. More...*sivrins*. A lot more."

Fig gave Dev a look, and he replied, "What? It's better they know."

Fiery coals seemed to gather in Furvin's belly again, and the dragonets all surged back together into formation. *How dare you bring that violence upon us. And you, the supposed king?*

"I didn't bring them here," Dev said, putting a hand on the hilt of the Sword of Morin. "We need to return this sword to the dwarves and find some bloodril to fix our friend's sword, and then—"

Furvin made a sound like a mix between a chirp and a growl, bobbing half a foot in the air in surprise.

That sword! That's what those sivrins *came to get months ago. We couldn't hear its song anymore.*

"It belongs to the dwarves," Dev said.

Furvin narrowed his scaly eyes at Dev and their assembled group. *I know not of that sword's tale, but Drakioryn knows it belongs in the Mountain. And if these dwarves were the ones who crafted it...*

He paused, and by the darting looks in the eyes of the group of dragonets, it looked like they were having a private conversation. Furvin kept his gaze on Fig and Emrah, as if they might burst into flames any second.

Finally, when the dragonets were done conferring, he said, *Very well. You may pass. But you will not go through our Mountain without an escort.*

Emrah looked like he was going to argue, but Fig raised her hand and said, "That's fine."

Furvin gave a whistle, and all the other dragonets disappeared —except the blue one eyeing Mairead and a red-and-gold one that hovered in the archway, still looking like it didn't want to let them pass through. Furvin hovered, eyes narrowed as he watched them.

Everyone looked at each other.

"Well," Ziggy said, "now that we have an official escort, we'd better go before the 'swords break down that tunnel."

DEV

"Quite the band of followers you have now," Ziggy said to Dev as they crossed the next bridge.

"And you doubted me for wanting to return to Tytan," he scoffed.

"For the wrong reasons, if you recall?" She gave his sword a pointed look.

He shrugged. He was ready to be rid of this Bard-forsaken sword—to exchange it for a proper alliance with the dwarves. Of course, they might be infuriated with him for stealing it from the tournament in the first place, but he had gotten it safely out of Rhivven's hands, hadn't he?

Ahead, Fig raised a casual hand, calling down her orbs of flame to follow them all into the tunnel. The enormous arch they approached had been carved with intricate woven borders, its ancient runes almost like those of the silverswords. The flames descended and hovered about ten-span above their heads as they entered the tunnel.

Dev glanced behind him at the enormous cavern, which Knoll had said was dedicated to their god, Baldwyn. How six such caverns could exist within these mountains, abandoned save for the dragonets, the Bard only knew.

Their dragonet "escorts" flanked the group from the front and back, keeping a watchful eye mostly on Fig and Emrah. The sound of footsteps echoed off the tunnel walls, illuminated by the flickering orbs. Identical niches lined both sides, with what looked like a thick rope running behind them. Knoll gave a grunt of surprise and veered over to inspect them as they walked.

"Do we know where this forge is?" Dev had caught up with Fig to ask. She walked beside Vaelor, letting the big Viren lean on her arm. He looked like he'd been to Malhela and back after meeting the darkest fiends that dwelled there. Dev was fairly certain they'd be carrying the man soon if the dragonhead forge wasn't close by.

A sudden *whoosh* was the only warning they got before a stream of firelight tore down the right wall—the rope running behind the niches ignited down its entire length.

Dev whipped around to spot Knoll by the wall, fiddling with something.

"Hmm," the dwarf said in surprise. He put away his flint.

"How did you possibly know what that was?" Dev asked incredulously.

Knoll shrugged. "Heard about them."

"I hope you know a way to put it out," Ziggy grumbled. "Once the silverswords get into that cavern, they'll see a nice beacon to follow us, eh?"

"I can put it out," Fig said. Her voice was quiet, which was unusual for her. She'd changed since they'd parted aboard the *Trevena*, when he'd left for Tirnalore. Her bond with Emrah had made her powerful and more controlled. But Vaelor's deteriorating condition had placed a mantle of melancholy over her shoulders. Dev didn't want to think about what would happen to her if they couldn't heal him—it was clear she and Vaelor were deeply in love. He'd known her long enough, had loved her enough himself, to recognize it. Bard's quills, it was probably evident to everyone around them, except perhaps Fig and Vaelor.

The group lapsed into silence as they followed the line of flames to the end of the tunnel.

To the right, across that bridge, and down the stairs of the tower, Emrah said. *That's where the dwarves are.*

"Shouldn't we find the forge first?" Mairead asked, twining her fingers together with a nervous glance at Vaelor.

"We need to go to the dwarves first," Fig said.

Dev stared at her. "Fig, the Sword of Morin isn't as—"

"We need bloodril," she explained. "The sword needs to be mended with something stronger. The dwarves will be the only ones who know where we can get some. And honestly, we should ask their permission."

"Let's go then," Dev said, nodding.

Fig raised a hand to the end of the flaming rope in the nearest niche; then, with purpose, she clutched the rope. It immediately went out, leaving them in darkness save for the two fire orbs floating above them. She sent the most powerful orb to hover high in the air, revealing a second cavern even larger than the first. Arching bridges pierced through the center, and the boundaries of the far side were wreathed in dusty shadows.

In the middle stood a tower much like the last, except the pattern of windows and the architecture had significant differences, flying buttresses jutting out from each level, and more statues carved into it.

They couldn't see the bottom of the cavern in the meager light, but a certain *shush* of sound, and the occasional clank told them that the dwarves were down there.

"Who's this cavern dedicated to?" Mairead asked Knoll.

"Corryn," he offered. "The goddess of justice."

"How do you know all of this?" she asked.

Dev gave a small smile. He could always rely on Mairead to ask the detailed questions, which he himself wanted answers to just as badly.

"Told you, Pan Vidda has better records."

"Records of dwarf history?" she asked. "Here on Tytan?"

"Aye," he replied.

"You're from Pan Vidda, then?"

"Born there," he allowed. "But we all come from the Mountain. Generations ago, when it was first taken from them, my ancestors fled Tytan."

"And now you've returned," Dev said.

Knoll grunted in the affirmative.

They reached the tower, going through an arched doorway and down the winding stone staircase inside. One of their dragonet escorts swooped back outside to watch their descent from outside the tower, while the red and gold one hovered close to Fig and Emrah. Emrah glared at it a few times when it got too close, and Dev was glad the blue one had gone outside; there wasn't enough room for a dragonet brawl, especially with all of the very flammable bystanders.

Each floor of the tower held aged remnants of a long-past era: heavy wooden furniture coated in dust, most of it overturned as if the inhabitants had fled. Tables, statues, desks, and chairs, mostly. With the very public bridge doorways, and stairs passing right through each level, Dev thought the tower must have been a public place—perhaps for learning, bureaucracy, or something else entirely. If Corryn was the goddess of justice, perhaps the space was dedicated to the study or execution of law.

He grew uneasy with every step they penetrated farther into the ancient Mountain, like something was creeping up his neck and if only he turned his head to look, he'd see it.

The silverswords had usurped the Mountain from the dwarves, that much they knew, but what was the great danger Knoll had spoken of? That which would destroy all of Tytan—all of Svora? Was that the real reason the dwarves had left?

His head began to spin a little as he weighed possible outcomes of this meeting with the dwarves as they descended step by step. Would they support him against the silversword enclave? Would they take the sword and use him as bait for the oncoming army? He had no intel, not even a hint from Knoll. The stairs seemed endless, his legs straining as they went down, down, down with only decades-old detritus to look at.

Dev paused for a few seconds on the last set of stairs to gather his wits, feeling a touch dizzy. Finally, he drew a steadying breath, reached the bottom of the tower, and faced the open archway.

An army of dwarves was pointing weapons at them.

They spilled out the open archway at the bottom of the massive staircase, and Dev walked forward, hands raised. He had known this was coming. Some of the dwarves pointed gnarled fingers at the dragonets, who had perched on statue plinths on the tower and were watching disinterestedly.

But most focused their attention on Dev.

"The Sword of Morin," the nearest dwarf growled, a woman with thick red hair braided down her back.

"What is he doing here?" another dwarf said, a hammer coming up into position faster than looked possible for an object of considerable weight.

More weapons were raised; those with torches brandished them in their direction, and the shouts all rang together so that none could be made out in the great echoing cavern.

"Silence, silence!" someone called from amid the gathered dwarves.

It took some time for the riotous shouting to calm. The dwarf army had gathered outside the tower in a large empty space, where massive natural rock formations were still intact.

Clang.

A hammer strike rang out, raining silence upon the cavern at last.

Dev spotted the figure who'd struck the hammer, high up on one of the elevated rock platforms, a natural dais of sorts. The dwarf woman stood tall, two dark braids framing her face and running past her waist. She wore an ornate helmet with dragon wing decorations jutting from each side.

"Silence," she called again, her voice as deep as the caverns themselves. "Do not sully the return to our glorious Great Mountain with pointless insults and violence. I am sure the traitor has some reason for following us here."

Dev stuck out his chin. "I am no traitor." Despite the adrenaline surging through his veins, he was pleased with how his voice sounded in the cavern—confident and sure. "I am the rightful ruler of the Rayvan throne, and I am here to return the Sword of Morin to its rightful owners."

Silence fell so thick it was like he was all alone at the bottom of the cavern, the tower and bridges looming over him with their dark and ancient presence.

The dwarf woman looked straight at Dev, the hand not holding her hammer propped on her hip. "And I thank you for it, my lord. But I was talking about that one." She lifted her hammer with an easy strength and pointed it at Knoll, who stood stone-faced at the side of the group.

DEV

"K noll?" Dev couldn't help but reply.

"Knoll Morinson," the woman intoned, "whose family fled Tytan like cowards when the silverswords stole these mountains from us, and would have let them crumble into Drakioryn's claws at the depths of Malhela. Knoll Morinson, who gave away the location of the very sword you hold, my lord, to the silversword briigards."

"I did no such thing!" Knoll interjected.

She quelled him with a look, raising her hand, still speaking to Dev. "I thank you again, my lord, for returning the sword to us. I must confess, we didn't know your intentions in Halvard's Pit, when you claimed it over the dwarf competitors, but I thank you for removing it from Rhivven Reynolt. Bring it here."

The army parted automatically. Dev squared his shoulders and started walking. This was why he was here. But what of Knoll?

It took longer than he expected to reach the end of the

crowd—even though he longed to rush through the rough-looking sea of faces, he forced himself to walk with dignity. Like a king.

He also made sure not to touch the sword, though putting his hand on its hilt had become second nature to him, its power calling to him in whispers. He didn't want the dwarves to think he had any intention of keeping it, and he didn't want to be accused of becoming too familiar with the weapon. Even Knoll had said he wasn't worthy of holding it. Dev *had* thought there was something odd about Knoll's appearance at the tower.

Nonetheless, the silverswords had located the sword, and Djuren had retrieved it from the Mountain. It was strange. Not only had Djuren stolen the sword, but his name had been on his brother Shad's lips back on Nithe. Perhaps after all of this was over, Dev should call upon the briigard and find out what he knew about Shad.

He finally reached the enormous rock dais where the dwarf woman stood. He bowed his head as befitted greeting another ruler.

"May I?" he said, gesturing with both hands to the Sword of Morin at his hip.

"You may, my lord." She was pretty—now that he could see her up close—her regal bearing befitting her curves and dark golden skin. Two long black braids framed her face and hung well past her stomach. She wore a long rust-colored gown with gold stitching, and her hammer was still raised and at the ready.

With cautious movements, Dev unstrapped the sword and held the sheathed weapon up with both hands. The dais she stood upon was at least four-span high, and he lifted it over his head for her to see.

"You may approach."

He did, stopping one stride from the edge of her stone dais. "I would give this sword to the dwarves, which I went to great lengths to recover in your name. In return, I have two requests."

She raised a bushy black eyebrow. "Very well."

"Well, three," Dev said, raising the corner of his mouth in a smile. "First, my lady, I request the name by which to address you."

He hadn't known there was any kind of leader among the clans. He'd only ever dealt with the Feijowa, and Firth had been set on getting the Sword of Morin as well. Giving the sword to this woman would solidify her leadership position, but he'd have to take that gamble.

A deep chuckle rumbled through her chest, and with the smallest of smiles, she replied, "I am Valencia Ferrinwright, Uniter of the Clans."

"That would certainly explain how you've gathered all of them here with such purpose, great uniter," Dev said. Sometimes a little flattery could sweeten very real requests. "I applaud your leadership."

"What is it you require?" she asked, a steely look in her eye telling him no amount of flattery would sway her in either direction.

"I have one among my advisors who is greatly ill. He is a silversword loyal to me, and his weapon was shattered in my service. To repair the connection between his sword, and, well, himself, we require bloodril ore, and the use of the dragonhead forge."

Dev paused for the briefest of seconds, and when she didn't say anything, he decided to soldier on and get it all out at once. "And, as I am sure you are aware, the Rayvan throne has been taken from me. I propose that we work together to make Tytan the country it should be. You have already returned to the Mountain, but if you will ally with me and help me take back the Rayvan throne, I will, without a doubt, support your return to the home of your ancestors, and help you keep it."

Valencia's bushy eyebrows rose, and she gave him a ponderous look as the dwarf army broke out into whispers.

"Those are some serious requests, my lord," she said, her great voice booming through the cavern. "But we shall not discuss them here. I hear tell of an army of silverswords bearing down upon us as we speak, and we need not all tarry on the cavern floor like ants to be crushed. Come! My lords and ladies—join me while our clans ready for battle!"

Dev swallowed. So his suspicions were true. The dwarves had led the silverswords to the Mountain with the purpose of instigating a fight. But who would survive, and what would be left of them?

He stood his ground as the clans burst into a flurry of movement. The clan leaders shouted orders, directing their clans into various chambers or to set up traps. Dev patiently stood with the Sword of Morin held tightly in two hands in front of him.

Somehow, Fig and the others managed to fight their way through the chaos and joined him a few minutes later. Dev thought he saw blood on Vaelor's shirt, but the big Viren shifted his cloak. Mairead caught Dev's eye and gave him a look that said as clear as day: *We need to hurry.*

He nodded and turned back to Valencia, who was now flanked by a dozen dwarves, including none other than Firth, the leader of the Feijowa. Dev gave the dwarf a respectful nod.

"Come," Valencia said, stepping to the edge of her dais and jumping the four-span down to the ground floor as easily as a child jumping into a lake, her hammer held tightly in one hand. She beckoned the dwarves and Dev's party away from the army's flurry of movement, and they followed, Dev still holding the sword in front of him.

In the shadow of the central tower stood another set of natural flat stone shelves, though here the dwarves of old had carved walkways between them, making statues of some of the taller stones. It reminded Dev of the gardens in Tirnalore, except these were wrought in stone. They followed Valencia to a bare circle in the middle, lined with heavily decorated benches carved into the rock. A perfect circle. The dwarf leader gestured for Dev to take a seat, and he did.

Fig sat on one side and Ziggy on the other. Everyone else followed suit except for Knoll, who remained outside the circle, arms crossed.

"Very well," Valencia began as she sat down, directly across the circle from Dev. "I can see why you're in need of help with this silversword in your company," she said, nodding at Vaelor—the deathly ghost of himself sitting at Fig's other side. "But I don't see how bloodril will help. Only one sword has ever been forged with it, my lord, and you're holding it."

Dev nodded solemnly. "We have with us a Sister of Morgha to aid in the reconnection of the weapon, but his weapon is shattered. Simple steel might not be enough. We believe if it is mended with something stronger than the original metal, the weapon will survive the process."

Valencia eyed Vaelor. "It will be incredibly painful."

"It already is, my lady," Vaelor said in a low voice.

Fig stiffened beside him.

"But the dragonhead forge hasn't been used in…well, a dragon's age, my lord," Valencia went on, holding out her palms. "I don't know if I have one among my clans who can light it and operate it, particularly on such short notice."

"I will do it," Knoll said, his arms still crossed. The clan leaders turned to acknowledge him.

"You are not welcome in these sacred halls!" one leader hissed.

"Silence," Valencia ordered. "We will try Knoll Morinson for his crimes after this battle is over. His ancestors deserted the clans at the fall of the Great Mountain, and he sold dwarf secrets upon his return to the continent."

Knoll was glaring at Firth, who shifted uncomfortably. Firth had given Knoll leave to camp out in Emrah's tower, which meant the two of them knew each other and had made some kind of deal. Had Firth wanted to become the Uniter of the Clans instead of Valencia? What deal had Knoll and Firth made?

"Please, Lady Valencia," Dev interjected. "If Knoll is willing to operate the dragonhead forge, do we have your leave to try? We don't have much time."

"No, you don't," Valencia agreed frankly, "and neither do we. The silverswords will have begun entering the tunnel by now, and you're about to be in the center of a battle you did not initiate. I suggest you go to the chamber of Morin-Song and do what you need to do and quickly. It is deeper within, so you should be safe for a time, but if all does not go well here... well... Knoll Morinson should know the location of the bloodril ore."

Valencia stared down Knoll. "But know this, *dwarf*," she spat. "You will answer for betraying the Mountain. When I am done cleaning the silver, I'll be back to find you."

Fig stood immediately, helping Vaelor to his feet.

Dev got up and held the sword out to Valencia, advancing forward. "Then please, take this. And about my other request—"

"We shall discuss it if I am still alive when you return. Now, out of my way, I've got silver-clad demons to slay, for daring to set foot upon my Mountain."

She took the sword from his hands and held it high. The clan leaders stared in silence for a moment. Then a chant in an ancient language unknown to Dev rose from those gathered around the cavern. It built to a roar, and Dev felt his blood rising in answer to the call of battle.

Valencia thrust the sword higher into the air and cried for all to hear, "For the Mountain!"

They roared in reply, and then, silence settled on the cavern like a snuffed-out candle thrusting them into darkness.

Dev watched as Valencia strode toward the gathered dwarves, the clan leaders falling into line behind her. Somehow, he was pulled along in the procession, with Ziggy a close step behind. He had been led onto the large stone dais beside Valencia and the clan leaders, facing the droves of dwarves. A sea of faces greeted him, with just as many weapons glinting in the firelight.

"The Sword of Morin has been returned to the dwarves—to the Mountain," Valencia called, her low voice seeming to vibrate through the very rocks themselves as she projected. "Forged in the very heart of the Mountain, in the great dragonhead forge, and built by the mightiest dwarves ever to pass through these halls, our ancestors knew there was great power in this sword. The gods know it is time to put that power to use!"

A battle cry went up. Dwarves shook hammers and stomped

their feet upon the cavern floor. A thundering not borne of feet vibrated through the very earth. Ground shakers.

"We lie fallow no longer. This Mountain is ours, and may Drakioryn burn whoever thinks otherwise, for beside me stands the true king of men in Tytan—Devryn Verrence!"

Suddenly she was beside him, and though he still focused on maintaining his royal demeanor, a quick smile flashed on his face at Valencia.

"At great risk to himself and his companions, he retrieved the Sword of Morin for the dwarves."

"*For the dwarves!*" the cry echoed.

She grabbed his hand and raised it, the sword in her other. "The silverswords are coming, yes. We made sure of that! And now, we claim this Mountain:"

"*For the dwarves!*"

CHAPTER 42

FIG

Fig hurried to catch up with Vaelor, who'd begun walking away from the conversation circle as soon as Valencia's rallying speech had ended. The cavern quickly shifted from reverent silence to the chaos of preparation once more.

Mairead had gone to have a hurried discussion with Dev and Ziggy, who were still among the dwarves preparing the Mountain for battle.

"Vaelor," Fig called, grabbing his sleeve.

He turned to look at her, and she had to work hard to keep her face from crumpling into sadness. He was practically in Morgha's outstretched arms. Dark circles dragged under his eyes, which were bloodshot, his usual ring of silver not only rust-colored but fractured and broken. When had that happened?

"Vaelor," Fig said again, holding his arm firmly. "We're on the right track now."

He nodded slowly.

Fig blinked back tears and distracted herself by surveying the cavern.

The red and gold dragonet scout was circling the cavern, but the blue one was nearby, watching her. Valencia had returned to the plinth where they'd first seen her, issuing orders to the clan leaders and anyone else who reported to her. Firth had disappeared, taking the Feijowa clan directly to the maintenance tunnel they'd all entered from, if Fig had heard their orders correctly. Fig had no doubt they would cut down whoever they encountered. But how many silverswords were on their way? And what about the red brother among their number?

She shuddered, bringing her attention back to Vaelor, her hand still on his arm. She waved with her other hand at Dev, telling him to wrap up whatever he was arguing with Ziggy about.

I'm sorry, Fig, Emrah said in her head as he came to land on her shoulder.

About what?

"Ziggy's going to stay with the dwarves to lend a hand," Dev told her as he arrived. He glanced at Vaelor. "Come on. Knoll's going to lead us to the forge. Now. Oh, and Emrah's going to stay here too."

"What?" Fig barked. "No. Why?"

So we can communicate between this cavern and wherever you're going, Emrah explained. *The dwarves need all the help they can get. You won't be leaving the Mountain alive if they lose.*

"It was Emrah's idea," Dev said apologetically.

Fig's chest constricted. She forced herself to nod. "Fine." She knew they were right.

Emrah bumped his snout against her neck.

She swallowed the lump in her throat. *I'll never say this with more seriousness than I do now, Emrah, but please, be careful.*

I will if you will, he said.

Of course, my friend. She closed her eyes, pressing out the moisture that prickled there.

Fig and Vaelor followed Knoll in the opposite direction from the bridge they'd used to enter Corryn's cavern. The blue and silver dragonet tailed them at a distance.

That red and gold dragonet's watching you, Fig warned Emrah.

Oh, I know, Emrah said darkly. *And if he tries anything, he'll get a face full of sparks.*

Fig snorted and continued on, dodging the dwarves who hurried about making preparations. Some carried what looked like mining equipment for blasting. Fig glanced back at Mairead and Dev behind her. Mairead looked worried—and a little scary with her black hood up and her glowing red face tattoos. Dev was adjusting his mundane sword, visibly missing the presence of the Sword of Morin.

A great roar filled the cavern. The dwarves banged hammers, hollering at the top of their lungs, the sound both wild and fearless. The very earth vibrated beneath their feet.

The silverswords entered the cavern then—not only through the large archway Fig and the others had used, but also through half a dozen other entrances, their weapons glinting in the firelight mirrored around the cavern.

The one leading the charge across the largest bridge with a mighty roar, her axe held high and covered in blood, was...

Dev faltered, and Fig thought he might drop to his knees.

"Is that..." He choked out the words. "Liess Astor?"

"Come on," Fig urged, grabbing his arm. "Time to go."

He shook himself, and they hurried after Knoll, running to catch up. Fig couldn't pretend she wasn't relieved to stay out of the battle; she had no desire to be caught in the whirl of blood and silver, of hammers striking and minor explosions now shaking the cavern. Except they needed the dwarves to win.

May the Bard's luck be with you, she thought to Emrah.

A small group of three silverswords advanced on them, having entered the cavern from a nearby tunnel. She cursed Valencia for making them dally with politics in the conversation circle.

"Bard strike it!" Fig cursed, whirling to face the oncoming 'swords. "We don't have time for this!"

Flames burst to life in her hands, and she sent massive bursts in their direction, a hot pull of fire coming from her core. It felt like her whole body now glowed with a pleasant golden light—her connection with Emrah strengthening her. She leaned into the glow, and her bursts of flame grew—gold and hot white—stretching a dozen feet farther and scattering the small group of silverswords.

The nearby dwarves wasted no time in engaging them, dropping their equipment and rushing the 'swords with a fervor Fig had never before seen. They had regained something upon reentering the Mountain—something visceral, as if the ancient magics of the earth had blessed them.

"Come!" Knoll shouted, and Dev yanked on Fig's tunic to pull her away.

She whirled back and ran toward the tunnel where the others had already gathered. Panting and sweaty from the heat of her flames, she glanced back into Corryn's cavern one last time. Fig felt terrible leaving Ziggy here, but if anyone could fight the silverswords, it was one of their own number. It was the dwarves she should be worried about. But even as they fled the cavern, she knew the dwarves had a fighting chance. One bridge had been rigged to explode—which required ripping apart an ancient edifice, but the result was worth it. A dozen silverswords plunged through the open space, falling longer than it took for Fig and the others to vanish into the dark tunnel.

Emrah, may I borrow your sight? she asked.

Green flickered over her vision without answer, and she grinned. Emrah could see far better in the dark than she could. She summoned a small ball of flame for the others, as they raced away from the battle as fast as they could.

She found Vaelor's hand in the dark and squeezed it with all her might. It was colder than she expected, but he squeezed back, saying, "Goldfire, I'm not sure..."

Her breath caught in her throat, and she hoped to the Bard he wouldn't finish that sentence. She couldn't hear the rest, not now.

They were so close. They'd trekked across Tytan to mend his sword, and they finally had everything they needed.

She clenched his hand tighter. She felt Dev and Mairead draw closer to Knoll, leaving her with Vaelor and his slower pace.

He didn't continue speaking, only caressed her hand with his thumb.

Out of nowhere, words bubbled to her lips. "We've got to try, Vaelor. The best we can do is try. Even if everything seems dark."

He nodded, and slipped his hand out of hers, only to wrap it around her shoulders. She blinked back tears, drinking in the feeling of his closeness.

Despite everything, they continued into the darkness together.

"Kind of reminds me of that night on the Twist," she said softly, after a few minutes of reveling in their closeness. They were the perfect height where she fit *just so* within his arm. She couldn't see his bloodshot eyes or how pale he was, just felt him beside her as they chased their last hope.

A rare chuckle rumbled in his chest. "Except a lot drier."

"And roomier, I suppose."

All she could do was try, and she had to. Because what was the point of living if she didn't?

CHAPTER 43

LIESS

Liess cut down another dwarf on the bridge and flung the blood from her axe with gusto. The scent of blood made her axe sing amid the sea of carnage. Her army had come together just in time to follow the idiot dwarves back to their Mountain. She had done her job.

And she had kept her mouth shut.

She raised her axe at the next dwarf in her way just as a bright flash of golden light on the cavern floor drew her eye.

If she didn't know any better, she'd have mistaken the massive flame burst for mythical dragon fire. But no, as she dispatched the dwarf and drew closer to the side of the bridge, she could see that those gold flames had come from Prince Devryn's outlaw mage, Fairaleigh, and right beside her was...

There. The prince himself.

Devryn Verrence, that kind-hearted fool, so unlike his brother, who was mixing cursed mage blood with the silversword ritual to create abominations befitting the deepest pits of Malhela.

She'd kept her word. She'd ridden like a dragonet on the wind across the country to gather Rhivven's army after Rokhold, and here she was. She'd been glad for the task, excusing her from Rayva and the tournament. She'd heard Rhivven had killed a dozen dwarves himself in the aftermath of Halvard's Pit.

And here was Devryn, fighting alongside the dwarves. Or not fighting—he and Fairaleigh were now retreating into a tunnel.

Did he know his brother was here in Tytan? Did he know what an abomination he was? Though she'd never forget Shadryn's threat as long as she lived, she wondered why he'd let her go, let her support the man sitting on the Verrences' throne.

Her hand to Morgha, Liess would much rather have Devryn take the throne than Shadryn if it had to be a Verrence.

She gasped at the sacrilegious thought. *Rhivven* was her king. And he'd promised her the throne as well should she return victorious. She cut down another dwarf who thought he could sneak up on her. Slashing in a fit of confused fury, she made up her mind. No matter her reason, she was certain of one thing: she had to get to Devryn. He was the center of everything. The prize for Rhivven. The should-be crown prince. The boy who'd always let her go first when she demanded in practice.

She stepped back a dozen paces from the side of the bridge, then dashed forward with a burst of speed her body relished, the delightful rush of adrenaline pumping into her muscles as her enhanced body reveled in the magnificence of sinew, speed, and strength.

A wall of dwarves and heavy equipment meant to blockade the entrance to a tower stood in her way, but nothing would stop her from getting to Devryn now. He was the key to all of this. Not these confounded dwarves.

With her burst of speed, she calculated the angle of the tower and the next bridge down, then leapt over the stone railing.

She windmilled her arms and, using her axe for leverage, dropped through the air, the wind whistling past her ears.

Before she slammed into the side of the tower, she threw her gauntleted hand out to catch the side, slowing her and adjusting her trajectory, falling, sliding, sparks scraping against the ancient stones. The smell of burned dust and hot stone flooded her nostrils as she fixed her gaze on the unguarded bridge below.

With one last push against the tower—and the momentum of an axe swing—she shifted her body midair to adjust her landing position, excitement rushing in her veins.

The bridge came to meet her feet faster than her eyes could follow. Shock reverberated up through her feet, and she sheathed her axe. Adrenaline surged through her, and she glanced up at the bridge she'd just leapt from. A scar marred the stones of the tower where she'd slid down. A grin curled her lips, and she ran into the tower—only to be confronted with a maze of stairs. Cursing the Bard, Liess ran as fast as her silversword blood would allow.

FIG

Across another vast cavern, and down several dark tunnels, Fig found herself half-carrying Vaelor—Dev supporting him on the other side—down a seemingly endless staircase.

The ceiling above their heads was roughly-carved but still high enough that it allowed for the fire orbs she'd brought with her to hang ten-span above her head. The dwarves of old had not taken the easy way.

"How much longer?" Fig demanded of Knoll, who walked silently ahead of her.

With Emrah's vision overlapping her own, she could make out every detail of the staircase. It looked like they were nearing the bottom, where a large half-circle of ornate flooring lay in wait.

Knoll didn't answer, he just kept going. Fig wasn't sure she actually wanted to know.

Legs wobbly, they finally spilled out onto the landing, which opened into a wide hallway, statues and braziers lining the walls on either side. Fig resisted the urge to light the braziers—not wanting to leave a trail for anyone who might follow—but raised her flaming orbs a little higher to shed light on the arched, gabled ceiling. The dust was thick down here, and the walls and flooring looked untouched, as if the hall had been new even in the dwarves' time.

Without discussion, Fig and Dev lowered Vaelor to sit on the bottom step. He tried and failed to suppress a groan, clutching his chest. Fig sank down to sit beside him, drawing in a deep breath and stretching her legs out before her. Emrah's overlaid vision flickered and went out, and she rubbed her eyes. Her own vision was almost blurry after the enhanced dragonet sight, but once she blinked a few times, it felt normal again. She knew Emrah needed to concentrate on the battle and tried not to worry. He'd been flickering in and out to check on them for the last hour.

"Was this a new section?" Mairead asked curiously, putting a hand on one of the walls. The intricate carvings decorating the corners and archways around the statue niches were sharp and detailed, the floors barely worn compared to countless others they'd trod to get here.

Knoll grunted, looking up and down the corridor

"You know," Dev said, getting to his feet and stretching with a groan. "Eventually, you're going to have to tell us what you have to do with all of this, *Morinson*," he said pointedly.

"You're smart for a Verrence," Knoll said begrudgingly.

"So your ancestors forged the sword," Dev said, arms crossed.

"Oh, aye."

"We're going to need a bit more than that, before we get back to Corryn's cavern."

If the dwarves are even alive when we get back, Fig thought to herself.

A small chirp in her mind made the corner of her mouth go up. Emrah. She wasn't surprised he could hear such a "loud" thought, even from this distance.

They're holding their own, he reported, *for now, just so you know. I don't think the 'swords knew it was an ambush.*

Good. I think we're getting closer, she replied. *I hope, anyway.*

"Oh, aye," Knoll said again. "My grandfather forged the Sword of Morin—King Morin."

"Then I should have given *you* the sword," Dev said. "Why didn't you tell us before?"

Knoll didn't answer.

Dev looked devastated. "But—"

"They said you...sold the location of the sword to the silverswords," Mairead said in a small voice.

"I did no such thing," Knoll growled.

"Of course not," Fig said, "but Djuren *did* find it somehow. Was it the Feijowa? I know they tried to pay Emrah to retrieve it."

"I've no idea in Malhela how the briigards found out about it at all," Knoll snapped. "King Morin forged it in near secrecy before the fall of the Mountain. The legend was passed down to me by my father. As soon as I was old enough to forge a sword, he told me. But he thought it was a lost cause, even though his father King Morin had forged the sword, he'd abandoned the dwarves.

"He said the bloodril was discovered before the silverswords took the Mountain. The 'swords would have taken it all for themselves two hundred years ago if they'd known about it back then."

"So, ultimately, the silverswords will be coming down here," Fig blurted out. "Since Djuren knows the location."

Knoll didn't respond, and Fig's insides writhed in apprehension. They were already walking a thin line keeping Vaelor from Morgha's arms while the battle waged above them.

"We should get going then," Dev said.

Knoll strode off down the right without another word.

"Vaelor, can you..." Dev began.

Vaelor stood on his own, the brief respite giving him enough strength to keep going. He gave Fig a tight smile, and she tried to return it.

They walked in silence, following Knoll. Fig wondered about the great danger Knoll had mentioned earlier, and if that was why news about the bloodril hadn't reached King Tesvier. Had the silverswords actually saved the dwarves from this great danger when they took the Mountain?

And were they just now delving into the depths of the Mountain, only to unleash it?

A sound behind them made Fig turn. The blue and silver dragonet winged around the corner of the stairs, still following them. She'd thought it had given up and returned to the others, but it persisted in silence. Fig narrowed her eyes at it and pointedly turned away, focusing on the tunnel ahead.

"And the dragonhead forge?" Fig prodded.

"Is in the chamber of Morin-Song," Knoll said. "King Morin discovered the bloodril when carving out the cavern for it, the forge that was meant to be his great legacy." He spat the last two words, self-disgust evident in his tone.

"But it's not your fault your ancestors fled the continent," Mairead piped up.

"I've known about the Sword of Morin and the bloodril for twenty years now, lass. In that time, I've seen the silverswords conquer yet another territory under their blades. And I cowered in Pan Vidda like the traitor to the dwarven honor they say I am."

They were silent for a moment, the only sounds their muffled footsteps on the dusty stone.

"But you came back," Dev said. "Why?"

"Your father," Knoll said.

"What?"

"When he was killed, I knew it was only a matter of time before things got worse for the dwarves of Tytan. And I had the only key to return them to power: the knowledge of the sword."

"And you paid the Feijowa to retrieve it for you?" Dev asked.

"Aye. When I returned to Tytan, I didn't want to be seen anywhere near the Mountain. I know most dwarves' opinion of the Morinson name—deserters and rightfully so. So I contacted an acquaintance, Firth, to locate the sword for me, hoping it could be of use to the clans in the upcoming fight that was sure to come. When a murderous briigard like Rhivven gets away with a coup like that, you know he's going to bring terror on his people."

"But Djuren got to it first," Dev mused.

"I don't blame Valencia for declaring me a traitor. I must have slipped up somehow with my instructions to Firth. How else would they have known?"

"And there's no way Firth sold out the information," Fig said. "The way the Feijowa acted when they thought Emrah had taken the sword…"

Dev nodded. "Djuren isn't just some silversword, either. He knows my brother is alive on Nithe, and he was part of the coup. Which means he's got far worse connections than just Rhivven. Maybe he found out through them."

Fig knew Dev meant Afrith, whose elaborate collection of spies spanned both sides of the continent.

Knoll grunted in surprise as Dev filled him in on their encounter with Shadryn—whose botched silversword crossover had made the news as far away as Pan Vidda.

The corridor was still—like the surface of a brackish pond, untouched for decades. Eventually, Mairead sidled up to Vaelor to inquire about his health. Fig and Dev drew back as the two talked in muted words ahead, giving them some semblance of privacy.

"How are you, Dev?" Fig asked quietly.

He shook his head. "I should be asking you that." He nodded toward Vaelor.

Fig swallowed. "Right now, I just want to focus on finding this forge." If she thought about anything else, she wasn't sure she could keep herself together.

Dev nodded and they walked on in silence for a few minutes. Eventually, he said quietly, the words ripping from his throat, "I thought I'd killed Liess Astor."

Fig chewed the inside of her lip. Privately, she would have been glad if the ferocious silversword was out of the picture, but by the way Dev spoke, she knew it had tortured him. Although, if he thought he'd killed her, that would explain his stricken look when they'd spotted her at the head of the invasion.

"Well, turns out she's alive," she said neutrally.

He huffed. "And I don't know if I should be glad for myself or disappointed. She trekked with us through the salt swamps, you know? Ziggy would have killed her, but I wouldn't let her for some Bard-forsaken reason. And then, to the surprise of absolutely *no one*, Liess turns around and betrays us. I should have killed her when I—"

"No," Fig said, reaching out and grabbing his arm, pulling them to a stop. "You shouldn't have. You're not a silversword, Dev, killing at every turn and taking what's not yours. And you don't need to be like them. Tytan will be better off if you're *not* like them."

He gently pulled his arm from hers and kept going, but she thought she heard the quietest of sniffles in the dim corridor.

Finally, Knoll's footsteps drew up fast.

Before them lay the curved arch of a grand chamber, its massive wooden doors flung wide, elaborate carvings etched into the frame. With silent steps, they followed Knoll into a chamber large enough to fit a small castle.

The blue and silver dragonet lingered outside, and Fig remembered the creatures had said they didn't go to the chamber of Morin-Song. She'd rather not have some dragonet spy seeing what they were up to, anyway. And maybe, just maybe, it would keep watch for them.

An ethereal sense of solitude and calm immediately washed over Fig the moment she entered the room.

The centerpiece of the room towered over them: a massive dragon's head with its mouth agape. Fangs like stalactites hung from the roof of its mouth, and the front teeth formed a ledge of sorts—one she imagined a blacksmith might use as an anvil. Its eyes were dark cavities, and the whole head was covered in exquisitely detailed scales. The walls of the circular chamber curved inward at the top, like they were standing in a massive dragon's egg, runes and braided carvings twining carefully up the walls at intervals. Water trickled in a narrow moat that bordered the entire room. Veins of a dark silvery metal wove among the smooth stones of the walls and floor. The dragonhead forge was made from the same silver-veined ore that lined the chamber.

The water in the small moat lining the room gathered into a pool just behind the forge. Fig wasn't sure where it was coming from. It would be helpful for the forge, though, which was surely why King Morin had directed its path here.

Fig looked down at the floor, feeling the stone under her feet. Power seemed to emanate from the chamber itself, much like in the Gold Wood, although this place held a different kind of power. She would bet on all the Bard's scrolls that it was the bloodril.

She came to stand beside Vaelor, and gently nudged him with her shoulder, hope leaping into her chest. They were so close. If there was any place they could repair his sword, it was here—in this sacred place.

Knoll set to work: assessing the forge, looking for supplies, and settling into what looked like a familiar rhythm. As familiar as lighting a gargantuan forge that hadn't been touched in decades could be.

Fig helped Vaelor get settled and tried not to watch as Mairead did a cursory examination of him. The red sister looked concerned, but that was nothing new. Fig cast around for something to do, but she didn't know the first thing about forges. Dev offered his services should Knoll need airflow adjustments in the chamber. The two of them hurriedly set to work together, Knoll muttering curses about how he wished he'd brought his own tools.

Mairead caught Fig's eye, and the two headed back to the mouth of the chamber to talk.

"What's your plan?" Mairead asked her quietly. "I know how to do a crossover, of course, but this... What did Mother Savidah tell you?"

Fig bit the inside of her mouth, thinking back to that horrid trip to Mar Nevan. "She said the crossover magic lay deep. That the magic was still there—at the time, anyway. Fix the sword first, and then strengthen the bond," Fig recited. "I'm just not..."

"Fig, could we have some more light over here?" Dev called.

She gave a reluctant smile. "That's something I can do," she replied, her voice echoing around the chamber.

Braziers sat in niches sunk into the walls of the chamber. Fig sent a dozen orbs of flame to settle in them, which—thankfully—sparked to life, their dusty coals igniting. Dev busied himself cleaning out the ancient ash in the dragonhead forge with careful whisps of amethyst wind, so as not to fill the air with the ghost-like ash. Knoll grunted in excitement when he discovered a stock of tools in a hidden compartment of the dragonhead and set to work assessing them.

"Incredible," Knoll muttered. "These were forged of bloodril as well." He raised the hammer high, and they all stared at it. It was arguably even more impressive than the Sword of Morin with the lines of runes and intricate details carved into the hammer's mighty head.

The light that had kindled in Knoll's eyes as he raised the hammer flickered and went out, and he set the hammer down on the lower jaw of the forge with reverence, shaking his head.

The silence of the Mountain pressed down on the chamber, carrying the weight of centuries.

Dev straightened from where he'd been clearing ashes and brushed dust off himself. "Knoll...I don't think it was your fault the sword was taken. Your grandfather created this place, these tools. And they are still yours to wield."

Knoll shook his head again, dark braids shifting.

Dev cleared his throat, then came over and placed a hand on Knoll's shoulder, looking more like a king than ever, despite a fine layer of ashen dust coating his clothes. "I cannot speak for the dwarf kings of old. But this Mountain belongs to the dwarves—it belongs to you. If King Morin made this forge and these tools—this chamber? They were built to last. They were built for his descendants, built to last millennia. When you put this much effort into creating a legacy, it's meant as a gift for those who come after. And that's you."

Knoll's throat bobbed as he swallowed and looked at the forge. He shook his head to himself, blinking fast. Almost without seeming to, his thick fingers brushed the nearest fang of the forge, stroking the bloodril with a touch as light as a feather.

"Fine," Knoll said quietly. "I said I would run the forge, and so I will."

He disappeared to inspect the rest of the forge, clearing his throat gruffly.

Fig caught Dev's eye and gave him a nod. She was so proud of him. Despite everything that had happened since his father was killed, Dev was more of a leader now than ever.

A sharp clank from behind the forge caused Fig and Dev to jump. Thick lumps of coal fell into the forge from somewhere inside. There was another clank, and the coal stopped, leaving a pile of massive black chunks in the heart of the forge.

Knoll peered out from where he stood beside the dragon's head and said, "Huh."

"Well, that solves that problem," Dev said. "I was afraid we'd have to go find some furniture to burn for fuel."

A surprising chuckle rumbled from Knoll. "There's a coal chamber in the back of the head," he explained, his eyes alight in wonder. "The lever is behind the ear. Looks like they filled it from a tube that comes out of that back panel there." He pointed out the workings of the forge, and Dev inspected everything with interest.

Fig rubbed her fingers together, letting some sparks fly free. "Looks like you'll be needing some fire soon."

Knoll wanted everything just so before he allowed Fig to light the dragonhead forge. He carefully inspected the coal, deeming it worthy of lighting. Evidently, the fuel chamber in the dragon's head had been airtight—no moisture had spoiled the coal over the decades. The dwarf set Dev to inspecting the airflow around the chamber, and the forge was filled with as much coal as Knoll deemed prudent.

Fig stood at the front of the dragon's teeth, gathering flames in her hands.

"How many times do you get to say you've lit an ancient dwarven forge made of bloodril?" Dev quipped from behind.

Fig ignored him, but the corner of her mouth drew up. Gold glowed in her core, and flames appeared at her hands with barely a thought. Heat rose inside her, intense but in a way she enjoyed, like the heat of the sun on a summer's day, warming her from the inside and out.

The flames leapt from her hands to the coals, and Knoll gave Dev some instructions about monitoring the airflow. Fig hoped King Morin had properly calculated the airflow around the forge and in the chamber, so they didn't all choke to death, but at least they had Dev to keep them alive should something go wrong.

As soon as the coals were lit, she leapt back, the flames in the forge leaping toward her and licking the fangs of the dragon's head unexpectedly.

A wild grin rose as her chest inflated painfully. She rushed over to Vaelor as Knoll set to work poking the flames, which had subsided to a more normal burn, with Dev's gentle assistance.

"Mairead, hand me the sword bag, would you? And you've got the holy water, right?"

"Right," Mairead said, touching the flask hanging from her hip and then handing over Vaelor's sword bag.

Fig tried to catch Vaelor's eye to offer him a reassuring smile but received no response. His listless eyes stared at the forge, and a spot of blood bloomed over his chest...

"Vaelor!" she hissed, dropping to her knees, pulling aside his cloak, and reaching into his shirt without hesitation.

A gasp drew her searching fingers up short the moment she saw the blood. The wound on his chest, where this very sword had pierced his heart and killed him, was open and bleeding freely. Not a deathly rush of blood, but enough to startle her to her feet and send her lurching toward Mairead. Something in the girl's expression crumpled. "You knew?" Fig asked shakily.

Mairead shrugged helplessly. "He made me promise not to say anything."

Fig stared at Vaelor, shaking her head. "Oh, Vaelor," she muttered, fingers fumbling with the sword bag. "Quick, we have to get the sword ready." She hastened over to Knoll. "We're running out of time. When will the forge be ready?"

Dev and Knoll shared a look. "Fig..." Dev began. "It could take hours to get to the right temperature, and the bloodril will need to melt down."

Suddenly the heat from the forge felt like too much, and she couldn't breathe. "We don't have hours. Vaelor doesn't have hours." She flung her hand to point; the blood was now trailing down the white tunic.

"Can't Mairead help him?" Dev asked, panic pitching his voice too high.

The red sister shook her head. "That's not a normal wound."

"Can't we try?" Fig asked.

Mairead's throat bobbed, and she nodded, uncorking the flask at her belt and pouring a few droplets onto Vaelor's wound. Then she lay her tattooed hands over it and muttered a prayer.

Knoll had disappeared, and Fig turned to look around for him. Had the blasted dwarf left them? She tried not to watch what was happening with Vaelor—torn between hoping that the holy water had worked and the black pit of fear that opened every time she let herself consider the possibility that it wouldn't work. Not on an enchanted crossover wound.

Fig stalked over behind the dragonhead in search of Knoll. They had to get the forge ready, they had to—

"Baldwyn's hammer!" the dwarf cursed as he ran into her, cradling something in his hands.

"I'm sorry, I—" Fig backed up, her hands raised in apology. "Is that...?"

"Oh, aye," Knoll said. "Bloodril ore."

Fig nodded, her heart racing. "Vaelor's in a bad way. Is there any way we can hurry the process along?"

"Not the forging, no," he said right away. "Rush and you'll ruin it. But heating up the dragonhead and melting the ore? I think we can try. With your help."

She rounded on the forge and her reluctant gaze swept over to

Vaelor and Mairead. His tunic was stained in bloody water, but his eyes were still open. That was good, at least.

"Dev," Fig called, "we've got the ore. Knoll says we can speed up the heating process. Can you help?"

He gave her forearm a squeeze, and the two of them took opposite sides of the forge, with Knoll positioned in front.

"Wait," Fig said, handing the bag over to Knoll. "Here's the sword. I've put it together once before, if you want help—"

"I can do that, lass," he said, his deep voice giving her a measure of reassurance.

Emrah, I really wish you were here, Fig thought suddenly with a glance at Vaelor.

When he didn't respond, she shook her head, wishing to the Bard she hadn't spoken in the first place, because now, with every second it took for the dragonet to respond, her worries increased tenfold. She forced herself to brush the fears aside. With their newly strengthened connection, she was sure she would know if something happened to Emrah. Maybe, once the forge's flames were hot enough, she could try to look into his vision again.

Wordlessly, she took Knoll's instructions to the letter, refining her flames to scorching white-hot gold as he pulled the coal lever once more. Wisps of purple wind darted through the forge at Knoll's orders, pulling the backdraft up through the vent in the top of the dragon's head with unnatural speed.

"More!" Knoll shouted at Fig. He was busy feeding a crucible into the dragon's maw with a long pole, the bloodril ore in its cavity.

She bent her knees slightly as more flames surged from her core, feeding the dragon. Flames danced before her eyes, the gold turning blue and white as they leapt from her control and multiplied among their brethren.

"Keep it up!"

Caught up in the glow and the heat, Fig wouldn't have spotted the silver figure enter the chamber if she hadn't chosen that moment to check on Vaelor. Even beside the great forge, the sharp scent of blood—of biting copper—hit her.

Liess Astor stood in the doorway, her axe drawn and a sneer on her cruel face.

FIG

Fig swayed as she stepped away from the forge, a sudden wall of exhaustion slamming into her. She was covered in sweat, and her legs wobbled as she staggered toward Vaelor, who sat unprotected in the middle of the chamber with Mairead.

Two silverswords followed behind Liess, swords raised and helms covering their heads.

Knoll couldn't move from the forge while he held the crucible in place with the pole. By the Bard's holy luck, Fig thought they'd gotten the forge hot enough. But—

Liess moved faster than Fig's eyes could track, hovering over Vaelor with her axe at his neck. The other two silverswords silently flanked her from behind.

Mairead had scrambled a few feet away, and Liess seemed content to ignore her for now. Vaelor, clutching his heart, was at least aware enough to know what was going on.

If they didn't get that sword fixed soon, nothing would matter anymore.

"Liess," Dev said, the purple wind around him dying out as he stepped away from the forge, sweat soaking his brow.

From the way the flames licked the insides of the dragon's maw, it seemed like the extra attention to air had created more than enough heat. Fig could see the ore in the crucible start to melt around the edges, black and silver in a sea of golden flames.

"My prince," Liess said, "come with me, and I might spare your Viren. Though he's not long for Morgha's arms if you ask me. I can barely hear his sword. Hardly a whisper."

"Why are you doing this?" Dev asked, brow furrowed. He extended his hands before him as if in supplication.

Liess glared at him, shifting from foot to foot. "I have my reasons."

"Bard's quills, Liess," Dev said, taking a step forward. "I saved you in the salt swamps! More than once! Malhela, you even saved me from that wood mage!"

"I did that for Rhivven," she growled.

Her arm jerked slightly, and several things happened all at once. Green light flickered over Fig's vision, then went away. A burst of amethyst bloomed in her periphery, and the two silver-sword backups lunged—one coming for Fig, the other for Dev.

Fig didn't have time to think before the silversword charged at her with inhuman speed. Flames burst to her hands—she raised them in front of her like a shield. She couldn't use flames to stop something like a sword from bearing down on her, but she shoved the flames at the silversword in desperation, ducking and turning away behind the man.

The silversword changed direction in a too-swift motion, catching Fig with a strike of his elbow to her stomach and causing her to double over. She felt like she'd been hit with a cannonball. Coughing and spluttering, she dropped to one knee and called on her inner flames, which felt even stronger after lighting the forge. Scorching hot white-gold flames burst from her palms as the silversword lunged in with his weapon, which he promptly dropped when it hit the flames. If touching a silversword's weapon was like pulling out their heart, then her scorching flames sent the man screaming to the floor, clutching his torso in apparent pain.

Fig didn't relent. She had to buy Knoll time—for him to fix the sword—and protect Vaelor and the others.

She brought the scorching flames closer and, with a roar of fury, pushed them at him all at once. He stopped moving. Panting, blood pounding in her ears, she turned to look at the others.

Dev had his man down almost as quickly. Though he couldn't move as fast as a silversword, he'd been trained to become one for most of his life. He used strong wisps of air to throw the silversword's balance off time and again, striking with his sword in between gusts and tripping the silversword with hard ribbons of air.

Mairead, fingers dripping in Vaelor's blood and holy water, drew a sigil in the air and shoved it toward Liess, who still loomed over Vaelor with an impassioned eye on her comrades' battles.

The silversword ducked, evidently familiar with the rune magic of the red brothers, and lashed out with a sweep kick, knocking Mairead off her feet.

The open flask of holy water fell with the sharp sound of broken glass on the floor, its contents spilling over the stones amid the shards. Mairead ducked to the ground, desperately clawing her fingers through the holy water to coat them, then signing yet another rune.

Liess aimed a swipe of her axe in the red sister's direction. The axe missed, and Mairead grinned, but she was rubbing her fingers together, now dry of holy water.

Fig felt like she was running through molasses as she tried to reach them, bringing the scorching flames back to her fingers. Liess had cost them their holy water. What use was fixing the sword now if they couldn't rekindle Vaelor's connection with it?

Vaelor, spurred on by the fight—or emboldened at the sight of Fig surging toward Liess with murder in her eyes—got to his feet and faced Liess, his mundane sword drawn with inhuman speed despite his condition.

Fig drew up next to him. "Vaelor, get back!"

"No, goldfire," he said in a low voice. "I have to try." He stepped forward, angling one shoulder in front of Fig.

Liess glared at the line of them. "A broken Viren, a disgraced priestess, and a fugitive mage. Quite the collection of outcasts you're hiding behind, Dev! I'm not going to kill you, you know."

"Why do I doubt that," Dev called back. Wind flicked through the chamber. From the forge, Knoll uttered a wordless yell of outrage at the air mage.

The amethyst wind flickered and went out, and Dev came up beside Fig, his sword ready.

As soon as he drew level with Fig, Liess lashed out with her axe. To everyone's surprise, Vaelor met her weapon with his mundane sword, grunting with the effort of holding her off. He staggered but held.

Dev tried to strike while she was engaged, but she twisted away, throwing Vaelor off balance and causing him to stumble back.

Sparks dripped from Fig's hands as she gathered flames to her palms, ready to strike back at Liess for all of the problems she had caused Dev—caused all of them—but Dev was too close now for her to risk throwing fire. He rose to meet Liess with his blade, and a dense swath of purple air seeped from his fingers as they clashed.

Fig was about to yell at him to stop, to protect the air currents in the chamber, but the purple wind wove like a ribbon down Dev's sword, careful, controlled. Liess whirled around, an armored elbow slamming into Dev's face.

Dev staggered back, blood dripping from his nose and mouth. He coughed, spitting blood onto the stone floor.

"Oh," Liess said, "I didn't—"

Vaelor had recovered; perhaps Mairead had been able to staunch the wound at his heart after all. Fig couldn't think about the loss of the holy water right now or she'd lose her spark altogether. He lashed out at Liess, who let out a cry as she swung her axe to fend him off. He staggered back a few paces to regain his balance.

Before Fig could surge in with the flames at her palms, Liess swung again and again, moving almost too quickly to be seen. Vaelor caught a few blows with his sword, one of them knocking him off balance again.

They'd taken the fight across the chamber back by the pool of water, and Fig edged forward, looking for an opening.

Dev was on his hands and knees, trying to staunch the flow of blood from his face. His eyes had swollen, and it looked like he could barely see between the bruises, swelling, and blood. Mairead dashed over, ripping off a piece of her cloak as she ran.

Flames glowed at Fig's core, but every time she inched closer to the silversword fight, Liess positioned Vaelor between them. Liess looked like she was barely putting forth any effort in fighting Vaelor—like she was toying with him. It was remarkable how he could barely stand half an hour ago, and now he was fighting one of the best silverswords. Fig knew that Liess could end it any second. She had to get in there.

She dashed forward when Vaelor's back was to her, then she darted to the right, flames dripping from her hands. A kick to the chest sent Fig flying to the stone floor. She gasped and stared up at the ceiling. Fig forced herself up on her elbows, dragging in breaths as she tried to scramble to her feet. She needed to reach Vaelor.

"Would you just—" Liess growled, aiming a swipe at Vaelor to force him back. But his reaction speed was too slow.

The sharp blade sliced through the air and cut straight through Vaelor's chest.

His fractured, rusty eyes opened wide, meeting Fig's for a brief second before blood spurted from the wound.

Then he fell.

He seemed to fall for ages, the back of his legs hitting the low stone wall around the pool of water meant for the forge. The fresh blood spread, joining what had seeped from his wounded heart. His eyes closed just before he slipped beneath the surface of the pool.

Fingers curling into flaming claws, Fig scrambled to her feet and rushed forward, seeming to lose all feeling in her body even though her legs were moving as fast as they could. Rising heat scorched her insides, her throat.

"No!" she roared. And she wasn't surprised when golden flames bellowed from her throat straight at Liess, the hatred and anger building within her like a forge of its own. "No!" The flames roared from her throat like the pain inside her scoured her insides.

Fig didn't see the silversword fall to the floor. She only saw Vaelor lying in the pool, the water splashing against the basin's sides lost to her ears. She could only hear the roar of the flames behind her—the dragonhead forge that was supposed to be their savior.

And the clank of a hammer like a heartbeat.

Heat surged in her throat once more, and she longed to roar flames in Knoll's direction. What did the sword matter now? The sound of the hammer mocked her, for the heart of the swordsman that was surely no longer beating.

Time caught up with her as she leapt into the pool, and the water met her skin through her clothes. She sank down to put her hands around Vaelor's shoulders, yanking his limp body close to her.

"Vaelor," the word sounded raw, her throat feeling like... feeling like she'd just breathed fire. She swallowed, the action no less painful. "Vaelor."

His eyes were closed, and he didn't move, blond hair floating serenely around his head.

The hammering continued behind her, and she tore her gaze from Vaelor to glare at Knoll. The dwarf still stood at the mouth of the forge, having united Vaelor's sword with the molten bloodril. He now hammered away at its imperfections, beating it, shaping it. The echoes of silver rang through the chamber around them.

Tears streamed from her eyes as she turned back to Vaelor, thinking it was fitting in a way. Vaelor could have his sword returned to him in the end, better than ever with the bloodril ore.

She...she would see to it he was buried with it. In Viren.

She'd failed to protect him, to fix his sword. The sword he'd broken in her defense, the same one that had caused his crossover wound on that battlefield in Viren years ago.

She put a hand over his chest and gaped. His tunic was torn from shoulder to hip. The scar over his heart—long healed. And nothing else. The blood was gone. The axe-wound, healed.

A gasp ripped through him, and he sat up, hands scrambling around him and then grasping her. Fig's shriek filled the cavern.

CHAPTER

46

FIG

Mairead rushed over, the hammering at the forge continuing behind her.

"Vaelor! W-what?" Fig stuttered, breathing so hard it hurt.

Mairead dropped to her knees at the edge of the pool, cupping the water in her hands. "*Holy water.* It's undiluted holy water! I can't..."

"*What?*" Fig repeated. She could barely breathe, barely... She searched Vaelor's face. The ring in his eyes was no longer broken, but the rust color remained. All the air rushed out of her and she flung her arms around him, almost knocking him back into the water. And then she drew back and kissed him with everything she had.

The fear and fury died as her lips met his, and his hands clutched her head as if she were the most precious thing in the world. Time froze around them. There was no more hammering at the forge, no battle above—only the two of them.

And then it was over with the *clang* of a hammer. Panting,

343

they drew apart, and she felt tears pouring from her eyes only to drip down into the water.

He was alive. By some lucky pen stroke of the Bard, he was alive. She flung her arms around him again, burying her face in his shoulder.

Then a low voice rumbled through her. "Now *this* is more like that night on the Twist."

A watery chuckle escaped, and she brushed tears from her eyes, pulling back to look at him. They were soaking wet and clutching each other, and she was scared out of her wits. Yes, it *was* more like that night on the Twist.

Out of the corner of her eye, Fig saw Liess Astor lying on the ground a few feet away, which yanked her unkindly back into the pit of Malhela they were still in. Burned strands of hair framed Liess's face, and the skin on her hands was also badly burned. She couldn't see the woman's face, which was turned away, but Fig thought she could see her chest rising and falling weakly. Somehow, that silversword had better luck than the Bard.

The other silverswords had not been so lucky. The one Fig had fought lay dead on his back, staring up at the chamber ceiling, burns ravaging his face and hands. The one Dev had fought lay in a pool of blood.

Mairead drew herself up stiffly, arms crossed as she stared down at the pool. Fig blinked, beginning to come to her senses. She and Vaelor were sitting in a large pool of undiluted holy water—probably the most sacrilegious thing they could be doing.

Dev, holding a piece of cloth to his bloody, broken nose, helped pull the two of them from the pool, but they couldn't stop the water from dripping across the floor as they got out. Fig cringed as she stood there, dripping. Mairead simultaneously looked like she was going to throw up and cry as she stood there wringing her hands.

"I'm sorry," Fig muttered, feeling terrible about defiling the holy water.

Mairead shook her head with a shaky chuckle. "It's fine. It's fine! Vaelor, I'm so glad you're alive. I just—Why is there a large pool of holy water here? I didn't think the Sisters of Morgha practiced in the Mountain before."

Clang. Knoll returned the sword to the forge, letting it regain its heat. Vaelor flinched at the sight of the sword entering the flames dancing off the white-hot coals. The warmth of the forge had already begun to dry Fig's clothing.

Even from here, Fig could see silver veins in the weapon that glowed through the flames with an ethereal presence, where the bloodril had mended the cracks of the original weapon. The dwarf pulled the glowing sword out, inspected it once more, and strode toward them.

Fig couldn't help but notice Vaelor was standing straighter than he had in days. That was what bathing in full strength holy water would do, she supposed. She herself felt better than she had in a long time, a veil of exhaustion lifted—she actually felt a little light-headed.

"Not holy water," Knoll said, stepping to the edge of the pool, the white-hot sword before him.

Mairead gasped when Knoll plunged it into the water. It hissed loudly, creating a cloud of steam that billowed over them all.

"Then what is it?" Mairead demanded, taking a step forward, a menacing look on her tattooed face.

"It's just water," Knoll said. "Water that's been touched by bloodril since before the gods walked the continent."

Fig's jaw dropped, gazing down at her and Vaelor, covered in the water. "No," Fig said. "It's holy water, like the pool at Mar Nevan. Vaelor's healed...he..."

Knoll looked at her pointedly. He turned his back and returned to reheat the sword in the forge, then he laid it on the flat anvil of the dragon's front teeth. *Clang. Clang.*

"Bloodril?" Dev said, coming closer to Mairead.

She jumped, shaken. "It can't be... Only holy water blessed by Morgha can heal like that..." Mairead whispered.

Fig stared at the pool along with the rest of them. "It must be..."

"No," Mairead said.

"It's the bloodril," Knoll said, striking his hammer again. "Bloodril in the pools down here. Bloodril in the pool at Mar Nevan."

No one spoke.

Fig's stomach roiled. The healing water had flowed over bloodril, which ran deep through the dwarves' Mountain. Was it so ludicrous to think there would be more bloodril deposits through the rocky highlands, as far west as Mar Nevan, where another large pool in an ethereal cavern had healed thousands upon thousands across the Svoran continent? Where water was carted to founts to be diluted, its priestesses blessed with the water's magic to turn diluted water into the kind that healed?

Mairead dropped to her knees, and Fig winced. She wanted to put a hand on Mairead's shoulder and tell her it was all right. That her world wasn't crumbling around her. That her goddess's healing powers didn't come from a stone that could be found deep in Tytan's earthen crust. That...

Vaelor swayed beside Fig, and she grabbed his arm, giving him a searching look. He appeared as light-headed as Fig.

"Knoll?" she called. Mairead's goddess would have to wait. "How's that sword coming?"

The dwarf grunted, coming back to the pool with the sword glowing hot once more. A hiss, and a cloud of steam, and he held it aloft in front of them.

Silver veins of bloodril glinted at them as Knoll held up the sword for inspection. The blade was smooth once more, whole and complete. He held it closer to Vaelor, who took it. Fig held her breath, which didn't help with the light-headedness.

"How does that feel?" Knoll asked.

Everyone watched as Vaelor reunited with his weapon, now reforged—stronger than ever. Knoll was practically glowing—not just with sweat, but with an overwhelming sense of triumph and something Fig couldn't quite put her finger on. The deepest sense of the earth, the veins of bloodril, the holy water—it all echoed through Knoll too, a profound magic.

Her chest lifted. This was it. The sword had to work. Fig searched Vaelor's eyes.

The rust pervaded.

The connection still wasn't complete. It felt like a bucket of water doused her inner fire. Of course she shouldn't have expected it would be that simple.

Mairead cleared her throat after a minute. "I've been thinking... Do you think we need to repeat the crossover ritual?"

"No!" Fig said at once, sparks flickering at her fingertips. "Absolutely not. I don't care if we have a whole cavern of holy water, we're not trying that—"

A growl and a snap at the door drew their attention, and Fig whirled to see her vision flooded with a pleasant green glow. Emrah had come, but apparently the blue and silver dragonet had been lurking outside the chamber of Morin-Song and was now locked scale and claw with Emrah midair in the doorway.

Fig rushed over. "Stop it! Stop! Emrah? What are you doing here?"

The blue dragonet growled, and Emrah's belly lit like a forge full of coals. The blue took the warning and backed off, retreating to the shadows once more. It was clear that the dragonets avoided this place for a reason—was it the bloodril?

Blasted briigards, Emrah grumbled. *I saw you were in trouble, that the silverswords had come down here—Oh. I see you handled them. Well, I hope Ziggy's not too mad I left her up there.*

"Oh, Emrah," Fig cried, rushing forward. He sailed over to land on her shoulder, enveloping her in the scent of smoke and dust. She ran her hand down his neck in reassurance. "You're here, thank the Bard and all his scrolls."

What in Drakioryn's scaly backside happened here, and why haven't you fixed the connection with Vaelor yet? You do look a bit better, Viren, but something's not right.

"I think we should do the crossover ritual again," Mairead said.

"And I think that's too great a risk," Fig countered. She couldn't stand the idea of that sword striking a killing blow on

Vaelor, not after he'd died once already. What if a second crossover wasn't possible? If only they'd been able to get their hands on the texts at Mar Nevan with all the crossover lore. Those wounds weren't simple wounds, she knew that much.

Dev, his voice thicker than usual due to his broken nose, said, "I agree with Fig. The water may have healed him, but who knows if the ritual would work twice..." He adjusted the scrap of fabric he had pressed to his nose to keep the blood from flowing.

"You know," Vaelor rumbled, "I am right here. I'm not quite in Morgha's arms yet."

Fig smiled weakly, meeting his rust-ringed eyes. "Then what do you think?"

He bobbed his head slightly, damp hair falling in thick strands over his shoulders as he gazed down at the newly mended sword he held before him. "I can't...*feel* the new sword. Not like it was before. Not yet. It's like it's just out of my reach—a light in a faraway room, while I'm standing in the dark. Before it was mended, it was like the faraway light had almost gone out."

Emrah twitched on her shoulder, and Fig's core warmed. *I'm glad you came back, my friend,* she told him privately. *I need you here.* She reached out with her mind and was intuitively able to show him flashes of her memories about what had just happened. It was just as easy as sending her thoughts to him—some new phenomenon with their full bond, it seemed.

He chirped behind her ear, one of his claws accidentally digging into her shoulder at the sight of the memories, of Vaelor being dealt a killing blow.

"Wait a minute," Fig said aloud, her thoughts reeling. "What if we don't repeat the whole silversword ritual? What if we modify it?"

Mairead looked at her like she'd grown scales. Fig studied her reflection in the pool of bloodril infused water, but she looked the same, if a little bloodied, wet, and dirty. But she'd breathed fire when facing down Liess, and she'd never heard of a fire mage doing that before—even Afrith with his advanced techniques. It had to have something to do with the bond, like Fig and Emrah's powers were enhancing each other with the connection.

Just like they needed Vaelor and his sword to do.

"I don't think that will work," Mairead said kindly. "The silversword ritual has been the same for centuries. If there was a way to modify it, wouldn't they have done it before?"

"When I completed the bond with Emrah," Fig explained, "do you remember what I said we'd been missing? Blood and fire. He'd taken blood from me and given me fire—giving us that partial bond. But to finish it, we had to complete the circle. I had to take his blood and give him fire too."

"I don't think that will..." Dev started. "Well, wait a minute. You, Fig, were obviously predisposed to bonding with Emrah. Fire, of course. But Vaelor isn't a mage, so—"

"The sword," Mairead said. "The sword cut him in the original ritual, and the water—"

"Healed them both," Fig finished. "Vaelor. What if you... make a mark on the weapon. And since it's a new sword, it should make a mark on you too, drawing blood. Nothing like the original ritual, just a symbolic cut." It was a reach, she knew. Without knowing the exact arcane magic behind the ritual, it might not work. But it seemed less risky than killing him again.

Vaelor's throat bobbed, and he nodded. "Whatever you say, goldfire."

As Knoll readied the tools Vaelor would need to make a mark upon the mended sword, Fig leaned against the pool of bloodril water with her eyes closed. Her throat burned something fierce. She wondered if Mairead would be offended if she used some of the bloodril water to heal herself. All of the bruises and sore muscles from her fight with the silversword were gone, healed in the pool. It was...a miracle.

Dev and Vaelor had moved the bodies of the dead silverswords out into the hallway. Somehow, by the hand of Morgha, Liess Astor still breathed. Dev wouldn't accept Knoll's suggestion to finish her off, and Fig had remained silent. A dark part of her wished her flames had accidentally ended Liess.

It was Mairead who came up with a solution. With a whispered prayer asking for forgiveness, she sank tentative fingers into the pool of water, then signed some kind of rune, ending with a pushing motion toward Liess's prone body.

"There," Mairead said.

"There...what?" Dev asked thickly. His nose had stopped bleeding, but it was broken, black and blue bruises blooming under his eyes.

"She's bound," Mairead said. "I—er—think. I know the bind rune from the crossover ritual, anyway. Maybe we should check." The last bit sounded more like a question, but Mairead didn't move.

Dev gathered amethyst-colored magic to his hands, thick and dense, and approached. The 'sword's axe had fallen when she'd collapsed, and he sent a ribbon of air to move it farther from Liess's hand. The woman didn't move. He nudged her with his toe and turned her over. Her arms stayed awkwardly where they were in relation to her torso and hung midair as she now lay on her back.

"Ah," Dev said. "That's much easier than binding with air. And that's permanent?"

Mairead nodded. "I think until I do an unbind rune."

Fig stared in awe. "A bind rune, did you say? Are the ones you used in the crossover ritual the same as the red brothers use?"

Mairead raised her tattooed hands in frustration. "Some of them, yes, but there's so many more that I don't know. Mother Savidah only teaches the crossover ones to the sisters, unfortunately."

"That's what we'll need to have Vaelor carve into the sword then," Fig said.

Mairead nodded slowly. "That could work. At least the holy water seems to have bought us some time."

Fig pressed her lips together in a tight smile. It would have to work. And at least now they had a surplus of the healing water—

whether it was blessed by Morgha or simply the bloodril of the ground was for the Bard to decide.

Dust fell from the ceiling as something exploded far above them in a distant cavern. Fig looked up while Dev was busy pacing the chamber, chatting quietly with Emrah.

Fig massaged her pained throat as she ambled over to see how Knoll was getting on. He practically growled at her when she peered over his shoulder while he looked through King Morin's tools, so she headed over to Dev, fighting to keep nervous sparks from jumping out of her hands.

The battle waged far above, and now that Emrah was down here, they had no way of knowing its outcome.

"Eventually, Djuren is going to lead the other silverswords down here if they succeed against the dwarves," Dev said quietly when she reached him. "They know how much the dwarves value King Morin's sword, though hopefully, not the *full* extent of the ore's properties."

Fig nodded, a sick feeling in her stomach. Liess had found the chamber, and Djuren knew about it too. How long did they have before more came?

"I don't think it would take them too long to figure out about the water," Dev said.

Fig's jaw dropped as everything fell into place. She rounded back on Knoll. "*This* was the great danger—" she said, pointing at the pool of water. "This was what King Morin discovered. That the holy water of Morgha was actually bloodril water. *That* was the great danger to life in Tytan, wasn't it?"

Knoll looked up from the tools, brows furrowed.

"And you knew," Fig went on. "You kept forging Vaelor's blade, even though we all thought he was dead. You knew it would heal him."

"Oh, aye," Knoll grunted irritably, gripping a fine-pointed carving pick like he wanted to shove it into somebody's eye. Fig took a step back. "And why do you think I let Valencia lead my people? She speaks the truth. I am a traitor, not just to the dwarves, but to all of Tytan—gods, even Tysaine. The water of bloodril will heal *any,* but that knowledge would crumble the foundations of the Sisters of Morgha and the very gods themselves. Only the descendants of Morin knew, and I am the last. The only one now."

He bowed his head. "The silverswords would kill every last dwarf for unfettered access to the water. I heard about what they did in Viren"—he flung a hand to indicate Vaelor—"forcing the Virenish to take the silver or die. And that was with the blessing of Mar Nevan. Without? They'll be unstoppable. Killing and converting until the continent is covered in silver. Which is why I kept this knowledge to myself."

Tears welling in her eyes, Mairead said, "But you're just one person, Knoll."

"One person is enough to change the direction of history," he said as another faint explosion from far above echoed through the chamber. "The Bard knows that much."

Dev cleared his throat. "You're not just one person, Knoll. You're a part of this—we all are. And Vaelor? Let's finish what we started, eh?"

Knoll handed a case of tools to Vaelor. "These were King Morin's, and I've no doubt they'll make their mark on your sword. Any idiot can tap a small hammer into a pick."

Vaelor gave him a rust-ringed look.

"Erm—not that I meant—"

Vaelor's mouth turned up in an unexpected smile, and he opened the case, pulling out the picks to examine them. Mairead came over and began to instruct Vaelor on which runes to carve, while Knoll oversaw the carving.

Fig sidled up to Dev once more.

"You want a dry-off?" Dev offered, amethyst wind coming to his fingers.

"That would be fantastic," Fig said, practically melting at the idea. The hot air in the chamber had mostly dried her, but she was still damp and humid, and her hair clung to the back of her neck.

The air that fluttered through her clothes was almost as refreshing as the healing water had been. Fig swayed a little, the light-headed feeling coming back, so she decided to sit down before she fell down. Dev did the same. They both sat cross-legged, watching the slow progress of the rune-carving.

"This had better work," Fig said quietly.

Dev bumped her shoulder, and Emrah sailed over them to land on Fig's other side.

No one said anything for a while. The gentle *tinking* of the hammer hit the pick as Vaelor sat with his sword across his lap, carving the various shapes that Mairead had drawn on the floor for him using a piece of charcoal. She wiped each one away with the hem of her cloak, clearly worried about invoking some sort of magic.

Out of nowhere, Dev said quietly, "We can't let the silverswords get down here. This chamber—the truth about the water? That needs to stay with us—and at most, the dwarves. It's their Mountain."

Fig nodded, her stomach a storm of nerves. "You're right." She kept her final thought to herself, in that they could already be on their way down here. Anxious sparks danced just under the skin of her fingertips.

The dwarves were prepared for this fight, Emrah told them. *They lured the silverswords here. Though, from what I could tell, the silverswords were prepared too. That army didn't seem anything like the one at Rayva, but a new force gathered from across Tytan with Liess at the head of it.*

Fig's neck cracked as she whipped her head around to look at Liess. The silversword lay prone, unable to move the outside of her body.

"What are we going to do with *her?* Leave her down here to her fate?"

Dev sighed, an uncharacteristically serious sound that made him seem older than his years. "We'll decide after the battle is won."

The Bard knew that depended on *who* won.

Fig cleared her throat and winced, the motion not escaping the notice of Emrah or Dev.

"What is it?" Dev asked.

She breathed fire, Emrah supplied with a snort.

"What?"

Fig massaged her neck. "Yes, and my throat is killing me."

"You're not turning into a dragon, are you?" Dev asked, though through his joking tone, she detected a sense of seriousness.

She shook her head. "Of course not!" *Erm,* she thought privately, *right Emrah?*

Sparks snorted from the dragonet, and he replied to both of them, *Of course not. I've heard of dragonet bonds before, even if it hasn't happened in centuries. But never anything about Svorans turning into dragons. I doubt even your Bard tells of any such tales.*

"Good. I like my body how it is."

"Seems like Vaelor does too—" Dev started.

Fig elbowed him rudely in the side, eyes rolling. "Enough out of you, my king." She rubbed her throat absently.

There's a whole pool of holy water right there, Emrah said.

"I know, I just feel...strange...getting it myself." She shrugged.

A chuckle rolled from Dev. "Fig, you were practically swimming in it a little while ago. Go, I think offending the gods—or more imminently, *Mairead*—is the least of our worries right now. Actually, I could use a healing myself." His broken nose had stopped bleeding, but his face was a black and red mess.

Fig gave him a small smile and rose to her feet. Emrah's wings fluttered as he took off from her shoulder, sailing high in the mixed air currents of the chamber.

She tentatively approached the pool. Her gaze cut toward Mairead automatically, hoping the priestess wasn't paying attention, but of course, Fig must have drawn her eye, and Mairead was looking right at her.

The red sister gave her a sad smile and nodded.

Taking that for as much of an invitation to use the water as she would get, Fig turned her back on everyone and reached into the water with a cupped hand. She wasn't exactly keen on swallowing water that had been running untouched through the

Mountain for decades, but she wasn't sure what else to do. There was no way in Malhela she could just gargle it and spit it out in front of Mairead, whether the girl had given her permission or not. Besides, the burning sensation went a lot farther than just the back of her throat.

So she threw the handful of holy water back, swallowing it. As it ran down past her raw throat, it immediately cooled the burning sensation with an unmistakably metallic sense of magic that seeped into her body. Thankfully, the light-headedness was starting to go away too, something she'd worried was caused by bathing in the bloodril water to begin with. More likely, she had been dehydrated. She blinked, an actual smile coming to her face as she turned around to check on Vaelor's progress, passing Dev on his way to the pool.

Mairead was kneeling beside Vaelor, sketching a rune with a long line and two forks leading off the top, the whole thing intersected by a half-circle. "This one seals the circle of magic, protecting the rune string as a whole," she explained, briefly meeting Fig's gaze in acknowledgment.

Vaelor nodded and began carving it, each clink of the hammer bringing them closer to the end. Then he paused halfway through finishing the circle and looked up at all of them.

Fig swallowed, her brow furrowed, "Vaelor—"

"Before I finish," he began, his deep voice rumbling through their small circle, "I wanted to thank each of you."

Fig's stomach tightened at the seriousness of his words. It sounded like he thought it wouldn't work.

"Knoll, I am forever in your debt for mending my sword, making it better than new. And for you to operate such a forge with such skill, I do not doubt that you are worthy of King Morin's heritage." He put a fist over his heart and gave him a respectful half bow from where he sat.

Knoll's beard twitched, and Fig thought she saw moisture in his eyes as he looked away and back toward the dragonhead.

"Mairead, I couldn't have done this without you," Vaelor said with emotion, shaking his head. "The sisterhood was wrong to cast you out."

Mairead gave him a watery smile and put a hand on his knee.

"Dev, my life is in service to you—"

"Nonsense," Dev interjected fiercely. "I thank the gods every day that you defied Rhivven at your crossover and swore your oath to my family instead of the enclave. I just wish I could have returned the favor better—"

"You've done that and more."

Pressure had been building in Fig's chest, so much that she was worried she would breathe fire with all the pent-up energy, when Vaelor finally turned to her.

"Fig... Nothing else would have kept me working toward mending the connection with my sword but you. And for that?" He looked down, blond eyelids fluttering as he resumed carving the half-circle. "I'm naming my sword after you. It was forged in your flames, after all. *Goldfire.*"

Fig swallowed, glad her raw throat had been healed, because now every fiber of her being swelled with emotion at the odd sense of finality in his words. "I love you." The words came out without thinking, and she was glad the heat of the forge had already made her face red.

"And I you," he said softly, meeting her gaze once more, then turning to finish the rune with a final *clink.*

Fig's heart surged into her throat as she waited for something to happen. Nothing changed, except tears threatening at the corners of her eyes. They'd come all this way... *No.*

"Oh!" she cried, "Now the sword needs to mark you—"

Vaelor nodded solemnly.

"And the runes filled with blood and holy water," Mairead said, "like the original ritual."

"Of course," Fig said nervously.

Everyone stood up, forming a circle, Vaelor pointing his sword out in the middle.

Without preamble, Vaelor lifted the sword in his right hand, admiring the grip and the runes carved along the bloodril sword for a moment before taking the blade to his left forearm. Fig's stomach clenched as blood welled from the cut.

Mairead lurched toward the pool of water and came back with a small handful. After exchanging a quick look with Vaelor, she held out her hand. He dripped some of the blood into the water.

The red sister quickly got to work, dipping her finger into the bloody water mixture. Fig tried not to think of the last crossover she'd witnessed, with Mairead desperately scooping holy water from the fount at the Nithe castle, to no avail.

This was different, though. It had to be.

Fig gasped when the bloody water met the first rune and a sliver glow emanated from the carving. Mairead repeated the gesture, tracing each rune carefully with the bloody water. Slowly the entire string of runes came to life, each glowing with the holy water that was not holy, but perhaps still contained more than just the magic of the earth. When the last half-circle was traced, Vaelor gasped and fell to one knee, the tip of his sword clanking to the ground as he gasped for breath, clutching his chest with his other hand.

Surging to his side, Fig put her hand on him, searching his face for—

A silver glow emanated from his eyes, bursting through the red-rust that had settled there. The silver ring was whole and unbroken. His skin seemed to glow too, the strongest at his chest where he grasped his heart—the scar from his crossover, physically gone, but the magic resided there.

Fig's breath was racing as she watched him.

Finally, finally the glow faded.

"Vaelor?" Dev asked, stepping closer.

"Aye, my lord," Vaelor rumbled, holding out a hand to Fig and lifting her up as he stood. He towered over her as usual, but he stood straight, power coming off him like the sharp tang of steel—or bloodril, more likely. Fig's heart lifted.

"Are you..." she began.

"I am whole." He reached down and stroked her cheekbone with his calloused thumb, silver gaze meeting gold.

An explosion rumbled above, sifting dust down from the ceiling. Vaelor's hand shifted to her arm, and she glanced at the wide-open doors of the chamber. It was time to go.

"Well?" Knoll said to Dev, hefting King Morin's hammer. "From one lost heir to another, like the mighty Baldwyn says: Let us crush our enemy into the ground with the force of our fury."

DEV

The cavern of Corryn lay ahead, and the five of them stood at the mouth of the tunnel leading into it—the two dragonets sailing high above, avoiding one another so as not to cross claws again.

Dev, the lithe air mage, stood with his hand on his sword, amethyst-colored air gathering in deadly pockets at his fingertips. Knoll, the muscled dwarf wielding the hammer of King Morin, radiated earthen magic. Vaelor, freshly united with his sword, practically glowed with strength. Fig had gained more than any of them yet realized from bonding with Emrah. And Mairead, her red tattoos glowing, now carried the power of rune magic.

They made quite the group.

A piece of a bridge collapsed in an explosion, sending a bevy of silverswords falling. A rallying cry went up among the dwarves, but the battle wasn't won yet. More silverswords had reached the floor of the cavern, where they could engage in close combat with devastating results. Dead dwarves lay by the score around the halls of their ancestors.

Without preamble, Knoll raised his hammer high and made to jump into the fray.

"Wait!" Dev called. "We need to keep the silverswords from coming down here at all costs."

"Aye, what do you think I'm doing?"

"We should get to Valencia and rally the dwarves. The silverswords appear to be converging on the main floor—what if this is their final goal?"

Knoll gave him a stiff nod, and he charged into the cavern, hammer raised.

Gathering purple wind as he went, Dev followed Knoll toward the tower—the place where the dwarves had concentrated their defenses and the most likely place for the dwarf leader to be. Fig called flames to her hands and followed, Vaelor at her side.

A silversword slammed into Knoll, and before Dev could come to his aid, a pair of silverswords closed in on Dev. He gathered the wind to his arms and condensed it to a thick band curling around his sword.

The bulkier silversword lunged first, his large claymore swinging right for Dev's midsection. Dev sidestepped, quick on his feet, while throwing his ribbons of air to trip up the silversword's legs.

The other silversword darted in with inhuman speed, faster than most silverswords Dev had ever seen or trained with. She wielded a sharp dagger—fast and stealthy. In the next heartbeat, she was on Dev's other side, the dagger coming up fast—aimed to slip beneath his ribs and pierce his heart.

It was mere luck that Dev happened to whip a ribbon of wind as he caught sight of her in the corner of his eye, throwing off her aim. The dagger shifted, lightly brushing his ribs instead. But even the light brush of a dagger bit like Malhela. He lashed out another ribbon of wind, whipping it around the silversword's throat.

He saw the surprise in her eyes as he yanked her toward him, and his sword sank into her gut.

Blood spurted onto his hands and his stomach roiled. Automatically, he put a hand on her shoulder and pulled out his weapon, letting her fall to her knees.

But he didn't have time to ponder what he'd done—he barely had time to summon another ribbon of wind, feeling more than seeing his other opponent charging once more. This silversword was prepared. When Dev tried to lash out with his wind again, the man swung his claymore in its path, letting go of his sword as the wind made a grab for it.

Dev watched, shocked, as the silversword let the sword go—it was no small thing for a silversword to be parted from their weapon, whether due to physical longing or mental agony, Dev wasn't sure. But this one had willingly let go—Dev realized the trick too late. The man lunged for Dev with his gauntleted hand, grabbing Dev by the shoulder and cocking back his other fist to aim for Dev's face, which had already been bruised and broken once today. It was too close for Dev to maneuver his sword, and the Bard strike it if he was going to let another silversword mangle his face today.

He winced, yanking on the air around him to converge on the silversword holding him. The wind yanked at the fallen claymore, which had clattered to the ground nearby.

The idea of using the silversword's own weapon against him slithered into his mind, but Dev wouldn't stoop so low. Instead, he used the winds converging on the silversword to force his limbs away, prying the man's fingers off Dev and stopping his fist—pushing him back, back—

With the slice of a dwarven axe, it was all over. A young dwarf let out a "Huzzah!" as she sauntered over to stand above the silversword, bloody axe resting on her shoulder, and she gave Dev a respectful nod.

"King Verrence," she called, her golden face lighting up in delight. Dev caught sight of brilliant red hair braided around her head like a crown. "An honor to assist you, Your Majesty!" Then she sailed back into the fight, axe swinging madly.

Dev wiped blood off his face, a punch-drunk grin forming.

Two down, not bad, he thought to himself. Knoll had defeated his first foe, and had already moved on to the next, his movements swift and sure. Vaelor hadn't left Fig's side, but the two of them were fighting with golden flames and the inhuman speed of Vaelor's sword. Dev didn't see Mairead anywhere, and he wondered if she had lingered in the tunnel entrance. Not that the ex-priestess had any experience in battle, so he didn't blame her if she had stayed back.

The dwarves were filled with a righteous fury—some to the point of glee, like the girl had been; others with serious intent, like Knoll. Their home had been abandoned for decades, for no apparent reason other than King Tesvier had wanted to take it. And now they were fighting for their lives to reclaim it.

Dev glanced back at the tunnel. So far it was still on the outskirts of the fighting, but if Djuren was here, then at least one silversword knew the location of the chamber.

Was it for the secret of the bloodril that Tesvier had taken the Mountain—and then left it abandoned all these years?

The implications of the bloodril water made his stomach roil, almost as much as all the blood spilling around him. Fig was right, Dev was no silversword. But he could still make a difference. The dwarves deserved victory. They just needed to get to Valencia, to unite and rally the dwarves.

Dev spotted a lone silversword regrouping after cutting down two dwarves, and he strode over, gathering powerful ribbons of air around him.

But before he reached the silversword, Dev noticed a figure in red launch himself off a bridge with practiced hand signals—no doubt the reason the red brother had floated down through the dusty air at a safe speed, instead of falling to his death. And it was clear to Dev where the red brother's attention was focused—the tunnel leading to the chamber of Morin-Song.

"Knoll, Fig!" Dev cried, pointing.

He yanked his arm back just as quickly before an approaching silversword could take it off with their sword, and Dev was soon locked in another battle for his life. As quickly as Dev dodged, the silversword followed. But Dev hadn't trained against silverswords until he was fifteen for no reason—except, of course, his original purpose had been to become one of them. He dodged each strike with assistance from more gusts of wind, until the silversword landed a blow with the butt of his weapon in an unexpected move to Dev's gut, knocking the wind out of him.

He stumbled away, quickly gathering his senses—not a second could be lost when fighting against a silversword. Every moment mattered. Every breath.

Dev whipped out a ribbon of air, wrapping it around the silversword's torso as the man lunged in for another attack.

The exuberant dwarf girl was back, whooping as she swung her axe with violent abandon, cutting down yet another silversword speeding toward Dev. The one fighting Dev turned at the distraction, and Dev chose that moment to give a pull on the ribbon of wind and sink his sword in through a gap in the man's armor.

"I think they've started to recognize you, Your Majesty!" the dwarf called.

"Dev's just fine!" he found himself calling as he turned to get his bearings again. Sure, he'd fought hand to hand with silverswords, but never in his life had he actually been part of a full-blown battle. Dev hadn't even known he'd had air magic during the years he'd trained to become a silversword, and he'd never fought with it so openly before. Everything he'd learned at the Carriage House had been practical—putting out fires by starving them of air or using small gusts of wind to perform what now felt like purely theatrical and superfluous magic.

No, the silversword enclave hadn't wanted any of the mages at the Carriage House to learn how to fight with magic. Not even the boy who would be crown prince.

"I'm Cordwen!" the bright-eyed dwarf called as she ducked under the swing of a silversword's axe. She was quite agile for a dwarf.

In the next instant, Cordwen had downed the silversword, but not without spurting blood in Dev's direction. He grimaced and swept it away with a wave of purple-colored wind, then readied himself for the group of silverswords now moving their way—widening his stance and siphoning some wind to make pockets around himself. Knoll, Fig, and Vaelor were nearby—whether because they hadn't wanted to advance without Dev or had simply gotten no farther, he was grateful for it. He couldn't tell where Emrah had gotten to, but occasionally spotted bursts of flame out of the corner of his eye, earning cries from the afflicted silverswords.

Dev, Cordwen, and the others braced themselves as a dozen silverswords barreled down upon them, armor covered in splatters of blood. Dev yanked at the air and shoved dense air pockets at the advancing 'swords. If they had been mere men or mages, it would have knocked them over as easily as a child rolling a ball into pins. But with their strength and heavy armor, it merely slowed the silverswords down. And yet Dev kept pushing.

Before he could let go, Cordwen let out a whoop and dashed forward. As he watched her charge the silverswords in frank appreciation and a little terror for her safety, he saw something curious. A small piece of the ground rose to give her a boost, and she flew through the air toward them, axe raised. The ground had risen like a stepping stone at an alarming speed, then sunk away as soon as it had catapulted its master toward the enemy.

With a cry, Dev rushed forward to join her, blood soaring through his veins. He wrangled the wind back to thick ribbons, intent on entangling the sword on the far left of the group, but before he could, a sword burst through a gap in the man's armor, spurting blood and causing him to drop to his knees.

Over him stood a blonde Virenish woman Dev knew quite well, her sword Mystic dripping in blood.

"Ziggy—"

A loud explosion threw them all to the ground, and only one of the silverswords remained standing—the 'sword engaging Knoll on the other end of the group.

Dev dragged himself to his feet just in time to see where the red brother had gotten off to. He was already halfway through the cavern and coming their way.

He whipped his wind ribbons at one of the silverswords who advanced on him with incredible speed, the blade nearly driving into Dev's neck. He forced his muscles to respond, pushing the man back with both wind and steel, but a distinct slowness had started to creep into his tiring muscles. Ziggy rushed to his aid, throwing the silversword off balance while Dev unleashed another burst of air to trip him up. He'd been using his air magic more than ever before—even lighting the dragonhead forge had taken a tremendous toll. He wasn't sure how much longer he could keep this up.

Ziggy and Cordwen danced about beside him—one with the inhuman speed of a silversword, the other borrowing momentum from boosts from the ground—Dev noticed they were fending off attacks on Dev. Had they noticed he was flagging?

As he stepped up to the next attacker, Ziggy's sword Mystic butted in, engaging the silversword instead.

"Come on, prince-king, you do realize it's my job to keep you alive, right?"

"Yes, but—"

The silversword gave a strangled cry as Ziggy brought him down. Dev was glad for the interruption, since he didn't actually have a response to that.

Another explosion rocked the cavern, but this time they all stayed on their feet.

A roar outside the cavern was their only warning before another wave of silverswords poured in through half a dozen bridge tunnels. Dev swore at the top of his lungs.

"Djuren is leading them!" Fig cried, coming up beside him. Her eyes had taken on a green, reptilian sheen, and Dev was startled he could see the effect of her bond with Emrah.

The silverswords around them renewed their attacks with a burst of enthusiasm, bolstered by the reinforcements. Dev looked up at the new charge, and his stomach sank. Was Rhivven himself here, or just his traitorous lapdog, Djuren? He knew Djuren had some connection to Shad, which didn't bode well for Tytan. Suddenly, the enormity of the Mountain and its significance weighed on him—the magnitude of this battle, the blood, the dust...

The look on Fig's face as she fought beside Vaelor—triumph, joy, hope.

He shook his head and got his bearings again, summoning a heavy ribbon of air to trip up the silversword charging at him, her sword raised and ready. The silversword skidded to a half right in front of Dev's feet where Ziggy finished her off. Dev looked away, ready for his next target.

The red brother fought a dozen paces away, felling dwarves by the half dozen with his quick movements, his fingers signing tirelessly—runic signs that only those blessed with the waters could see. Valencia stepped into the red brother's fighting range, her dark braids swinging in contrast with her hammer's path. The brother was faster. A rune blocked Valencia, throwing her back.

Dev lunged forward, Ziggy at his heels. Fig, Vaelor, and Knoll were locked in a battle of flames and steel, but Cordwen followed Dev, and the three of them surged into the small clearing around the red brother. None of the other dwarves seemed willing to engage him, and the silverswords were steering clear as well.

"Your Majesty!" Valencia cried heartily as she recovered from the blow.

"Watch out!" Dev cried, but the dwarf was quick on her feet. She dodged the next set of runes the brother sent her way, laying her hammer's head on the ground and leaping aside as she held the handle.

Runic tattoos glowed from underneath the brother's hood, his fingers moving in intricate sigils as the brother darted forward, his black leather armor shifting over his red tunic.

"Don't let him get too close," Ziggy warned Dev. "I saw him take down a dwarf with one direct hit at the throat."

"I wouldn't dream of it," Dev said, summoning air to his command and pummeling the red brother from all directions, knocking his fingers askew mid-gesture.

An invisible force slammed into Dev at that moment, and he realized his mistake. Even an interrupted signal was dangerous.

The dark cavern ceiling wavered in his vision. He was flat on his back, the battle raging around him. He couldn't breathe, couldn't draw in any air.

In his blurry periphery, he watched Valencia take on the red brother alone, while he stared up at the ceiling, a weight on his chest like a tagor was sitting on it. He could move his fingers, but the force that had stolen his breath sent stars across his vision and edged it with blackness. He still couldn't draw any air into his lungs. Air!

Slowly, because his life depended on it, he fed small wisps of air into his lungs, hoping that whatever magic the red brother had sent his way could be undone. The popping at the edge of his vision eased as he carefully eased more air into his lungs, and he could finally see properly again. His chest still felt like he'd been mauled by a tagor.

Fig and Vaelor had found them, and now—with Cordwen—were all defending his position at the edge of the red brother's circle. But another body lay on the ground, parallel to his.

Silver-ringed eyes blinking furiously, Ziggy lay gasping beside him—no doubt felled by the same misfired blow. Dev surged up, hands on either side of her as he listened for breath. Nothing. The red brother had collapsed both their lungs with his misfire. And judging by the shallowness and pain in his own breathing, he'd need healing when all this was over.

Trusting the others to protect them, Dev put one hand on the center of Ziggy's chest and reached out with his senses. His own lungs were one thing, but he could just as easily kill Ziggy if he wasn't careful.

Slowly—so slowly—he fed wisps of amethyst-colored air in through her mouth, down her throat, and into her lungs, gently letting them expand. One of Ziggy's hands reached over and clasped his other wrist, and from the look in her eyes, he could tell it was helping.

The process felt like it took ages, but the battle still raged behind him, clangs of metal echoing through the cavern like incessant hammer blows. Finally, her lungs felt as full as he could make them, and he felt her chest rise under his careful hand.

She managed a nod, and he felt her breathe on her own. He gave her a tight smile and lifted his head.

The others fought with all their might to keep the silversword army and the red brother from encroaching on the two of them. Dev lurched upright. Ziggy lifted a weak hand, and he helped her to her feet. What was stopping the red brother from collapsing all of their lungs on purpose? They had to stop him. Dev drew in a ragged breath and summoned the winds to him.

They scoured his core—cleansing him, yet strong enough to make every breath ache. But instead of hurling them at the red brother and risking more damage, he turned the air inside out.

A vacuum of air shot straight for the red brother's head—much like Dev had done before to threaten Liess. That got the brother's attention. The man's hands paused as his eyes bulged, and his gaze swept the clearing in search of the culprit.

A triumphant and angry smile came to Dev's face as the red brother met his gaze. But distracted, he didn't see Valencia's hammer coming. The man collapsed to the floor, his skull broken.

Valencia shouted in triumph, lifting her hammer high and calling to the dwarves around her. But a fresh wave of silverswords pouring out of the tower onto the ground floor saw that as a challenge, and the sea of silver began to move their way.

"Dev—" Fig cried, rushing toward him.

She didn't see the silversword's strike coming.

The dagger went right into Fig's side, buried up to the hilt. Blood bloomed quickly around the wound. Fig opened her mouth in surprise, the sparks at her fingertips flickering out.

The silversword callously yanked out the dagger with a parting twist, and then, assured of her kill, she tossed Fig aside and moved toward Vaelor.

CHAPTER 48

FIG

Pain throbbed through her side like she'd been bitten in half by a tagor. Dev's shocked visage swam in her vision, and he clutched her to him, his hand pressed painfully against her wound. She was vaguely aware of Vaelor fighting her attacker, as her knees buckled from the pain. Blood poured from the open wound, past Dev's fingers.

A haze of green settled over her vision as her head swam. *Fig? Fig? What's wrong?* Emrah cried. She could feel him soaring toward her; even though she could barely keep her eyes open, the fuzzy green glow above her persisted. It hurt so much... She just wanted to close her eyes.

"Fig, no!" Dev cried, shaking. "No!"

The pain in her abdomen was subsiding, and she knew that meant the worst—the last time she'd been so gravely injured in her gut, she'd lost all feeling there. She blinked back tears and looked up at Dev, then Vaelor, who was still fighting the silversword. In two more movements, Vaelor finished her off, stronger than ever.

369

He was a beautiful, shining knight from one of the Bard's tales. She smiled drunkenly. For a precious hour, she'd known the warm glow of happiness, knowing that they'd saved him. It had been an impossible task. And now...

Fig grimaced, knowing her thoughts had grown fuzzy. She was about to black out—or... or...

"I'm going to get you to Mairead," Dev was rambling. "She's at the mouth of the tunnel, I think. I hope. But I don't know if she can..."

She was being lifted—first into Dev's arms, then, after some jostling, pressed against the hard muscles of Vaelor's chest. She sank into him, content. It was where she had always wanted to be. The Viren's strong arms carried her as easily as a doll. A doll that could breathe fire—but had been felled by a single dagger.

She sighed and nuzzled her face into his chest. The Bard would tell a good story. Maybe it wasn't Vaelor's arms at all, but Morgha's carrying her. It felt as though all the pain had left her...

In fact, she felt fine. She didn't mind it at all. She was warm. Whole.

Wait a minute. Whole? With furious fingers and renewed energy, she tried finding the wound in her side, but it was no longer there. She'd been healed, but they hadn't yet reached Mairead. Besides the girl didn't even have any holy water—the flask had shattered on the bloodril floor of the chamber of Morin-Song.

Fig? Emrah demanded. She felt him swoop nearby but couldn't see him over Vaelor's wide shoulders blocking her vision.

She squirmed in Vaelor's arms, suddenly realizing how fast he was moving through the battle, the others surrounding them as a vanguard. The edge of the cavern was coming into view—he must be bringing her to the nearby tunnel.

Fig tried to scramble down, and Vaelor's arms loosened in surprise. She found her feet with an unpleasant swoop of her stomach, but it was merely because Vaelor was so much taller than she'd calculated.

"Goldfire, no, you shouldn't—" Vaelor began.

"I'm healed!" she cried, pointing at where the wound had been. "It must have been..." Before she could finish the thought, a group of silverswords crashed into them, thrown back by two dwarves using earth-shaking magic.

Fig leapt out of the way, letting Vaelor and the dwarf girl handle the fighting. Dev and Ziggy looked worse for wear, both dragging in pained breaths and withdrawing with Fig to a safer place. She let them drag her closer to the cavern wall in a daze. Fig stuck her fingers through the hole in her tunic, the fabric covered in blood. Her skin was intact.

Sure, her clothes had been soaked in the bloodril water back in the chamber—but even Vaelor sported a few cuts here and there, and he'd been in it too.

But he hadn't drunk any. *She* had.

A leathery wing struck her in the face as Emrah collided with her. She reached out automatically trying to help him land and found herself half-hugging, half-helping Emrah onto her shoulder. *Fig, you're alive!*

"Emrah!" she said in relief, backing farther and farther toward the tunnel. She didn't want to draw the silverswords to it, but she needed to get to Mairead.

What happened? Emrah demanded. *I felt you dying.* It sounded like an accusation.

The bloodril water! Fig told Emrah. *We need to bring it up here for the dwarves!*

Vaelor nearly crushed her as soon as he helped dispatch the nearby silverswords, wrapping his hands around her upper arms and inspecting her. But the wound was no longer there. He let go, then encircled her in his warm arms, covered in sweat and dust.

"Goldfire," he murmured in her ear, sending tingles up her spine as he stroked her hair.

"I'm all right, it *healed*," she said. "I think drinking the bloodril water did something..." She pulled away, taking his hand and pulling him toward the mouth of the tunnel where Dev and Ziggy had already withdrawn.

Something black darted into her vision, and she found herself enveloped in a hug from Mairead next, who'd inched out from her hiding place. They pulled away, and Fig saw tear tracks on the girl's face.

"I saw you get stabbed!" Mairead said, eyes wide in her pale face.

"I know," Fig said, "but I...I drank some of the healing water earlier. I think that's what healed me." She put a hand over her former wound.

Dev stared at Fig like she was a ghost. The dwarf girl who'd been following them sauntered back into the fray as soon as the others were safe. She launched herself off the ground with a boost from the earth and slammed into the back of a silversword with a joyous war cry.

"Fig!" Dev cried, taking a tentative step forward. "I thought you..." He flung his arms around her.

"I thought *you* were for a second there too," she said in his ear, giving him a squeeze. He pulled back, his eyes glistening. She gave him a nod and squeezed his arm.

"Listen, everyone," Fig said, "we need to get more bloodril water from down below."

"What in the name of the gods for?" Dev asked, "I thought we wanted to keep it from the silverswords."

"Because drinking it earlier made this wound heal, I'm sure of it," she said, pointing to the bloody rip in her tunic. "We can turn this battle in the dwarves' favor. Their wounds will heal."

For a moment they stared at her, the sounds of battle raging behind them. Dwarf bodies were falling to the ground, never again to stand on the earth they had commanded so deftly. The second wave of silverswords had tipped the battle—the dwarves hadn't been prepared for the numbers. The enclave must have emptied its reserves from Rayva.

Scanning the cavern before them, Fig knew the dwarves would lose if they didn't do something—and they wouldn't just lose the Mountain, but all their people. Rhivven wouldn't allow a single dwarf to live free after this.

"But how will we get it up here?" Mairead asked.

"We'll figure it out along the way—" Fig began, grabbing Mairead's arm.

"Wait, Fig," Mairead began, "if you can't be wounded…"

Realization dawned on Fig as she said it, and her mouth popped open in surprise. "You're right," she said quietly, a strange elation brimming in her. "I should stay here and fight." Emrah chirped in agreement.

"Are you sure?" Vaelor asked, his gaze sweeping her up and down as if to make sure the wound hadn't reopened.

"I'm sure," she said with a slow-forming smile. "It's not every day you become invincible. Well, you're a silversword, so I guess that *is* everyday for you, eh? Dev, Ziggy, you should go with Mairead."

Dev and Ziggy looked at each other, and though it looked like the silversword wanted to protest, Dev nodded.

"We could both use the water ourselves," Dev said with a hand to his chest.

It was better to keep him away from the fighting, anyway. The three of them started walking into the dark tunnel, when Fig called, "Wait! Emrah, you should go too, so the two of us can communicate—"

Sparks flashed from the dragonet's claws, and he growled, clearly eager to get back to the fight.

"How do you think I felt last time?" she shot at him.

You're right, Svoran. We'll be fast then.

Here, you three—let's get farther in, then I'll light the way so we can look for something to carry it in.

And with that, her friends headed into the darkness, leaving her alone with Vaelor on the fringes of the battle.

It would be so much better to sink into the darkness, to go to the chamber of Morin-Song, hidden from the battle. But they wouldn't remain hidden for long. Particularly now that they knew for sure Djuren was here.

Though she had ingested the bloodril water, she doubted it would last forever, otherwise the dwarves of old would have never let the silverswords take the Mountain. As much as she didn't want to, she turned back to face the battle.

She glanced over at Vaelor, clutched his hand in hers, and said, "I bet this is going to hurt like Malhela, but there's no one else I'd want to go back into battle with."

He squeezed her hand, and they left the safety of the tunnel. Cordwen was dancing about nearby, with the help of the stones beneath her feet, nearly as quick as a silversword. She used her innate dwarven abilities to trip her attackers and push herself into a better position for her surprisingly quick axe strokes. Fig stoked her inner flames, not wanting to release them until they'd gotten clear of the tunnel entrance.

Vaelor squeezed her fingers once more, then dropped her hand, lunging into battle with a war cry. Fig dashed forward, challenging the next silversword in line. A renewed sense of energy zinging through her, she let out her own war cry—but with her inner flames stoked to bursting, it erupted as a roar of fire. Just as expected, it *did* hurt like Malhela, but her body began healing it as soon as she stopped.

This bloodril water is dangerous, she thought, euphoria rising as she turned to her next attacker. She was practically invincible with her newly strengthened fire magic and the ability to heal.

They fought tirelessly—Fig, with the renewed sense of wholeness, and Vaelor, his silversword abilities restored tenfold. Fig saw him slam another silversword back twenty paces with a kick to the chest. Wave after wave of silverswords came their way, but none of them made it past Fig, Vaelor, and Cordwen.

She couldn't tell whether they were actively coming for the tunnel, or if the relentless silverswords had run out of dwarves to fight.

As she wiped sweat and blood from her brow, a green haze settled over her vision. Emrah said nothing as he checked up on her. In the brief moment of enhanced vision, she spotted the briigard Djuren locked in battle with Valencia, a dozen paces away.

"Can't have that," Fig growled, signaling to Vaelor. "Valencia and Djuren!" she explained. He nodded.

She stalked through the battle, flames dripping from her hands as she went. Vaelor guarded her from behind as the two of them found Valencia, not far from where they'd fought the red brother earlier and had to flee.

"You're alive!" Valencia cried in surprise, spotting Fig, who gave her a grin, her inner flames fit to bursting.

Valencia swung her hammer at Djuren, but the silversword was much faster than the heavy weapon and easily evaded it.

A silversword with a short sword rushed up behind Vaelor, and Fig shouted a warning. He turned just in time to engage the attacker, who struck with incredible speed and accuracy.

Fig whipped her head around. Valencia had tried the trick of slamming her hammer on the ground and leaping over it to get more momentum, but Djuren was faster. He lunged out with a crescent kick and slammed her to the ground. He stalked toward her.

With a growl, Fig leapt back into the fight, fire roaring from her insides straight toward Djuren. But the silversword was fast, dodging again, and then he turned unexpectedly, slamming into Fig from the side and pinning her to the ground.

Djuren's hand clamped down on her mouth. "Ah, the gold fire mage. Shadryn sends his regards, you filthy Svoran." He spat on the ground beside her. "He wanted me to take you, but I'd much rather kill you." His ugly face—a nose broken more than once and folds of dark skin beneath his eyes—twisted in amusement.

"You briigard," Fig tried to growl around his hand. He had a knee on one of her hands, pinning it down, but the other hand was free. She grasped for a discarded weapon, and found nothing.

White-hot rage boiled within her. She called on the flames she'd summoned in the dragonhead forge, tapping into the power inside her. Just as he lifted his sword to strike her neck, she wrenched her free hand upward, fingers curled into claws, and drove it straight toward his face.

Flames encased her fingers—shaped into claws of their own, hardened by her will.

She raked her fire claws through his eye before he could deliver his killing blow.

He writhed, clutching his face, and she tried to shove him off, lashing out with more swipes of her claws. The flames had become so powerful they burst from her mouth unbidden in a roar worthy of a dragon. Djuren continued to writhe in agony, pulling away—allowing her to finally aim a kick at his chest and push him off her.

She wrenched herself free and struggled to her feet. Vaelor was still engaged with the attacker with the short sword, but Valencia was coming to after hitting her head on the ground. A wall of dwarves had formed at her back, keeping their uniter safe. The dwarf rubbed the back of her head, rage like the fires in the forge below kindled in her eyes. "He was coming for the Sword of Morin," Valencia said in a throaty voice, grabbing Fig's arm for support.

Fig helped her up, and said, "Well, he's not getting it."

The dwarf put her hand on the sword buckled at her waist as she looked down on the body of Djuren. She left her hammer where it had fallen, and drew the sword, a renewed fervor visibly washing over her features.

Their theories about Djuren working with Shadryn had been confirmed. Fig knew Shadryn had wanted her to convert to a "silvermage" like him, but had he really sent Djuren to abduct her along with the Sword of Morin? Fig looked at the sword with wide eyes. No one had Welded with the weapon yet. Was Shadryn really still hoping to convert her to a silvermage? But that couldn't be his entire play, sending Djuren here. Djuren had brought what looked like Rhivven's reserves from Rayva, and it was clear that the false king didn't know he had a traitor in his midst.

Well, not anymore.

Fig took a moment to brace herself as the bloodril water healed her throat. It took longer this time, sending a jolt of unease through her.

Green invaded her vision. *Fig, we've reached the cavern but found nothing to carry water on the way. The chambers down here don't appear lived in—they're practically empty.*

Fig scanned Corryn's cavern and the tower looming over them. Surely there were barrels, buckets, or something else that could be used to carry water to the dwarves. But how long would it take for them to find such things and bring them all the way down to the chamber of Morin-Song and back? She wished she'd thought this ridiculous plan through better.

Another wave of silverswords crossed the largest bridge arch, earning a roar from their comrades. The dwarves were flagging, many of their hammers and axes too slow to properly engage the silverswords with their incredible speed.

She groaned, working to keep the flames from pouring out. Bonding with Emrah was like being in a thrice-powerful Gold Wood, her flames magnified beyond measure. While her vision was still overlaid with Emrah's eyesight as he waited for her to answer, she spotted the blue and silver dragonet that had tailed them earlier. It now lurked in one of the tower windows, watching the battle with silver eyes.

The dragonets had been content to watch this battle unfold. But this was their home too.

Vaelor lurched to her side, panting from the fight, and she pointed to the window. "We need to talk to that dragonet."

He didn't question her, only charged forward, clearing the way. Hope flittered in her chest as she followed his sure strides, forging a way through the battle. Vaelor was well and truly healed. Every time she saw him—the silver ring in his eye, the strength in his posture, the emotion in his voice—her heart leapt. She didn't want to let him out of her sight for a moment. And somehow, she knew it was the same for him too.

He parried a silversword's strike, saving a dwarf from the blow as they went, and Fig ran in his wake, her eyesight still enhanced by Emrah, who clearly wanted to know what was happening up here.

The blue dragonet was in the third-floor window, watching Fig with a dispassionate eye.

Fig waved her arm to catch its attention. The dragonet merely stared at her.

"Please!" Fig cried. "I need your help!"

The dragonet turned tail and fluttered to the window above.

"Bard strike it!" Fig groaned, sparks surging at her fingertips.

That little— Emrah seethed as he watched through her eyes. *How dare she!*

"Into the tower, then," Vaelor said with a nod.

She hurried after him. They encountered no one on the ground floor, save the bodies of two dwarves and one silversword. The last wave of silverswords had poured out of the tower already—no one would linger in such a dark cramped place.

It was a dark moment of comfort to be out of the battle again, even for a brief respite. The outside sounds of metal clashing, groans of pain, and a distant explosion kept Fig moving quickly. They needed to end this, or there wouldn't be any dwarves left.

She lit a fire orb and threw it above their heads. It would announce their position to anyone who might be on the next floor, but Fig would rather see the attackers coming than not.

The second floor was clear. She could hear others fighting on the higher levels, but the distance was impossible to determine. It was likely closer to the bridge levels, so they kept going.

They spilled onto the third floor, where the dragonet had originally perched, and looked around—then a shadow moved.

Or more accurately, a silversword who'd discarded his armor lurched from the shadows, practically invisible without the trademark silver glinting from head to toe. Vaelor was fast, engaging the man with his bloody sword, the clash of their weapons a force Fig could feel radiating through the floor and into her feet.

Then a second shadow moved.

Fig spun just in time, summoning fire claws without a second thought. She swiped at the attacker but misjudged the distance. The silversword, who wielded two daggers, one high and one low, managed to strike Fig in the leg as she tried to spin away. Fig yelped, falling onto hands and knees, claws of flame still solid. She rose up on her knees as fast as she could, knowing the wound in her leg would slow her down, and managed to swipe her claws along the silversword's torso.

The silversword yelled in pain, blood and singed flesh slicing upward from her hip. She crashed backward, dropping a dagger— presumably not her Welded weapon.

The woman stumbled down the stairs away from Fig, clutching her torso, the wounds partially cauterized, which kept her from bleeding out.

Vaelor dispatched his attacker at the same time—who was less fortunate and would retreat no farther than death.

"Cowards. Hiding in the dark," Fig spat, even though not less than half an hour ago she'd wanted to do the same in the tunnel. But here she was with Vaelor beside her and friends to protect.

"Come on," she called, trying to stand, then promptly lost her footing as her leg gave out. The wound hadn't healed yet. It was busy gushing blood thickly down into her boot. She knelt again, not trusting herself to sit in case she couldn't get back up. Fig twisted to look at the damage. The dagger had sliced through the back of her calf, and the wound showed no signs of healing.

Fig drew in a deep breath and waited.

Vaelor studied her. He ripped off a handspan of the bottom of his tunic and quickly tied it around her calf.

"It's deep," Vaelor said, worried. He pulled his tunic off entirely and ripped it into more scraps, tying one above her knee to slow down the flow of blood and using another to replace the already sodden first scrap.

"I guess the bloodril water's reached its limit," Fig said softly.

Fig glanced up at the opening to the fourth floor in frustration. Every second they were down on this floor it would take even longer to bring aid to the dwarves.

"Pick me up, will you?" Fig asked. "We need to get up there."

Vaelor finished tying off the next rag, which didn't stain with red as quickly, then bundled her into his arms. She was suddenly aware of his naked chest—an *entirely* inappropriate thought in the middle of a battle—and she couldn't help but smile at the feel of his skin under her hand. His skin was flaming, or was that because she was losing blood and her hands were cold?

He raced up the stairs to the fourth floor, and Fig hoped to the gods that the blue dragonet had stayed in place.

Her fire orb went up first, and with a wave of her hand, she made it hover around the large circular room, shining light on all the shadows. The dragonet was the only living being there, and she was still perched on the window.

Fig sighed and pressed her hand into Vaelor's chest. He brought her over to the window and carefully set her down. Fig sat on the floor with her legs stretched out before her, not wanting to stand and allow more blood to seep out through the wound—not even knowing if she *could* stand.

"Hello?" Fig tried. "We need your help. I know you watched us in the chamber of Morin-Song, and your kind don't seem to want to get involved in this battle, but—"

The blue dragonet growled and turned to face Fig. *And why would we help anyone who wants to take our Mountain from us?*

"Please," Fig said. "If the silverswords win this battle, you will lose *everything*. But the dwarves... The dwarves know the value of dragonets and history—and they know firsthand what it's like to have their ancestors' home taken from them. I know they will treat you fairly. Surely these mountains are big enough for all of you?" Fig clenched her fist, feeling like a child on the floor, but they were running out of time, and it didn't really matter *how* she pleaded, as long as she could convince her. They needed help.

The blue dragonet stretched her wings as if to take off again, and Fig's stomach sank. But the dragonet merely hopped out of the window and onto the floor, out of view of the battle.

Only because you are like us, dragonkin. Furvin wants to know what kind of help you want. The blue dragonet eyed her, still a little distrustful.

Vaelor crouched by Fig's legs, examining her wound. She hissed when he touched the bandage, and he frowned, pulling out his last clean scrap.

"Down in the chamber of Morin-Song," Fig explained. "Some of my friends are there, and we need to bring some water up here to give the dwarves, as fast as we can. The dwarves probably won't know what it's for, but if you can get them to drink it, it'll keep the silverswords from winning."

The blue dragonet chirped and quirked her head. *The water? From down below? What in Drakioryn's fire-loving—Never mind. Furvin says fine. Only because you're dragonkin.*

And with that, the blue dragonet leapt into the air to sail out the window, leaving Fig on the floor, her heart racing, wondering if the dragonets would make enough of a difference...and whether they were actually going to help.

DEV

The dragonets are coming, Emrah reported in a suspicious tone.

"But we've searched down here," Dev said in frustration, a gust of wind sending dust clouds billowing around the empty chamber they were searching.

King Morin and his people had only just begun to carve out these lower corridors before they were all deserted. Some of them were half-finished, with entire walls of rubble or rough-carved ceilings covered in the dust of decades.

Sparks burst from Emrah in surprise. *They're in the upper chambers gathering...cups,* Emrah said. *One of them just informed me.*

Mairead let out a surprised gasp. "That'll work!"

"But how many dragonets are there?" Ziggy asked.

Emrah swooped overhead, leading them out of the barren room in a shower of sparks. *None of our business, I've been informed.*

They followed, empty-handed.

"I wish I still had a flask," Mairead said ruefully. "The rune magic only works with holy water. I was...useless in the battle."

"No one is useless, Mairead. We all have our purpose," Ziggy said. "Just like you all keep me around for my good looks."

Dev snorted as they passed the prone form of Liess Astor in the corridor before turning back into the chamber of Morin-Song. The silversword's eyes bulged in anger. Though she couldn't move, it was clear she was still alive. They ignored her and went inside. He couldn't deal with that right now.

"What you did to save Vaelor and bind Liess?" he said to Mairead. "That was far from useless. Amazing, I'd say."

She ducked her head, the tattoos on her face hidden for a moment. "In all my years training at Mar Nevan, I never thought..." She lowered her voice to a whisper. "Mother Savidah must have been desperate, blessing me with these powers. The red brothers have turned on her."

The dragonhead forge still burned, and would for a long time with how much coal Knoll had put in. The chamber was hot, but not as uncomfortable as it had been hours ago.

"It certainly appears so," Dev said, shuddering as he remembered the fight at Emrah's tower. "How did Rhivven win them over, I wonder?" he mused aloud.

"Fear. Why does anyone ever let those with evil in their hearts take control? And now the brothers turn their fear against others."

Dev sighed.

Just then, a strange whistling came from the corridor. Dev reached out with his senses and felt an immense change in the air pressure outside the chamber. He shifted to get a better look. A blur of scales fluttered to a halt just outside the room. Blues, browns, silvers, reds and greens, and even a dark amethyst dragonet—more than they'd seen when they'd first entered the Mountain.

Emrah sailed over to land on the wide-open door of the chamber.

Oi, a blue and silver dragonet stood at the front, clutching a flask in her claws. *The dragonkin up top said you needed help.*

"Dragonkin? Fig, you mean?" Dev said, brow furrowed.

Breathes fire? Bonded with that one? She pointed at Emrah with the tip of her tail. *Aye. Now, fill these up, why don't you? I thought this was important?*

Dev shook himself, rattled by the blue dragonet's bluntness. "Of course," Dev said, holding out his hand. But the dragonets remained where they were.

We do not enter this place, the same voice said, the blue one. *It is forbidden.*

"But you'll carry the water?" Mairead asked, taking a few steps forward to approach the gathering.

Dozens of scaly heads nodded seriously.

Mairead reached out to take several goblets and mugs from the dragonets, as many as she could loop around her fingers. Dev and Ziggy did the same, and the three of them were soon filling vessels by the pool. Only a few carried buckets, which was a shame.

Ziggy and Dev had each drunk a handful of the healing water as soon as they'd reached the chamber earlier, and the weight and burning pain in his lungs had disappeared. Dev had even convinced Mairead to drink a handful for her own protection. Though she'd looked thoroughly scandalized, she had done it.

"Here," Dev said, handing Mairead the ancient flask one of the dragonets had given him. The cork was crumbling at the edges, but it was better than nothing. "In case you want to use your sigils."

A smile graced Mairead's pale face, the first he'd seen in a while. As they brought full vessels back to the dragonets, the creatures took off, carefully balancing the open containers in their claws.

"I have to say, this is not how I pictured spending the rest of the battle," Dev muttered after his third round at the pool.

"Me either," Mairead chuckled. Emrah had taken to helping fill one mug at a time, since Fig had bid him stay here so that they could all communicate. He was clearly itching to rejoin the fight or carry up the healing water himself. Ziggy also looked as if she wanted to head upstairs again, but she said nothing.

Finally, all the dragonets were gone except for Emrah.

Dev sighed, rubbing his aching muscles. "Waiting is worse than battle."

CHAPTER 50

CORDWEN

Feet planted securely on the floor, Cordwen commanded the stones to jut upward twenty paces away, slamming right into the chin of the oncoming silversword. All the dwarves around her lay dead, except the one called Knoll Morinson, whom both her parents had touted as a traitor.

Her father had been guarding the west maintenance tunnel at the start of the battle, and Cordwen knew deep down from the sheer number of silverswords who'd penetrated the Mountain that it was unlikely any of those dwarves had survived. But with his stock of blackjack and affinity for the explosive powder, he'd felt he had no choice but to stop the silverswords from penetrating the Mountain.

And her mother...well...

Slam. Another shaft of stone jutted up, smashing into a silversword's armored kneecaps, causing him to tumble forward with a cry of pain. The earth was always stronger than armor. The earth was stronger than anything that came before or was still to come.

Another helpful jutting stone sent Cordwen flying forward, axe raised to aim a killing blow at the pain-stunned 'sword, but she miscalculated her trajectory by a fraction, landing three paces short.

The silversword recovered, and she was locked in a fight with one wielding an axe like her. Except the silversword's axe reverberated like the grinding of metal in her ears, the unholy cacophony of Welded steel. One of the silversword's swings managed to slice Cordwen's forearm, cutting through her leather guard like it was hot steel through butter. She hissed and aimed another swipe, dancing back a step.

Knoll Morinson entered her periphery. Cordwen aimed two strikes of stone at her attacker before delivering the silversword to the goddess Corryn to await judgement. The silversword fell with a clatter, and Cordwen released the stones at their feet. Knoll was watching her as they both guarded the outskirts of the tunnel entrance.

Cordwen hadn't been commanded to do any such thing, but after following the Verrence heir around the cavern, she'd picked up that something important was through this tunnel, and stones be broken before she let the silverswords penetrate this far.

She'd been at the tournament in Rayva, watched with her parents as King Devryn had won the Sword of Morin, yanking it from the grasp of that beastly usurper Rhivven. She'd seen the tornado of glass the two mages had created together.

Cordwen had wanted to enter the tournament, but her father had insisted she was too young. Her mother had looked pensive but let Father's word stand.

Just then, something shot out of the tunnel, a blue and silver dragonet. And water splashed in Cordwen's face right into her open mouth.

She spluttered. "Wh-what?"

It's better if you drink it, earth-dweller, a voice came into her head, and the blue and silver dragonet turned tail and headed back into the tunnel.

Cordwen had, indeed, drunk some of the water that had

splashed into her mouth in surprise. She swallowed reflexively, then stood stunned for a moment, watching as more dragonets emerged from the tunnel—each carrying a goblet or mug filled with what she could only assume was water. Some dragonets brought the cups to the dwarves, appearing to speak mind to mind. Then, with a beat of their leathery wings, they hightailed it back into the tunnel, empty vessels clutched in their claws.

"What in the name of..." Cordwen stopped, looking down at the slice in her leather bracers, where her skin suddenly felt strange. The bloody wound was gone, replaced by the fresh skin of a new scar. "...the Bard is going on?"

Knoll had been one of the dwarves to receive a cup and drink properly, and he now fought the swords with a renewed vigor, an aura of energy radiating around him.

He dispatched his enemy with gusto, the mighty hammer landing a sure blow. He seemed to sense Cordwen's gaze, and they shared a look. Something in that water...the thing Prince Devryn was protecting down there...

Knoll nodded at her, and she bobbed her head eagerly back. This was it. The mighty hammer of Baldwyn had swung back in their favor. Knoll's hammer, forged of black ore with silver veins running through it, slammed on the ground with a deafening clang, and he called, "Dwarves, to me! To me! Or we will never hold this Mountain!"

Confusion rattled through the cavern, but the confident timbre of the dwarf's cry made even Cordwen stand a little taller. A rallying cry went up, starting out low and building throughout the massive chamber. The fighting continued, but Cordwen could see a definite shift in movement toward them.

Yet it wasn't merely the dwarves heading toward them—the silverswords were advancing in their direction as well.

"You fools!" someone called from beside them. It was one of the dwarves from the Feijowa clan, and he had a bloody gash on his upper arm that had turned into a fresh scar.

Knoll had rallied the dwarves with his call—despite his ancestors' desertion at the pivotal moment when the Mountain fell into the bloody hands of the enclave, despite having alerted the silverswords to the existence of the ancient Sword of Morin. Cordwen had the nagging feeling that she was missing something about the histories of the dwarves, and it likely started with what must be holy water down below. But this wasn't the time to think about such philosophical quandaries, with the dwarves gathering tightly around her and the silverswords spilling toward the cavern wall like a storm at sea.

At that moment, though, another cloud of dragonets appeared from the dark tunnel. Chirps and growls pervaded the air as they realized the dwarves had gathered closer, easier for dousing.

Cordwen began running through the crowd; she didn't want the silverswords to hear her pronouncement, so she grabbed fistfuls of dwarves' clothes or beards as she went and pulled them in close to say, "Take the water the dragonets bring! Drink it if you can! You'll heal!"

She kept running, kept whispering, and a sea of whispers followed in her wake, amid the groans of pain. Most were wounded, and from the weakened energy sifting off them, Cordwen thought the dwarves had retreated here for a last stand. And it certainly would be their last stand. Their numbers had been more than halved; the silversword force had been an overwhelming miscalculation on her mother's part.

And she hadn't seen dear old Valencia in over an hour.

The clash at the front line shifted. It was incremental—a slow push outward from the cavern wall—but Cordwen noticed. The dwarves who had received the haphazard holy water dove to the front with renewed energy, driving the 'swords back. Cordwen could practically feel the energy radiating from her and the others who'd received the water.

Something metallic but powerful—like the force of an earthquake, like the bones of the earth.

FIG

Fig tapped her fingers relentlessly on the tower windowsill, watching the battle. Perched on her knees, she could see the far side of the cavern, where the tunnel led to the chamber of Morin-Song. "What's taking so long?" she muttered. Vaelor didn't answer. He'd taken to silently watching the stairs to make sure they weren't disturbed. It hadn't taken Fig long to realize she couldn't walk without getting lightheaded. She'd lost a lot of blood. Her brief moments as an unkillable force were gone—just as dead as she would have been without the healing water the first time she'd been stabbed.

"Do you think the dragonets actually listened to me?" she asked.

Vaelor came to the window and put a tentative hand on her shoulder. "*Va*, I think they did."

She straightened as a wave of scales and claws emerged from the tunnel.

Emrah, I could use your eyes, she thought quickly. *The dragonets are here.*

A green sheen flooded her vision, which had become so clear that she could make out each dragonet from across the cavern. The sassy blue and silver one had a goblet in her claws. She dumped it over a dwarf girl instead of convincing her to drink it, but it must have worked, because the girl ran off with renewed vigor.

There were dozens more dragonets than she'd imagined, nearly fifty of them—Furvin must have called on all the dragonets hiding in the Mountain to help. Pressure built in her chest, and it took a few minutes to realize what it was.

Hope.

They watched as Knoll rallied the dwarves, who, with their renewed bodies and a new sense of purpose, drove the silverswords back and back and back.

More dragonets came, and more silverswords fell. Fig clenched Vaelor's hand on the windowsill, her grip tense.

Chest fit to bursting, she tore her eyes away from the fight, almost wanting to delay seeing the outcome. What if they still lost?

Her gaze trailed to the battlefield, scanning the stone floor of the cavern. Large pieces of rubble—great chunks of the bridges— littered the floor amid scores of bodies. Which were dwarves and which were silverswords was made evident by the silver glint of armor. So many dwarves lost.

She took a deep breath, her gaze rising back to the far wall.

She couldn't have missed the cry that went up next, even if she'd covered her ears.

It felt as if the very earth was singing—at once dark and tumultuous, yet fertile and welcoming. A rising exaltation of liberation. The dwarves had won.

Cradled in Vaelor's arms, Fig was carried down the stairs of the tower. But once they emerged back into the cavern, she asked him to set her down, limping on her good leg with his help.

He drew his sword again, and a smile drew up the corners of Fig's mouth.

She wanted to ask how he felt. If the sword was any different. Whether the bloodril's effects were evident in some way. She wanted to ask if he missed his *mazir*, and if after the battle they could go stay at the tower for a few days and pretend the world of Tytan didn't exist around them. Or down to the *solanse* to bask in its verdant glory along with his family.

Her lips remained closed, however, knowing there would be time for those questions later. The bodies they stepped over, the pools of blood slick under their boots—the ancient silence of the caverns had descended on them once more. A proper silence for the dead.

Save for the groans of the dying.

Fig focused on two things as they passed through the carnage: breathing and reaching the mouth of the tunnel. Vaelor kept a sharp eye on the bodies at their feet, and Fig realized belatedly that she should do the same. The groans meant that not all the bodies were dead, and should a silversword choose a moment for revenge, now would be the time.

Vaelor slowed halfway across the cavern, and Fig hopped to a halt on her good leg.

Writhing on the ground before them was a silversword Fig had thought she'd killed with claws of flame.

Djuren.

"Djuren the traitor," she whispered. Vaelor shifted his stance protectively in front of her. "Tell me, whose side are you on here at the end? Shadryn's?"

A wet cackle and then a bloody cough. Djuren didn't move other than the cough that wracked his prone body. His face was turned toward the ground, but from where she stood, Fig could see the burn marks stretching from his face into his hair. His legs curled up painfully toward his core, his sword several feet away.

Against her better judgement, Fig took a step closer. Vaelor cleared his throat and went over to kick Djuren's sword farther away.

Djuren grunted when his Welded weapon clattered across the blood-soaked stones.

Fig shook her head, knowing they wouldn't get any answers out of him.

He cackled again, gurgling as he cleared his throat. "Did us a favor, fire mage, killing all these 'swords." Hacking now, Djuren's body seized and contracted with wracking wet coughs.

A deep sense of dread built in Fig's stomach, and she looked at Vaelor. Only the sight of his silver-ringed eyes brought her any sense of comfort.

After a few minutes, Djuren's coughs went silent, and he moved no more. They made sure Djuren was dead, with a swift dispatch from Vaelor's sword.

They moved on through the battlefield until they found the dwarves, Fig with a renewed sense of unease. What had Djuren meant?

Valencia, covered in blood and dust, one of her braids undone because a handspan had been cut from the bottom, was busy arguing with Knoll at the head of the tunnel leading to the chamber of Morin-Song.

Vaelor helped Fig over to where the two dwarves argued, and a dwarf girl Fig recognized stood nearby, bouncing on her toes.

"Cordwen, right?" Fig whispered.

The dwarf nodded, beaming.

"What's going on?"

"My *mother* wants to go down there." The look in her wide eyes made it clear that Cordwen wanted to know what was going on in that deep chamber as much as Valencia.

Fig bit her lip. The secret of the bloodril water would create chaos across Tytan and Tysaine if it left this Mountain. But they'd destroyed massive reserves of silverswords in the battle; what use was keeping it a secret now?

Either way, it wasn't her decision. Fig remained silent and watched Knoll, Vaelor's arm steadying her.

"Just trust me—" Knoll was saying.

"Trust you?" Valencia thundered, reaching for her hammer, which was lying on its head nearby. "*You* who told the silverswords about the Sword of Morin in the first place?"

Cordwen huffed in what sounded like embarrassment and impatience.

Knoll's eyes flashed dangerously, and he took a step toward her.

Then, another dwarf emerged from the crowd—Firth, the head of the Feijowa clan. Fig narrowed her eyes. She'd never forget the bite of Firth's axe for all her days, after the wound had nearly killed her twice.

"Valencia," Firth said, shaking their head. "Knoll isn't at fault for that, and you know it."

Valencia bristled, her shoulders raising. "Don't you tell me—"

"You think the silverswords don't have spies, the untrustworthy forgers who'll sell any speck of gossip for a silver?"

"You made a deal with Knoll after he returned to Tytan," Valencia accused, hands on her hips.

Knoll cleared his throat. "When I returned, the Feijowa gave me a place to reside where I had access to a hearth, in exchange for weapons. That was all."

"Ballast," Valencia said.

"What does it matter?" Firth said, rolling their eyes. "We've taken the Mountain!"

A cry went up between the dwarves, but even Fig could sense the unfinished business in the way it lingered like an unwelcome ghost. Whispers wove through the crowd like a light breeze.

"Why did the dragonets help?" a dwarf asked, and a cacophony of questions burst from the crowd.

"Where did they even *come* from?"

"Aye! And how did they get their claws on holy water?"

Valencia glared at Knoll.

He bowed his head, muttering, "Very well, if you wish me to reveal it to *all*, on your head be it." Then he spoke louder. "Below, in the chamber of Morin-Song, hallowed halls carved by my ancestors, sits the dragonhead forge, a gargantuan beauty of blacksmithing made of the purest element known to dwarfkind—bloodril. Just before King Tesvier took the Mountain, King Morin forged the Sword of Morin, the first weapon of this element, other than this hammer I retrieved from beside the forge.

"A pool of water sits in this chamber steeped in bloodril. It is incredibly powerful, possessing the power to heal...just like the holy water the Sisters of Morgha oversee at the monastery of Mar Nevan—that is because these waters are one and the same. Steeped in bloodril, the bones of the earth.

"King Morin discovered this before the 'swords took the Mountain, and, fearing that the secret of the holy water and bloodril would be the undoing of Tytan, fled the country and revealed the secret to his child alone when the boy came of apprenticeship age. And this was how I learned of it when I became my father's apprentice at the forge."

He stared at Valencia as if daring her to challenge his words, and damning her for making him speak them.

Valencia, to her credit, remained stoic, as if this revelation was expected—and perhaps the keen dwarf had figured it out already after everything that had happened, and was merely looking for confirmation of the miracle.

"Then it is well that we reclaimed the Mountain when we did," her voice boomed over the crowd. "It is done. Beneath the gaze of the great Corryn the Just, we reclaimed our home. The Mountain is ours."

FIG

The bloodril water healed her leg almost immediately after the battle ended. It was Emrah who raced up through the corridors and delivered a gobletful, almost spilling it on her in his apparent relief to see her alive. He'd stayed down in the chamber of Morin-Song to keep the connection with the cavern but winged it up as fast as he could when she told him the battle was ended.

He perched on her raised knees, and she scratched behind his ears as the water did its work. Then she bumped her forehead to his, closing her eyes.

More dragonets came. Wounds were healed, and with a renewed sense of purpose, those who remained began the arduous task of removing the fallen dwarves from the battlefield. But with bloodril water running in their veins, and the weight of the ancient Mountain seeming to look down upon them, there was no other way forward. Valencia directed them to the ancient dwarven burial chambers to be given proper rites.

Dev, Ziggy, and Mairead emerged from the tunnel, tentative smiles on their faces as they rushed Fig and Vaelor. Fully healed, Fig got to her feet and flung her arms around Mairead first. Emrah sailed overhead. Fig could sense his position without looking at him, and she knew he'd gone to speak with the other dragonets, who perched in the windows of the tower.

Mairead pulled away, tears glistening in her eyes. "I was worried when Emrah said you'd been injured and didn't heal."

Fig shot a look at the retreating dragonet, and her mouth curled into half a smile. "I don't recall actually telling him that..." she mused.

"He didn't think there was any other reason you'd have stayed out of the battle," Mairead said with a sly look.

"Oh," Fig chuckled, flexing her fingers. Her inner fires were calm, and no sparks attempted to break free.

Dev clapped a hand on Fig's back and put his arm around her, uncharacteristically saying nothing.

Fig reached up and squeezed his hand. "You did good down there."

Dev scoffed. "Don't think I didn't see through your plan to get me off the field, Fairaleigh. I'd like to see you take on a hoard of cantankerous dragonets."

"Well, since I summoned the help from those dragonets, I think I'd be well suited."

"Of course, dragonkin."

Fig balked.

"You know that's what they're calling you, right?"

"Yes," Fig said quietly.

"Is it because you can breathe fire and attack with claws like a dragon?" Cordwen had appeared, a smudge of blood on her face —presumably someone else's, judging by how fiercely she had fought in the battle. Fig didn't respond.

"Who taught you to fight like that?" Dev asked, pulling his arm away from Fig and giving her a light bump with his shoulder in parting.

Vaelor moved in just as quickly, putting a hand around her waist. Fig's heart lifted, filled with warmth.

"My father," Cordwen said quietly. "My mother doesn't have much affinity for the stone." Her gaze cut toward Valencia, who was holding a quiet conference with the clan heads on the other side of the tunnel entrance. No one had yet ventured down to the chamber of Morin-Song, and no doubt the revelation had rocked the dwarves, no matter how they pretended.

"Your mother is the Uniter of the Clans?" Dev asked.

Cordwen shrugged. "It wasn't hard to get the clans to agree that what the silverswords were doing was wrong. Most dwarves just want to go about their lives in peace, you know? But getting them all to issue the challenge by marching on the Mountain? I'll have to admit she was convincing on that front."

"Indeed," Dev agreed.

Even though none of them had eaten in ages and, ever since entering the Mountain and becoming encased in the earth, weren't even aware of what time or even what day it was, they'd all just imbibed the bloodril water, and so the task of helping the dwarves with their dead didn't seem as daunting as it should. Ziggy and Dev went off together. Mairead walked alone, whispering prayers under her breath. That left Fig and Vaelor to walk close together among the fallen.

Several days later, Fig emerged from her chambers with a contented sigh, scratching at one of the many new scars her arms boasted.

Vaelor was still asleep, his long limbs tangled amid the white sheets of their bed in the chamber the dwarves had assigned them.

Knoll had insisted she meet him this morning, and she didn't have it in her to wake Vaelor, when he was resting so peacefully.

He'd been through enough, since their perilous trip to Mar Nevan. They all had.

Now, in the depths of the Mountain, with the earth as their sentinel against whatever remained of Rhivven's forces, she felt some semblance of calm. How long it would last was anyone's guess. She hadn't forgotten Djuren's words before he died.

Emrah found her without a word, fluttering up the corridor behind her and landing on her shoulder.

"Up all night with the dragonets?" she asked, reaching up to scratch behind his ears.

Sylryn's shirking her duties, he complained. It was a long-standing issue at this point, a whole week after the battle. The blue and silver dragonet had been ordered to escort Emrah around the Mountain to the territories the dragonets had used for generations. Emrah, in turn, would communicate with Fig, so she could make an agreement with the dwarves. When she'd asked the dragonets why they wouldn't speak with Valencia herself, he turned up his snout and gave as close to a scoff as a dragonet could.

"So you're exploring on your own?"

Fig snapped her fingers, and a ball of flame appeared at her side, hovering down the corridor with her as she walked. Her new clothes chafed a little, but there hadn't been much to choose from, and she'd had to put up with tailored dwarven clothes. The patterns of stitching were incredibly beautiful, but the fabrics were rougher than she was used to, and the alterations had been rushed. It wasn't as though many seamstresses had accompanied the dwarves to the Mountain—Fig was lucky she had any clothes to wear at all after what she'd worn in battle had been discarded and likely burned.

More dwarves trickled into the Mountain every day. Fig had worried when so many new faces appeared at first, but Knoll had assured her that he and Valencia had created and guarded secure entrances for the dwarf refugees to seek shelter.

King Rhivven had declared all dwarves traitors of the crown, for their deliberate attack on Tytan, crippling the enclave. Fig hadn't heard the reports from the dwarf war council, but what she'd picked up from Knoll and Dev made it sound like the countryside was writhing in unrest after news of the Battle of Corryn's Cavern got out, thanks to Mairead's friend Derrin and his printing press. It had been Mairead's idea to send a dwarf soldier to Derrin to get the word out—with Valencia's permission, of course.

Fig's footsteps finally led her to her meeting place with Knoll: down in the chamber of Morin-Song. Though blood had been spilled here, and Vaelor had almost succumbed to that deadly wound, Fig found the place oddly comforting. Perhaps because they'd sought solace here before the battle, or because Vaelor had regained his life here—but as she stepped through the doors and inhaled the ethereal scent of the bloodril essence lingering in the air—the magic imbued in the very floors and the water—she was surprised to see Dev, Ziggy, and Mairead turn her way.

"Knoll's not here yet," Ziggy said, hands on her hips as she examined the dragonhead forge, which was dark and unlit.

Emrah fluttered off Fig's shoulder to swoop about the round chamber above their heads.

"What do you think—" Fig began, but then she heard footsteps behind her.

Knoll appeared, followed by Cordwen. The girl had taken to following Knoll around, even though the blacksmith rarely spoke unless spoken to. The girl's father had fallen during battle, and Valencia was as stoic as ever, so Fig was glad Cordwen was busying herself.

"Good. You're here," Knoll rumbled. "Where's Vaelor? No matter, he already has a sword."

A smile pulled up the corners of her lips.

"And it's a magnificent sword," a smooth voice came from the corridor. Vaelor stepped into the chamber, said magnificent sword belted at his hip, and the laces on his tunic loose. The sides of his hair had been shaved just yesterday, and she'd watched him set a few braids just last night.

Fig's smile grew. "I'm sorry, I wanted to let you sleep in."

"It's no matter, goldfire," he said in a low voice as he approached.

Knoll cleared his throat. They turned to look at where he stood by the forge, holding a long wooden box. He offered it to Dev.

But before Dev could take it, someone else bustled into the room, followed by the clan leaders. Valencia wore a black and silver cloak and had the Sword of Morin strapped to her hip. She had re-braided her hair and cut the rest to match what had been removed in battle. She still wore two thick braids, and another set of braids was wrapped around the crown of her head like Cordwen's. Now that Fig looked at the two of them, they did bear a strong resemblance, though Cordwen had red hair and golden skin. The girl's father had been found in the rubble at the west maintenance tunnel. Fig hadn't seen Valencia shedding any tears over the dwarf, though from what she gathered, the two had ceased to be romantically involved long before the battle.

"I thought you were going to wait for me," Valencia intoned.

"You're late," Knoll said with a shrug. Then he pushed the box toward Dev. "This is for you."

Valencia took a step forward. "To Devryn Verrence, the true king of Tytan, for giving up the Sword of Morin, and for following through with your promise to the Feijowa to help take back the Mountain. We dwarves do not forget a bargain. You will have aid when the time comes for you to reclaim your throne."

Dev nodded regally and accepted the box. Fig cocked half a smile, recognizing Dev's formal training kicking in. He opened the box and found a sword nestled in white fabric. Valencia took the box from him as he withdrew the weapon in awe.

"Bloodril," Valencia supplied pointlessly. They could all see the silver veins running through it. Fig could also feel the power radiating off it, and a new essence washed over Dev's aura. Powerful, deep, and inviting.

"I thank you—and your people—for this incredible gift," Dev said formally, acknowledging both Knoll and Valencia with a bow of his head.

Knoll had retrieved another box, and he was looking at Fig. Her eyes darted left and right. No. She didn't do anything to deserve...

"For your role in liberating the Mountain and discovering the natures of the bloodril, we present you with this gift, Fairaleigh Veil," Valencia said. The dwarf leader had refused to address Fig as such, having wrinkled her nose in distaste at the moniker upon formal introductions, citing something about the unseemliness of nicknames.

Knoll pushed the box into her hands, and Fig opened it, hardly daring to believe her eyes as her gaze landed on two daggers nestled in the simple box.

The weapons called to her, and she barely noticed Valencia taking the box as Fig lifted the daggers from it. They fit into her hands perfectly, as if crafted for the curve of her fingers, the nestle of her palms. Delicate veins of silver ran through them just like Dev's sword, forming unique patterns on each, and on the hilts— carved patterns like dragon scales. Fig's mouth opened in awe. It was a long time before she could speak. "I—thank you."

She knew not to say more—to try and reject such a gift would be the gravest of insults. And besides, she didn't know if she'd ever want to part with these beautiful weapons as long as she lived. Was this what it felt like to be Welded with a weapon?

They were perfect. Perhaps during her long hours in her new chambers with Vaelor, she'd convince him to teach her how to fight better with traditional weapons. That is, if she could drag herself away from other activities with the Viren.

The rest of her time had been spent making the Mountain inhabitable again. There was clean drinking water to be found, chambers to clean, food to ration. Mirrors needed to be polished and angled to bring more light in for food growing conditions, and then, of course, there was the war council. Valencia and the clan leaders, with Knoll and Dev as representatives. Dev spent long hours strategizing with Valencia, even though a lot of her plans involved bringing Tytanian dwarves to the safety of the Mountain.

"They're my people too," Dev had said one evening after staying late with the war council.

Fig, Vaelor, Ziggy, Mairead, and Dev had taken to eating their dinner rations together in one of their chambers, away from the raucous dining hall where the dwarves burst into song each night like the bawdiest of taverns.

But who could blame them? They'd reclaimed their home.

Knoll had one more box. Of course, Ziggy and Vaelor had no use for further weapons, so the blacksmith approached Mairead.

"Now, I have no idea if this will work for you," Knoll began. "Well, just open the box."

Mairead's brows quirked as she accepted the small square box from him. Inside was a small vessel—a flask forged of delicate bloodril. Mairead cradled it in her hands, admiring its beauty.

It was fitting that Mairead hadn't been gifted a weapon; though the girl was deft with a blade, that wasn't in her true nature. This though...

"It's perfect," Mairead said. "Unbreakable. Just what I need."

"And we thought," Cordwen piped up, "it might be able to imbue water that you put in it from anywhere. We didn't test it though."

We? Emrah commented to Fig with a snicker. *Seems the dwarfling has been lurking around the forge as well.*

Hush, Fig told him, trying to keep her face straight. *The poor girl's lost her father, and I don't think her mother is the comforting sort.*

To wit, the dwarf leader nodded at Knoll and said, "Now that that's over with, it's time to go see the prisoner."

DEV

Liess Astor stared up at Dev from her cell, rage rimming her silver eyes. Her axe had been moved to the next cell, both compartments carved into the wall of the cavern where prisoners were kept. The axe was also a prisoner, it seemed. But it would have been cruel to part them any farther than that.

"Tell us," Valencia commanded. "You said you would speak."

Liess spat, her bloody lip making her wince at the movement.

Only after the dwarves had discovered her bound body outside the chamber of Morin-Song and transported her to the prison had they informed Dev and the others. Mairead had come right away to unbind the woman, but Liess hadn't said anything, until now, apparently. He suspected it had something to do with the new wounds that had appeared from the dwarves' inter-rogation.

Dev's gut clenched. There were so many answers he wanted from Liess. That had been the whole point of traipsing across the salt swamps with a disdainful 'sword in tow. He'd wanted answers about Rhivven, about the tournament.

And now? A sinking feeling in his stomach made him wonder if he wanted to hear any of it.

"I'll tell *him*," Liess said so quietly they could barely hear. "Only him."

"Not an option," Valencia said, chin high.

Dev looked at the dwarf leader. She pretended not to see his gaze. "Please," he said quietly.

Wordlessly, Valencia snapped her fingers, and her entourage followed her out of the prison corridor. Fig and the others stood nearby, but Dev gave them a look as well.

Fig furrowed her brow as if to say, *Really?*

He nodded.

The four of them followed in Valencia's footsteps, leaving him completely alone with Liess Astor.

"Thank you for speaking with me," he said quietly, a current of electricity running through him.

Liess growled. "I came to the forge chamber to warn you."

Dev scoffed. "Warn me? I can hardly believe that. You *killed Vaelor*."

She crossed her arms, looking unsure herself. "He wouldn't back off. And I see he lived anyway."

"That's hardly an excuse from someone allegedly warning me of something."

"Look, I didn't know what to think, I—" She turned her back on him and was silent so long, he thought she'd changed her mind about speaking. "Your brother is alive."

Dev froze. "And how do you know that?"

"I saw him," she whispered, glancing back over her shoulder.

"Where?"

"Rokhold. I followed Djuren there."

"Rokhold," Dev said, grasping the only firm idea in his mind. "And what business would Djuren have up there that you followed him?"

Liess's silver-ringed eyes went dark for a split second, and he realized she was rolling her eyes. "Not silversword business, Prince. Something else. Something worse."

"My brother."

She nodded tightly.

Fig had spoken of Djuren's last words in his death throes. That Djuren had wanted silverswords dead didn't make any sense, unless... Had Shad wanted to let the dwarves kill as many 'swords as they could to clear a path to the throne?

When Dev thought he'd taken one step closer to the throne, his brother took two more. What had they won during the battle? The deaths of hundreds of dwarves?

No. They'd won the Mountain, the rightful place for the dwarves. They'd restored their ancestral home. That had to mean something. It had to.

"Very well," Dev said quietly. His brother was on Tytanian soil once more. "Then I will be ready, and you're going to help. As I've heard the dwarf war god Baldwyn says: Let us crush our enemy into the ground with the force of our fury."

THE END

LIZ DELTON

GLOSSARY

PERSONAE

FAIRALEIGH VEIL	Also known as Fig, a fire mage with gold flames who no longer trains at the Carriage House.
DEVRYN VERRENCE	Heir to the Rayvan throne, an air mage with amethyst colored magic.
VAELOR RESBROK	A silversword in the employ of the Verrence family, from one of the last clans to fall during the Slaughter of Viren.
RHIVVEN	A bloodthirsty silversword who led the Silver Slaughter.
EMRAH	A dragonet with a possibly shaded past.
NIEL GANIVAN	A silversword from Thornkill.
LIESS ASTOR	A silversword from Southmarch, Weld with a formidable axe.
GAN WROGHSLEY	A silversword Weld with a shortsword.
QUEEN EILEIGH	Deceased, mother to Devryn.
BRUNA	A paper mage who Fig lives with.
COLLIS	A dwarf of the Feijowa clan.
FIRTH	A dwarf of the Feijowa clan.
MAIREAD JOIROS	A Sister of Morgha.

MAELCHIOR	A silversword posted in Nova Istra.
FENRA	A swamp dryad of the de Wald gathering.
ELDER ELIZARETH	An elder of the de Wald gathering.
VILVAN	A swamp dryad of the Lokin gathering. Friend of Fenra. He is on his pilgrimage out of the swamp.
ZULA RESBROK	Vaelor's grandmother.
AIDIENNE TASKOR	Tutor at Resbrok Manor.
PERRIN RESBROK	Adopted son of Zula, he is technically Vaelor's uncle.
MARLOWE	A dwarf who works at Resbrok Manor.
MASTER AFRITH SENAKA	Fire mage with green flames who taught at the Carriage House.
ELFIE	A svorcat, Afrith's pet.
ZIGGRUNE ASHBROK	Also known as Ziggy, a silversword who was turned at the end of the Silver Slaughter.
VINNIEL	A silversword posted in Viren.
SISTER STERINWAIT	A Sister of Morgha with a fount in Verindas.
ELFRAR	A swamp dryad, Fenra's brother.
LADY ATRICIA	A noble of House Griveen of Viren.
LORD ONALDE	A noble of House Weirbrook of Viren.
LORD ELESTE	A noble of Viren.
CAPTAIN FELRAS	A silversword posted in Viren.
ISHI AND EVVY ASHBROK	Ziggy's younger sisters.
FANGALORE	Also known as Fang, part of the Fienn-Da.
URSA	Fang's dog.
THOMAT EVANDAHL	The leader of the Fienn-Da.
KING ARTAXIS	King of Tysaine.
QUINNETRA	Part of the Fienn-Da.
KERAFINA	Part of the Fienn-Da.

ALLIFREY	A knife mage.
ESTILL	A water mage.
KING BAILEMOR	Historic Verrence king, who took the Gold Wood for the crown.
KING TESVIER THE RELENTLESS	Historic Verrence king, who took the Mountain for the crown.
MOTHER SAVIDAH	Head of the Sisters of Morgha.
KNOLL	A dwarven blacksmith.
SISTER AVELINA	A Sister of Morgha stationed at Mar Nevan.
HARRYN	A mage with object-moving powers.
FLOURICE CONHAM	A color mage who worked in the palace in Queen Eileigh's retinue.
JAFFID	A forger in Black End.
FOLLY	The Joiros family dog; a goldhound.
HOWARTH JOIROS	Mairead's great uncle. Lives in Thoan at the family goat farm, making soap.
DERRINAHL	A childhood friend of Mairead's; runs the family print shop in Thoan.
SISTER FRANCINE	The Sister of Morgha assigned to Thoan.
VALENCIA	The Uniter of the Clans, a dwarf.
CORDWEN	A young dwarf with an earth-moving affinity.
MIDRUNA	A mage from the Carriage House.
MINNA	A dryad toddler.
ELDER SPRATE	A dryad elder with magic and botany training.
BJORN CONWELL	Captain of the guard at Southmarch Keep.
TORRY CONHAM	Husband of Flourice Conham, spent one year in Queen Eileigh's retinue as a tailor.
SHIPMAN	A silversword captain in Ghorvost.
MORANDRA	A water mage.
CHAMILLE	A crystal mage in Ghorvost.
FURVIN	A bronze dragonet.
SYLRYN	A blue dragonet.

MORGHA	The goddess of healing and death, who takes souls into her arms upon their death.
THE BARD	He records the story of everyone's lives to share with the gods.
DRAKIORYN	In dragonet lore, a mighty dragon god.
CORAVA	A Virenish goddess. Corava's Day is celebrated in the fall, with black streamers on doorways like the wings of Corava's crows, to prevent wandering souls from entering homes they used to live in. It is said she was chained to a watery grave in the *solanse.*
MALHELA	The dark place, where dark creatures of myth reside, and a soul may go if not taken into Morgha—or Corava's arms, depending on the belief.
CORRYN	Dwarf goddess of justice.
BALDWYN	Dwarf god of war.

FLAURA & FAUNA

VIRRENISH EIFDALES	A large horse breed originating from Viren.
AFFERVATZ	A type of stone.
LYRESTONE	A type of stone.
AURAN TREES	Endangered trees with gold bark and gold leaves, which emit gold sparkles in the right light. It is said they enhance the powers of mages.
VORSE EAGLES	A large brown and white eagle breed.
WHORLTHORNS	A bush with thorns in the shape of spirals.
BLOODRIL	A type of stone.
SVORCAT	A gold cat, originally native to the Gold Wood.
TAGOR	A large and vicious swamp reptile.
SILVERSAP	A healing plant.
VIRAGROVE TREES	Native to Viren, they only grow in the water of the salt swamps. Natives make a strong tea with the leaves.
ANDISIA MOSS	An invasive air plant from Andisia, which grows easily on any surface and favors the trees of the salt swamp.
KAFYE	A drink made from hard beans that grow on bushes, originating from Kafyetta in Tysaine.
FIREMOTHS	Green glowing insects in the salt swamp.
ILDERBERRIES	Purple berries found in the salt swamp.
SHAFRA	Woolly creatures kept by farmers for their fur and meat.
FOLI-LEAF	A Virennish plant which is not safe for animals.
ETRU	A Tysainian plant that is a mild sedative.
ASHBAR	A plant for smoking.
EMBERGOLD LEAVES	Found in the Gold Wood, can be made into tea.
SORATILLO	A Tysainian spice.
BRIARWOLVES	A type of wolf native to the continent.
FALLONDIR	A flower used in teas and perfumes.
VITALE	A bubbly spirit made only in the Vitale region of Pan Vidda.

VIRENNISH LANGUAGE

Solanse	"so-lonse"	The salt swamps
Voixage	"voy-yahj"	A pilgrimage that the swamp dryads take out of the solanse for fifty years
Grimazir	"gree-ma-zeer"	Grandmother
Mazir	"ma-zeer"	Mother
Brozir	"broh-zeer"	Brother
Ida moz'n	"ee-dah moe zin"	I'm here/I'm with you
Visat	"vis-sat"	Is that
Mo desz	"moe dess"	My god
Mo der	"moe dehr"	My dear
Va	"va"	Yes
Meve	"meh-vee"	Maybe
V'rai	"vray"	An exclamation of surprise or awe
Vir dan	"veer-dahn"	A greeting
Mir	"meer"	Look
Merda	"mare-da"	A curse
Drixia	"dree-sha"	A dragonet

ABOUT THE AUTHOR

Liz Delton writes and lives in New England, with her husband and sons. She studied Theater Management at the University of the Arts in Philly, always having enjoyed the backstage life of storytelling.

World-building is her favorite part of writing, and she is always dreaming up new fantastic places.

She loves drinking tea and traveling. When she's not writing or reading, you can find her baking in the kitchen or out in the garden making valiant attempts at keeping her plants alive.

Visit her website at **LizDelton.com**

ALSO BY LIZ DELTON

<u>LEGENDS OF GOLD AND SILVER</u>

Flames of Gold

Echoes of Silver

Gods of Obsidian (2026)

<u>REALM OF CAMELLIA</u>

The Starless Girl

The Storm King

The Gray Mage

The Starlight Dragon

The Fall of Azurite

<u>COZY COTTAGE SERIES</u>

The Witch at the Edge of the Wood

The Library at the Edge of the Wood

The Tea Shop at the Edge of the Wood (2026)

<u>SEASONS OF SOLDARK</u>

Spectacle of the Spring Queen

The Mechanical Masquerade

All Hallows Airship

The Clockwork Ice Dragon

Seasons of Soldark Novella Collection

<u>EVERTURN CHRONICLES</u>

The Alchemyst's Mirror